Margarita Malevolence

Tanya Westlake

Impractical Press

ISBN-13: 979-8-9997112-0-5

Cover design by: 100 Covers

Chapter One

"What's the best way to catch a suspect in a lie?" Kalliope Brooks's best friend, Tess Russo, asked, as they studied from their new Private Investigator textbooks, assigned by their mentor, Reggie Cornwallis. She reached for a loaded nacho and pointed it at Kallie.

"Bring them another Long Island Iced Tea?" Kallie suggested, with a smile.

"That would probably be faster," Tess agreed. "But we're not going to be toting booze on stakeouts."

"Sad but true," Kallie sighed. "Ask them the same question a bunch of times, but worded differently," she answered the question, seriously. "Because they're more likely to feel pressured to embellish the details and mess up."

"And then?" Tess asked.

"Hmm. . ."

Tess crunched her nacho, somehow managing to avoid getting any of the melty cheese on her perfect nails, waiting for her best friend to continue.

Kallie looked down, thinking, and Tess teased,

"No looking at the book!"

Kallie lifted the heavy, slightly tattered paperback defensively and rebelled, "It's not even open!" She'd bought a used copy of the book, which their mentor had requested, off eBay. "Watch their eyes, because they're more likely to look left if they're lying."

Tess verified the answer on her e-reader and nodded. "Cornwallis says that trick isn't always reliable, but the book says it's right." A moment later, she added with a smile, "But ever since I read that, I've been watching everyone like a hawk, to see where their eyes go when they answer me."

"Me too," Kallie laughed. "I was at the grocery store this week, and when the customer service guy said I missed the sale on avocados, I swear he looked left!"

"He probably wanted them all for himself. They've gotten so expensive," Tess agreed with a frown. She looked back at her digital copy of the book. "The other answer was to tell them what you think really happened, as if you have proof. If you're wrong, they might correct you. And if you're right—"

"They might just break down and admit the whole thing! Cornwallis said that's worked for him before. He just made up some crazy explanation, on the fly, and he got it right," Kallie laughed.

"And the guy confessed to everything right there," Tess said, shaking her head with wonder.

"It's not all fun and games, though," Kallie pondered, suddenly serious. Thinking about their shocking and often frightening experiences in the past few years.

We've been through a lot, in a short time. Risked our lives.

"No, but we can handle it," Tess murmured, and Kallie knew she was waiting for her response, watching her carefully.

But it was all worth it, to find the killers.

"It's a *little bit* fun and games," she joked.

Tess nodded with a gentle smile. "Just a little. And as long as we keep finding ourselves in the middle of murder investigations anyway, we might as well go pro."

"Exactly." Kallie grabbed a nacho and lifted it like a champagne glass. "To going pro!"

Tess clinked her nacho against Kallie's and agreed, "Heaven help us. Owhiro's first all-girl, professional private investigator team."

***

The next morning, after an evening of studying, Kallie stood behind the bar at The Lazy Gecko, smiling at her regulars. She seemed perfectly sane and composed, compared to the patrons who were cheering

3

and whooping in their seats like lunatics.

It wasn't a sports bar, but local University of South Florida was in the March Madness Championship, and everyone in town was going crazy.

In celebration of the playoffs, The Lazy Gecko was serving special USF-themed Margaritas, decked in green and gold garnish. She mixed up a batch, with dark green salt on the glass rims, for two couples sitting at a booth by the window who were engrossed in the game. Naturally, another couple ordered a pair of her famous Bloody Marys—with bacon, asparagus, a dill pickle spear, and lots of Cholula Hot Sauce all around—and she placed them all on a tray. Pouring a beer for her regular in the corner, completely oblivious of the game, she added it to the tray and delivered the drinks.

She walked back behind the bar just as a loud cheer rose from the room, and turned to see that the USF Bulls had made a three-point shot. Kallie wasn't really watching the game, but she was glad her customers were happy, and impressed by the local athletes.

She caught a wave from across the room and gestured back with two fingers and pointed at the table. *Two of the same?* Her patron nodded with a smile, so she poured another glass of white wine and a glass of beer from a popular local brewery. She knew this couple usually wanted food, so she picked up two menus as she carried their drinks to the table.

Turning away, after taking their order for chicken nachos and coconut shrimp, she jumped as a chorus of loud boos suddenly filled the room. She chuckled at her nerves and scurried back out of the way, so she didn't block anyone's view. One of the players had been called for a foul—apparently in error, judging from the crowd's reactions.

She placed the food order with the kitchen on the bar computer and reached for a water bottle under the counter. She liked the business from the local games, but they sure kept her busy. She took a deep swig from the straw and leaned back against the rear railing, hearing the crowd grumble again. This time, they were looking around, confused.

The game had gone silent.

Oh no. Don't tell me the cable's gone out right now!

Kallie quickly grabbed the television's remote control. Marcy, her boss, didn't usually leave it out in the bar because it caused arguments. But during sporting events, Kallie often needed to adjust the volume. She quickly verified that the volume and channel were unchanged, so she walked out into the room to see what was happening on the screen.

"What's going on?" one of her regulars asked. "Did you change the channel?"

"No," Kallie answered, equally confused. "Look, it still says the channel name in the corner. And the sound's on."

Suddenly, two local newscasters appeared on the screen, looking a little disheveled as if they, too, had just been called from watching the game.

"We apologize for interrupting your local presentation, but we need to go to a press conference," the male anchor announced.

The crowd groaned unhappily, and Kallie grimaced along with them. But not for the same reason.

Press conferences are never about good news. And it must be a doozy to interrupt the big game.

One of the anchors nodded to someone offscreen, and the station cut to an outside shot. The sky was a dazzling blue, and Kallie caught a glimpse of the sparkling Gulf of Mexico water between three police cars in the background. Pinellas County's Sheriff Nelson Hall was standing at a podium, already speaking.

"—was found this morning at the Celebration of Sandcastles site in Owhiro before they opened—"

Not again!

Kallie groaned miserably and closed her eyes. *Of course, again.*

Did you think there would be no more murders, Kalliope? Anyway, this one isn't your problem. So relax.

"—has been identified as—"

One of the patrons in her section, whom Kallie didn't recognize, shouted, "Can't you change the channel?!"

The others shushed him aggressively. Most of her regulars knew about the other crimes Kallie had experienced lately, and a few of them glanced over at her sympathetically.

She shook her head to clear it, and then fumbled with the remote.

He's right, Kalliope. Just change the channel.

They don't want their afternoon spoiled, and this game is a big deal. See if it's on one of the premium sports channels.

She looked up at the screen and pointed the remote, but her thumb froze over the channel button. The beautiful sandcastles on the Owhiro shoreline, so carefully carved and shaped by artists from all over the world, were in disarray.

Some of them were unforgivingly trampled behind the crime scene tape. One castle's graceful tower was knocked askew, barely remaining attached. To its right, a huge, stylized pagoda had been clawed by someone who had obviously been trying to escape. Another castle, straight out of a fairy tale, was almost completely destroyed.

Kallie's heart dropped, and her eyes teared up a little at the damage. Not just because so many artists had worked for days to complete the masterpieces, but because the annual festival was in her hometown. She'd been to Celebration of Sandcastles almost every year since she was a kid.

The news channels were usually very discreet, but she thought she could see blood in the sand. She closed her eyes and took a deep breath.

Her hands gradually stopped shaking and her heart rate slowed back to normal.

This is your life now, Kalliope. You can't become a private investigator if you're going to panic every time there's a murder.

She took one more deep breath and nodded to herself.

It was just a surprise, coming up at work like that, she thought, trying to cut herself a little slack. *And so nearby. That's all.*

Trying to shift her mind from fear to curiosity, she listened to the reporter.

"—believed to be a vagrant, but we've located his family and are working to contact them. After that point, we'll update you with further information."

"So, there's a murderer running loose, here in Owhiro?" a woman at a nearby table whispered loudly to her friend.

"I'm sure they'll catch him. But you'll stay at our house in Palm Harbor tonight anyway, Norma. You don't need to be in the middle of that," her friend replied, without looking away from the screen.

"Thanks, Barb," the woman sighed. "I don't know what's happening to my little town."

Tell me about it, Kallie thought, grimly. *And that's just a mile up the beach from here.*

The reporters on the scene were clearly thinking the same thing, as one asked, "Sheriff Hall, is there a threat to the public?"

"We haven't determined yet whether it was a targeted attack or not. We're speaking with a person of interest, who was staying with the victim—"

That's a relief, Kallie thought, fiddling a little with the remote. *Hopefully, that person of interest can identify the killer.*

Or maybe it is the killer, even if the police haven't proven it yet.

"We've already increased patrols in the area and gone door-to-door in that section of Owhiro's waterfront. We don't believe there's a current threat. The assailant had plenty of time to get out of the area before daybreak," the sheriff replied. "Unfortunately, the security camera coverage near and under the tents at the festival is minimal."

Another reporter called out, "Are you locking down the beach during the festival?"

"We are *not* going to impose a nightly curfew at this time, since there's no indication that the killer has remained in the area," the sheriff answered. "But we'll have another press conference at six o'clock this evening. We'll determine by then whether to change that plan. If any residents or visitors saw anything suspicious, or caught anything on their cameras, we ask—"

Kallie suddenly realized her arm was still sticking out, awkwardly frozen, holding the remote in the air. She blinked several times and finally changed the channel.

It's March Madness, Kalliope. This game is probably on at least four of the premium sports channels.

Focus.

She clicked through the channels until she saw green and gold uniforms, and heard the squeak of tennis shoes on a hardwood court. A murmur of appreciation rose from her patrons, and a few of them smiled at her. Several signaled for more drinks, too, so she replaced the remote in its hiding place under the bar and got back to work.

A smile cracked her face as a cheer went up following another three-point shot, and she took a moment to recognize her calmness.

Tess will be so proud of me. Heck, I'm proud of me!

Not that she was a timid, fragile person, but she'd been through a lot in the past few years. It felt good to be healing. And toughening up.

She took another deep swig out of her water bottle and then loaded up her tray with half a dozen drinks. The rest of the afternoon swept by, as folks ordered appetizers and some meals—The Lazy Gecko was famous for their food—and more drinks. USF won the game, and her patrons left happy—the way she liked to see them.

After she wiped down the bar and cleared the tables, turning the televisions back off, she was surprised to hear a ding from her phone. Tess and her dad knew she couldn't take calls at work, but this was a known number. The sender's name filled her with excitement and nerves at the same time. She touched the screen and read the message.

Cornwallis

Ready for your first test, Kallie? Let's all meet at my office when your shift is over.

***

Kallie could barely concentrate for the rest of her shift, and the customers began to clear out after the game, which made it even harder to focus. She and Tess had originally hired Cornwallis to help with a previous case, but he'd been so impressed with them that he offered to mentor and train them, until he retired. Kallie didn't think she was ready for a test yet, though.

And she certainly didn't want to disappoint him.

What does he mean, our first test? I haven't even finished the first book yet.

I knew I should've read faster, like Tess. What if I don't pass the test? Will he kick me out?

She changed the music on the sound system, then changed it back. Cleaned the bar counter again. Cleaned the touch screen on the ordering computer. She had just run hot water into a cloth and started for the nearest table when a voice called from the corner.

"You only clean like that when you're nervous."

Kallie laughed out loud, embarrassed. "I swear, you've got us all figured out, Barry. How's your book coming?"

"This is the *third* book, actually," he replied with a smile, looking over his wire-rimmed glasses at her. "Why are you nervous?"

Barry Hunter was one of Kallie's longest-serving regulars, since she'd joined the day shift, and she knew he'd been writing a book about all of them at The Lazy Gecko—though she didn't know he was on the third book in the series already.

Now I'm even more nervous! I hope my character in the book is nice.

"Oh, I just found out that I might have to take a test of some kind," she answered. "Pop quizzes are always a little stressful, right?"

Barry looked every bit the studious author, with his grey goatee and tweed jacket, as he closed his notebook, using his pen as a bookmark. He looked at her seriously. "You're a smart lady, Kallie. I'm sure you'll ace it." After a moment, he added, "Is it something you can study for?"

"It's in. . ." —she looked at the clock on the ordering screen— "two hours. So not really."

"Well, I won't complain if you sneak behind the bar and do some last-minute cramming—and it looks like everyone else is gone." He continued, with a smile, "Could I get another beer first, though?"

Kallie beamed. "That's a good idea! And, absolutely, another beer coming right up!"

***

After her shift ended, Kallie was getting into her car, when Tess called to ask about the text from Cornwallis.

"What do you think he wants?" Tess asked, sounding a little concerned herself.

"I think it's a pop quiz."

"But we haven't learned enough to take a quiz yet," Tess complained. "Do you think he's going to do this with every book?"

"I hope he's not tired of teaching us, and looking

13

for an excuse to stop our training," Kallie admitted, her fear growing.

Tess sat ominously silent on the phone for a second, considering, and then replied, "Nah."

"Was that the voice of reason?" Kallie asked with a chuckle.

"He's really not that subtle. If he was sick of us, he'd just tell us."

Kallie thought back on their first meetings with the private investigator, and then laughed. "That's true. He doesn't really have much of a filter. That actually makes me feel a little better."

"Good," Tess answered. "Come by my house and we can take my car to his office. You can read the chapter summaries out loud, while we're driving. It'll take a while to get across the bridge at this hour, so we'll do some last-minute studying."

Kallie agreed and hung up, then made the quick drive to Tess's house. Owhiro was a small town, so almost every drive was a short one. Tess met her in the driveway with a bag of pretzels and two Diet Cokes, and they climbed into her car for the trip to Cornwallis's office in Tampa.

After they got onto the highway leading to the bridge across Tampa Bay, Kallie pulled the heavy textbook out of her bag.

"Skip over the first chapters," Tess advised. "We've already talked about those. Start around chapter seven."

"Surveillance photography?" Kallie asked.

"Sure, let's start there. Wally said that's where he makes most of his money, even though it's usually boring. So we might as well get good at it."

Kallie smiled crookedly at Tess's reference to their instructor and friend as 'Wally.' She couldn't believe Cornwallis allowed the nickname, but she was sure he wouldn't take it from anyone but Tess.

Each chapter of the textbook had a summary section at the end, so Kallie read them out loud. They'd go back and read the full chapters later, of course; they just wanted the high-level details for tonight's surprise test. By the time they'd crossed the bridge and arrived at the dark and obnoxious-smelling walk-up office, they were both feeling better about their chances.

"Ladies, come in," their mentor called, as Tess opened the door. He was reading something on the dusty computer monitor, but waved them to their usual seats at the desk.

"You're testing us on the book already?" Kallie asked. Cornwallis looked confused as he glanced away from the computer. "What? No, you haven't even had time to finish the first book, have you?"

Kallie and Tess looked at each other. "Not really–" Tess began to answer.

"But you said there was going to be a test?" Kallie added, quizzically.

"Oh, not that kind of test," he answered, as the office door opened behind them. A young blonde woman entered the office and sat down in a small chair by the dingy window. Kallie thought she was probably in her mid-twenties, but her eyes were much older. Her hair was dirty and she was wearing a pair of men's trousers and torn-up shoes. She looked tired and sad, but there was an air of quiet dignity about her.

The woman smelled like cigarette smoke, and Kallie realized she must've been outside smoking in the grimy, little courtyard downstairs.

Tess and Kallie looked at each other in surprise, then back at Cornwallis. They'd never seen anyone else in his office before.

"This is Prudence Lawson, ladies."

"Hi Prudence," Tess greeted the young woman with a friendly smile and a small wave across the room.

"Prudence rode the bus to my office this morning, all the way from Owhiro, where her father was murdered last night," Cornwallis explained, in his normal matter-of-fact tone.

Kallie gasped quietly and clasped her hand over her mouth, remembering the press conference she'd seen at work.

This is the daughter of the Celebration of Sandcastles murder victim?!

"Prudence is your test, ladies. Welcome to your first case."

16

Chapter Two

"Oh, Prudence," Tess whispered sincerely. "We're so sorry."

The young woman nodded, averting her reddened eyes awkwardly.

"She can't afford to pay us," Cornwallis explained quickly. He made eye contact with the woman for a moment, clearly not wanting to offend her by discussing her financial situation. "But her father was a good informant for me in the past—and this will be a good learning experience for you. So we're working pro bono."

"Sure, of course," Kallie replied quickly. They didn't expect to get paid until they had their P.I. licenses, at least. They were basically just students at this point. Barely even able to truly assist.

Although we did fine as amateurs on our own, Kallie thought, with a little well-earned pride.

That's why he has faith in us.

"Just a reminder, we'll be working *with* the police, not around them," Cornwallis added, with a raised eyebrow.

Kallie blushed a little, but Tess saluted him cheerfully. "It's *way* easier to be honest. And then we can ask them for help—"

"When you inevitably get into trouble," Cornwallis finished her sentence with a wry smile. "Lesson one starts with trying to *avoid* danger, from now on."

"Career goals," Kallie mumbled with a facetious smile. "So what's the story? How are we involved?" They didn't usually talk to the victim's family, and she didn't want to make this young woman go into gory details about her father's murder.

But we need the gory details.

"The police didn't contact me about this case," Cornwallis explained, "which is usually how I get involved in official county investigations. But I cleared it with the sheriff's office. We can work with Prudence, as long as she goes to the station and files her statement." He glanced at the blonde woman and added, "I'll be driving her down there in the morning, so she doesn't need to take the bus. She'll also need to appear for any other questioning they might have. But we'll be handling her direct case, as it applies to her father's affairs—"

He stopped speaking, apparently also a little protective of her feelings. She remained silent, so he continued. "Prudence was just a kid when Oscar—her father—was working with me. So this is an unusual case. We don't really know each other personally, and yet, we do."

Prudence's eyes teared up a little, and Kallie could see how grateful she was for the investigator's help. And his decency.

It must've been so hard for her to ask him—practically a stranger.

I'll bet he seems like a knight in shining armor. I wonder how long it's been since anyone went out of their way to help her.

Well, we might not be the most expensive agency in town, or have the nicest office, but I know we can help.

"Why don't you go back down to the courtyard, Pru," Cornwallis suggested. "You don't need to hear us talk about the details."

She looked like she was going to argue—defend her courage, perhaps. But she didn't. She nodded and sighed, walking to the door and slipping out of the room silently. A moment later, they heard her footsteps on the noisy old stairs.

"I talked to your boyfriend, actually," the investigator told Kallie, with a smile.

She started to argue, but then smiled serenely back, and blushed a little.

He really is my boyfriend now, so I guess I can stop arguing with everyone about it.

"Morrison approved your case?" she asked with surprise. "That's good to know."

"You think that means he won't tell you to be careful every five minutes?" Tess asked glibly.

"Oh, I'm sure he will," Kallie replied with a smile. "But at least he can't pretend to be surprised."

She had been dating Detective Morrison for about a month, having previously worked on a murder case together. After being completely oblivious to his romantic interest for all that time, it still seemed slightly surreal to her.

"He was able to give me a few minor details which haven't been released to the press yet." Cornwallis sighed and added, "And, of course, Prudence is the victim's next of kin. The police were having trouble finding her, considering their living situations. She doesn't have a permanent address, either. So I was able to facilitate that step for them."

They'd previously learned that Cornwallis wasn't just a 'handler' to his informants. He genuinely cared about them and was obviously personally troubled by this case—the death of a friend and ally.

"I saw the press conference while I was at work," Kallie explained. "It came on during the USF game. The sheriff called him a vagrant—"

"I'm not sure that's the right word," Cornwallis replied, stiffly. "He's been living in the Tampa Bay area consistently, even if he couldn't always afford his own apartment. And he was sober, and hadn't committed any crimes in at least ten years."

"You wouldn't hire him if he did," Tess replied, knowingly.

"Detective Morrison said they think he was staying in Owhiro with a few other guys, to work the tourist crowd who came to the festival."

Kallie nodded, waiting for him to continue.

"He didn't panhandle when he was working with me. I guess he didn't need to," he sighed again. "But it's good money. His friends told Morrison that he was an honest guy. No pressure, no thieving, no cons. So maybe he was just in the wrong place at the wrong time."

"Is that what they think, Wally?" Tess asked quietly. "The murder wasn't targeted?"

Cornwallis nodded. "That's their theory so far, but it's only been a few hours."

"It sounds like you disagree?" Kallie asked.

"I'm not so sure. I saw one of the crime scene photos, and it looks. . . personal. To me, anyway. Like he'd been beaten up, too. Though he might've gotten in a few defensive blows before he lost the fight."

"So, someone he knew?" Tess suggested.

"I hope it's nothing worse," he added, grimly.

Kallie and Tess exchanged glances, but remained silent.

What's worse than murder?

Probably better if you don't go down that ugly rabbit hole right this second, Kalliope.

"But this isn't the time to speculate. Let's start with what we have," Cornwallis added, suddenly sounding every bit the schoolteacher. "Kallie, go."

"Oh," Kallie faltered. "Okay, um. We have a murder. On Owhiro Beach, at the annual Celebration of Sandcastles exhibit. Um. . . Male victim, aged—"

"Fifty-one," Cornwallis filled in her pause.

"Oscar Lawson. No recent criminal record, no spouse, one daughter."

Cornwallis nodded appreciatively, then pointed at Tess.

"The victim was semi-transient and staying near the festival. With, um– Known associates?" Tess hazarded a guess.

"Yes, with known associates. I have their names."

"But the murder was committed during the night, so he was outside after midnight," Tess continued. "He wasn't *staying* outdoors, correct?"

"They were staying with a male cousin in a studio apartment, apparently for a few days," Cornwallis acknowledged. "The cousin is being questioned by the police as a possible suspect."

"But you don't think it's him?"

22

"Prudence is convinced that it's not the cousin. She said they're as close as brothers, and they knew how to work out their disagreements."

"But they *had* known disagreements?" Kallie asked, frowning.

"Everyone does," Cornwallis replied with a shrug. "But I'm willing to take her word for it at this point. She knows him better than I did, obviously, so she knows the family dynamic. But she said there were others at the apartment. A woman and another couple, near her father's age."

Tess cringed. "Five people in a studio apartment sounds like a fight waiting to happen."

"Indeed, it does. And Prudence doesn't trust any of those three. She didn't come straight out and call them suspects, but she called them 'junkies and thieves.' She thought they were leading her father back down the wrong path."

Kallie nodded. "Okay, it's a stretch to go from 'junkies and thieves' to murder, but—"

"But it does happen, sometimes," Cornwallis continued, tapping his pen on the desk thoughtfully. "Morrison only mentioned the cousin, so I'm not sure if the police know about the others yet. Prudence can give them all the details when I drive her over there in the morning."

"Do you have their names?" Tess asked. "I can start checking for them online when we get home, so we have a head start."

"She only mentioned that the younger woman was called Peaches. She didn't identify the others. But I'll get the names from her later and send them over to you."

"Peaches is probably a nickname, anyway," Tess agreed. "If she knows their full names, that would help. I'm sure the police will be interested in talking to them too."

Tess was a stunningly beautiful woman, and Kallie was one of the few people who knew that she was also secretly a total nerd, as well as a certified genius. Her best friend would be strategically scouring the internet for any suspects as soon as they had some names.

"What other questions do you have, *class*?" he asked, dryly. "What do you need to know in order to start investigating the case?"

"Why did he go outside during the night?" Tess pondered, continuing the analysis.

"If not for drugs, then maybe just insomnia? Someone snoring too loudly in that crowded space?" Kallie suggested.

"Let's not speculate on that, quite yet," Cornwallis replied. "We don't have enough information. Prudence doesn't think he was on drugs, although neither of us had seen him for a while."

Good. That would complicate the case, in a big

way.

"What else?" Cornwallis encouraged them to continue.

"Did he have anything in his pockets?" Kallie asked.

"Good question," the investigator replied, pointing his pen at her. "That can be a great clue, but we don't know yet."

"Oh," Kallie mumbled.

"No, that was a good question," he reassured her. "But they won't release that until after the medical examiner is done with her assessment of the victim."

Tess was apparently also out of ideas, which was unusual for her. "We don't have many facts yet. Do we know the cause of death?"

"Morrison couldn't tell me. Word on the street says it was a shooting, but until the medical examiner releases—"

"Yeah, that's speculation too," Tess sighed. "This is *hard*, Wally. Did anyone hear gunshots?"

"Nothing reported yet, but that area of Owhiro's beach isn't heavily populated, except by tourists. The police are pulling their ShotSpotter reports, but they—"

"More speculation," Kallie grumbled. "We're obviously on empty, when it comes to solid facts. What options do we *have* right now?"

"Well, it was a full moon—"

"*Werewolf!*" Kallie chirped.

"Oh, and a silver bullet!" Tess replied immediately.

Cornwallis rolled his eyes theatrically, replying, "I just meant that there would've been good *visibility*, you weirdos. We'll check with the hotels and shop owners of buildings facing the beach—maybe we'll find someone who was awake and happened to see something."

"That's *way* less interesting than werewolves," Kallie grumbled.

"There's apparently a big pre-teen cheerleading competition starting on Monday, so there are even more tourists in the area," Cornwallis noted. "All of the hotels were full. We can check with the parents and chaperones, in case they went out during the night."

"Would they do that? When we were kids, our chaperones never went out partying after we went to bed on school trips," Tess frowned.

"They probably did, though," Kallie replied with a chuckle.

"You think so?" Tess shook her head, but considered the suggestion for a moment. "On that school trip to St. Augustine, maybe."

"And the track meet in Miami," Kallie added.

"Oh, right. That was when Betty's mom and her best friend stayed with us." Tess turned back to the investigator. "Never mind, I rescind my argument. We'll go check with the chaperones."

"Oh, thank you so much for your approval," he answered, jokingly. "We can check with those little shops and restaurants on the pier as well. Maybe we'll get lucky and someone was up late—or up early—restocking their shelves, and heard something."

Kallie and Tess stood up to leave, and Tess added, "I'll see what I can find on Oscar Lawson, but send me any other names you find, okay?"

"You'll be the first to know," Cornwallis replied, also standing up. "I'm going to get Prudence a hotel room for the night, here in Tampa. I'll meet you at the pier tomorrow morning, after we talk to the police."

***

Kallie and Tess met up again with Cornwallis the next morning at ten thirty, and started their interviews on the Owhiro pier, since the shops usually opened early on the weekends. It wasn't a huge pier, but it was popular enough to keep a few stores, a bait shop, and two small restaurants, in business.

"I guess the restaurants were the most likely to still have employees inside late at night, but they aren't open quite yet," Kallie noted, checking the time on her phone.

"Well, we have a few hours before I have to be at the office. Let's check the stores first," Tess suggested.

"The bait shop might've been open early," Kallie added. "When my dad goes fishing, he always wants to be out before sunrise. He says that's when the fish are most active."

They started walking out to the bait shop, which was closer to the end of the pier, but quickly turned back when they saw a lot of people inside.

"It's still too crowded. The owner won't be able to talk to us when he has so many customers waiting," Cornwallis explained.

"No problem. I'm sure it'll calm down later, when the day gets hotter. Let's start with this shop." Kallie read the ornate wooden sign, Darja's Dolls.

The store seemed to specialize in handmade wooden dolls, as well as wooden dishes and bowls. They could see an older woman inside, wearing a colorful, old-fashioned dress and writing in a notebook near the register. Her silver hair was pinned up in a scarf.

As the trio entered the shop, they discovered a pre-teen girl who was sitting just inside the doorway, painting one of the dolls. In contrast to the other woman, she wore jeans and neon pink sneakers. Her dark hair was swept up in a messy but pretty ponytail.

"These are beautiful," Tess said with a smile, approaching her. "Do you make them all?"

The girl didn't smile, but nodded. Her

paintbrush delicately touched the wooden face, adding long eyelashes to the rustic but lovely doll. She added curious eyebrows next, making the small face even more interesting. But the girl's own face was impassive, bored.

"You look like you'd rather be at the mall," Tess added with a smile.

The girl looked up, confused, and pulled off a pair of inexpensive headphones. "Why would I go to the mall?"

"Oh, it's where we used to hang out when we were. . . Never mind. I just meant you look like you'd rather be somewhere else."

"I have to do this for my grandmother," the girl explained, gesturing toward the older woman without looking up. "I was supposed to practice for the soccer game tomorrow, but she made me come here instead."

"And now you're worried about your game," Tess concluded.

"Sure, and I miss my friends." The girl continued painting carefully, but Kallie heard her sigh. "I don't want them to think—"

Kallie looked at Tess curiously, and they both waited for the girl to finish her sentence.

That you don't miss them?

That you don't care about soccer practice?

That you care more about painting than

winning?

"You don't want them to blame you if you lose," Tess stated quietly. "But you know you need to be here."

The girl suddenly looked up. "Don't tell my grandmother I was complaining. *Please?*"

Tess shook her head—no way.

"She can't paint the dolls anymore. She can't see so well, and her hands shake a little." She scowled and mumbled, "Why am I even telling you this?"

"You have to tell someone, and it's easier to tell a stranger," Cornwallis replied, and they all looked over at him in surprise.

"We need the money," the girl concluded with a shrug of her shoulders. She went back to painting, as if they hadn't spoken, and pulled the cheap headphones back over her ears.

"Aren't we going to ask her if they saw anything?" Kallie whispered.

"Not today," Tess whispered back.

Kallie shrugged, and started to walk away from the little stall, toward the next shop on the pier. "So are we coming back tomorrow, then—?"

But Tess had stepped inside the shop and was picking up one of the dolls. A redheaded one in a green dress, Kallie noticed. She carried it to the register and paid the older woman, chatting briefly as she waited for it to be wrapped carefully.

They both watched her—Cornwallis squinting in annoyed resignation and Kallie with a smile, hoping the purchase might mean the girl could get to her soccer practice, after all.

"Should we head out to the bait shop?" Tess asked when she rejoined them.

"Not yet. I'm starving, and I don't want to smell fish guts on an empty stomach."

"Great, then let's eat at one of these restaurants, and maybe we'll get some information from the staff."

They stood looking at the two places, and Cornwallis joked, "Should we have fish or fish?"

The one closer to the beach was more of a snack shop than a restaurant. There was a counter where customers could order, and outdoor seating where they could eat under umbrellas.

"They have more than just fish," Kallie explained, since she and Tess had eaten there dozens of times when they were growing up in Owhiro. "But pretty much everything's fried."

"Let's get sushi instead," Tess replied. "I don't want a bunch of fried food in my stomach when we're going to be walking around in the heat later. They have a lunch special that's not too expensive."

Kallie and Cornwallis agreed happily, and they entered the cool, darkened sushi restaurant. The owners recognized Tess and seated them at the counter.

"Three lunch specials, please," Tess requested, without picking up the menu. "How's your wife doing, Mr. Hayashi? Is she out of the hospital?"

"Yes, and I will let her know that you asked, Tess," the older man behind the counter replied, as he reached for the rice. "She went home to stay with her mother for a few weeks, near Kyoto."

I swear, she knows everyone, Kallie thought to herself, always impressed by her best friend's kindness. *And everyone loves her.*

"Do you still have family there, too, like your wife? In Japan?" Kallie asked.

"Not anymore, a tsunami destroyed my hometown," the chef replied, without looking up from the fish he was slicing.

Kallie was startled into silence for a moment. "I'm so sorry."

"I remember hearing about that on the news, years ago," Cornwallis mentioned, without a pause. "Wasn't there a nuclear accident caused by the tsunami, too?"

"Yes," Mr. Hayashi replied, simply. After he finished making their sushi, he added, "I have never been back there. Sometimes life is like that. Everyone wants to return to some part of their past, but sometimes the way back is gone."

Kallie sighed. "I feel like that sometimes. Not that *my* past is radioactive and dangerous. . ."

"Some of it is," Tess whispered, with a smirk.

"My family is all here now," the chef continued. "My brother was already here, in Chicago, and my parents escaped from our village after the earthquake. My father spent a lot of time at sea. He was a geologist, and he knew the tsunami would come, even before the alarms began."

The trio sat quietly, listening to his story in wonder. He passed the sushi across to them, adding, "They were lucky. They fled with only the clothes on their backs, but they survived. They live in Palm Harbor."

"Are you homesick?" Kallie asked, still feeling slightly in awe.

"Not too much anymore. We go to California every year." He didn't explain what he meant, and Kallie didn't pry.

"My son has never been there," he gestured at an attractive young man in a grey linen suit, who was studiously doing paperwork behind the register. "I hope we can go back when his children are born."

"No pressure, Pop," the young man replied with a laugh. "I don't even have a serious girlfriend."

Tess, who clearly knew the son as well, looked at him questioningly.

"Pop can't let me off work for a long vacation," the young man continued. "But, believe me, I'd rather go to Japan now, than take a screaming toddler in five years."

"That sounds very sensible," Kallie answered with an involuntary shudder.

"My son Ren doesn't want people to think he depends on his 'old man,'" the chef added with a subtle smile.

"Don't talk their ears off, Pop. They're trying to eat."

"Actually, we wanted to ask you something, Mr. Hayashi," Cornwallis responded, getting serious. "Are you often here late at night?"

"Yes," the chef replied. "We serve dinner until ten, and we're often open until midnight."

Kallie frowned. *That's not late enough. The murder was in the middle of the night.*

"And do you stay much later than that?" their mentor continued.

"We have to clean up and close out the registers," Ren intervened, standing up from behind the counter. "What's this about?"

"I'm a private investigator," Cornwallis replied. "We're looking into the murder that occurred at the festival."

Mr. Hayashi shook his head. "It was such a shame. When we opened this restaurant, there was no violence here, in Owhiro."

"We were here that night, but we were working.

34

We didn't see anything." There appeared to be a sharper edge to Ren's words this time, and Kallie noticed him tensing up. "Or *hear* anything," he added.

Is he getting defensive, now? I wonder why. . .

"Do you have security cameras?" Tess asked, looking around the small restaurant.

"Yes," the chef replied calmly, with no sign of his son's apparent discomfort.

"Pop, we shouldn't get—"

"Did the police already ask you for the camera footage?" Kallie asked.

"No, we're so far away." Mr. Hayashi gestured toward town, even though the murder scene wasn't visible from inside the restaurant.

"Could we see the video?" Kallie asked. "We're not with the police. We're just trying to help the victim's daughter."

Ren started to argue, but his father interjected, "It's just a camera that I bought online, so I don't think it will show you anything helpful. But it saves seven days' worth of video. I can check the video card after we close tonight and send it to you." He didn't sound hopeful, but he added, "If you think it would help."

The son rolled his eyes and sighed, but Kallie was thrilled. "If it's not too much trouble, that would be great." He handed her a small notebook, and she wrote down Cornwallis's e-mail address and then added her own. "Even if the festival grounds aren't visible, maybe it will show something else."

The sushi chef nodded and smiled, seeming a little more encouraged. He glanced at his son and added, "If it were my father, I would want someone to help me."

"That's how we feel too," Tess replied.

They finished their lunch and Tess paid the bill, chatting with Ren at the register for a minute or two.

Why was Ren so hesitant about helping us? Is he worried about the murder affecting their business? Or is it just a generational concern about law enforcement?

Or does he have something to hide?

"Should we go out to the bait shop now?" Tess asked when they left the restaurant and stepped back out onto the pier.

"I think my nose is ready for the smell now," Kallie replied. "But they're even farther from the beach. They're almost out on the end of the pier."

"Yeah, they wouldn't have seen anything from way out there. And unless they have a really good camera, they wouldn't have filmed anything either," Cornwallis agreed. Kallie thought he probably didn't want to endure the stinky bait shop either. "But that's the only place that might've been open at that hour of the morning."

"I doubt they have a thousand-dollar camera and off-site video storage to guard a bunch of worms and chopped-up fish chunks. This place doesn't even rent boats," Kallie sighed. "But maybe they saw something when they drove up."

"It won't hurt to ask them," Tess insisted. "They're probably not too busy this time of day."

The three of them strolled out to the end of Owhiro's cute pier. It was a lot less impressive than the expensive piers at some of the bigger beach towns—but they loved it. Kallie remembered fishing out here with her dad as one of her earliest memories.

The smell of dead fish and bird droppings hit them from thirty feet away, but they were determined. Pelicans and seagulls sat quietly on the railings, ignoring them, waiting for someone carrying a fresh catch—or possibly French fries from the little snack shop near the beach.

"Ready?" Tess asked.

"Ready as I'll ever be."

Cornwallis opened the door, and Kallie tried not to breathe.

Wow, I didn't think it could possibly smell any worse than it did outside. Holy moley.

The bait shop owner looked up from his magazine behind the counter when he heard the door open. His skin was deeply tanned from the Florida sun, especially against his white butcher's apron. Kallie presumed he'd changed it after the morning rush of bait buyers—it was surprisingly clean. "Afternoon, folks. Are you looking for. . . a fishing pole?"

Kallie frowned, confused, and then looked down at their clothes. Tess was wearing a lightweight skirt and bejeweled pink flip-flops. Kallie was dressed a little more sensibly in nice jeans and tennis shoes, but she certainly didn't look like she planned to bait hooks and wrangle live fish.

"We actually just have a few questions for you," Cornwallis intervened.

The shop owner pulled up the brim of his faded baseball cap and leaned back in his chair. "Is this about the murder?" he asked, stoically.

"Yes, sir," the investigator replied. "Were you here late on Friday?"

"Not late that night. But early the next morning, sure. Business starts picking up a little after five a.m. this time of year, so I have to be open when they get here."

"We thought that might be the case. Do you remember seeing or hearing anything that morning? Anything unusual?"

"I've asked myself that a dozen times. And my wife's asked the same thing at least a *thousand*." He shook his head. "I'm usually out here alone. I have two part-time employees, but they aren't out here before daybreak. Wife's convinced that it could've been me."

"Did the police speak to you?" Kallie asked.

"Not yet."

"We're not involved in their investigation, but the sheriff's latest announcement sounds like they don't think it was a random, indiscriminate killing," Cornwallis clarified. "In case that makes your wife feel any better. But it wouldn't hurt to watch your back, I guess."

"The whole pier was closed while the police were checking out the crime scene, so this is the first time I've been back out here," the shop owner continued, pulling down his baseball cap again. "I'm sure they'll get around to interviewing me in the next few days. They probably have better witnesses keeping them busy, right now."

"Did you remember anything you might've seen?" Kallie asked. "And do you remember what time you got here?"

"I always leave home at four o'clock, and it usually takes about seven or eight minutes to get here."

Cornwallis raised an eyebrow. "That's pretty precise."

"Well, it's only about two miles. Owhiro ain't that big, and I've been making that drive for nearly twenty years. It's pretty predictable in the middle of the night. Just depends on whether I hit the light at Main Street green or not."

Wow, that's dedication. He seems like a really

observant guy, but I wouldn't notice anything at four a.m.

Cornwallis nodded and allowed him to continue.

"I keep asking myself if I saw anything when I parked. Were the sandcastles completely covered? Were the tent drapes down?" He shook his head. "I'm a pretty sharp guy, for what it's worth. I might not have the fanciest job, but I notice things. I *think* I would've noticed. . ."

"It's possible that it hadn't happened yet," Cornwallis replied, sympathetically. "The medical examiner hasn't released a time of death yet. You might've already been out here in the shop before it happened."

"I guess so," the man replied. He didn't sound convinced, and Kallie wondered if he felt guilty.

I know that feeling, my friend. And it's not your fault, any more than our first murder was my fault.

"They keep the festival site really well-lit at night, so no one can mess with the sandcastles," the man explained. "I took my grandkids over there one night, last year, and it was almost like daytime."

I didn't think about that. It's pretty brazen to kill someone out in the open like that—but even more so, when it's so well-lit.

"Under a big spotlight like that, anyone could've seen them," she agreed.

"Well, I hope someone did," the man replied. He sounded angry and frustrated about this murder in his hometown, much like Kallie felt.

Cornwallis handed him a business card. "Will you call me if you remember anything?"

"That's all I remember," the shop owner replied quietly, but he took the card.

"You never know what might trigger a memory. If anything comes up, let me know. We're happy to come back out and talk to you."

Kallie felt like she should say something, since he seemed so despondent, but she couldn't think of anything helpful.

It's not the same thing you experienced, Kalliope. He might've been able to actually help Oscar. He must feel awful.

As they made their way back to the beach, most of the fishermen along the pier were packing up and leaving. Spring was always the hottest season in Owhiro, and the day was heating up uncomfortably. Kallie wished she'd worn shorts.

Apparently, even the fish want to be somewhere cooler.

"Anyone else we should talk to, while we're out here?" Cornwallis asked, looking around the quaint little pier.

"I'd like to talk to the folks in the snack shop,"

Kallie replied. "They might've been out here early that morning, since they have such a busy kitchen. But they're too crowded, since the pier just reopened."

"Busy enough to be out here in the middle of the night, though?" Tess asked.

"We open for lunch at eleven at The Lazy Gecko, and I know some of the kitchen guys get there at eight. So they might've been there a few hours early," she reasoned. "I can't remember if this place is open for breakfast or not."

Tess pointed out a sign showing their business hours as they approached the little food stand. "It says they open at eight." She considered for a moment. "They probably don't get there before six. We could ask them, but not right now."

"We can't interrupt their business like the police can," Cornwallis added. "I mean, we could try, but—"

"That'd be rude," Kallie agreed.

"Especially when the police probably already spoke to them," Tess added. "They're right alongside the festival grounds, after all."

"I'll check with Morrison, but I'm sure you're right," Kallie replied. "If he says the police didn't talk to them, then we can come back out tomorrow morning before they open."

"Good plan, you two," Cornwallis concluded. "Where should we go next?"

"I have to get to the office," Tess answered, sounding a little sad. "I told Winchester I'd transcribe some notes for him today. Will you email us the video from the restaurant when you get it?"

Tess's boss – Cornelius Nicodemus Winchester, Esquire – was a mostly-retired attorney, who no longer took legal cases unless they interested him personally. Tess was his assistant, although she didn't have a law degree, and spent most of her time picking out the more intriguing calls, and getting rid of everyone else.

"You betcha," Cornwallis answered. "Good job today. No regrets so far?"

"None at all," Tess replied, as they made their way to the car. "This is really interesting."

Kallie added, "I'm glad we studied first. I noticed so many things that were in the book."

"Great! I agree, it's going well so far, and I hope I'm being a good mentor," Cornwallis replied. "Let me know if you think of anything else. And feel free to go on interviews without me, if something occurs to you."

They thanked him and walked back to the car, feeling like the morning's excursion had been a success, even if they hadn't found the killer quite yet.

Maybe tomorrow, Kalliope.

Chapter Three

Kallie and Tess were playing Parcheesi with Kallie's dad, Benny Brooks, after dinner when both of their phones dinged in unison.

"That must be Cornwallis," Kallie noted, hesitating long enough to move her man on the board.

"He has the video from the restaurant already," Tess replied, sounding surprised as she read from her phone. "He said Mr. Hayashi downloaded the video before they reopened for dinner. He's emailing it to me now." She walked over to the couch and pulled her laptop out of her work bag, taking a moment to plug it in.

"Well, let's see it!" Benny exclaimed. "I'm kicking both of your butts at this game, anyway."

"As usual, Mister B," Tess agreed with a laugh. "The video will take a few minutes to download. Does anyone want dessert while we're waiting?"

"There's part of a lemon chiffon pie in the garage fridge," Kallie replied. "I'll go get it and start some coffee."

Ten minutes later, they gathered around Tess's

computer and watched as she opened the folder showing the first file. "There are a bunch of separate, short videos," Tess explained. "The camera must be set to only record when it's triggered by movement, which makes sense if he bought it online."

"At least we won't have to stare at four straight hours of dark sand," Benny added.

"The timestamps say they're between two a.m. and six a.m."

"That's about daybreak on the beach, so that should be all we need," Kallie agreed.

Tess counted the files and said, "There are fourteen files, so let's start at the beginning."

She clicked on the first video file, and her player came to life. They all blinked at the dark screen, needing to adjust their eyes. Kallie got up and turned off the dining room's overhead light.

"I don't know why I expected to be able to see anything," Kallie added, discouraged. "It was filmed in the middle of the night, so of course it's dark."

"It's easier to see with the light off, though," Tess replied. "That was a good idea. So it looks like the camera is pointing the wrong way, which Mr. Hayashi said would probably happen. It's filming from the front of the restaurant, across the pier, and over the edge at the beach."

"It's kind of a fisheye lens," Benny added. "So the area right in front of the restaurant is a little distorted, but it gives a wider view. That's good for us."

"I think this video was triggered by those seagulls, though," Tess replied with a sigh. "There's nothing else going on."

They all sat back and got comfortable as they made their way through the files—pausing and rewinding occasionally. They were each under four minutes, and a few were only thirty seconds long. Kallie deduced that there was a minimum recording time, but the cameras would record longer if something continued moving within the field of view.

Most of them were videos of seagulls, unfortunately. Someone had apparently dropped a slice of pizza on the pier the night before, and the gulls were picking at the last bits of crust and cheese.

By the fourth video, Tess was getting annoyed with the birds. When the fifth showed more of them, she snapped, "These stupid birds. This is a waste of time!"

Kallie leaned on her shoulder and said, "I'm sorry, I thought this was going to be a good clue, too." The feathery feast ended, and she clicked on the next video. "Do you want to go sit with Sherman while I finish watching the 'Best Supporting Seabird in a Drama' nominations?

Sherman, Kallie's rescued border collie mix, opened his eyes at the sound of his name and looked at Tess expectantly.

Tess laughed and replied, "No, I'll finish

watching them with you. I'm sorry, I'm just disappointed."

"It's never this easy," Kallie replied, hugging her best friend crookedly from her seat. "Can you imagine if we caught the killer on the first day of the investigation?"

"I'd be okay with that," Tess replied, sheepishly.

"More seagulls," Kallie complained when the video ended. She clicked on the next one. "And *more* seagulls. . ."

"Wait," her dad interjected. "They're flying away."

Kallie and Tess both leaned forward to view what was happening, only to see the blur of a striped stray cat run through the screen.

"No killer, but at least it was an interesting break." Kallie clicked the next video.

"More seagulls. Maybe I *will* go sit with Sherman," Tess grumbled.

"Hang on," Kallie mumbled, leaning toward the screen.

"Nope, Sherman and the couch are calling my name," Tess joked, standing up.

"Seriously, look at this for a sec," Kallie insisted. "I think there's someone on the beach."

"What?" Tess sat back down. "Where? What time is this?"

Kallie maximized the window, making both the video and the recording time bigger. "Four twenty-seven. And that's definitely someone down on the sand. It looks like they're running, too."

"Could it just be a jogger?" her dad asked.

"Maybe," Kallie answered. She clicked on a few options in the video viewer and then found the zoom button. The picture enlarged but became blurrier. "I don't think those are jogging clothes."

"And joggers don't usually run in the loose sand. They run on the waterline, where it's solid," Tess agreed, staring at the screen. "I think we might actually have something here."

"I can't really make out anything else," Kallie complained. "Does he have something in his hand?"

"This is just the laptop's built-in video player," Tess explained. "Let me open this file in a better application, so we can see more of the details." She quickly clicked a different icon and allowed the professional viewer to open. "I mean, he's really far away, and this camera doesn't have the greatest resolution..."

"I'm sure it'll be great," Benny reassured her. "We can give it to the police and let their technical forensics team work on it, but I want to see it first."

Did my retired, easy-going father just say 'technical forensics team?' We are such a bad influence!

48

"Me too, Mister B," Tess replied. The much-slower application finally opened, and she started the video. "Here we go."

The shadowy figure ran across the laptop screen again – but in the better viewer, they could make out more details. He was in dark clothing and seemed to be sliding a little in the loose sand, and. . .

Tess paused the video.

"He *definitely* has something in his hand," Kallie added, when the still image was zoomed in. "Can you play it, in this close-up mode?"

"Not really," Tess replied. "It's too grainy. Let me zoom back out a little and try it."

They watched the video again, all of them leaning forward over the table with their heads together.

"There's something in his hand, but it could be anything," Benny sighed. "A water bottle, or a phone, maybe. Some people run with dumbbells—"

"A gun?" Kallie suggested.

"It could be a gun," Tess replied, tilting her head and squinting. She frowned and shook her head in annoyance. "Heck, he could be holding one of those seagulls. I can't tell."

"We're pretty sure it's a guy, though, right?" Kallie asked.

Tess zoomed back out more, and then played it

again. "Yeah, that's a guy. That height, build, and running form? Definitely a guy."

Benny nodded, "I agree."

"Okay, well, that was worth watching ten thousand seagulls," Tess concluded with a smile, obviously feeling better. "I'll make a better copy and send it to Wally. We'll let him take it to the cops, since he's working with them."

"I can't wait to tell Morrison. He's going to be so proud of us."

Benny coughed awkwardly and put down his phone. "Okay, yeah. I'll let *you* tell him."

"Oh, thanks, Dad," Kallie answered with a laugh, adding, "I guess that's what I get for dating my dad's best friend."

***

"What exactly do you think we're going to find out here?" Kallie asked grumpily, as they walked down Owhiro's main beach the next night. She'd had a table of four rude customers at work right before her shift ended, and she was still annoyed.

"Probably nothing," Cornwallis replied, swinging his backpack onto his shoulder. "But I thought we should come out here and look, anyway. There are worse places to be than this pretty beach at night."

Kallie was struck again by his odd accent. She didn't usually notice it anymore, but the way he pronounced 'pretty beach' was unusual. She still couldn't place it.

Tess probably already asked him, Kalliope. Would it kill you to be a little nicer?

What's 'nice' from Tess just sounds like 'nosy' from me.

"It *is* beautiful out here tonight," she agreed with a sigh. "I'd rather be here than behind the bar, anyway."

"I doubt we'll find anything, since there have already been two high tide cycles since the murder," he added. "But we can get a feel for what our runner saw, which way he was going, and where he was in relation to the crime scene."

"You said the moon was full that night, right?" Tess asked. "Then the tide would've been even higher than normal."

They were approaching the pier from the side, and as they walked into its shadow, the night seemed to get even darker. The Gulf water—still chilly even though the days were getting hot—lapped at their feet. Kallie paused as Tess sighed and took off her shoes, walking peacefully into the deeper water. A moment later, she did the same, noting that her tired feet felt better already.

For about thirty seconds.

"Ow!" Kallie winced and grabbed her right foot.

"What?" Tess asked in surprise. "Are you okay?"

"I just ran into something."

"Were you doing the stingray shuffle?" Tess asked, seriously, making Kallie laugh despite her pain.

Cornwallis was looking at them both like they were crazy. The locals always shuffled their feet in the water to scare away any hidden stingrays before they were accidentally kicked.

"It wasn't a stingray. It was something metal. Come over here and see."

Tess was quickly by her side, standing in the knee-deep water, and Cornwallis finally took off his shoes and joined them.

"It does look like metal," he concluded. "Don't touch it. It looks mangled, so it might be sharp."

"What is that thing? It looks like a robot exploded."

Algae had started growing on one end of the metal pole, making it look even weirder.

"A robot who's growing green leg hair," Kallie added.

"Maybe it's scaffolding from one of the renovation projects," Tess suggested. "They just finished restoring the façade on one of the old churches in town. Maybe someone scavenged it for money, and then couldn't find anyone to buy it."

52

"Could be," Cornwallis replied. "The scrapyards are getting wary of thieves." He tilted his head to look at the metal, trying to examine it without touching it. "Oh. I think it might be one of those e-scooters that they rent in town. The motorized ones."

"Really?" Tess asked doubtfully, tilting her head, too.

"It doesn't look like a scooter to me," Kallie agreed, squinting.

"Come stand over here," he instructed. When they moved closer, he knelt down and pointed into the deeper water. "I think that's the front wheel."

"Ohhh," they both whispered.

"Definitely don't touch it. These things have lithium batteries, and they can explode when they touch salt water." After a moment, he pointed and added, "And that would be the handlebars. It's already starting to get barnacles."

"If we could get the serial number, we could find out who rented it. Do you think it's written on the handlebars?" Kallie asked.

"If so, it's already totally covered," Cornwallis replied, with a sigh.

Tess already had her phone out and was scrolling. Kallie smiled a little, and they both waited patiently.

She's our own technical forensics team.

"Can you see the kickstand?" Tess finally asked. "This says the serial number should be on the deck, by the kickstand."

"The deck," Cornwallis repeated. "So that should be something that looks like a skateboard. . ."

"Maybe it floated away?" Kallie considered aloud.

"Maybe." He took a heavy security flashlight out of his ubiquitous backpack and pointed it at the water, trying to see what was hidden below the surface—but the dark water just reflected the blinding light like a mirror. They all flinched and quickly looked away from the glare.

"Could the deck still be attached to the front wheel, down there?" Kallie asked.

"I don't see it. And I'm not getting down there to find out."

"Yeah, good call," Tess sighed. "If it was near the surface, I was going to take a picture of the serial number and blow it up."

Cornwallis chuckled. "That's how I read the expiration dates on my groceries."

"Exactly, it makes tiny details so much easier to see," Tess agreed. "But I doubt it would help, with all those barnacles. And certainly not with parts that have already drifted halfway to Texas."

"Well, I'm taking photographs anyway. And the

police will be able to find the company that rented it," Cornwallis responded. "The renter can't have ridden it far—it's probably from right near the beach."

He proceeded to take photos with a professional digital camera, and then frowned at the view screen.

"What did you see?" Kallie asked, pulling out her phone and taking some photos too.

"Nothing specific, I just wish we could see what's down there in the deeper water. I'm afraid it'll be gone with the tide by morning."

"But you have an idea," Tess stated, not a question.

"Well, sure," he replied with a quiet laugh. "But that doesn't mean it's right. I'll come back out here in the morning, when the tide's back out. Hopefully, it won't float away. Maybe it will make sense in the daylight."

"It might be unrelated to the case," Kallie suggested. "Right?"

"Oh, of course," Cornwallis agreed immediately. "Almost certainly, in fact. Barnacles grow fast around here, but not in forty-eight hours. So there's a ninety-five percent chance that it's totally unrelated."

"But you don't think so," Kallie continued.

"Nope," he smiled.

"Let's hope you're right."

***

They'd planned to go back to Cornwallis's office to drop him off and pick up some files, so Tess drove toward Tampa, while they all dwelt on their own thoughts.

Tess made the left turn toward the bridge and asked, "Do you want to stop for takeout before we go back to your office? There's a good Greek place about a mile from here."

"Sure, I could eat," Cornwallis replied. Then he suddenly looked to the left and added, "Oh, wait. Pull in here." He pointed to a small, dirty parking lot beside the road. "I recognize that car."

A deserted strip mall with boarded-up windows was the only thing visible from the street, but Tess followed his instructions. The old, orangish overhead lights lit up the dingy parking lot surprisingly well.

"A friend of yours? Do you think they're having car trouble and need a lift?" Kallie asked, as Tess parked next to a spotless, black, late-model Cadillac with a license plate that read BN2QLT, and got out of the car.

"No, it's Mrs. Jackson, the blanket lady," he replied cryptically, walking off into the shadows.

"What's a blanket lady?" Kallie asked.

"Beats me, it sounds like something from a ghost story," Tess replied. "Where's he going?"

They hurried to keep up with Cornwallis, and Kallie added, "Oh, Born to Quilt. That's what her license plate means. She must literally be a blanket maker."

"But what's she doing out *here*?"

Cornwallis was walking away from the car, toward the end of the old strip mall. The empty space at the end of the building was overgrown with weeds, but he stomped through them and walked out of sight into the darkness. Kallie heard him call out, "Hello, stranger."

They turned the corner and found the investigator talking with a tiny old woman, who was carrying armfuls of shopping bags. Behind them, Kallie saw a small homeless encampment beyond the trees.

When they reached the chatting couple, Kallie took the opportunity to appraise the packages. What she'd been carrying were inexpensive woolen blankets from a chain store, not quilts.

Wait, blankets or quilts? What's happening? And why is this poor woman in the woods behind a crumbling old strip mall, in the dark?

"This is my friend, ladies. You can call her 'Mrs. Jackson,'" Cornwallis explained. "She's an exceptional seamstress, and she makes prize-winning quilts."

Kallie nodded, still confused but not ready to admit it quite yet.

"She sells them in online auctions for a lot of money," he added, beaming at the old woman with obvious fondness and respect. "Then she uses the money to buy blankets, to bring out here."

"Oh. That's pretty cool," Kallie exclaimed, suddenly clear on the process.

"I'm not an expert on quilts or anything," he added. "But they're apparently really something special. Anyway, that's how I met her."

Kallie looked over at the tiny, elderly woman, who had been quietly enveloped by a group of strangers from the woods, and was handing out warm blankets to everyone in the camp.

"It's usually hot this time of year, as you well know. This incoming cold snap the weathermen are predicting caught the county off guard, so here she is, helping them out as usual."

"I'd be nervous if my mom were out here with this crowd," Tess confessed. "There have been murders in these homeless camps in the past few years."

"They all know her," Cornwallis replied. "Of course, that doesn't mean it's without danger. Some of these folks have serious mental health issues, and nowhere to get their meds. I keep an eye on her, if I see her out volunteering. I think others do too."

"I'd love to see *my* mother out here," Kallie sneered.

Tess laughed. "Can you imagine?" She started giggling and several people looked over at them. "I'm sorry, I just got a vision of your mom out here. Trying to get someone to break a hundred for her."

Kallie grinned, but Cornwallis was frowning in disapproval.

"It'll make more sense once you meet her," Kallie explained.

"If you're ever so unfortunate," Tess added.

"Sorry, it's been a stressful couple of months," Kallie added, trying to stifle a giggle. "We'll get it under control."

"She's almost done," Cornwallis noted, once they'd stopped laughing. "Let's catch her before she leaves." He took off in her direction without waiting for them.

"—to see you, Mrs. Jackson," they heard him saying, when they caught up with him. "It's so generous of you to come out here to help these people."

"It's not *my* money, Reginald. You know that," she corrected him, with a gentle smile.

Whoa, did she just call him Reginald? He must really like her.

Cornwallis chuckled. "If you insist, Mrs. Jackson. But those folks will be warmer tonight because of you."

"I hope to Heaven they are." As Kallie's eyes adjusted to the dim light of the waning moon, she could see the elderly woman's still-clear, dark eyes sparkle with kindness behind her thick glasses. She wore a long dress, and the million tiny braids of her hair were swept up into an elegant chignon. "Did you need to talk to me, Reginald?"

He blushed, as he must've realized he was holding her up. Kallie was surprised but charmed to see the P.I.'s normally grumpy face turn red. "Yes, ma'am. I wanted to see if you'd heard anything about the man who was murdered in Owhiro?"

"Well, I knew Oscar, of course. But I hadn't seen him in years," she explained. "I thought he'd moved away, in fact, until a few weeks ago."

"You just saw him a few weeks ago?"

"I saw him with some other men when I was leaving the farmers market. He wasn't asking for help or money, but I recognized him. From the old days, you know." Her face was sad, and she looked disappointed but confident. "I never forget a face, Reginald."

"I remember that about you, ma'am," he replied with a shy smile. "Did you know the men he was with?"

"I knew one of them. Name's Endicott, or that's what they call him. A decent man. About the same age as Oscar." She tilted her head in thought and paused. "But the other two were younger. Looked like they had money."

"Were they giving money to your guys?"

"No, they were just talking. Didn't seem to be any trouble. I only noticed them because I hadn't seen Oscar in so long." She sighed at the memory. "And then

I saw him on the news, of course. Was he one of yours, Reginald?"

"Yes, ma'am," he answered simply.

She nodded. "I thought so. I figured perhaps he'd saved up enough money and moved away. I recall a few of yours have done that."

"A few, ma'am," he mumbled. "Would you recognize the other two men if you saw them again?"

"Perhaps. I only saw them from a distance. But Endicott might be able to tell you who they were. He's quiet, not very sociable, but he's been known to return a favor."

Cornwallis nodded. "That's good to know, ma'am. Thank you for your help."

"Of course, Reginald." She gave him a tiny smile and patted him on the arm. "We're on the same side, you and I." She walked away without another word, and they trailed behind her until she was back in the parking lot and returning to her Cadillac.

"Do you know this guy Endicott?" Kallie finally asked.

"Never heard of him," Cornwallis sighed. "But I'll put out some feelers. Someone has to know him."

Chapter Four

Kallie plopped down at the small table outside the charming little café with a slight grunt. "Sorry I'm late."

"I was wondering if you'd stood me up, Brooks."

She pushed her auburn hair messily out of her face and looked up, exhausted, to see Detective Morrison smirking across the table at her. His handsome brown eyes twinkled in amusement, and her stomach did a tiny somersault. She grinned back.

"I must look terrible. I'm sorry, I was up late studying."

He shook his head. "You never look terrible. But you're not usually late, either."

Justine, their usual waitress, came to the table and brought two glasses of orange juice, taking Kallie's order for a bacon and cheese bagel with hash browns.

"How's the case treating you?" Morrison asked. She'd told the detective that she was intent on learning her new trade the hard way, and she could tell he was trying not to offer suggestions, trying to let her learn organically unless she asked.

"It's a mess," she laughed. "When I think we've found a great clue, and do a bunch of research, it turns out to be nothing. And then we're afraid to discard any ideas, even if they seem stupid, in case they turn out to be important."

Morrison nodded sympathetically. "I know the feeling. I mean, sort of. When I was on my first case, I had a whole department behind me."

"I have Tess," Kallie replied with a grin.

"Yeah, that's practically the same thing," he agreed, picking up a strip of bacon. "So, Investigator Cornwallis is letting you handle it on your own?"

"He's trying," she replied with a laugh. "But he's been really helpful."

Morrison nodded and reached for the jar of orange marmalade, smiling down at his plate.

"You've been keeping tabs on us, haven't you?" she asked, suddenly suspicious.

"No!" Morrison insisted, hands up in surrender. "No, I haven't even spoken to him, except when he asked for leeway on investigating Oscar Lawson's case. But I'm glad to hear he's looking out for you a little."

Not that Kallie minded a little protection. She'd had enough close calls in the past few years, and wouldn't mind having a bodyguard hiding in the shadows—even if it was a grumpy, secretive one.

She smiled up at Justine as she delivered her

breakfast. She'd been serving them for several years, and Kallie was sure they must seem like a bizarre team. Had she been following their mysteries, and speculating on their evolving friendship, like all of her other friends? Probably.

"So who are you harassing now, Miss Busybody?" Morrison asked.

"You will be proud to know that we aren't harassing anyone, *Detective*," she answered, archly, cutting her bagel sandwich carefully into quarters.

"That's an encouraging change. What brought on this wave of maturity?"

"Cornwallis has been counseling us on the best way to treat suspects," she replied, seriously. "It's not what I thought—"

"Not like on TV, huh?"

"Nope," she agreed, as Justine returned with a pot of coffee and refilled their cups. "And we haven't been attacked or sued yet, so I guess he must be right."

"I wish I could help you, but Owhiro PD is the primary on this case. I'm not up to speed on the details."

She raised an eyebrow at him, as she dumped milk in her coffee.

"Not help. I didn't mean help," he replied in a panicked tone, teasing her. "I would never offer to *help*. But I could read your case notes out loud to you, if you want. Like murder flash cards."

Kallie laughed as she splashed hot sauce on her hash browns. "Hmm, murder flash cards. That's not a bad idea, actually."

***

After their early breakfast, Kallie texted Tess and asked to meet and discuss their plans. Tess was waiting with a pitcher of iced coffee, watching the news.

"Come sit down," she called. "They're having a press conference."

"Ooh, my favorite," Kallie replied, only half-joking. She poured a glass of creamy coffee and sipped it happily as the Owhiro chief of police stepped up to the podium.

"Thank you all for coming," he began speaking to the press. "We have some additional information on the Celebration of Sandcastles case for you. The victim's name is Oscar Lawson, age fifty-one, and a long-time resident of the area." He spelled the victim's name patiently as the reporters took notes. "We can confirm that he was shot on Owhiro Beach, at the site of the annual Celebration of Sandcastles festival, but the medical examiner hasn't finished her work yet, so we don't have much more on the cause of death."

"Is it true that you caught the killer?" one of the reporters yelled. "Was it the victim's own cousin who shot him?"

"We have a suspect in custody, and we no longer believe there's a threat to the community," the chief, Cab Patterson, replied. "I can't give out any other information on the suspect at this time, but I can confirm that he was known to the victim. It wasn't a random act."

"Can you confirm that two of his roommates were also involved? There was a report that—"

"I can't discuss the suspects, Sharon," Patterson repeated to the reporter from Tampa News Twelve, the 24-hour news channel they were watching.

"Will the festival be reopening?" another reporter asked.

"The forensics team has finished their work, so—after some consideration—we're planning to allow the festival to reopen. We're aware this is a major tourist destination, especially for a small town like Owhiro, and we don't want to cause any economic strain." Patterson paused for a moment and looked to his left, and then added, "The Owhiro mayor will speak next."

Kallie recognized their long-time mayor, Rebecca Torres, and smiled warmly as she stepped up to the podium.

"I love Mayor Torres," Tess echoed her thoughts.

"As Chief Patterson said, the main tent will reopen shortly, at nine o'clock this morning, and we're going to allow the food trucks to return to the festival site at eleven," the mayor explained, looking polished in a cream suit and black heels, her dark brown shoulder-length bob impeccable. "But we want everyone to be aware that there will be a candlelight vigil for the victim at sunset tonight. Mr. Lawson may not have been wealthy, but he was blessed with friends—"

It's so kind of the city to hold a tribute for Oscar. I only wish they could've helped him sooner.

"—and they've asked to hold it on the sidewalk near the pier." She added, seriously, "The vigil will *not* be allowed into the Celebration of Sandcastles area. Some of the sculptures have already been damaged, and we don't want any other destruction."

"I guess we know where we'll be at sunset," Tess mentioned with a crooked smile.

"Definitely," Kallie replied. "I wouldn't mind going down there and having a look around during the day. A killer sometimes returns to the scene of their crime, looking for validation."

"It'll be *packed*, if they're reopening it today," Tess noted. "But we could walk down there and see who shows up. Parking will be a mess."

"Sheriff Hall is busy with his investigation," the mayor added. "But he wanted to remind everyone that there's no curfew in place. So if you're in town visiting, it's a perfect day to get down to the festival and spend some money, and then check out the nightlife. The vendors lost a few days of sales, and I know they'll be thrilled to see you all."

The chief returned to the podium, as Mayor Torres waved at one of the reporters and then stepped aside.

"We'll have another press conference when the medical examiner releases her findings. That will probably be tomorrow or the next day. Thank you for—"

The television cut back to the news station desk abruptly, and Charles, the lead morning anchor, began summarizing the press conference. Tess muted the television.

"If you want to go down to the beach, let's go now," Tess suggested. "She said they're opening at nine, and I'm sure every tourist within fifty miles of the mayor's voice will be driving down here."

"Good, maybe they'll go to The Lazy Gecko too, and spend lots of that happy tourist money," Kallie added with a laugh. "Mama needs a new pair of. . . Well, not shoes, obviously," she quipped, looking at her sneakers. "A new pair of scuba flippers, I guess?"

"Are you working today?" Tess asked.

"Yeah, but we have two hours before I need to be there for the lunch rush."

"Great, then let's go now, and we can go back for the vigil later."

Tess put on her shoes and ran to the kitchen,

while Kallie grabbed hats and sunscreen for the beach. She hurried back, and then stood still beside the front door, staring outside.

"What's going on, Kallie?" Tess called as she hurried out of the kitchen with two bottles of water. "We're going to be late."

Kallie stood looking out the window, stunned. "It's raining."

She heard Tess snort behind her. "Right, Kal. Come on, let's go." She reached for the door, but stopped as soon as she opened it. "What the–?"

"I know," Kallie whispered, forcing back a weird giggle. "When has it ever–?"

"But it's *April*," Tess groaned. "I can't remember the last time it rained in April. It's *pouring*."

The driving rain sounded almost like hail, pounding on the metal overhang above the door.

"I hate to complain. We really need the rain— my lawn is downright crunchy," Tess added, staring out at the deluge. "But this totally throws a monkey wrench in our plans. How can we stake out the festival site in the pouring rain? We'd have to stay in the car, and the main tent's way too far from any parking lot."

"Poor Mayor Torres. They'll have to pull the tent flaps down, with it raining *this* hard," Kallie sighed, looking out at the growing puddles. The sculptures were built under an enormous tent, both for initial secrecy, and for protection from the elements and vandals. But they rarely needed shelter from rainstorms.

Tess tapped on the door, thinking. "This is the first chance the killer's had to come back to the scene of the crime, after it was roped off for three days. So he's bound to show up. And tonight's vigil will be *outside* of the festival grounds."

"And packed with cops, too, I'm sure," Kallie added.

"Way less enticing," Tess reasoned.

"But we're just doing surveillance work now," Kallie noted. "And we can't see into the crime scene with the tarps down."

"Right. This stupid rain."

"What if, instead of doing surveillance from the car, we went in closer?" Kallie suggested. "We'd just look like lost tourists."

"Lost tourists, stuck in the rain," Tess finished her thought. "I think Wally wanted us to stick with surveillance to be safer, but we should be perfectly safe in a crowd, as long as we're subtle."

"I'm the Queen of Subtle," Kallie replied. "But where could we hide?"

"How about *inside* the festival tent?" Tess suggested. "It's going to be packed, especially with the tarps down. But let's try it." She opened the hall closet and dug around until she found an old golf umbrella. "My good umbrella is in the car, but this should keep us dry for the moment."

They made a mad dash for Tess's car, where the pouring rain was already standing a few inches deep in the driveway. Despite the umbrella and their quick actions, they were both soaked by the time they shut the doors.

"The gutters must all be full of dead leaves. What a mess," Kallie complained.

Tess took off her shoes and frowned at the soggy fabric. "I think these are ruined." She tossed them into the back seat, and then turned on the car's heater and pulled out of the driveway. "I have flip-flops in the trunk. I'll get them after we find a parking place. At least with the rain, maybe we'll be able to find a spot."

"I should've rolled up my pants before we came out," Kallie added. "My shoes will survive, but I'm soaked from the knees down."

Tess laughed. "At least the killer won't suspect us. We look like drowned rats."

Lightning flashed across the darkening sky, and thunder clapped loudly a few seconds later.

"Yikes. That means we can't hide out at the pier either. That lightning was way too close for comfort."

"When thunder roars, go indoors," Kallie replied with a smirk and a wag of her finger.

She was teasing, but it was a serious lesson in the Tampa Bay area. It was the lightning capital of the

US, and people were sometimes killed by a lightning strike from up to twelve miles away. Especially on the beaches, where storms had a habit of sneaking up from the land side—the direction no one was looking.

Kallie took out her phone and checked the weather radar, as Tess continued driving slowly toward the beach. "It's just a small storm. We can wait until it passes," she suggested.

"Will you call Wally?" Tess asked. "I don't even want to use the hands-free phone mount in this weather. The road's so slick after no rain for a few months."

Kallie called Cornwallis and told him what was happening, only to find out that it wasn't raining there. "He asked if I was kidding," she told Tess.

"I wish," she replied, squinting into the downpour through the rapidly flicking windshield wipers, looking for the nearly invisible lane lines.

"He can't meet us right now. He said he's meeting with Badger," Kallie announced after she hung up.

"Badger?" Tess asked, with surprise. "Is he involved in this?"

"I think Cornwallis is just following up on a lead."

"Well, that guy knows everything. And everyone."

"I'm glad Cornwallis is going without us," Kallie whispered. Badger was an informant for Cornwallis, and a great resource. But he was unpleasant at best. Downright creepy, if she was being honest.

"Me too," Tess agreed.

***

The rain had indeed chased away some of the tourists, and Tess was lucky to find a parking spot near the main festival tent. When the pop-up storm passed, they grabbed Tess's flip-flops from the trunk and walked down to see the displays.

Kallie had visited the Celebration of Sandcastles festival many times over the years, since she'd grown up in Owhiro, but the sculptures were amazing every year. Artists came from all over the world to create their majestic works of sand.

As they entered the main tent, the massive, towering sandcastles loomed over their heads, seeming to be held up by magic. There were statues of elegant pagodas, fanciful palaces, and replicas of buildings from fantasy and science fiction films.

Kallie stared in wonder at a statuesque tower with a dragon wrapped around it, seeming to defy gravity.

"This never gets old," Tess stated, raising her

voice a little over the crowd. "I don't know how they create these things out of plain old sand." They'd watched the artists one year, as they piled tons of wet sand, and then carved it away to reveal their masterpieces – but it still seemed amazing.

"Do you see anyone acting strangely?" Kallie asked, looking around.

"It's mostly parents with kids," Tess replied, sounding discouraged. "Definitely no one who looks dangerous or threatening."

"For all we know, it could be one of these parents," Kallie suggested. "This is silly. Did we think there was going to be some guy in a trench coat, twirling his moustache and ogling the crowd?"

"Like Snidely Whiplash," Tess agreed with a laugh, pretending to twist an invisible moustache.

"Let's stay and look at the sandcastles, anyway. At least until I have to leave for work," Kallie added. "Maybe the murderer will come back since the rain stopped."

Kallie and Tess spent another twenty minutes admiring the sculptures, but no dastardly villain appeared. In fact, they didn't even see anyone who seemed to be alone in the festival tent – and they couldn't imagine the killer bringing a date, or his kids. And finally Kallie needed to leave for work. The Lazy Gecko was nearby, so Tess dropped her off, but they were both disappointed.

After work, Tess called just as Kallie finished cleaning up her section for the next shift. "You have amazing timing. How do you always know right when I'm done?"

"Years of practice," Tess replied with a laugh. "They showed the Celebration of Sandcastles site on the news, and there are about twenty uniformed police officers there."

"Already? The vigil doesn't start for almost another hour."

"Yeah, they have it totally locked down. The cops must've had the same idea, that the killer might come back. I hate to say this, but I don't think there's any reason for us to go," Tess replied. "The experts can handle it, and the killer probably won't show up in front of all those cops, anyway."

"And I'd have to walk there from the Gecko. No way we'd find parking," Kallie agreed, adding, "Ugh, we just can't catch a break, today. What should we do, then?"

Tess gave that some thought. "Let's go see Cornwallis. I haven't heard from him all day, and I don't feel like studying. So let's go pick his brain instead."

Kallie agreed, and Tess picked her up ten minutes later for the rainy, thirty-minute drive to Tampa. Tess pulled in to the drab parking lot outside of Cornwallis's office. As she parked the car, Kallie checked her phone again. "It's weird that he hasn't texted us all day. He usually reaches out at least once."

"He's probably just busy. He has to take other cases to pay the bills while he's training us, remember?"

"Yeah, you're right," Kallie agreed with a nod, watching the rain streak down the car windows, and trying not to worry. "He's probably just out taking pictures of some adulterous spouse in a cheap motel."

"Gross," Tess replied with a jaded laugh. "Suddenly, I'm glad we just stick to investigating murders."

Cornwallis's office door was open a crack when they reached the top of the stairs, and Tess pushed it open. Kallie frowned, but Tess shrugged. "He must be downstairs."

"We didn't see him—"

"He's fine, Kal. He's probably in the courtyard." Tess stepped behind the desk and gestured for Kallie to follow her. She pointed at a framed photograph and nodded that Kallie should look at it.

"Who's that?" Kallie whispered, looking at the faded old photo.

"That's his first wife. She died about fifteen years ago," Tess answered.

"She was beautiful. She looks like that actress—"

Tess looked at her quizzically.

"You know. She was in that movie with Paul Newman. She looks just like her."

Tess tilted her head and squinted at the photograph.

Kallie sighed and let it go, reminding herself to look it up online later. "I wonder how many times he's been married. . ." she pondered.

"Just the two."

Kallie's eyes widened. "How did you get him to talk about his personal life? He's so private."

"I just asked him," Tess replied with a shrug.

Kallie snorted. "He won't even tell me what kind of coffee he likes. You didn't *'just ask him.'*"

She probably really did, though. Tess just has a way with people, making them feel seen and understood—like they're the only person in the room.

Something you'll never have, Kalliope.

Kallie shoved that thought aside and continued, "So no pictures of the ex-wife?"

"Would you keep pictures of your ex?" Tess asked with a laugh.

"Heck no," Kallie replied. "I'd have to shovel them out of the fireplace, anyway." She looked around the office and added, "Did he clean in here? It smells better, too."

"Yeah, I think he—"

The door opened, and they both jumped, guiltily. Cornwallis walked back in, soggy from the rain and unsurprised to see them.

"I thought that was going to be the FedEx delivery guy, but it was actually one of my contacts," he told them, as he returned to his seat.

"Out there in the rain?" Kallie asked. "It's pouring."

"He could've come inside," Tess added sympathetically. "Do you want to go get him? We don't mind waiting."

"He's already gone," Cornwallis replied. "He rides his bike all over town. Even into different counties."

Kallie looked out the dirty window at the driving rain again.

"I don't see him very often, but when he's in the area, he usually brings me some information he's collected," Cornwallis explained, leaning back in his chair.

"Does he keep a folder for you or something?"

Cornwallis smiled. "Nope, it's all up here." He pointed at his temple. "I don't know how he does it. I guess he has a photographic memory."

"Did he tell you anything useful?" Tess asked, curious.

"I'm not sure yet." He held up his phone and

added, "I always record him. *He* might be able to remember a sliver of information he heard six months ago, but I can't even remember it long enough to get up the stairs." He laughed at himself.

You and me both, Kallie thought to herself, feeling a little less like an amateur.

"It's usually fifty-fifty. Or maybe more like forty-sixty, really. Some information is helpful and some of it's totally random." After a moment, he added, "But sometimes the random stuff makes sense later. So I always transcribe the whole recording and save it. One time, he told me about a wounded lady he saw. In the middle of a bunch of other stories. Injured. Bleach blonde with a tattoo of a dragon with the name 'Tommy' under it."

"That's so specific," Kallie whispered.

"Yeah, and he saw her about a month before he spoke to me. I never found anything about her, not even from the cops, so I wrote it off as one of his misses. Maybe even a figment of his imagination—which happens sometimes, too. But she turned up dead a year later."

"Wow," Tess sighed.

He slammed a desk drawer a little harder than was necessary. "I mean, it'd be a lot more '*wow*' if I saved her from getting killed in the first place—" he grumbled angrily.

Kallie leaned back, surprised at his sudden

change of mood, but Tess replied, "It sounds like you tried. You even went to the police."

He ignored her and opened a second desk drawer, tossing the phone inside. Kallie supposed he'd transcribe the conversation later, after they left. He slammed that drawer, too, and then turned away toward the window.

"It's not like you could go door-to-door looking for her. . ." Tess continued, sounding miserable.

Kallie looked at both of them, stunned by Cornwallis's reaction. At his impatience with his own perceived failure, when he was so patient with them. But then he shook it off so quickly, she wondered if she'd imagined it.

"Anyway, I'm still waiting for the FedEx delivery."

"How did it go with Badger?" Tess asked. Kallie thought her voice sounded like she didn't really want to know.

"Oh, it went well, actually." Cornwallis replied. "He said he saw Oscar the weekend before he was killed."

"Seriously?" Kallie asked. "Man, that guy's everywhere."

"Yeah, he gets around. That's why he's such a good contact."

I'd like him better if he wasn't so creepy.

"Where did he see Oscar? Was Badger in *Owhiro*?" Tess asked, sounding alarmed.

Yikes. Please say no.

"No," Cornwallis replied, tapping his pen on the desk thoughtfully. "Down in Pinellas Park. Outside the convenience store across from the flea market, he said."

"The flea market? Was he buying something?"

"Badger wasn't sure. And that's a long way from Owhiro too. I asked him if he was sure, but. . . Well, Badger doesn't make mistakes."

"And I'm sure he wasn't thrilled that you doubted him," Tess added.

"You're right about that," Cornwallis replied, chuckling. "But he said the flea market was open, which means it had to be a Saturday or Sunday. Probably morning or early afternoon."

"Was Oscar alone? Maybe he was with his killer," Kallie suggested.

"Badger said it was too crowded to tell if he was alone." Cornwallis looked at them both and emphasized, "He wasn't *looking* for Oscar, you know. He just *notices* things. And people."

And that makes him even more creepy. Kallie glanced at the office window, chilled by a sudden, eerie feeling of being watched.

"So you're going down there to ask if anyone saw him?" Tess asked.

"Yeah," Cornwallis answered. "It's probably pointless, but I'm going to try. Some shopkeepers have sharp eyes."

"Okay, good luck," Tess replied. "Have you heard anything from your police contacts?"

"Not really. They're still focused on the cousin, apparently. I watched the press conference this morning, and that was the only person they mentioned." He shrugged and added, "That doesn't mean he's their only person of interest. But I haven't heard about anyone else."

"Prudence was pretty sure it wasn't him, though," Kallie mentioned.

"Yeah, but a murderer is always more likely to be a family member, especially when it's aggravated. The police have to check."

"Did she tell the police about the other roommates? The ones she suspected?" Tess asked.

"Yes. I wasn't allowed in her interview, but she said she told them. So hopefully they're looking into them too. I doubt they had enough time to check them out before the press conference, in any case."

"How about that Endicott guy? Do any of your contacts know him?" Kallie asked.

Cornwallis shook his head. "No leads on him yet, either."

Tess nodded and stood up. "Okay, good to know.

We're going to head out, unless you need us for anything else."

"Actually, before you go. . . I'd like the two of you to visit this individual tomorrow," Cornwallis replied, opening another desk drawer.

Cornwallis rarely asked them to visit someone specific, unless it was a suggestion to recheck someone they were already investigating. He held up a printout photo of a middle-aged woman with a likable face.

"Who's that?" Tess asked, obviously also surprised by his request.

The investigator smiled crookedly. "I'm not telling you. Just go see her, okay?"

"Is she a psychic or something?" Kallie asked, taking the paper and looking at the woman. "Why are you being so cryptic?"

Tess leaned over to look at the photo, and then back at Cornwallis.

"This business can be pretty cryptic—in case you hadn't noticed," he replied, giving up nothing. "Sometimes you just have a gut instinct."

Tess looked at Kallie and smiled. "We know all about gut instincts," she told Cornwallis. "So is this mystery lady just a hunch of yours?"

"No, I've dealt with her before," he answered, but didn't elaborate.

"Okay, so either she's a suspect, or one of your

helpers," Tess pondered.

Now Kallie shrugged. "Okay, well, we need all the leads we can get right now, so we'll talk to her." She studied the photograph again and saw a fairly nondescript brunette, mid-forties, no makeup. She looked tired but not unkind. The lines around her eyes were the type that came from laughing, not anger. "Renee McGuire," she read from the paper. "Is this a mugshot?"

Cornwallis nodded.

"Even the good guys have mugshots in Wally's World," Tess replied with a smirk.

Kallie thought back to a few of his friends and colleagues they'd met previously, and smiled. "Yeah, some of your criminals are pretty cool. Should we tell her you sent us?"

"That's a good question," their mentor answered. After a moment of consideration, he added, "No. It might influence her answers, if she knew I was involved. Tell her you got her name from Bonnie at the Humane Society."

"She's not on the Humane Society's radar for crimes against animals, is she?" Kallie asked, tensing up. "We're both animal lovers, you know."

"Not at all," Cornwallis reassured her. "Now, no more hints for you. You'll see. Be at that address by nine a.m. so you catch her. Now go on, I have to meet Oscar's daughter in twenty minutes."

They finally left the office, and made their way back down the rickety staircase.

"Do you think this McGuire lady knows something about the case?" Kallie asked.

"She must," Tess replied. "He wouldn't send us off on a wild goose chase."

"Wouldn't he?" Kallie asked, sarcastically.

Tess laughed. "I mean, of *course* he would. Even if only to teach us a lesson about the trickiness of this business. But in this case, I think she's involved somehow."

"I'll do a search on her name when we get to your car," Kallie offered.

"It's a pretty common name—I doubt you'll find her, unless she has a major online presence. Or she's an axe murderer. But it's worth a try," she added, hopefully.

"Well, it's only about twelve hours until we meet her. It can wait."

"Maybe we should call Bonnie at the Humane Society first?" Tess suggested. "She might give us a hint."

"That's actually where I adopted Sherman," Kallie replied. "But I don't know her. And I don't want her to think we're crazy, asking about her friends."

"Good point. We'll just follow Wally's instructions and go to this address in the morning. She can't be any scarier than Badger."

Chapter Five

"This address Wally gave us says it's in Clearwater," Tess noted the next morning, as Kallie got into her car. "But I've never heard of this street."

"Just put it in the GPS," Kallie reasoned.

"I already did, but look—it's in a pretty nice area of town."

Kallie looked at the GPS, and her eyes widened. "That doesn't look like the kind of neighborhood where any of Cornwallis's contacts would hang out."

"Unless they were robbing the place," Tess replied with a smirk, as she backed out of the driveway.

She's kidding, right? I hope she's kidding.

Tess was right, it was a nice house in a nice neighborhood. And in Del Oro Groves, no less—that meant *expensive*. They parked on the street and rang the doorbell, and were surprised to see the woman in the photo open the door.

Oh no, Cornwallis didn't tell us what to ask her. Now we're standing here like idiots, with no way to—

"Hi, Mrs. McGuire?" Tess asked in her usual

charming fashion. "Bonnie at the Humane Society said—"

"Oh, of course!" the woman interrupted, beaming. "Come in, come in! You're a little early. I was just getting ready to go."

She turned and walked back into the house, leaving Tess and Kallie blinking at each other in surprise.

That was easy.

They followed behind the woman, as she called back to them, "Could you pick up those two black bags? I'll drive."

Two black bags? I hope we're not really getting involved in a robbery, like Tess said. I know she has a criminal record. What if she's some kind of cat burglar, who's gotten rich off her crimes?

What has Cornwallis gotten us into?

Tess picked up one bag, hesitantly, and handed the other to Kallie. She shrugged and then followed McGuire.

Tess is confused too. I guess we just play along, for now.

Carrying the bags through the house, they met McGuire by the back door. She was carrying an expensive camera and waved for them to keep following her.

Seriously, is she casing a bank with that thing?

Did we just walk into a heist? I couldn't afford that camera with a whole month's paycheck, plus tips!

The trunk popped open on an Audi sedan in the driveway, and she waved them forward with the bags.

"Thank you so much for the help. Hop in."

Once they were all loaded into the car and pulling out into the street, she asked, "So what made you ladies want to work in this industry?"

Kallie kept her mouth closed, knowing she'd blow their cover. Plus, she knew Tess would have the perfect answer in mind already.

"Well, you know, Kallie and her father have already been so involved," Tess bluffed, convincingly. "And I have a minor background in a similar field—" Kallie knew her best friend was making up nonsense, but she sounded completely sincere.

Honestly, how does she do that? She sounds so genuine, and so vague at the same time!

"Oh, that's wonderful," their host exclaimed. "So nice when it's a family affair."

Is this lady really a criminal? She seems so sweet. And what's in the bags?

A few minutes later, they pulled into the parking lot of a strip mall and McGuire turned off the car.

Well, this is it. If this lady's going to be a problem, this is the moment when we need to have our guard up.

She looked at Tess, who raised a curious eyebrow. *Seems like she still isn't sure, either.*

"Could you ladies grab the bags again, please?" She pressed the trunk release button.

Kallie and Tess both slipped out of the car and went back to the open trunk. Picking up the bags, they followed the woman into the back door of an unmarked store in the strip mall. Kallie mentally prepared herself to fight or run, depending on what they found inside the building.

Walking from the sunny street into the dim storefront, it took Kallie's eyes a moment to adjust and—

"Spike! Duchess! Come back here!" a woman's voice cried out. "Buddy, don't pee on that! *No!*"

Puppies?

"That's my assistant," McGuire laughed awkwardly. She knelt and casually picked up both of the fluffy mixed-breed puppies that were dancing around her ankles. "Hello, my dears. Ready for your big day?"

"Thanks, Renee. They got away from me," her assistant called.

"This way," McGuire waved to Kallie and Tess. "You can put the bags over there."

They followed her into the next room and found a huge digital photography backdrop, currently showing a lush green meadow of dew-covered spring flowers.

"She's a pet photographer?" Kallie whispered, confused.

Tess was struggling not to laugh. "She's *not* exactly Wally's normal type of contact."

"You can say that again. I wonder why he wanted us to meet with her?"

"Grab that puppy, will you?" McGuire called to them. "He's trying to get into my camera bag!"

Kallie quickly scooped up the fluffy, round dog. It looked like a lab mix, and was only about ten weeks old. She snuggled him for a second, scratching his ears. "You're too young to use a camera, little one. And you don't even have thumbs."

"Thanks. What did you say your name was?" McGuire asked.

"I'm Kallie, and this is Tess."

"And Bonnie sent you?" She crossed to her camera setup without waiting for an answer, so they didn't reply. "I take photos of the available pets for the Humane Society's website," she explained, absently. "Better pictures help with adoptions. But I can only get over there once a week, and even that's getting more difficult as my business has grown. Bonnie said she was looking for someone new."

Oh, that explains who she thinks we are.

Now, what did Cornwallis want us to discuss

with her? Not puppies, surely.

It must be something related to the murder. So what do we say? 'So, nice murder we're having!' Or, 'Did you catch the murder playoff game on TV last night?'

Kallie was cracking herself up now and struggled not to laugh.

'Traffic on the highway was murder this morning!'

"Sorry we were late," Tess explained calmly. "There was a big police presence down by the Owhiro pier, and it took us a while to get past it."

How does she say things like that, so nonchalantly? If I tried to tell that lie, she'd never buy it!

"Are they still down there?" McGuire asked. "There was a nasty incident down at the pier on Saturday, but I figured they were already done cleaning it up."

"Oh, I think I saw something about that on the news," Tess continued bluffing. "Did it effect you all the way out here?"

"Not here," the photographer sighed, looking up from her camera. "But I was actually driving past there for an early shoot on the beach on Saturday morning, and I got caught up in it."

"Oh, no," Tess commiserated. "What a mess.

Were you just stuck in traffic?"

"No, I had to talk to the police and everything! They thought I might've seen something."

Bingo!

Kallie tried not to look at Tess, focusing on the puppy in her arms and feigning disinterest, as they kept talking.

"Oh, wow," Tess replied, as the photographer went back to focusing her camera. "So did you?"

"Hmm? Did I what?"

Tess laughed. "Did you see anything?"

"Oh, no. I don't think so. It was dark—only about four thirty in the morning. So I couldn't see much anyway," McGuire replied. "We had a couple getting married on the beach on Halfway Island, at daybreak, and the baker and the violinist and the setup crew all got stuck in the police blockade too. They were ahead of me."

"Wedding photography seems like it would be so boring, after playing with puppies," Tess suggested.

"Oh, I don't do traditional wedding photography. The bride and groom wanted to use their dog as the ring bearer." She chuckled, and added, "I'm sure it seemed like a good idea at the time."

"It didn't work out?" Kallie asked.

"Oh, the pictures came out great," McGuire reassured her. "Pets are my specialty, and their bulldog

Zeus looked great in his little tuxedo. But it's a lot of work, and they were both pretty frazzled and out of sorts by the time we got him down the aisle."

"I'll bet," Tess sighed.

"At least he didn't try to bite the minister. . ." She leaned toward the door and called out, "We're ready for Spike and Duchess, Mary!"

As the photographer and her assistant prepared for the photo shoot, Tess and Kallie whispered together.

"So now we know why Cornwallis wanted us to talk to her. . ."

"But what is he trying to find out?" Tess wondered aloud. "He must think she really saw something."

"Maybe something she doesn't even realize she saw?"

"Then it must've been something in the street. Not at the pier."

"And how do we get her back on the subject without sounding like obsessed murder fans?" Kallie pondered.

McGuire snapped away with her camera, cooing happily at the puppies and directing her assistant, until she was sure she had the shots she needed. Then she called Kallie and Tess over. "Why don't you try a few shots? Get a feel for the project?"

"Oh, thanks," Kallie replied. "This equipment is

much better than my skill level, but I'd love to try it."

Although I'll bet a sugar-addled monkey could take good pictures with this fancy camera.

"Still photography is one thing, but learning to work with kids and pets is. . . Well, it's not always something that can be taught." She attached the camera to a tripod and stepped back. "Of course, Bonnie won't be paying you. It's a volunteer position. So she won't expect you to have professional-level skills—"

"Oh, no, of course not," Kallie replied. "We'd be happy just to help the animals find good homes."

She stepped behind the camera and watched as McGuire's assistant wrangled the puppies, squeaking toys at them to keep them engaged. Kallie took a dozen or so pictures as they romped and frolicked in front of the colorful backdrop. It was a fun undercover role that she'd actually love to play in real life. She thanked McGuire and stepped away.

The photographer thanked her back, and checked the shots. "These are actually really good," she responded with a smile. "Mary, come look at these," she called to her assistant.

"Seriously?" Kallie asked. Renee and Mary flipped through Kallie's photos on the screen and talked quietly together.

"The Humane Society will be lucky to have you, if Bonnie takes you on as the new photographer," Mary told her sincerely. "You should consider getting some good equipment, though—you've got a great eye."

"Thanks!" Kallie replied, blushing. "I'll look into it."

The photographer and her assistant went back to work, and Kallie and Tess left the studio. Tess quickly ordered a rideshare on her phone to take them back to their car at Renee's house.

"Well, if she didn't see anything at the murder scene, maybe we can find the baker and the setup crew," Tess sighed. "She said they were stuck in the traffic that morning too."

"I don't think we should ask Renee anything else about the murder, unless we get some other information first," Kallie mentioned. "She seems really nice, but she *does* have a criminal record. She's likely to get spooked, and we'll blow our cover. If she knows we're investigating her, she probably won't talk to us again."

"And we might *need* to talk to her again," Tess agreed. "That's a good point. Well, we know the date. And we know it was a sunrise wedding on the island."

"Oh, that's a good point," Kallie noted. "If she got stuck in the traffic at the festival grounds, heading for the causeway, then she was going north."

"Hopefully there weren't too many weddings that day, and we can find the details online."

Owhiro was connected to the beautiful Halfway Island by a two-mile causeway, and weddings out there were popular. But limited licenses were issued, since the island was actually a state park, and the beaches were pristine, unspoiled and mostly unoccupied.

"Yeah, not like in June," Kallie agreed. "And it's a small area. We should be able to find the wedding details. I wonder if they're still reported in the newspaper?"

"I don't think so. But she said it was on the beach. Aren't beach weddings usually affiliated with hotels?"

"On Clearwater Beach, they are. But there are no hotels on Halfway Island," Kallie replied. "Although I think there are some rental cabins."

"Has someone been researching *wedding* spots?" Tess teased.

"No!" Kallie exclaimed, blushing to the roots of her hair. "I was just looking for scuba locations."

Tess laughed and nodded. "Sure."

"I think we should start looking for leads, to find the baker," Kallie quickly changed the subject.

Tess was already on her phone, searching, and still chuckling to herself quietly at Kallie's reaction. "There are a bunch of companies that organize weddings out there. We can check their social media. Maybe they'll have photos."

Their rideshare arrived, and they self-consciously stopped discussing the murder during the drive.

No need to freak out our driver, Kallie thought to herself. *But I have a feeling this is a solid lead!*

***

"I read in the car that you can rent a no-frills private section of the island from the city, for a wedding," Tess explained when they got home.

"Hmm. That sounds. . . secluded."

"Yeah, so if the couple went that route, they're probably really private. We won't find pictures on any company websites."

"And we don't have the credentials to ask the city who rented a spot, either," Kallie agreed with a sigh.

"Maybe Cornwallis can help us with that, if we run out of options. In the meantime, we might as well start looking at the other possibilities." She took out her laptop and sat down on the couch to begin searching.

"I don't think they'd dress their bulldog in a tux for a super-private wedding," Kallie considered.

"It does seem like a lot of work, if they weren't going to share it. And they did hire *two* photographers."

Tess checked an online map and quickly made a list of the companies that scheduled outdoor weddings. Then she started methodically checking each website, following links to their social media accounts.

Kallie made coffee and then began looking for news articles on the murder—to see if the police had released any new leads.

An hour later, Tess stood up and stretched. As she twisted to unwind her back, Kallie asked, expectantly, "Find anything?"

"Not yet. I can't believe how many places offer weddings on that one tiny island," Tess answered. "I've checked seven, and there are at least ten more to go."

"They don't have any wedding posts?"

"Oh, sure. They all have tons of photos on their social media. But most of them offer beach weddings in a dozen cities up and down the Gulf coast," Tess explained. "That's why it's taking so long. Most of them are in Clearwater Beach and Anna Maria Island."

Kallie nodded agreeably. "I'd love to get married on Anna Maria Island."

"So would half the world, apparently," Tess grumbled.

Standing up, Kallie went to the kitchen to get them both a glass of iced tea. She hadn't found anything helpful in the news articles, either, so she sat back down grumpily and thought about other options.

You're not going to find anything that Tess didn't find, Kalliope. Stick to searching for news articles. She's the tech genius, not you.

But I've already read every news article and

checked every blog. What else is there?

She opened one of the social media sites and quietly searched on #halfwayisland—not wanting to interrupt Tess.

I might as well try to learn. Tess can't be stuck doing everything.

Ugh, way too many results to check. Are these even sorted in any kind of order?

#halfwayislandwedding

Still too many. And I don't see any dogs. Hmm.

#halfwayislandweddingdog

#halfwayislanddogwedding

#halfwayislanddog

#islanddog

#weddingdog

#halfwayislandbulldog

Stop it Kalliope, you're going to drive yourself crazy. All of these searches either have zero results or a million. You can ask Tess to teach you some other day. Now go make an ice cream sandwich or something useful.

Kallie sighed, agreeing with the voice in her head. *Tess is on the right track, looking for the host company. I'm sure ten thousand people post wedding photos every day.*

As she got up for another glass of iced tea, she

took one last, hopeless stab at it.

#bulldogbestman

She laughed to herself and leaned back in the chair, viewing the adorable photos of chunky, wrinkly-faced dogs in tiny tuxedos and bow ties.

These are so cute! Sherman would totally do this.

She blinked hard and waved her hand. "Tess, come here and look at this for a second."

Her best friend stood up and yawned. "What did you find?"

"Is this—?" She pointed at the screen.

"That's definitely an English Bulldog in a tux," Tess replied with a broad smile. "And that is some seriously white sand on that beach." She grabbed the mouse and scrolled down. "And it's the right date."

"Did I—?"

"You found it, Kallie! It says #zeus, and I'm *sure* Renee said the dog's name was Zeus! That's our mystery wedding!"

"Wow," Kallie mumbled to herself. "I found it. Now what do we do?"

"I have no idea," Tess laughed. "But right now, we're going to send the bride a direct message and hope for the best. Great job, Kallie!"

***

Kallie walked back into Tess's house with burritos half an hour later, for a late lunch, and found her on the phone.

Tess waved and added, "Kallie just got here, Mom. Thanks for the update. I'll call you back later."

"Hi, Mrs. Russo," Kallie called out with a smile.

"Kallie says 'hi,'" Tess added, and then a moment later turned around and blew her a kiss. "From Mom. I'll talk to you later. Love you."

When she hung up, Kallie noticed that she looked serious, even sad.

"What's up, Tess?"

"Somebody broke into my parents' house," her best friend replied angrily.

"Oh my gosh, are they okay?"

Tess nodded. "They weren't home. And the alarm scared the robbers away, so they didn't get much—except some stuff that was next to the back door."

Kallie sat down and put the burritos on the coffee table. "Well that's good. Is your mom scared?"

"She seems okay. She's shaken up, but now they know their expensive alarm system really works."

"Thank goodness for that," Kallie replied with a

sympathetic smile.

"There wasn't much for them to grab, but they got my dad's telescope that he bought when he retired. And he had one of his military medals out because he wanted to have it repaired."

"Oh no," Kallie sighed. "Your poor dad. What a terrible thing to have stolen."

"They called the police and filed a report, but she said the cops didn't sound very hopeful." She added, "There are so many pawn shops in downtown Atlanta, it would take a miracle to find the medal, unless it's still with the telescope. No serial numbers."

"I'm so sorry, Tess."

"Well, she said they took fingerprints, so maybe they'll find something. I'm going to ask Wally if he recommends anything else for them to do."

"Good, maybe he'll have an idea. He knows the criminal mentality better than anyone outside of the police."

Tess's phone dinged and she sighed. "What *now*?"

When she checked the screen, though, she smiled through her lingering anger. "Hey, it's the bride."

"Wow, that was fast. You just sent that DM right before we ordered the burritos. She must be an influencer or something."

"Or she just wants to keep talking about her wedding day," Tess replied with a smile.

"Probably. What did you ask her?"

"I told her I was considering Halfway Island for my wedding, and asked if she could recommend a baker and a photographer," Tess answered. "I actually feel a little bad for lying to her."

Kallie snorted. "She'll survive. And if you ask her for more pictures of that cute dog in his tuxedo, she'll probably volunteer their phone numbers."

Tess laughed and added, "She actually said she didn't like the wedding photographer they hired, but she loved the pet photographer."

"We'll have to tell Renee!" Kallie replied with a laugh.

"I'd love to, but I'm not sure how we'd explain why we were talking to the bride. . ."

"Oh, that's a good point. We can't blow our cover as Humane Society photographers—"

"Yeah, in case we need to talk to her again," Tess added.

"Did she say who she hired for the cake?"

"Not yet. But she just replied about the photographer a few minutes ago. I'll give her some time."

"Do you think it's someone in Owhiro?" Kallie asked, hopefully.

"That'd be really convenient—but judging from her social media, I think she lives in Clearwater." Tess refreshed the screen, and then nodded. "She just replied. Her cake was from 'Patisserie du Patti,' in Clearwater."

"Hey, I'm in the mood for a *patisserie*, now that you mention it."

"Sounds good to me," Tess replied, picking up her car keys.

***

Half an hour later, Kallie and Tess were walking in downtown Clearwater, looking for the bakery. They'd had to park almost half a mile away, and were looking for the correct street.

"Come in, come to my shop," a sing-song voice called, as they walked past the next storefront.

Kallie ignored him, still looking for the bakery, but she saw Tess turn back.

"Tess, that's not—"

"Maybe he can help us find the place," Tess suggested. "I mean, we've already been down this street twice. We're obviously not going to find it ourselves."

Sighing, Kallie followed her best friend into the shop, which turned out to be a record store. She let Tess do the talking with the elderly but edgy proprietor, and walked to the nearest bin to check out his wares.

"A friend of ours said there was a good bakery down here," she heard Tess explaining. "We thought it was on this street, but we can't find it. Do you know where it might be?"

"I'm gluten intolerant, myself," the owner explained. He looked about seventy but had at least four earrings that Kallie could see. "But I can check with my wife. Give me a minute, and I'll go ask her." He started to walk into the rear of the shop, but called back to Tess, "Have a look around."

"There's some good music in here," Kallie noted, as Tess joined her. "Some of it's new, but there's a lot of retro stuff too. Frank Sinatra and Ella Fitzgerald. Oh, and the Beatles."

Tess pulled out a Fleetwood Mac album with a tattered cover, obviously a relic. "My mom loves this album. I should buy it for her." She considered aloud, "I wonder if it's playable, though. The vinyl's probably scratched after all these years, right?"

"Beats me," Kallie replied. "I don't even have a record player, but I think my dad still has one in the garage."

"Twenty-five bucks," Tess whistled, looking at the price tag. "That cute little thrift shop in Palm Harbor used to sell old records for a dollar each. When did they get so expensive?"

"My wife said the bakery is on the next street

over," the store owner called, returning from the back room. "She agreed that it's a good one, too."

"Thanks so much," Tess replied. "No wonder we couldn't find it, we had the wrong street name. Which way?"

The man pointed toward the back of the store. "You can get there through the restaurant breezeway two doors down. She said it's next door to one of those art studios where you drink wine and paint." He walked over to where they were standing. "Did you find anything? This section is on sale for thirty percent off."

"Neither of us has a record player," Tess explained. "When did they get so popular again?"

"Some of the newer artists started releasing albums on vinyl a few years ago, and the younger generation apparently got hooked on the sound."

"I do love that scratchy, poppy sound," Tess agreed.

"Well, good luck finding your bakery," he added. "And if you ever get a record player, come back. I'm happy to play any of the older albums on our store system, so you can be sure there are no scratches."

"Thanks, we were wondering about that," Tess replied.

They walked back outside and continued down the sidewalk, looking for the breezeway he'd mentioned.

"After all this, I hope it's the right bakery," Kallie mumbled.

"There aren't that many private bakeries anymore," Tess reasoned. "I'm sure this is the one Renee McGuire mentioned. Here's the breezeway."

The restaurant didn't open until six p.m., so they quickly cut through their breezeway to the next street, and then stood looking both ways.

"Do you see it?" Kallie asked.

"No," Tess replied. She looked both ways again. "Oh, there's a sign for the art studio. On that sandwich board on the sidewalk."

A colorfully painted chalkboard sign showed a drawing of a wine glass with a paintbrush and palette. At the bottom, it announced kids' events on Saturday mornings.

"'Brushes and Booze.' We should try that," Kallie considered as they approached the sign. "Marcy's done it, and she said it was fun."

Tess nodded noncommittally.

As the record store owner had noted, the bakery was right next to the painting studio. They could smell the delicious baked goods while they were still half a block away.

"Yum, I'm definitely buying something here," Tess added with a laugh. "I can live without records and bad paintings, but I *need* whatever I'm smelling right now."

They entered the bakery just as a young employee was taking a sheet of fresh croissants out of the oven, and they both sighed audibly.

An older gentleman was decorating cookies at another counter, and he smiled and said, "Wait 'til you smell the chocolate croissants in the next batch."

"That sounds delicious, but we're actually here to see Patti," Tess replied.

"Oh, she'll be back in at four, to oversee the after-work shift." The young woman at the counter looked at the clock by the door, and added, "That's only fifteen minutes. Do you want to wait? Or is it something I can help with?"

"We'll wait," Kallie answered. "It's about a wedding cake, but it's. . . complicated." After about fifteen seconds of resistance, she added, "Could we have two of those croissants, please?"

"You bet," the girl answered with a grin, wrapping two warm pastries in paper. "That was some valiant self-control. Most people don't make it five seconds after walking in the door."

Kallie and Tess took the croissants outside to the patio seating while they waited for the owner to arrive. Kallie tore off one flaky end and watched the steam escape with a sigh. "What do you think?"

"I think these are the best croissants ever," Tess replied.

"Agreed. But what about the murder?"

"I think we should—"

The bakery door jingled suddenly, and a short brunette with an easy smile leaned out. "I'm Patricia. I'm the owner. Betsy said you wanted to talk to me about having a wedding cake made?"

"Hi!" Kallie replied with surprise. "We actually wanted to ask you about a previous cake."

The shop owner pulled up a chair and sat down. Her hair was secured in a hairnet, but she was in a flowing purple dress and wore several natural stone necklaces – turquoise, lapis, jade, and a few others that Kallie couldn't identify. She wore no rings—probably because they'd interfere with the dough—but wore heavy silver bracelets on both wrists. "Oh, that's what I like to hear. You tried our cake at a wedding?"

"Actually, it's kind of a long story," Tess began. "We're working with a private investigator on a murder case—"

"Oh, that's not nearly as fun as wedding cakes," the owner responded doubtfully, with a shake of her head.

"No, I'm afraid it's not," Kallie agreed. "We spoke to the wedding photographer, and she said you both got caught up in the aftermath?"

"Aftermath?" Patricia asked with a frown. "I'm not sure what you mean."

"She said you were on the way to a wedding on the beach—"

"Oh, right! The wedding out on Halfway Island last weekend," she finally replied, nodding. "That was a Dutch chocolate and white ganache day, with gold leaf buttercream roses. We were stuck in that backup for half an hour, which was weird because it was before daybreak."

Kallie nodded, thoughtfully.

"We ended up being so late, I was about to tear my hair out," the baker added. "The sky was already starting to turn twilight blue when we got there. That's bad news for a *sunrise* wedding."

"Did you see anything?"

"Well, no. I mean, the police spoke to us, but they didn't tell us what was going on. I heard the murder was that same day, though."

"You didn't know about the murder?"

"Not until Monday, when we were back in the shop. Then all the customers were talking about it." She blushed and added, "I don't listen to the news very much."

Kallie looked at Tess, but her friend remained strategically silent.

After a moment, the baker added, "This is sort of my dream job." She scratched at a sticker on the table, awkwardly. "That probably sounds silly. But I worked in a corporate job for thirty years, and retired with a pension and a bleeding ulcer."

Ah, that explains her bohemian dress and jewelry. They look a lot more comfortable than a pencil skirt and pantyhose.

"So I like my silly wedding cake life," she concluded, sounding more confident. "And I try not to spoil it with social media and 24-hour news."

Tess smiled at her sincerely, but still didn't respond.

That makes perfect sense, actually. There are plenty of days that I'd rather not turn on the news, either.

"The police just stopped us—me and my assistant—and asked us to open the back of our delivery van." She pointed at the van, which was parked at the curb, and the sun flashed off her bracelet, which had a large amethyst stone in it. Kallie noticed the one on her other wrist had a similar turquoise stone.

Pretty, but I'll bet they're awkward for baking.

Patricia continued, "One of the officers checked the back with a flashlight, and the other stayed with me. That part only took a few minutes." After a moment, she added, "I thought they were looking for drugs or something."

"They didn't ask if you'd seen anything?"

"No," she replied, shaking her head. "Although

they could see that we were coming from the south end of town. But it was dark. What could we have seen?"

"Anything unusual?" Tess suggested. "Someone suspicious?"

"Oh. I guess they didn't want to scare us."

"Do you remember seeing anything, now?" Kallie asked.

"No, but now it's been, what? Almost a week? If I remembered something, I wouldn't be able to swear it was that morning. This time of year, we drive in the dark a lot."

Kallie sighed. *Another dead end.*

"Well, thank you for your time," Tess replied, and Kallie thought she looked dejected too. "If you remember anything, could you please give us a call?" She ripped off part of the receipt and wrote her number on the back.

"Of course," Patricia replied.

You really need to get business cards, Kalliope.

They strolled back to the car, and Kallie asked, "You think she's telling the truth?"

"Yeah," Tess grumbled. "She was in the right place at the right time—but if she saw anything, I don't think she remembers it."

"Well, maybe she'll remember something, now that she knows what happened."

"Hopefully. Because all of our clues are looking

113

pretty thin, right now."

Chapter Six

"Wait, so we're going back to see the bakery lady *again*?" Kallie asked, stopping mid-stride in Tess's kitchen, the next morning.

"Yeah, I want to ask her a few more questions, and I don't want to call her," Tess answered.

"I mean, I certainly don't mind eating another croissant or three. But why not call her?"

"I want to see her face when she answers," Tess explained.

"But—"

"I know she's not a suspect," Tess continued, anticipating Kallie's question. "I just have a feeling she knows more than she's saying. Besides, I talked to Wally, and he thinks she might be in danger, if the killer thinks she saw something that morning."

Kallie shrugged. "Fine with me. I can't go right now, but I have tomorrow off."

Tess looked at the clock. "I wanted to go today, but I don't have time either. Let's plan to go tomorrow at noon. I'd rather go earlier, but I don't think she ever gets there until the lunch rush."

"Okay, maybe we can go to lunch in Clearwater after we see her. If we're not completely stuffed on croissants. I hope they have the chocolate ones."

"Ugh, stop it, I'm starving," Tess laughed.

"All I have is a protein bar," Kallie pouted. "Want to go to the Chinese drive-through before work? They're fast."

Tess nodded and quickly grabbed her keys. "Let's go. I'll drop you off at work."

They rushed to Wok 2 Go, a local Chinese takeout with reasonable food but incredibly fast service, and were soon settled in the parking lot with two small orders of shrimp fried rice. No egg in Kallie's, of course.

"So what do you want to ask Patricia?" Kallie asked, after she'd taken a few bites.

"Renee McGuire said she didn't see anything by the pier, because it was too dark," Tess explained. "But we thought Patricia might've seen something as the murder happened, because Renee said she passed by there *earlier*. Ahead of her."

"Sure, that's why we went to see her," Kallie nodded.

"But Patricia said the sky was already starting to turn light when she got to the wedding spot, with the cake."

"Renee didn't say she was *that* late."

Tess nodded. "Exactly. So one of them is either confused—"

"Or lying," Kallie finished her thought. "Interesting. Maybe Renee set us on Patricia's tail to shake us off her own?"

"That's the thing, though. Neither of them is a suspect. They both have alibis and neither of them has a motive—"

"That we know of," Kallie added.

"Exactly," Tess repeated.

"So maybe one, or both, of them is covering for someone else."

"Or maybe they're just confused. It *was* before five a.m., after all. Anyway, we'll find out tomorrow." Tess finished her fried rice and tossed Kallie a fortune cookie. "It's late, we'd better get you to work."

***

Kallie took a tray of beer and wine to a table by the window, and quickly returned to the bar, where the night shift manager was eating lunch. "I'm not sure about the main suspect, Mike. The cousin Oscar was staying with. I know the police are focused on him, but I don't see it. And neither does his daughter."

Mike nodded, sipping his glass of ginger ale. They'd been friends for years—since the days when he was a security guard at The Lazy Gecko, and Kallie felt comfortable bouncing ideas off of him.

"You have good instincts, Kal," Mike replied. "What does your gut say?"

"I can't tell anymore," she sighed. "Before I started studying, I trusted my gut a lot more. Now I always wonder if I'm being influenced by the last thing I read."

Mike nodded again. "The cousin does seem like a pretty obvious suspect, and criminals aren't usually that bright. That's why they usually get caught. If he's guilty, the police have got him covered."

"True." Kallie refilled his soda while she thought about that. Her section of The Lazy Gecko had emptied out after lunch, and the happy hour crowd hadn't started filling in yet. She looked around to make sure she wasn't neglecting anyone, but even her regulars seemed engrossed in their phones or conversations.

"Well, that guy Cornwallis obviously didn't decide to train you for the *money*—"

"Since I don't have any," Kallie added with a laugh.

"—so he must think you have what it takes," Mike concluded seriously. "You solved a few murders without all these books, so I think you should trust your instincts. When you find the killer, I think you'll know."

"I guess," Kallie mumbled, trying not to sound pitiful. "I just hope the killer doesn't get away, while I'm being indecisive."

"He won't. You have Cornwallis and Tess on your side. And I'm sure Morrison has his eye on the case too."

"Oh, no," Kallie insisted. "He *promised* he wouldn't—"

"Mm-hmm," Mike interjected with a slight smile. "Anyway, just be careful. Okay?"

"I will," Kallie replied.

"You might be a good investigator, but you're not always the most subtle."

"What? I'm *perfectly* subtle—"

"I just don't want the killer to notice *you,* before you notice him, Kal," Mike insisted. "Promise me you'll remember what your dad and I taught you, too, okay?"

"Elbow to the nose, yes, sir!" Kallie replied with a chipper smile, and Mike grinned back at her.

"That's my girl. If you and Tess want to go through any self-defense drills, let me know."

"Okay, thanks. I'll ask her," Kallie agreed with a nod. "We might take you up on it."

"Carlos can practice with Tess," Mike added with a chuckle. "She's *mean* when she's angry."

"She's tiny, Mike," Kallie replied with a laugh.

He mumbled something that sounded like 'poison dart frogs are tiny' and took a drink from his soda.

**

"We have to do something. Is there anyone else we can interview?" Kallie groaned. She'd had a busy happy hour at work, with no further chance to think about the case. Now she was frustrated by going back to it.

"Well, since we've already checked most of the shops on the pier, and the snack shop doesn't have cameras, I thought maybe we could check out this hotel." Tess pulled up an online map of the Owhiro coastline and pointed at a hotel near the pier. "Maybe interview the staff and ask if they saw something?"

"Oh, right. Cornwallis said we could check with the guests, too, and ask if anyone saw anything. There's some convention in town."

"Right, the cheerleaders," Tess recalled. "That's great, maybe we can catch the staff and the visitors at the same time. There are other hotels in the area, but that's the only one with a direct line of sight. And I'll bet they have some security cameras."

"Sounds perfect. Do you mind driving?"

They made the quick drive down to the Owhiro pier and parked in the hotel's lot. Kallie was struck by the glamorous old hotel, which had been renovated to its former glory about ten years earlier.

"This is an expensive place to stay for a sports conference," Kallie noted. "My mom says the McCormick Hotel is the nicest hotel in Owhiro, since they fixed it back up. She stays here when she visits Jack."

"Maybe they have a special rate for conferences and stuff," Tess suggested. "I've heard they have a great restaurant with a beautiful view at sunset."

Breezing confidently through the McCormick's side door, they took the elevator up to the second floor without attracting any attention.

Tess reoriented herself in the upstairs hallway, and pointed to the left. "The front of the building is this way, so let's see if anyone's still in these rooms."

"I can hear girls laughing, that's a good sign," Kallie replied with a smile.

"But we can't just start knocking on doors. They'll have us thrown out."

"Excuse me, sorry," a voice behind them called, and they stepped apart to see a woman awkwardly carrying four sodas and an ice bucket. She started to drop a soda, and Kallie grabbed it before it hit the floor.

"Thanks," the woman laughed. "That was the last one in the machine, and I would've had a riot on my hands. Are you here with the tournament?"

"No, we're actually here about an incident that

happened on the beach," Kallie explained. "Have you been here all week?"

"Oh, we heard about that," the woman replied, frowning. "The hotel had security walk us outside every time we needed to take the shuttle to the tournament. But all of the other hotels are completely booked up, so we had to stay. We're going home on Friday morning."

"Did you see anything that night?" Tess asked. "Or were you outside at all?"

"I never left the room after nine o'clock, because I have two girls in the competition," she answered, with a sigh. "I'd love to see the sights, but they need to get their sleep. If I left, they'd be up giggling until midnight."

"We understand completely," Tess replied.

"But a couple of the moms brought their husbands, and I know they left the men behind and went out for a girls' night a few times," she explained. "I'm sorry I'm not much help, but they might've seen something. Check with Liz in room 212."

"Thanks, we'll do that," Kallie replied gratefully.

"The murder happened at around four a.m., and I doubt any of these moms were out that late," Tess mentioned as they walked toward the suggested room.

"Not if they had to be at the competition first thing in the morning," Kallie agreed. "But it's worth checking. They might've been watching the beach from the room, if they had jet lag or something."

"Oh, hang on," Tess stopped her. "Let's talk to these ladies from housekeeping. If they're here this late, maybe they work the night shift."

Kallie glanced down the hall where three women were talking animatedly around a cart full of towels and toiletries. The youngest woman was pointing and giving instructions to the other two in Spanish. They nodded back at her respectfully and returned to their work.

As Tess and Kallie approached, she greeted them warmly. "Good evening. Can I help you with anything?"

"We're working with a private investigator," Tess explained. "Looking into the incident at the festival by the pier."

"Is there some concern with the hotel?" she asked, with a hint of worry in her voice.

"Not at all," Tess replied. "Or not as far as we know, anyway. We wondered if someone might've seen something that night. We talked to one of the guests, but we thought the night shift workers might be more likely to have seen something."

The woman nodded. "I'm the night manager, and I can tell you, everyone's been gossiping about it. But I don't think any of my staff saw anything. I think they would've told me." She smiled and added, "Or, well, they would've told *everyone else*, and it would've eventually gotten back to me."

Kallie smiled in understanding.

"The night shift just started. I could introduce you to the ladies who work on this end of the building, if you think it would help."

"Thank you, that would be very helpful," Tess replied.

"The sooner this is solved, the sooner things will get back to normal around here."

She walked to one of the rooms and waved for the housekeeper to come out into the hall. Kallie wasn't fluent in Spanish, but you don't grow up in Florida without learning the basics. The woman explained that they weren't police, but they had a few questions about *el incidente*.

Just as the housekeeper was beginning to speak, though, a large man burst out of the elevator, stomping angrily toward their little group.

"You need to leave, both of you," he demanded, still closing the distance rapidly. He reached for Tess's arm, but she pulled it away and took a step back in surprise.

"Stella, get back to the desk," he snapped at the night manager, ignoring the housekeeper entirely.

The young woman bristled at the order. "We weren't doing anything, Simon. We were just talking about—"

"Nobody needs to be talking to the staff." He

took another step toward her, getting in her personal space, and ordered, "Get back to the desk."

This time, she cringed and backed away toward the elevator.

What a bully! I don't blame her, that guy's enormous.

In a moment, the night manager was gone, and they were left alone with the hostile security guard.

"This is a private business, and I'm not going to ask you again. Leave now."

Kallie looked at Tess, who shrugged. Without another word, they began to return to the elevator, but saw that it was still off on another floor—so they walked to the staircase door, instead. Opening the heavy door, they started down, with the security guard close behind them. He followed ominously until they were outside, and watched them until they were getting into Tess's car in the parking lot.

"What in the heck was *that*?" Kallie asked.

"I don't know, but I'm definitely calling it a clue," Tess replied, fuming.

***

"I found some information on that hotel," Tess called from the living room, as Kallie was fixing hot chocolate in the kitchen later that night.

They'd made the short drive home in record time, with Tess seething the whole way.

Kallie opened the garage door and called to her dad, then went to look over Tess's shoulder.

"It's just a hotel, right?" she asked.

"No, it's over a hundred years old. And it has a pretty amazing history—good and bad. Hi, Mister B!"

"Hi, Tess," Kallie's dad waved from the kitchen. "It smells great in here, so you two must be solving mysteries."

"I do my best cooking when we're investigating," Kallie agreed.

"But it's mostly because we get obsessed, and don't stop working until we're starving," Tess added with a laugh.

"Are you still working on that murder down at the sandcastle festival?"

"Yeah, we just got chased out of the McCormick Hotel, Mister B. By a giant, angry security guard."

Benny Brooks smiled. "Sounds like the McCormick is going back to their old ways. That place used to be a smugglers' den back during Prohibition."

"Really?"

"That was before my time, of course," he added. "But it still had a reputation when I was growing up."

"Now I really want to check it out," Tess replied with a laugh.

"Me too!" Kallie agreed. "I wonder if there's a speakeasy tucked behind a hidden wall or something?"

"It wasn't that glamorous in my day," Benny replied, shaking his head. "But if there's anything to find, I know you girls will dig it up."

"Most of the smaller hotels and motels on the coast have been bought out by the big corporations. I wonder how this place stayed in private hands for so long?" Kallie considered.

"That is strange," Tess agreed. "Now that you mention it, Clearwater Beach is all massive Hiltons and Marriotts and Hyatts. It's a much more famous beach, obviously, but I'm surprised this place hasn't sold out for a multi-million dollar paycheck."

"Either they have a lot of skeletons they don't want uncovered—"

"Or they already have so much money, they don't need the windfall," Kallie's dad finished her thought.

Tess typed quickly on her laptop for a moment and then nodded. "The place changed hands in the 1990s. It's owned by some rich businessman named Barton Donovan, now."

"Ah, the shady story gets shadier," Kallie noted. "And wealthier, too. We definitely need to go see Mr. Donovan."

"My thoughts exactly," Tess replied. "I'll pick you up at eight o'clock tomorrow morning, and we'll see

127

if we can arrange an interview."

***

"Whoa, how do they have so much glass on the front of this building, when they're right on the Gulf?" Kallie wondered aloud, staring up at the elaborate, gleaming front of Donovan's office building, the next morning.

"I'm sure they're hurricane-proof windows," Tess replied, opening the door.

"Oh, I'm sure they are," Kallie replied, lowering her voice as they crossed the lobby toward the elevator. "But they're insanely expensive. That must be at least a million dollars, just in glass."

"I guess it's worth it to them. It's a heck of a view, and very *prestigious,* my dear," Tess added facetiously. "Besides, they obviously have plenty of money."

"True, and I'm sure it's all insured."

They entered Donovan's office and checked in with the receptionist, taking a seat in the waiting area.

Kallie was still staring across at the windows. "I wonder how they keep them clean, though. They must need window washers every night, with all the sand and salt blowing in."

"Oh, I hope the police aren't already looking into

this guy," Tess wondered aloud, changing the subject. "Wally doesn't want to step on their toes."

"Hang on, I'll check with Morrison," Kallie replied, taking out her phone.

Kallie

Hey Morrison, we're interviewing a guy named Barton Donovan about the murder. Have the police spoken to him?

Morrison

The billionaire? No, I'm sure I would've heard if he was being questioned. He's not our biggest fan.

"Understood, Mr. Donovan," a woman's voice suddenly intruded, startling Kallie and Tess. "I'll book the suite at Rooftopz for next Saturday night, and let him know." The receptionist wrote a quick note at her desk and then approached them. "Miss Brooks, Mr. Donovan is ready for you."

Kallie and Tess stood up, and followed the receptionist into an office, where an older gentleman was waiting. His expensive suit was almost the same color as his steel grey hair, and he was quite handsome. But something about his eyes and the way he looked at them was unsettling. He wasn't finishing a call, or handling papers, or even checking his phone. Kallie was a little flustered at how he seemed to just be waiting for them.

Like a shark in the shallows.

Calm down, Kalliope.

"Mr. Donovan, thank you for seeing us," Tess began. "We just wanted to ask you a few questions."

"Of course," he accepted calmly. "I'm so glad I could squeeze you in."

"There was an incident down in Owhiro last weekend, adjacent to a property that you own—"

"Yes, I've been talking with the police about it regularly."

"You have?" Kallie asked, surprised.

But Morrison said. . .

"Yes, the incident damaged my property. Several of the outdoor art pieces were damaged, and a priceless Asian Pear tree was destroyed. It had history going back centuries."

"Oh, I didn't—"

"They're taking their sweet time getting a police report ready, so that I can file an insurance claim," Donovan complained. "Has there been any progress?"

Kallie glanced over at Tess and saw that her best friend's usually impassive face was slipping into a sneer of dislike.

"We were actually talking about the murder," Kallie explained carefully.

"Oh, I really don't know anything about that," he

replied, brusquely. "Who did you say you were working for? You're obviously not with the police."

"We're working with a private investigator—" Kallie began.

"Yes, my receptionist told me that. But I thought it was concerning the damage on my property."

"We're investigating the *murder*," Tess repeated. "We'd just like—"

"I'm sorry, I really don't have time for this right now," Donovan interrupted. His manner abruptly became ice-cold, and he added, "I think I've been helpful, and I carved time out of my day to assist you. But I really don't know anything about a murder."

"If you could just—" Tess began, but he cut her off, again.

"Miss Melnyk," he called to his receptionist. "We're done here."

The young woman came back, less friendly this time, and escorted them out of his office. She quickly thanked them for coming, and showed them to the door.

"Well, that was final," Tess grumbled, as they walked away from the building.

"Good thing it was only a dead guy, and not a priceless Chinese apple tree or anything," Kallie sneered.

Tess frowned in agreement. "I guess we're doing

this the hard way, then."

"What else is new?" Kallie sighed.

"Winchester said he'd help us if we needed it," Tess concluded. "Maybe it's time to put pressure on them for the hotel's video cameras."

"Good idea. And I've been wanting to check out that new Rooftopz restaurant too," Kallie added conspiratorially. "I hear they have great food."

Tess shook her head. "I don't think we can afford that place. But it sounds like our next good lead, so maybe Wally can figure out some way to get us in there."

They climbed into Tess's car, both still in grumpy moods caused by Donovan.

"And I'm hungry too," Kallie announced, as Tess pulled out into traffic.

"Me too," Tess agreed. "I've been craving one of those chocolate croissants from Patricia's bakery."

"Let's go right now, then. It's only twenty minutes from here, and you can ask her about the timeline issue. Maybe she's remembered something from the morning of the murder."

"Good idea. I wonder if that means we can expense the croissants?"

"I doubt it," Kallie replied. "Anyway, I think they're less than three dollars each."

"Hey, we should ask her if she saw that guy who

was running on the beach too," Tess added.

"It's worth a try, I guess. You can't see his face or anything, so I'm not sure how she'd be able to tell."

"Well, there aren't too many runners out at that time of night," Tess answered. "Although, for all we know, he's just a jogger with insomnia. I downloaded the picture to my phone, so we can ask her."

Parking is often a challenge in Clearwater, but they found a spot that was only a block away from the bakery. Soon they were inhaling the decadent scent of pastries and chocolate.

"Hi girls!" Patricia called out to them when they walked into the warm shop. "Come back for more of my tasty treats?"

"Yes, ma'am," Tess replied with a smile.

"Or are you in detective mode today?" she added.

"A little of both, actually. Your croissants were our original plan, but we'll probably pick your brain while we're here."

"As long as you can pick while I work, that's fine with me," she replied, selecting two fresh pastries and ringing them up.

They paid for the order and each took a decadent bite, and then Tess continued, "We got some video footage from a restaurant on the pier. It's about the right time, and it shows a guy running on the beach."

"That's lucky," Patricia replied, without looking up from a batch of snickerdoodle cookies that she was placing in the oven.

"You can't see his face, but we wondered if you might remember him?"

"Sure, let's see," the baker responded, brushing off her flour-covered hands on her apron.

Tess held up her phone and played the short snippet of video.

"You know, I think I *might* remember that guy. While I was talking to the police, someone came past my van on the driver's side. I didn't get a good look at him because the officer was on the passenger side, so I was looking in the wrong direction. But he bumped into my side mirror."

"Really? Do you remember anything about him?" Kallie asked.

"No, the mirror bounced back into place and made a loud noise, so I looked to see what happened. I just saw that he was wearing dark clothes." She hesitated, then added, "I think he was pretty tall."

"So, a big guy in all black?" Kallie asked.

"Hmm, not *big*," she replied. "Just tall. I think I would've noticed if he'd been big and muscular – since he was right next to me in the dark."

"Tall but lean."

"Yes, that's a good word. Lean. Nothing else – I only saw his back." Patricia paused. "I remember because I thought it was weird that he'd walk in the street, instead of on the sidewalk. At that time of night, that's just downright *trying* to get flattened. Some drunk driver, swerving home from a wild night, would never even see you."

Kallie and Tess looked at each other thoughtfully, and Kallie suggested, "Maybe he was avoiding the police?"

"I guess," Tess replied with a frown. "But it'd be easier just to stay out of sight, down by the water."

"Yeah, that's true."

"Wait, was that guy involved in the *murder*?" Patricia asked, breathlessly. "Oh my gosh, he was *right next* to me."

"We're not sure yet. He was definitely in the area, so we're just following up."

"But you wouldn't have been in any danger, with a cop standing right next to your van," Kallie added, sympathetically.

"I don't think the police officer even noticed him, actually. My van's pretty huge. You know, for carrying big wedding cakes." Her voice was getting lower and lower as she rambled. "And I was following the band—they have a big van, too, for the drums and stuff." Her eyes were starting to tear up, and Kallie could tell she was getting scared.

"He was probably just a jogger, Patricia," Tess reassured her quickly. "Really."

"Do you think so?" Patricia replied, but she didn't sound relieved. "It still gives me the creepy-crawlies."

"That's understandable," Tess replied. She looked at the video again, lips pursed. "You didn't happen to notice if he had anything in his hands, did you?"

"I wish I'd thought to look. I was so distracted by the police." Patricia took a moment to think about the question, hands fiddling with her apron. She shook her head. "No, I don't recall. I only remember his dark clothes, because it seemed. . . foolhardy. You know, to be walking in the middle of the street in the dark, in dark colors."

"Sure," Tess replied, sounding sympathetic now too.

We came into this poor woman's business and stressed her out for no reason. Now she's going to be worried all day.

At least we know she saw the jogger, if we can figure out who he was.

Customers were starting to fill the shop more quickly now, so Tess said, "We'll let you get back to business, Patricia. Thank you for your time."

"Could we get two éclairs for the road?" Kallie added.

"Of course," Patricia replied, laughing for the first time all morning. "I knew I'd get you hooked on my bakery." She rang up the order and circled the total on the receipt with a purple marker.

"Don't hesitate to call us if you remember anything," Tess added. "Or if you just want to talk."

"I'll do that. Thank you. And please let me know when they catch the guy, would you? I haven't been sleeping well ever since this happened."

I know that feeling, believe me!

"We'll do that. Thanks again," Tess replied.

***

"Well, at least we have one success, even if it's a small one," Tess noted, as they reviewed their notes later.

"Weren't you going to ask her about the time difference in her story?" Kallie asked.

"That was my idea," Tess answered, blushing. "But she was so *worried.* I didn't want to make it worse for her."

"And she's not even a suspect. I know what you mean."

"I was afraid she'd start crying," Tess sighed. "I guess we're just not as hard-boiled as Wally. Maybe that comes with time. . ."

"Maybe. I'm not sure if we want to aspire to that, but it probably helps with the job." Kallie thought about the rest of their morning. "I wish we could go back to Donovan's office and talk to his receptionist alone."

"We could try it, sometime when he's not there. Do you think she'd tell us something new?"

Kallie reconsidered. "No, she's obviously committed to him. She wouldn't sell him out."

"But you think she knows something?"

Kallie laughed, "Well, I *always* think everyone knows something. Or they're hiding something. Or they saw something they haven't told us."

Tess tilted her head. "Sometimes they do. If you get an intuitive spark, you have to follow it."

"Even if I'm wrong?" Kallie asked sheepishly.

"Even if you're only right one percent of the time, that might catch a killer," Tess replied pragmatically, shrugging.

"Thanks, Tess." Kallie blushed.

"I mean, that's what we're trying to do. And we've done it before. It's worth a little craziness."

"And a little danger?"

"Hopefully this is the part where we minimize the danger. Wally can teach us how to investigate *without* antagonizing the killer."

"How's that working out so far?" Kallie grouched.

"It's been at least a month since someone tried to kill us," Tess teased. "That might be some kind of record for us."

"But going back to Donovan's office would be stupid, wouldn't it?" Kallie asked.

"Not necessarily. This just isn't the right time."

"How do you mean?"

"We both have a bad feeling about Donovan. But he doesn't have any obvious motive for killing Oscar."

"True," Kallie conceded.

"If we assume that the receptionist *isn't* a criminal, then she's just defending Donovan out of plain old office loyalty. Because he's her boss," Tess suggested.

"Okay. . ."

"But if we're right, and *he's* a criminal, then he'll eventually burn her," Tess theorized. "And loyal people don't like being burned."

"Oh. So if we give Donovan enough time and matches—"

"—he'll burn his *own* bridges. Without our help," Tess concluded. "We don't have enough evidence to approach her again right now, either. But we should make sure she has our contact information, for when both of those days eventually come."

"I'll call her and leave a message," Kallie replied.

"Exactly what I was thinking. And maybe a

text."

"And if he's actually innocent, then we haven't made any enemies," Kallie added.

"See? Safe as houses," Tess replied with a nod. "I love it when no one's trying to kill us."

"Let's check with Cornwallis about Donovan, though," Kallie suggested. "Maybe he'll have some other ideas."

Chapter Seven

"Have you ever seen a swimming pool that big before?" Kallie asked as they peeked out of the woods at the enormous, garish mansion, later that afternoon.

"Sure, but only at a hotel," Tess replied. "This guy must really be loaded."

"And there's no way it's all legal. Donovan's a world-class jerk, but I'd bet a week's worth of tips he's into something illegal too."

"I think I'm getting the hang of this thing," Tess replied, moving the left controller a little and squinting at the tiny view screen. "Look at that cute little cabana by the wall. I need a pool like this, one day."

"Remember that place we stayed near Disney World that had that huge winding river around the patio?"

Tess nodded, pushing the right control switch up.

"And it ended at the swim-up bar that made those incredible mango smoothies! I loved that place," Kallie continued. "You need to pester Winchester for another bonus, so we can go back there."

"That was *way* bigger than this, though. But I've definitely never seen one this big at a house."

Kallie daydreamed for a moment. "If you had a pool this big, I bet you'd have at least three of those giant, blow-up unicorn floaties."

"Why are you looking at me?" Tess scoffed. "You'd be *in* one of those giant, blow-up unicorns."

"That's true," Kallie replied with a laugh. "And I'd bring a portable blender, so I could make my own smoothies without going back to land."

"I love this cool drone that Wally lent us." Tess gushed. "Although I don't think he meant for us to use it *like this*."

"I'm not sure if anything we find would be admissible in court," Kallie considered. "I mean, it's outside, so there's not really an expectation of privacy..."

"But they aren't likely to have incriminating evidence sitting out by the pool, either."

"You never know," Kallie replied with a shrug.

No way are we ever getting back into Donovan's office, so we'd better hope there's some evidence out here. This guy's up to no good.

"I wish the monitor screen was bigger," Tess complained. "I can't really see what I'm filming. But at least it's all recorded."

"We can check it out later. At least we know we're in the right spot."

They'd confirmed the video resolution on the drone before they left Kallie's house, and it was surprisingly high-quality. There was no sound, but the footage they'd recorded from her back yard was crystal clear.

"I love being safe down here on the ground, while we're investigating," Tess added. "Can you imagine how much trouble we'd be in if we climbed up on that wall?"

"Plus the hospital bill, after we *fell off* the wall," Kallie agreed, wincing.

"Exactly. I wish we'd thought about buying one of these things back when we were investigating for ourselves. They aren't that expensive anymore."

"And they're so much safer," Kallie nodded sagely. "But then we wouldn't have had nearly as much fun."

"Fun being almost killed? Repeatedly?" Tess asked with a raised eyebrow.

"Oh, stop. We were barely even in danger."

"You have officially lost your mind, Kalliope Brooks," Tess laughed. "Do you want to drive this thing?"

"Yeah, but steer it out of his yard first. I don't want to drop it in the hot tub if I mess up."

Tess took one last lap around the pool, swinging close to the house to make sure she got everything – and then steered the drone back over the wall. When it landed in the side yard, she handed the controller to Kallie.

Kallie pushed up the lever to launch the drone again, and then looked at the view screen. Tess was right, she couldn't really see what she was filming, because the monitor was so tiny. But flying it around Donovan's backyard was a blast.

"It's funny that they don't have a motion-sensor security system that picks up a drone over their property," Kallie noted as she fiddled with the controls, getting the hang of the different levers.

"Oh, I didn't even think of that," Tess replied, and then whimpered audibly, looking over her shoulder. She took Kallie gently by the arm and pulled her away. "Try to look innocent, and let's just wander back over here into the neighbor's yard."

"I don't think we—"

But then Kallie noticed the police car rounding the corner, and saw Tess cringe.

"Too late."

"Oh no. Let's get out of here," Kallie urged her, but Tess held her in place.

"We can't run, Kal. Just play dumb."

"What? We can't—"

"Just keep steering it," Tess whispered. "And messier. Make more mistakes."

Kallie followed her best friend's directions, making the drone dip awkwardly and almost hit a pink crepe myrtle—as a woman in an apron opened the front door and pointed them out to the officer.

In thirty seconds, the black and white cruiser stopped next to their spot on the sidewalk.

"Good afternoon, ladies. The homeowner here said you were spying on them with your drone," the officer stated without preamble.

"Oh, hi officer," Tess replied, sweetly. "My boyfriend gave me this stupid drone for my birthday. I said I wanted to fly to Key West, and I guess he thought this was a funny substitute."

"And you're flying it over your neighbors' houses?" he asked suspiciously.

"Well, not on purpose," she laughed. "But if this is my only birthday present, then, by gosh, I'm going to figure out how to use it. But I'm not very good at it yet. I've crashed it so many times, I'm surprised it still flies at all."

The officer took another look at the drone, seeming suspicious, but replied, "Well, try to keep it closer to yourselves, and out of your neighbors' yards, ladies."

He took one last look back at them as he walked toward the house. The woman, who appeared to be a housekeeper, was still standing at the door, watching them.

Kallie landed the drone carefully in the grass and sighed. "Thank goodness. I thought he was going to confiscate it."

"So did I," Tess agreed. "And the video card is in there, so we would've lost all that work."

And been caught fibbing to the cops, even worse.

"That was way too close for comfort. Let's get out of here," Kallie whispered. "We can pick up some empanadas on the way home, and watch the video on your laptop."

Tess took a shortcut to avoid the highway, so they were home in twenty minutes with takeout. Kallie carefully removed the video card from the drone and handed it over to her best friend.

"Here goes nothing," Tess replied, slipping it into the card reader on her laptop. "I hope it worked."

Kallie grabbed two Diet Cokes and two plates and joined her at the table, just as Tess was hitting the 'play' button.

The screen came to life with bright green grass zooming by, and then a cinderblock wall, and finally the huge swimming pool they'd watched on the tiny screen earlier.

"It worked!" Kallie cheered. "Now I hope we got

something useful."

Tess maximized the video so it filled the whole screen. "Don't get your hopes up. I doubt Donovan has a pile of heroin and stolen guns sitting on a lounge chair by the jacuzzi."

"Thanks for spoiling my daydream, Tess," Kallie teased. "You don't think he left the murder weapon on the diving board for us?"

"Probably not, but we're about to find out."

They'd only filmed for about ten minutes, so they watched the whole video, from beginning to end, first. Despite her earlier joking, Kallie was disappointed.

She was right, the cabana is really pretty. But I hope we didn't waste all that time and effort for landscaping ideas.

"Let me open the video in a better viewing application, now that we've got our bearings. I have a few places I want to zoom in. . ." Tess clicked her mouse a few times while Kallie took another sip of her Diet Coke. "Here we go."

"Wow, this is way better," Kallie replied, leaning in for a closer look.

Tess forwarded the video until the drone was over the pool, and then slowed down the playback speed. She effortlessly manipulated the keyboard, making the picture zoom in and out, and then refocus. "I just want to check the tables and chairs, and this place by the door to the house—"

Kallie watched carefully as Tess inspected the footage, and offered a few suggestions. "Could you check the table with the sun umbrella? And are those towels by the cabana, or something else?"

But after fifteen minutes of reviewing the short video, they were both feeling dejected.

Did we really get nothing?

Tess switched the video back to normal speed as the drone zoomed out of the yard, moving toward where it had landed.

"Hang on, when you steered it around for that last loop—"

Tess reversed the video while Kallie was talking, and the footage zipped backward for a few seconds.

"—Did you see something inside that window?" Kallie asked. "I thought I saw something move."

"I wasn't even looking at the window," Tess replied. "I was focused on the hot tub. Hang on. . ."

The video started again, and Kallie watched as the side window returned into view. There were vertical blinds over the window – giving a little privacy but probably still allowing a nice view of the enclosed courtyard and pool.

"There," Kallie pointed.

"I saw it, that time. Something moved inside the house." Tess zoomed in a little, and focused the video.

Now Kallie could see the edge of an oversized club chair and a side table inside. As they watched again, an arm reached into view and picked up something from the table.

"What was that?" Kallie whispered.

"I think they just picked up a book or something," Tess replied. "Maybe a wallet. It wasn't very big." She zoomed in more and rewound it again. Paused. "Yeah, it's a book. Does Donovan have kids? It was small, like a kid's book."

"Oh, yeah," Kallie agreed. "I can see it now." She tilted her head. "A little book. Is it red?"

"I think it's—"

The picture zoomed in again and focused. Kallie squinted. "Oh wait, there are two of them. One's red and— Wait, Tess, are those *passports*?"

Tess frowned and rewound the video until it was showing the side of the house again. Then she let it play in slow-motion through the whole shot of the window.

"They *are* passports," Tess murmured. "Two or three of them."

"He's a rich guy, I'm sure he travels a lot," Kallie considered.

"Yeah," Tess agreed. "But why does he need three? And why are they different colors?"

"And this video is *definitely* not admissible," Kallie sighed. "So what do we do with it?"

Tess took a screenshot of the video and replied, "The *first* thing we're doing is sending this to Cornwallis. Even if it can't be used in court, I'm sure there's something we can do with it."

Tess sent the screenshot, and her phone rang a minute later.

"This *wasn't* how I meant for you to use the drone," Cornwallis admonished them, without even saying hello.

"We know," Tess replied, quickly. "We thought there might be something outdoors. This shot was an accident."

"Are those passports?" he asked, brusquely.

Oh man. He sounds really mad this time.

"We think so," Kallie replied, as Tess put her on speaker. "But they're different colors."

"Let's not jump to any conclusions. The other ones might belong to someone else. And a guy like that might have dual citizenship," Cornwallis explained, still sounding testy. "Even if he wasn't born with it, some countries will allow you to petition for citizenship if your parents were born there."

Kallie glanced at Tess and frowned.

"Although, I think that second one's black," he continued. "There aren't very many countries with a black passport."

"Really?" Tess asked, sounding hopeful.

"Only about five, I think."

"So the odds of him having dual citizenship are—"

"Remember the part where we're not jumping to conclusions?" Cornwallis replied wearily. "This isn't going to be admissible in court, but let me see what I can find out."

Kallie leaned toward the phone, with another idea in mind, "But couldn't we try tricking him into—"

"That's entrapment," he snapped, interrupting her.

"It's only entrapment if the police do it," Tess corrected him gently, and Kallie was surprised to hear him laugh.

"True," he agreed. "And the student has surpassed the master—"

Now Tess laughed, too. "Hardly! We're still on the first book. We just thought maybe—"

"Before we try *tricking* Donovan into anything," he stopped her again, "Let me just contact a friend about these passports, okay? Then we can talk about covert operations, I promise."

They agreed, half-heartedly, and he added, "Give me two hours."

***

"Thanks for coming on my walk with Sherman, Dad." Kallie sighed as they left their yard and began walking on the path around the lake. "I'm so frustrated with this case, and I knew Sherm needed a walk."

"I'm sure it'll help clear your head, kiddo. When I'm stuck, a nice walk and a chance to focus on something else usually does the trick."

"I'm sure you're right. It's so much more complicated when it's someone else's case, and we don't know all the facts," Kallie complained.

"I'll bet," her dad replied. "But it seems like you're doing pretty well."

"It sometimes seems like it to me, too, but we can't tell if someone is lying to us. Even the people we're trying to help."

"Do you think his daughter is lying?" Benny asked with a concerned frown.

"No, it's not Prudence. We haven't had a chance to speak with her again yet, anyway," Kallie sighed. "But everyone's stories seem to contradict each other. When Tess and I were personally involved in a case, we *knew* what we saw."

"But when it's someone else, you have to just trust they're telling the truth."

"Yeah, and that's always hard to do, even when there's *not* a murder involved!" Kallie added with a laugh.

"Well, if they're lying to you—that's on them, kiddo."

Kallie agreed, "But I'm the one who's losing sleep over it."

"I know," her dad commiserated. "But you'll stop taking it personally after a while. It'll become a job."

"I don't know if that'll be a good thing or a bad thing," she sighed.

"A little of both, I suspect. What did Mr. Cornwallis say about—?"

Kallie's phone rang, and she stopped her dad. "I need to take this call from Tess."

"Sure," her dad gestured for her to answer the phone, and took Sherman's leash.

"Hey Tess," she answered. "What's up?"

"I talked to the records department at the library, and they were able to pull some old city blueprints and news articles about the McCormick Hotel for me, from the private collections," her best friend replied immediately.

"Oh great!" Kallie replied, hurrying to catch up with Sherman and her dad. "That was fast. Did they find anything unusual?"

"It helps to be friendly with your local librarians. The old newspapers said there used to be a smuggling operation from that location."

"Smuggling? That has to be what they're hiding!"

"Wait, but it was over a hundred years ago, Kallie."

"Oh, but it could still be going on, right?" Kallie suggested. "Or, maybe it stopped and restarted. If it was during Prohibition, like my dad said, then they were probably smuggling alcohol. But maybe Donovan found some old secret passageways, and now he's trafficking something worse?"

"She said there was originally a tunnel that ran under the building," Tess added.

"*Under* the building?" Kallie asked.

Her dad looked at her quizzically. She felt as doubtful as he looked.

"That doesn't make sense. It's right on the beach. Anything underground would be *underwater*."

"Yeah, it would've had to be waterproofed. Maybe a tunnel encased in cement or something."

"That doesn't sound like something that would've lasted a hundred years," Kallie sighed. "It must've collapsed by now."

"Probably," Tess agreed. "But I'm going to ask Wally if he wants to check it out."

Sherman suddenly dashed after a squirrel, pulling her dad along as it ran up a statuesque oak tree by the lake.

"Sherman, stop," Benny told him, pulling him back. "You can't catch that squirrel, he's already gone."

"If the old tunnel collapsed, it would've damaged the hotel itself," Kallie reasoned. "We should be able to find some records about that. News stories or insurance claims, maybe."

Sherman pulled again and barked at the squirrel, distracting Kallie. "Sherman, stop it. The squirrel's way up in the tree. There's no reason to bark."

"What?" Tess asked. "Did you say we're barking up the wrong tree?"

"What?" Kallie laughed. "No, I was talking to Sherman. Actually, I think this might finally be the *right* tree."

"Do you?" Tess sounded relieved.

"They've got a history of smuggling and bootlegging, secret tunnels, hostile security guards, and an ice-cold owner who's more concerned about an old tree than a murdered man," Kallie concluded. "Something's going on in there, and they're barely even trying to hide it. And I'll bet it's something Donovan thought was worth *killing* over."

"I'll talk to Wally about it, and see what he wants to do."

"Since he's been so chatty with you lately, do you know if he found out anything else about the hotel cameras?" Kallie asked.

"No, they're still stonewalling him. I think he's going to try forcing them to hand it over, legally."

"So he thinks they're hiding something too?" Kallie asked, hopefully.

"He thinks they've probably just got some shady operation going on in the hotel. Drugs or hookers or something."

"In *that* neighborhood?"

"*Expensive* drugs and hookers, I guess," Tess replied with a chuckle.

"I'm just sure Donovan's involved, somehow."

"I think so, too, but Wally's been doing this a lot longer than we have. He's probably right, and it's just a boring, old million-dollar meth lab."

"Do you think Winchester would help us get the security footage?"

Tess laughed. "He'd probably get a kick out of that, actually. Working on an old-fashioned street murder again, after all these years. But Wally has his own lawyer."

"His own lawyer? Like, on call?" Kallie asked with surprise.

"I think it's someone he helped in an old case. He didn't go into the details."

"See, *that's* more like the secretive Cornwallis I know," Kallie responded with a nod.

***

"I can't believe Cornwallis is coming *here*," Kallie sighed, as she shoved a few glasses into the dishwasher the next morning. "He hasn't been here in months."

"Kallie, you've seen his office. It's a pigsty," Tess replied. "Why are you cleaning?"

"I don't know. I can't help it." She picked up a cardigan and threw it into her bedroom.

From the couch, Sherman looked up at her questioningly, but she shook her head. "You're fine, Sherm. I wouldn't ever make you move for some silly old investigator." She straightened the dining room chairs, though.

"Kallie, relax," Tess insisted. "He's only coming here because he's picking us up to see the hotel in person. It's not a test."

Cornwallis arrived five minutes later, carrying an umbrella and three plastic shopping bags in each hand. The bags were full, nearly rupturing, and he was wearing a huge hiking backpack. Kallie could see that there were newspapers rolled up in the place that would normally hold the sleeping bag.

I hope he doesn't think we're going hiking in this weather.

"Kallie's already got a roommate, Wally," Tess

quipped. "And I don't think Mr. B is giving up his room."

Cornwallis smiled. "I'm not moving in, just planning for a long stakeout."

"Excellent! But you don't have nearly enough food," Kallie replied, scanning the bags. "I don't see a single bag of chips."

"And no Mountain Dew at all." Tess squinted at him, looking highly critical. "Are you some kind of amateur?"

"I have a jar of instant coffee in my backpack," he replied, a little defensively. "That's all I need. If you two need high-octane caffeine and fancy grub, you can order delivery before we leave." He hoisted the heavy bag onto the couch and took out a laptop. "We don't need to leave for an hour."

Tess and Kallie looked at each other, considering.

"I could eat real food," Kallie decided.

"Yeah, me too," Tess agreed. "No gas station snacks this time. Let's order sandwiches."

"Good idea. If we order subs from Fred's, we can get cheesecake too."

Cornwallis grudgingly agreed that he'd eat a turkey and Swiss. He wanted tuna salad but they quickly and sincerely talked him out of it.

Who knows how long this stakeout will take?

And tuna doesn't have a great shelf life.

Kallie could tell he felt like a wimp for ordering real food for a stakeout, instead of just surviving on bad coffee, but they couldn't have him sidelined with stomach ulcers when he was supposed to be teaching them.

Tess ordered three subs, a couple of two-liter bottles of soda, and three slices of cheesecake. Cornwallis drew the line at strawberry cheesecake, and insisted on plain.

Really roughing it, poor guy.

"My lawyer's trying to encourage a judge to issue a demand for the hotel's security cameras, hopefully in the morning," he told them, changing the subject abruptly. "He thinks the police are working a different angle. Or maybe they just think the hotel was too far away from the crime scene."

"Great," Tess replied. "Let us know if you hear anything."

"Speaking of security," he added, "I checked to see if any of the local businesses caught Patricia's bakery van on their cameras, when she was talking to the police."

"Good idea!" Kallie replied. "Did anyone get a better picture of the runner?"

"I'm afraid not," he replied. "I only found one antique store with a security camera pointing that way, and I think their equipment is almost as old as the vintage dishware." He pulled a manila envelope out of his bag and passed it to Kallie and Tess.

"A picture?" Kallie asked. "Not video?"

"Their camera only takes one picture every thirty seconds." He saw their dismayed facial expressions and commiserated. "I *know*. But at least it's a clear picture."

Kallie opened the folder and saw a perfect photo of Patricia's bakery van. The rear doors were open for the police inspection.

Tess snorted back a laugh.

"Something funny, Miss Russo?" Cornwallis asked. "It's not a bad picture. And it's better than nothing."

"I'm sorry," Tess replied, quickly. "I wasn't laughing at the quality. It's just this other SUV!" She pointed at the photo.

In the foreground, a stocky black Bentley SUV had almost passed the bakery van in the right lane. It was easily a two hundred-thousand-dollar car, but it was tricked out like a high school kid's first Hyundai. In the high-quality photo, they could see a silly-looking spoiler on the back, and a brightly-lit purple neon license plate holder.

Cornwallis put on his glasses and frowned at the photo. "That's tragic," he muttered.

"So what changed your mind about checking out

the McCormick Hotel?" Kallie asked, bringing them back to the previous conversation.

"I talked with a friend in Pinellas County law enforcement, and he said there've been rumors swirling about that hotel for years. Drugs, prostitution, money laundering," Cornwallis explained "But Donovan's bulletproof. When they try to infiltrate the hotel, or press charges, nothing sticks."

I knew it! But is he going to get away with this, too?

"But you think we have something now?" Kallie asked. "How could we catch him, if the police couldn't find anything?"

"Well, because *you* managed to catch him with his hand in the cookie jar."

"But the video won't be allowed in court, Wally," Tess replied, sounding crestfallen.

"That might not matter. I got in touch with a friend—a very *thorough* friend – and asked him to look into Barton Donovan's nationality—"

"And—?" Kallie asked.

"And, he verified that Donovan doesn't have dual citizenship."

"Then why did he have a bunch of passports?" Tess asked.

"It doesn't *prove* anything. The others could still belong to someone else. Maybe he was just keeping them in a locked safe for his travel partners."

"Or—?" Kallie encouraged him to continue.

"Or he could be dealing in stolen passports. Or fake passports." He shrugged. "Or worse."

Or worse? Maybe those passports belong to girls who were looking for a better life, but got tricked into working at his hotel? And maybe not as housekeeping staff. . .

"No way of knowing," Cornwallis continued. "But between the history of that hotel, his own background and shifty behavior, and an assortment of mismatched passports in his house. . . Well, I'd just like to keep an eye on him."

"I found something else shifty, Boss. Come see this old map of the area near the hotel," Tess called to them while they waited for the delivery guy. "The library gave me a printout of the blueprints. It shows a service entrance on the south side of the building, but it's not in the modern photos."

As they looked at the old documents, Tess pulled out her phone and checked the map online. Squinting at the screen as she zoomed in, she frowned. "I can't see it on the street-level map. It looks like there's a garden in that spot now."

"It looks like the parking spaces are gone, but the old door might be there," Cornwallis added.

"Yeah, the angle isn't quite right," Tess agreed. "I can't see what's in the shadows."

"But even if there's an old door there, it wouldn't be open, would it?" Kallie asked.

"Unless it's been bricked over, I'm not giving up," Cornwallis chuckled. "Workers can be bribed to open doors."

"Oh, I like *these* kinds of lessons," Tess replied with a laugh.

Cornwallis grinned and added, "And customers don't even need a bribe, most of the time. If you look and sound official, most people will fall all over themselves to help."

"Ah, the pencil skirt lesson," Kallie nodded sagely at Tess. "Looking official worked like a charm for us too."

"So then, do we try that door first?" Tess asked.

"No, we'd better try the easiest option first. If they're doing something illegal in the hotel—especially if it's worth killing over—then they're probably jumpy about strangers poking around," Cornwallis noted. "You two can try the lobby first, and see if you can get a good look at the place."

Tess and Kallie nodded.

"I'll stick behind in case we have to do this the hard way. Then they won't associate me with the two of you if I get caught."

"You've given this a lot of thought," Kallie noted.

"To be honest, I've never really worked with

partners before," Cornwallis explained. "I have informants all over town, but they don't run operations like this with me."

"But this is a good thing?" Tess asked, hopefully.

"Well, half and half. Three pairs of hands are always better than one. But I have to keep you out of trouble too."

"Us? Trouble?" Kallie replied, looking shocked.

"Don't try that innocent routine with me, young lady. I know better," he chuckled. "I doubt the hotel itself is dangerous, but I don't know who'll be watching us."

"Well, that security guard is onto us, but we saw him there late at night—after nine o'clock. He shouldn't be there at noon. I doubt anyone else would recognize us," Tess added. "Would anyone else in town know we're investigating the hotel?"

"I haven't discussed it with anyone but you, but we're all doing internet searches and poking around down by the waterfront," Cornwallis replied. "I've talked to a few of my contacts, too, but didn't share any details."

"And we've been talking to people in the area too," Tess agreed.

"Just shop owners, mostly," Kallie retorted.

"But you don't know who the shop owners might have told," Cornwallis replied.

"Oh," Kallie leaned back on the couch. "So maybe we're already moving targets."

"He's just being thorough, Kal," Tess reassured her. "Better safe than sorry."

"Exactly," Cornwallis agreed. "Don't worry."

"I'm not worried," Kallie replied. "Heck, this is—What, our third murder?"

"Fourth, I think," Cornwallis mumbled.

"Fifth, if you count—"

"Exactly," Kallie interrupted quickly, her shoulders tensing involuntarily. "So I'm not *worried*. I'm just being thorough too."

"The delivery guy's here," Tess noted with surprise, standing up to get the door.

"Make sure it's really the delivery guy, and not a serial killer," Kallie quipped.

Tess rolled her eyes, but Cornwallis shrugged. "It's not a bad idea."

"Fine, you two jokers, I'll wait until he leaves." She looked out through the peephole, tapping her foot with impatience. "Are you ready to go?"

Cornwallis started reloading his backpack, and Kallie collected three plastic cups with lids and built-in straws from the pantry.

Tess brought the food inside, and the house immediately smelled like fresh-baked bread and cheesecake.

Even Cornwallis's stomach growled, this time. "Fine, I'll admit it. I'm glad you convinced me!"

***

Cornwallis drove Tess's car into town, since it was less conspicuous – and ten minutes later, they were sitting in the parking lot of the McCormick Hotel again, discussing their options for the operation.

"I'd rather sit and watch who's coming and going," Cornwallis explained. "I know it's less exciting, but we need to see if anyone we've interviewed is involved."

"But we need to find out what's around that missing door, on the south side of the building," Kallie complained. "Let's at least go check that out."

Cornwallis sighed. "Fine. But only that one place. Don't get on the elevator, or try to infiltrate any of the rooms."

"Awesome, let's go," Kallie cheered, reaching for the door handle.

"Slow down," Cornwallis grumbled. "You're investigating a murder, not going to a birthday party."

Kallie and Tess left the car, much more stoically. Crossing the parking lot, they made their way into the lobby. Kallie barely dared to breathe, but no one stopped them. There were no security guards in sight, and only a few guests checking in.

So far, so good.

"This way is south," Tess whispered, turning down the hallway to the right. "That old doorway was in a space with no windows, so there must be a storage room or something down here."

They walked all the way down the hallway into the southern wing of the McCormick Hotel, and came to another fork, but saw only guest rooms.

"There's an unmarked door down there," Kallie noted, squinting. "Let's go see if it's open."

"Excuse me, you can't go that way," a hotel worker called out to Kallie, as they walked down the hall.

She ignored the woman and walked faster. She was within ten feet of the door, when another hand grabbed her arm, holding her tightly.

"That room's off-limits," an impatient-looking manager explained. He sounded calm, but his grip tightened.

Wow, that guy came out of nowhere.

This has got to be a lead! The only room in the building with someone guarding it, that means it must be important.

Kallie looked around, and saw that Tess had escaped.

"I was just following my husband up the hall,

and I lost him," she bluffed. "I think he must've come this way, and gone through that door."

The manager shook his head in visible annoyance. "No one came this way. And no one's allowed in that room."

Kallie laughed, trying to sound flirtatious, and hoping she didn't just sound desperate. "What's in there? The owner's golden arm?" she teased.

But the manager didn't bite. Didn't even acknowledge the joke. "This way, ma'am. I'll walk you back to the hallway." He pulled her gently but unrelentingly away from the mysterious door.

Well, at least I can tell Cornwallis where to start. No telling how he'll get in there, but if there's a clue to Oscar's murder in this building, then it's got to be in that room.

Or maybe the owner really does have a golden arm. Or the bodies of his thirty ex-wives.

The manager walked her back to the main hallway and made sure she was heading for the front door. Kallie glanced back, but he was still standing there, arms crossed, making sure she left.

Donovan isn't Bluebeard the pirate, but he's up to something sinister.

"I'll bet Tess could've gotten past that guy," she muttered to herself as she crossed to the car, out of sight. "I obviously need to work on my flirting skills."

***

"Well, that was an unmitigated failure," Cornwallis muttered. "I need to get inside myself, and see what's in that room, if it's behind that old service door."

"They know my face already, so I can't go back," Kallie reminded him. "I don't think they got a good look at Tess, though."

"This dress is pretty memorable," Tess added. "But if I changed clothes and put my hair up, I think I could get past them."

"Great, let's try that," Cornwallis agreed. He drove Tess's car to a gas station on the corner, and parked on the farther side in case anyone happened to be watching.

Kallie and Tess quickly opened the car's trunk, where Tess grabbed a cardigan. Then they headed straight for the restroom, where Tess quickly braided her naturally curly black hair into two pigtails. She threw on the cardigan and posed expectantly.

Kallie gave her a thorough review and was pretty sure she looked like a different person. But after another thought, she told her best friend to wash off her eye makeup too. "Half the guys in there were ogling you. Most of them are probably gone by now, but any guy in his right mind would remember those smoky eyes," she

169

teased.

Tess batted her eyelashes dramatically and then pulled out a packet of makeup remover wipes from her purse. Twenty seconds later, she looked like the girl next door.

If you lived next door to a 1960s bombshell movie star, that is.

"That's better. With the cardigan, you look totally different."

Tess shrugged. For a bombshell, she wasn't overly concerned about her looks. "We can't afford to attract any undue attention."

They met Cornwallis back at the car, where he'd changed into a linen suit that looked casual but expensive.

Where was this side of Cornwallis hiding? And did he have that suit in his backpack?

"We'll go in together and rent a room," Cornwallis explained, when they were back inside the car. "That will make us look more legit. Tess, you'll be my wife."

Tess raised an eyebrow, and Kallie stifled a laugh.

"What, I don't get a ring or anything?" Tess scoffed.

"I'd hold out for a prenup, if I were you," Kallie advised her, straight-faced.

"A prenup and a bended knee," Tess agreed. "I've gotten more romantic offers from my neighbor's six-year-old kid."

Cornwallis blushed and laughed. "Fair enough, you can be my mistress, and your code name'll be *Toots*."

Tess looked a little green at that. "Fine, I'll be your wife. Just don't call me Toots."

Kallie laughed, but tried to refocus them. "We're running out of time. What's the plan?"

"Okay, while Tess is renting the room, I'll pretend to be looking for the lobby bar," Cornwallis explained. "And once you get the keys, Tess, we'll pull the old switcharoo."

Chapter Eight

Kallie watched nervously from Tess's car as the two of them crossed the parking lot and walked into the hotel.

Calm down, Kalliope, it's just a hotel. They're just looking around.

And Cornwallis can take perfectly good care of Tess. She'll be fine.

That didn't work, of course. Kallie was still nervous and worried about her best friend. But her part in the charade was coming up soon. She checked the clock on her phone about twenty times in the next five minutes. When it said 1:26 p.m., she closed her eyes, took a deep breath, and got out of the car.

It was pouring buckets of rain, again, but she figured that would help with her part. Without even trying to cover her clothes or hair, she stomped angrily across the parking lot and into the hotel's lobby. She had just a moment to take in the beauty of the place – its spectacular tile floor, carved hardwood desks, and gorgeous vintage light fixtures and moldings. But she had a job to do. Dripping wet to the skin, she whipped her head around in a fit of rage.

She glimpsed Tess in the hallway outside the lobby, near the elevator bank, and made eye contact for just a millisecond.

"Where is that manager that kicked me out of here?!" she fumed, stomping toward the reception desk.

The girl at the desk cringed behind the elegant marble counter. "He's—he's gone."

He's not gone!" Kallie raged, leaving a trail of water on the floor from her dripping clothes and hair. "Don't lie to me, lady. I told my husband what he did, and he's going to come down here and kick—"

The manager who had ejected Kallie finally had the guts to leave his office and defend the desk clerk, though he looked like he wished he hadn't. Every visitor in the lobby was staring at them in alarm, and one was edging toward the doors. Kallie had never been prouder to look like a crazy redheaded Amazon-Valkyrie warrior.

"I apologize for the commotion earlier, and we'd be happy to have you stay," he simpered.

Any legit hotel owner would call the police and have her removed—or arrested—but Cornwallis was apparently right. The hotel was glamorous and historical, but it had a seedy underbelly. This guy couldn't afford to have the cops in here, poking around.

Out of the corner of her eye, she saw Tess reenter the lobby. With her change of appearance, the manager wouldn't recognize her, but Kallie knew their mission had been completed. If Tess was back, that meant Kallie had caused enough of a distraction to get Cornwallis down to the mysterious door.

She accepted a gift card and a worried apology from the manager, and swept irritably back out to the car—getting soaked again in the process.

It was all on Cornwallis from here. She climbed into the driver's seat and opened a bottle of Diet Coke, settling in to wait and worry.

Ten minutes later, Tess returned to the car. She'd been waiting sensibly for the rain to stop.

"Did he get into that room?" Kallie asked breathlessly, as soon as the door was closed behind Tess.

"He hadn't come back to the lobby when I left, so I guess so. Either that, or he got caught. . ."

"Don't even say that," Kallie whimpered, looking out the foggy car window at the hotel.

But Cornwallis strolled casually back out of the hotel five minutes later, as if everything was completely normal.

"What happened?!" they both clamored, as he sat down and started Tess's car.

"I couldn't get into the room, but I got a good look around," he replied, pulling out of the parking lot. "I want to get a little distance between us and the hotel, in case someone mentions us at the desk."

Kallie and Tess waited patiently while he drove back into the side streets of Owhiro.

"That room is definitely in the same location as the external door in the old photographs. But it's locked and wired with an alarm," he explained. "I thought it might be some kind of storeroom, possibly for drugs or cash. But it's too small. I think it's an office."

"Where Donovan keeps his incriminating evidence?" Kallie suggested.

Cornwallis shook his head. "*Donovan's* way too careful for that. He wouldn't keep anything incriminating at the hotel. Whatever's in that room wouldn't have his fingerprints on it. He'd let someone else take the fall."

"So we didn't learn anything?" Tess asked with a sigh.

"We can tell the police about that room, and see if it helps them get a warrant," he suggested. "It might not help our murder case, but that whole empire will topple if they can get Donovan."

"Great, I guess," Kallie grumbled, finding herself disappointed again.

***

"Morrison's coming over for dinner, Sherman,"

Kallie called from the kitchen. "Go get your ball."

Her beloved pup raised his head and looked at her to verify the magic words.

"You heard me," she added with a laugh. "Morrison's going to be here in a few minutes."

Sherman slipped gracefully off the couch and walked to the back door, carefully taking his favorite squeaky tennis ball out of the toy box. He held it up hopefully and looked back at Kallie.

"That's right, he'll throw it for you. Bring it back in here." She went back to stirring the chili and checked on the cornbread in the oven, but a moment later, she heard a tiny, tentative squeak from the living room.

"Making sure it still works, sweetie?"

Sherman wasn't sure about Morrison at first, and apparently had seen enough unpleasant men to distrust them so close to Kallie, his favorite human. He was perfectly friendly, but always kept an eye open when they got too close.

Of course, he warmed up quickly and decided that Morrison was one of the nice humans, like his Auntie Tess and Grampa Benny. There may have been some bacon involved in this decision, but only a little. Morrison's kind nature and inherent way with animals sealed the deal. Now, Sherman couldn't get enough of his new friend.

Sherman set the ball between his feet and smiled happily up at his mistress in the kitchen. "I saved you some ground turkey, too, don't worry," she reassured him.

She heard a car door slam outside, and Sherman jumped up.

"Don't harass him," she admonished him. "He just got off work, so let him sit and rest for a minute."

The doorbell rang a moment later, and she looked back at Sherman, who seemed to agree. He was smiling happily again and nodding at the front door as if to say, "Answer it, already!"

Kallie opened the door and was met by Morrison's smiling face.

How did life get this perfect, so fast?

She smiled back, and he picked her up and spun her around. Sherman barked happily, and Morrison stopped to scratch his mismatched ears.

"I'm just finishing dinner, have a seat." She waved him toward the couch. "How was your afternoon? Did you find that lost kid's mother? I saw it on the news."

"We did, and it was a happy ending, but I don't want to talk about work." He sat down, adding, "It smells great in—"

Sherman had officially spent his last ounce of patience, and he skidded across the hardwood floor, jumping awkwardly onto the couch. He snuggled in next to Morrison and peacefully rested his chin on his friend's knee.

"Traitor," Kallie added, laughing. "I can't believe he waited that long. He was so excited that you were coming."

***

"I swear, it feels like it's been raining for a month," Kallie sighed, as she and Tess drove home from taking Sherman to the park the next morning. There had been another cloudburst, and the windshield wipers were on high, again.

"It's not even the rainy season yet," Tess agreed. "I think I'm going to melt if I get soaked one more time."

They jumped out of Tess's car and ran for the door of Kallie's house, but were all drenched by the time they got inside.

Kallie yanked three towels out of the linen closet, and they mostly dried Sherman's fur and their own hair. Then, annoyed but drier, she tossed them all into the bathroom hamper.

"I'm hungry," Tess finally stated. "Do you want to order takeout or something?"

"Yeah, I'm definitely not in the mood to cook. Pizza?"

Tess took out her phone and called the little pizzeria on the corner. "I'd like to place an order for delivery," she told them immediately.

"Good call, Tess. No way we're going back out in the rain."

After placing an order for a large pepperoni and mushroom pizza, with a side of garlic bread, Tess hung up and walked back to the garage. She cracked the door open and called out, "Mr. B, I just ordered pizza!"

As Kallie was getting plates ready, her phone dinged, and she sighed.

I love learning this stuff, but I'd also love to eat one meal without being summoned by Cornwallis.

Cornwallis

I found a lead on our mystery guy Endicott. A cop friend knew him a few years ago and said he lived in a squatter house near Fourth and Osprey.

Tess was reading her phone, too, and they looked at each other. Kallie started typing back.

Kallie

Here in Owhiro?

Cornwallis

Not anymore. Doesn't know where he is now.

Kallie

Okay, we'll go over there after dinner. Waiting for the rain to stop.

"We're going over *there*?" Tess asked softly, her voice a little squeaky.

Kallie looked up at the sound. "It's close to here. I thought we could—"

"You don't remember, do you?"

"Remember what?" Kallie asked, confused. "Do you know where Endicott lived?"

"You don't remember the old Reeves house on Osprey Street?" she asked, voice barely above a whisper. "I'm *sure* that's the house he's talking about."

"Tess, are you okay?" Kallie asked, surprised. Her best friend was a little pale and seemed worried.

Tess suddenly shook it off, and laughed at herself. "I forgot I'm a grownup, for a second there. We can go after dinner. But we're driving, not walking."

Kallie frowned. "Okay, sure. But I don't—"

"You'll remember when we get there. Trust me."

***

Kallie turned right onto Osprey and drove slowly up the road. "Fourth Street is two blocks up, so the house must be near here. I'm not sure how we're supposed to guess which house it is."

Tess shook her head. "I can't believe you don't remember."

Feeling slightly judged, Kallie kept driving, scanning the surrounding houses. At the next stop sign,

180

Tess put her hand to her mouth, but stayed silent.

"Stop it," Kallie whispered, laughing awkwardly.

She drove halfway up the block and then stopped suddenly, in the middle of the street. "Oh my gosh," she whispered.

Tess giggled like a nervous eight-year-old.

"Is that—?"

Her best friend nodded.

A derelict old house sat in the middle of a dozen slightly run-down but otherwise intact houses. The broken windows were covered with cardboard and duct tape, and a rotting two-by-four crossed the damaged front door. The paint was dirty and splotched with moss and mold.

But in Kallie's head, it looked just like it had when they were thirteen years old.

"We're not going in there," she stated definitively.

Tess giggled eerily again and covered her mouth. A car behind them honked, and Kallie bolted upright in her seat. After a moment of shock, she pulled over to the curb to get out of their way.

Kallie croaked, "That's the place where—"

Suddenly, they were thirteen, and it was Halloween. Tess was dressed as a vampire, and Kallie was a 1960s hippie wearing bell-bottoms and a giant peace sign necklace. They'd been trick-or-treating at some of the boutiques on Main Street, and their friends dared them to come down to Osprey Street.

Kallie didn't know about the rumors and, of course, Tess wasn't afraid of anything. And that's how they wound up at the Reeves House for the first time.

The most haunted house in Owhiro.

"There aren't really ghosts, you know," Tess chirped, cringing in the passenger seat.

"I know," Kallie whispered.

"We don't even have to go in there," Tess added, her usually calm voice sounding slightly like a plea. "We can just ask the neighbors if they've seen him. Endicott."

"That sounds like a great idea," Kallie replied, realizing she'd been holding her breath. She put the car back in gear and drove away from the creepy old house. She immediately felt lighter, as soon as it was out of sight.

"Maybe they won't even remember him," Tess suggested. "Or maybe this isn't even where he was living."

"Yeah. Nobody could've lived there. It's in terrible shape." Kallie pulled over again and parked. "It's probably some other house."

Both feeling less anxious, they got out and walked up the sidewalk to the nearest house. Tess even smiled.

"Hopefully, folks will be home from work by now," Tess added as they started up the first walkway to a faded purple door. Many of the houses had fallen on hard times, but they had good bones. Nothing a little love and a few gallons of paint couldn't fix.

No one answered at the first door.

"I mean, how could a house in Owhiro even be haunted?" Kallie asked, flippantly, as they crossed to the next house. "It's not like we have a ton of crime, and the houses aren't old enough to have hundred-year-old ghosts."

Tess didn't answer, but walked to the next door and knocked. No answer here, either. The drapes were drawn, but Kallie could see that it was dark inside.

"Maybe we're too early. Let's try one more house, and if there's no answer, we can go into town and get ice cream. We'll come back a little later."

Tess nodded and turned back toward the sidewalk.

"You okay?" Kallie asked.

"There was a fire," Tess replied quietly. "I looked it up in the library after Halloween, that year. The whole family died. Mom, Dad, and two kids. The cat. It was back in the sixties."

"Oh man," Kallie replied with a sigh. "No wonder it's haunted."

"Somebody eventually built a new house on the

same spot, and another lady was murdered there, too. Some guy robbed a liquor store and was looking for a place to hide, and she surprised him." Tess stopped on the sidewalk. "She'd just gotten married and she was pregnant."

"You read all this in the library? When we were just *kids*?" Kallie groaned. "Tess, oh my gosh."

"I couldn't ask my parents. They didn't like to talk about stuff like that," she continued, barely speaking above a whisper. "I didn't expect it to be— I guess I thought it would be some dusty old ghost story from the 1800s."

"I'm so sorry."

"The neighbors were interviewed for the newspaper article, and they said the husband went crazy with guilt and despair."

"And it's just been sitting there empty, ever since?"

"Unless Wally's right about the squatters," Tess suggested.

Kallie took her hand. "Do you want to go get ice cream and just wait for the neighbors to get home? We can do that."

"I'm not really in the mood for ice cream anymore," Tess replied. "Let's get it over with."

The door of the next house opened suddenly with a loud creak, and they both jumped.

An elderly woman stuck her head out, and called, "Can I help you girls with somethin'? There's no solicitin' around here. We've all got signs."

"No, ma'am," Kallie yelped, recovering first. She grabbed Tess's hand again, and pulled her across the lawn. "We'd love to ask you a question, though."

The woman crossed her arms, looking annoyed, but didn't close the door.

"Have you seen anyone in that old house across the street lately?" Kallie asked, deciding not to mention Cornwallis unless it became necessary.

"Y'all some kind of ghost hunters, like on TV?" the woman asked, with a scowl.

"Oh, no ma'am," Tess replied quickly. "We meant humans."

"I haven't seen anyone over there in years. Used to be a bunch of drug addicts over there, or that's what my late husband called them, but—"

"Who's at the door, Debra?" a voice called from inside the house.

"No one, Mama. Go back to bed," she yelled over her shoulder.

A moment later, an even older woman appeared in the doorway. "You sellin' somethin'?"

"No, ma'am," Tess replied again, speaking a little louder. "We were wondering if you ladies had seen anyone in the abandoned house across the street."

"Funny you should mention that," the older woman yelled. "I hadn't seen anyone over there for years, until about a week ago."

The first woman chided her, "You're imaginin' things, Mama." She looked back at Tess and added, "Her mind's goin'. Don't listen to anything she says, miss."

"Saw two men carrying a big, heavy bag. Draggin' it, really. They were tryin' to hurry, but it was too heavy, and they dragged it right into the front door." The older woman pointed at the other house. "Crawled right under that old board." After a moment's hesitation, she glanced at her daughter and added, "I was takin' my medication, 'cause I couldn't sleep. I saw 'em through the bushes."

Her daughter rolled her eyes. "I'm tellin' you, Mama. You dreamed that."

"I didn't dream it, Debra," the older woman insisted. She drifted back into the house, and her daughter followed her. She reached back and swung the door closed without another word.

"Okay, that was. . ."

"Different," Tess completed her sentence.

"Do you think she was imagining things?"

"Yep. Almost certainly."

"Wanna go over there?" Kallie asked, hesitantly.

"Sure, I guess. It's too sad to be scary, anymore."

"Tell me that again when five ghosts come screaming out of the attic," Kallie grumbled.

"Maybe six, if there was a dead body in that heavy bag."

"The *imaginary* heavy bag, you mean?" Kallie teased.

"That's the one. Let's go look," Tess agreed. "But we're calling Wally first."

They crossed the street, as Tess quickly called Cornwallis and told him where they were going. Checking the back of the house, they determined that the front door, though partially blocked, was their best option.

"He advised us not to go in, Kal," Tess mentioned, as they stood peering through the space under the diagonal board.

"Okay," Kallie replied, absently, as she knelt under the board and lowered her head. "I think I can get through here. And it'll be even easier for you."

"He said it's probably trespassing, even though it's abandoned."

"Trespassing is our middle name," Kallie replied with a jaded laugh. "Besides, who's going to press charges? The ghost, or her bereaved husband?" she mumbled.

"Yeah, he didn't sound hopeful about stopping us. He'll probably be mad."

"Then we'd better find something really good, huh?" Kallie asked, as she crawled under the makeshift barricade, into the derelict house.

Like Tess said, get it over with, before you chicken out, Kalliope.

"Okay, but let's be fast."

Once they were inside, their eyes adjusted quickly to the dim light. There was an old sleeping bag in one corner of the dining room, but it was covered in chunks of plaster, where part of the ceiling had fallen down. It clearly hadn't been used recently.

"I don't think anyone's squatting here now," Kallie replied. "Let's look around. Maybe there's something here that can help us find Endicott."

"Well, we know the money's in here somewhere, if they didn't come back out with it."

"*Money*? What makes you think it was money?" Kallie asked.

"Well, it was heavy, and important. And hopefully not a dead body."

Kallie cringed. "Right, *money*. Let's focus on it being a ton of *money*," she agreed with a nod.

And definitely not a dead body, Kalliope.

"If I were running from the cops, and I needed to hide a bunch of cash, where would I put it?" Tess mused.

Kallie nodded and played along, "If I thought I

could get *back* here quickly, I'd hide it somewhere fast and easy. A shoebox, a closet. The fridge."

Tess nodded, and they walked toward the kitchen. It was a mess as well, and they could see signs that rats were the primary tenants here now.

Kallie grabbed the refrigerator handle and whined softly.

"It's been a long time, Kal. It won't be anything gross," Tess whispered reassuringly.

She pulled the handle, and the old rubber seal around the door crumbled quietly to the floor. Kallie saw Tess's phone flashlight out of the corner of her eye, beaming into the old appliance.

"No piles of cash," Tess sighed.

"But no body parts either," Kallie whispered. "I'm calling this a draw."

Tess nodded in agreement. "Okay, let's check the closets and the couch cushions."

After quickly checking all of the other simple hiding locations, they began considering other options.

"If I knew I *couldn't* get back here quickly," Kallie continued, "If I knew the cops would check the place, or I'd be out of town–"

"Or in jail–"

"Or if I knew I was going to need to send someone else to come find it—I'd hide the money better. Someplace no one would find it accidentally."

"Under the floorboards. In the attic," Tess suggested.

"In the toilet tank?" Kallie reasoned.

"Like in *The Godfather*! Good call."

They ran to the bathroom, but the old toilet was empty and covered in dust and mold. Nothing behind it or in the lidless tank.

They tapped on the floorboards and the walls, looking for a hiding space without doing any damage, but didn't hear anything that sounded hollow.

"I'm not really sure what a secret hiding place is supposed to sound like," Kallie complained.

"Like the difference between a full box of oatmeal and an empty one," Tess answered sensibly, making Kallie laugh.

"I've never tapped on a box of oatmeal, Tess."

"Not even to play the drums?" her best friend quipped. "I highly doubt that."

"Okay, maybe once or twice," she answered, blushing. "But none of these walls sound like oatmeal."

"The witness said she saw someone come in here with a duffel bag that was almost too heavy to carry, dragging it. So if we presume that was the *cash*—"

"—and not a dead body," Kallie repeated.

"Not to be gross, but if it was a dead body, we'd—"

"Okay, yeah. It'd be obvious by now, in this tiny space. So let's say it *was* cash."

"If they left it in the bag, there's no way they'd be able to lift it onto a shelf or hide it in the attic," Tess considered.

"So they'd have to either split up the money, which would take time, or hide the whole duffel bag somewhere on the floor—or *in* the floor."

"No basements in Florida, at least not south of Tallahassee," Tess added. "And I doubt they dug into the cement slab foundation with a jackhammer."

"So let's look for hiding places *on* the floor. Dressers, kitchen cabinets, maybe a pantry? I'll take the bedroom, I guess," Kallie volunteered.

Tess nodded and headed toward the kitchen, but Kallie chased after her. "I changed my mind, stay with me."

Tess grabbed her hand. "Good, I didn't want to go by myself either. This place is *creepy*."

"We've been in some seriously weird spots before, but this is different. No horrible dolls or crazy men chasing us–"

"–currently," Tess whispered.

"It's more of a soul-creepy," Kallie continued. "I can just feel the awful things that happened here, even though right now it just looks grungy and. . . damp."

"Why *is* everything damp?" Tess asked,

suddenly sounding concerned.

"I thought at first that it was because there's no air conditioning. But everything feels like it was *wet*."

"Could it have been flooded? The Gulf is at least four blocks from here, so I don't think it's that."

"It could've just been a burst water pipe or something. Maybe the roof leaks?"

"You're right," Tess replied, shaking her head. "Of course, the roof probably just leaks. And it's been such an unusually rainy spring."

They entered the kitchen quietly—Kallie wasn't sure why they were trying to be quiet, but the place was downright eerie—and checked the bottom cabinets one by one. Most were collapsing from dry rot, and one had surprise guests—a family of rats feasting on an old box of Saltines. But no giant bag of money.

"I'm starting to think this theory is crazy, Tess. Even if someone came in here with the money, someone *else* would've stolen it by now," Kallie sighed. "The place is sitting wide open, and everyone in town knows about the ghost stories. It's probably still the top place in Owhiro that kids go on a dare."

"Well, we're already here, so let's just finish checking all of the rooms. No floors and no ceilings—just knee-height down. Okay?"

"Sure, okay," Kallie replied, opening the pantry door. She closed her eyes and held her breath as about a million cockroaches scattered at the motion, and disappeared into the corners and crevices.

"Gross," she whispered to herself.

They had been trying to be subtle with any lights, so the neighbors—and probably the cops—didn't see them in here, but in the pantry, she felt okay using her phone's flashlight. It was pitch dark, and no one could see it from the street. In the glaringly bright light, she saw that the pantry was filled with tattered and chewed bags and boxes of dried goods. Empty boxes of pasta and cereals, shredded bags of rice, and even a bin that seemed to be growing some kind of plant, probably from a discarded onion. Everything seemed to have at least one bite mark from some critter or another.

But still no bag of cash.

She considered pushing the refuse aside and continuing into the back of the pantry—briefly holding her phone up to shine it into the space beyond—but she couldn't make out anything in the shadows.

Looking around for something to use as a broom—

I'm not sticking my hands in there. . .

"Find anything—?"

Kallie let out an involuntary screech as Tess joined her in the pantry.

"Eww, you weren't going back *in there*, were you?" Tess asked, incredulously. "There are probably rats the size of a Great Dane back there."

"But what if the *money's* back there?" Kallie asked.

"What if it was really a *body*, in that bag?" Tess replied, raising an eyebrow.

"Okay, you win," Kallie quickly conceded, backing out of the horrible pantry. "Let's get out of here. I feel like I have spiders crawling all over me."

Tess turned on her phone's flashlight too, and shone it into the back of the pantry. "There's nothing back there, anyway. See?"

"Why is your light so much brighter than mine?"

"Because my phone wasn't made when dinosaurs roamed the Earth," Tess teased. "Let's go home. We've checked everything, and it's getting too dark to see, now."

"That's the best idea I've heard all day," Kallie replied, with relief.

***

"I don't know whether to yell at you or hire you," Cornwallis sighed, when they called him later that evening. "You checked every room?"

"Yep, if it's there, it's not anywhere below waist height."

"Where else can it be?" he asked with audible annoyance. "I checked on the women who spoke to you, and they're both retired teachers, so I'm considering them legit, for now. But if that bag was too heavy to lift into the attic, and the house is on a concrete slab, then where is it?"

"The neighbors would've noticed if they burned it, and the water's turned off. So they couldn't flush it down the toilet," Tess agreed.

"There's no water near there, right? No river or lake?"

"Nothing closer than the Gulf," Kallie agreed. "And no fresh digging spots in the yard."

"No new concrete poured?" Cornwallis asked.

"Nope," Kallie sighed.

"Well, the only reason we were interested in this house is because Endicott was seen there, and that was years ago," Cornwallis concluded. "So I'm pulling you off this one."

"What?!" Kallie and Tess both cried, in unison.

"I don't want you to get in trouble for being there, when we don't even have any evidence that those men were related to our case."

"I really feel like we were onto something, though," Tess complained. "Can't we just talk to a few more of the neighbors?"

"We won't go back into the house," Kallie added. "We promise. But Endicott is our best link to the victim, in the last few days of his life. We need to find him."

Cornwallis sat in silence for a moment, then sighed. "Fine. You can both use more experience with interviewing witnesses. But *don't* go back in the house."

"Thank you! We won't let you down!" Kallie replied cheerfully, hanging up before he could change his mind.

Chapter Nine

"Good morning, ma'am." Kallie greeted the older woman who was dragging her trash bin to the street, the next morning.

The woman grunted at her, but didn't reply.

"We're sorry to bother you so early, but we're investigating a crime in Owhiro, and we think there may have been a situation here too."

"Not talkin' to cops," the woman muttered under her breath as she left the trash bin at the street and started back to the house, which appeared to be a duplex.

"We're not with the police, ma'am," Tess called after her. "We're working for a private investigator, and we think there may have been a person of interest at the house across the street from you." She gestured at the deserted, ramshackle house.

The older woman sighed and turned back to them. "Nothing good happens in that house. Been squatters and drug dealers in there for years. And there were old stories—" She paused for a moment, but then snapped, impatiently, "What happened now?"

Tess and Kallie looked at each other quickly, and Tess continued, "We're investigating a murder, and we think someone who knew the victim lived here previously. We're concerned for his safety, and would like to speak with him."

There would be no security cameras in this neighborhood, Kallie knew. There was no point in asking. Even the grocery and liquor stores wouldn't have any kind of security, not even the kind that sold for fifty bucks online.

"We heard someone was hanging around," Tess added. "Someone who would've been carrying a heavy bag, dragging it. Late at night."

"I don't stay up late at night," the old woman shook her head. "I got diabetes, and it makes me tired." She said it with finality and started walking away again.

Tess didn't follow her, but called, gently, "Thank you for your help. We'll find the guy."

The old woman paused and shook her head. "Try Gibson. Two doors down." She waved to her left, without looking back at them. "He likes to sit on his porch and smoke at night."

Tess raised her eyebrows at Kallie and shrugged.

Might as well.

They walked to the house two doors down, an old Craftsman bungalow from the 1940s—which had seen better days—but there was no one outside. A brindle pit bull stood watching them through a crack in the old fence, but it didn't bark, so they walked up the stairs and knocked on the door.

After a few minutes, the door opened a crack. They saw an old man with bleary eyes, but he didn't speak, nor unlock the chain."Mr. Gibson?" Tess asked.

"Just Gibson," he replied, brusquely. "Not Mr. Gibson."

"We wanted to ask you about a house across the street. Two houses down?"

"What happened there now?" he asked. "Last time the police were out here, I asked them to clear that place out."

"What did they say?" Tess asked.

"They said they'd try, but they couldn't find the owner," he growled. "This used to be a nice neighborhood, you know."

Kallie could tell from the style of the houses that it had once been a charming neighborhood. Her dad's father had built a Craftsman home with his own hands, and she knew they took a lot of care and love.

"Yes, sir," Tess replied, simply. "We're looking for an older man, who used to live there. We heard there was some activity lately. Some men dragging a heavy bag?"

"I didn't see anyone dragging a bag, but there's been more activity over there," he added. "Younger kids, though. Nobody I recognized from the old days."

Mrs. Jackson said Endicott was older, closer to Oscar Lawson's age. So maybe he wasn't involved after all.

At least we can be pretty sure he wasn't in the bag. That's one piece of good news.

"Could you call us if you see anything?" Tess asked.

Gibson chuckled as he shut the door.

"I guess not," Kallie replied with a smirk. "This sounds like a dead end, anyway."

"Yeah," Tess sighed, as they returned to the car. "Let's go back to my house and brainstorm for a while. I'm so mad at myself for telling Wally that we wouldn't let him down," Tess grumbled as she looked around and started to pull away from the curb. "This morning was a total failure."

"It wasn't really a *failure*, exactly," Kallie retorted. "At least we found out something."

Tess made an annoyed face, and started to reply, but quickly jerked the wheel back as an older sedan screeched its tires and its horn honked noisily.

"Where did that guy come from?" Kallie asked in shock. They were still on a quiet side street, where there was very little traffic.

"I didn't even see him," Tess agreed. "Maybe he pulled out of a driveway." She drove on and continued toward home.

"Even if it wasn't what we wanted to hear, at least we know Endicott hasn't been seen around that house lately," Kallie continued, as Tess made the left onto Main Street. "That Gibson guy sounds like his own personal Neighborhood Watch group."

"It still feels like a failure," Tess replied with a sigh. "I really thought—"

Another screech of tires and a loud, droning honk, and they both jumped, startled.

"Was that the same car?" Kallie gasped.

"I think so," Tess replied, staring after the other car, which was speeding away.

"What kind of lunatic goes all *road rage* at eleven a.m.? There's not even any traffic on the road."

"Did he come back, just to harass us again, though?" Tess asked. "That's insane."

"Is he making a u-turn up there?" Kallie asked, squinting up the road. "Maybe you should go the back way."

"That's a good idea." Tess took a quick left and pulled into the side streets of Owhiro, and then took another right so they'd be more hidden. A moment later, they saw the sedan pass again.

"He definitely came back for us," Tess concluded.

"Do you think it's related to the case?"

"I don't think we've uncovered anything worth killing us over, do you?" Tess joked. Kallie thought she looked a little worried, though.

"It doesn't feel like we've uncovered *anything*," Kallie grumbled. "Period."

"So it's probably just your average run-of-the-mill Florida road rage psycho." Tess added, "His windows are tinted too dark to see his face, anyway."

Kallie nodded. "Let's go the back way, anyway. I don't want him knowing where you live."

Tess drove the rest of the way home, and then parked in the garage – something she didn't often do.

"Hang on, I'll move my bike, so you can get out," Tess laughed, after she'd rolled the garage door closed behind them. She ran around to the passenger side and moved a bicycle out of the way, so Kallie could open the car door.

Kallie peeked out of the small garage windows and whispered, "I think that sedan just passed again."

"What?! Are you sure?"

"No, it's just an old sedan. I haven't even gotten a good enough look to identify the model," Kallie conceded.

"Well he obviously didn't see us, if that was even him. Let's get inside."

Once they were safely in Tess's home, they checked the front windows.

"Do you think he's still out there?" Kallie asked, peeking through the edge of the curtain.

"Probably not," Tess replied. "But we're not going to find out. Let's order lunch and let that freak calm down."

She placed the order with their favorite Thai restaurant, and the owner—who knew them well—yelled for the delivery driver to pick up the phone. After a short discussion, he agreed to stop at Publix for a half-gallon of raspberry cheesecake ice cream.

Kallie would pay for it and tip him extra, of course.

"We're lucky you have that garage," Kallie told Tess.

"It's especially good for eluding psychotic drivers who try to follow me home," Tess joked. "And for storing kayaks."

"I don't remember this kind of thing ever happening *before* we started chasing murderers," Kallie considered aloud.

"It's just the perfect maraschino cherry on top of the other weirdness," Tess replied, with a gentle smile. "Do you want to stop? Is it stressing you out?"

"Nope," Kallie replied with just a hint of forced cheerfulness. "Bring on the psychos."

After they'd eaten lunch, and everything seemed calm outside, Kallie asked, "Hey, do you want to go to

Clearwater? I changed my mind – I want to buy that Ella Fitzgerald record for my dad."

"Sure," Tess agreed. "The owner said he'd play it for us, to make sure it's not scratched."

"Good, I made sure his record player is still working."

"And we can stop for croissants, too," Tess added.

"Why, the thought never crossed my mind," Kallie replied with an ironic smirk.

They made the short drive to Clearwater and found a parking spot not too far from the shops, since it was still early afternoon. As they were walking to the record store, Kallie suddenly pulled on Tess's sleeve. "Hang on, let's go to this plant store. Anna's birthday is on Wednesday, and I want to get her a gift."

Benny Brooks was dating Anna—a lovely woman—and Kallie adored her, but she was the sort of woman who had everything. Notoriously hard to shop for.

Tess followed her into the little store, asking, "Does Anna like plants? I've never heard her mention it."

"She loves them, but mostly keeps them outdoors. I want to get her something to keep in the kitchen."

"That would be nice, something colorful," Tess

reasoned.

"And something easy—"

"How about a plastic one, in a pretty pot?" Tess teased.

"Cute. I thought I'd get her a nice little cactus, or a violet or something."

"I think those are actually both hard to keep alive," Tess replied, frowning. "I killed a bunch of violets when we had our first apartment, remember?"

Kallie was looking at the small display tables, and didn't answer.

"They're really easy to overwater," Tess concluded, looking at another table.

The trendy little shop only sold small houseplants, mostly succulents in adorable pots the size of coffee cups. An employee saw them and walked over to offer her help.

"My dad's girlfriend is an experienced gardener, but doesn't have any houseplants," Kallie explained. "What's something that's easy for a beginner?"

"Is she more likely to over-care or under-care?" the young lady asked.

"I'm not sure—" Kallie replied.

"Most people under-water. But sometimes people who are very busy accidentally overwater, because they can't remember when they last watered," she explained.

"Oh, that makes sense, I guess," Kallie answered. She was already regretting this shopping foray.

"You know what's really easy?" the girl finally asked, gently. Kallie could tell she was sensing her confusion. "Everybody says orchids are really difficult, but most of them are easy, in our climate."

"Really?" Kallie asked, surprised.

"There are a lot of different varieties, and some are easier than others." She took Kallie to a section of brightly colored orchids. "You can keep them outside, or in a sunny kitchen, and just dump water on them when you think of it," she explained.

"That sounds easy," Kallie responded.

"Root rot is what usually kills indoor plants that are overwatered. But you can keep orchids in a little root cage, instead of a pot—so the water runs right through. And it's so humid here, they can absorb some of their water right out of the air."

"My mother always said orchids were so complicated," Kallie mused.

Although my mother thinks anything except being pampered is complicated.

"If you live up north, it's a lot harder," the saleslady agreed. "But we have the perfect climate for them. And we have some pretty ones that aren't too expensive."

As Kallie checked the multi-colored options, Tess quietly grabbed her sleeve and whispered, "Does that guy at the register look familiar to you?"

Kallie glanced over at the checkout desk, trying to use her new sleuthing skills to be subtle—only slightly succeeding. "He does, but I'm not sure from where."

Tess nodded in agreement and pointed out a lovely lavender and green orchid. "I think green flowers are so unusual and pretty."

"Anna's unusual and pretty, too. I bet she'll like it." She picked up the plant, noticing—as the saleslady had mentioned previously—that there was no soil in the pot, just some small bark pieces.

"Oh, he was working in the bakery, wasn't he?" Tess asked, suddenly.

"What?" Kallie asked, confused. "*Who?*"

"The guy at the *register*," Tess whispered, nudging her shoulder to make her turn back in his direction.

Kallie turned carefully, trying not to stare. "Oh, I think you're right. I wonder why he's working here too."

"Working two full-time jobs, that's tough."

"He probably only works until the lunch shift at the bakery, and comes here after that. That's not really two full-time jobs," Kallie replied, considering.

It still sounds like a long day, she thought to herself. *Although we're doing the same thing, working a job and then studying for a new career.*

Kallie walked toward the register with her orchid, hoping silently that the salesgirl was right about it being easy.

The young woman must've sensed her lingering worry, because she returned to her side and explained, "That's the shop owner, over there." She gestured toward the cashier and added with a laugh, "He'll back me up on orchids being easy. I couldn't keep a plastic flower alive before I started working here."

Interesting. The flower shop owner moonlights as a cookie decorator at the bakery?

What's the story with that? This store is really popular—so he can't be doing it for the extra cash.

They checked out quickly, taking a few more simple plant care tips from the shop's friendly owner, and then waiting for the salesgirl to wrap it up carefully.

"Why would he be working two jobs?" Kallie asked, after they'd left the shop.

"I was wondering that too," Tess answered, shaking her head. "But it could be anything. He probably knows Patricia, so maybe she had someone out sick and he offered to cover for her."

"That makes sense," Kallie shrugged.

"You think it's something else, though?" Tess

asked.

"I'm probably just getting paranoid after studying all of these sleuthing techniques," Kallie replied with a wave of her hand. "But, yeah, a little."

Tess nodded. "We can look into it. I'll just add him to the growing list of people we need to. . . stalk."

Taking her wrapped package, Kallie and Tess were continuing down the sidewalk to the record store when a man's voice behind them called out, loudly, "Hey, that's them!"

Glancing back, Kallie didn't see anyone. "I hope he didn't sell that record," she considered aloud, as they kept walking. "We probably should've called first."

"If he did, I'm sure you'll be able to find—"

Suddenly, there was a metallic crash, and two men sped around the corner and ran headlong up the sidewalk toward Kallie and Tess.

Kallie's heart lurched, and a moment of panic set in.

Is that the guy who tried to hit us in his car? It must be!

He found us! And he brought an accomplice. . .

"Tess, I think that's the guy from this morning, who tried to follow us home!" she hissed. "Run!"

Tess didn't question her, but took off running. They dashed around the next corner and then ducked into a shop doorway. When the men didn't follow,

Kallie peeked out.

"I think we lost them," Tess noted, stepping out of hiding. "What was that about?"

The voice yelled again, angrily, "Back that way!"

Kallie grabbed Tess's sleeve and started running again.

No more intersections, Kalliope. Find a place to hide, quick!

But there was nothing along this stretch of sidewalk. No oversized plants, no trash cans. Not even a random sandwich board with lunch specials.

Out of options, Kallie ducked behind a row of bicycles chained in a rack, in front of a trendy local health food market. She dropped to her knees, as Tess followed her. It was almost useless for cover, but it was their only hope.

This thing doesn't hide us. If they look over here, they'll see us, Kallie thought, ducking her head even lower as one of their pursuers stopped just a few feet away.

The man was looking in the shop windows— probably hoping to find them—and from that angle, Kallie could clearly see his face. *Dark hair, light brown eyes, an eyebrow scar*, she noted to herself. *And, what is that? A tattoo of a book on his neck? No, a playing card*. She squinted. *The ace of diamonds*.

She flinched as he turned away from the shop

windows, but he didn't look their way. A moment later, he ran off down the street.

She barely dared to sigh in relief as the man disappeared behind the crowd, but Tess's hand was clammy when she grabbed her arm.

I wasn't the only one who was worried, then.

"Those guys were really following us, right?" Kallie whispered.

Tess nodded. "I don't think they were going to kill us or anything, but I'm pretty sure they were following us."

"Wait, that's toward the bakery," Kallie reasoned. "Do you think they're after Patricia Evans, like Cornwallis said?"

"We might be overreacting, and imagining the whole thing," Tess sighed. "It wouldn't be the first time. But we could call her, just in case."

"Just in case," Kallie repeated, encouragingly.

Tess already had her phone out, and was hitting the redial button—but a few moments later, she sighed. "No answer."

"They shouldn't be too busy," Kallie replied. "The lunch rush should be mostly over."

"I hope there are some people left. Maybe those guys won't make a scene in front of a crowd."

"Oscar Lawson was killed at a more popular tourist spot than this—"

"Ugh, that's true." Tess agreed. "Wally did say she might be in danger. But it's daytime, and a bakery full of very hungry people is a little more conspicuous than an insomniac homeless guy," she sighed.

"What about calling the little painting gallery next door? We could ask them to go over there."

"You don't think that'll sound completely nuts, huh?" Tess asked, a little harshly. "Good morning, sir. Your cheerful, doughnut-slinging neighbor is about to be murdered by a nefarious, unknown villain and his henchmen."

"You could just say there's an emergency at home, Tess," Kallie snapped in a similar vein.

Tess sighed and immediately looked up the number of the painting shop. "Sorry, I didn't mean to be snarky."

"We're both under stress," Kallie agreed. "I hope we're wrong, and she's safe. Even though it will make us sound completely bonkers—"

"Hi!" Tess was saying on the phone. "I'm a friend of Patricia's son, and he asked me to call. It's an emergen—"

She paused.

"No ma'am, I'm not demanding money and this isn't a scam—"

Kallie sighed loudly.

"It's an emergency, could you please ask her to

come to the phone?" Another pause. "Yes, I know it's lunchtime. It will only take a second, and Betsy can handle the orders until she gets back."

Kallie's shoulders tensed. *Those men must be there by now.*

"Thank you."

Tess tapped her perfect nails on the edge of the bike rack, impatiently. "Patricia! It's Tess Russo! Listen, I need— No, your son's okay. I need you to hide. There's a man after you!"

Kallie thought she heard laughter, and then Tess added, "This is serious, Patricia. Cornwallis thinks you saw something on the morning of the murder. Or that someone *thinks* you saw something." She listened for a few seconds and then added, "I know *you* don't think so, but we think you're in danger. Could you please just hide in the painting studio until we get to you?"

Kallie leaned closer to the phone, and although she couldn't make out the words, she could hear that Patricia was getting annoyed.

"Your team can handle the customers," Tess insisted. "It will only be a few minutes. We're on our way right now, I promise." A moment later, she hung up and immediately took off at a fast pace up the sidewalk.

"Did she agree to stay there?" Kallie asked, as she grabbed the wrapped orchid again, and hurried to keep up with Tess.

For a shortie, she sure is fast.

"Yes, but only for five minutes, so we have to hurry."

"It's less than five minutes from here. If she's not in the bakery, then hopefully those creepy guys won't know where to find her. They can't just go charging into all of the shops in broad daylight. Someone would call the cops."

"I hope so," Tess replied, hurrying around the corner onto the bakery's street. "Heck, I hope we're wrong about all of this. I hope we're massively overreacting, and she's totally safe, and we look stupid."

"Me too."

They hurried down the long street, going as fast as they could without crashing into people on the sidewalk. Two minutes later, they turned quickly into the painting studio, Brushes and Booze.

"Thank goodness, she must be hiding in the back, like you asked her to do," Kallie breathed a sigh of relief.

The shop owner, a brunette in her mid-thirties with white paint on her hands and her colorful smock, came out and greeted them. She introduced herself as Alicia Elliot and asked if she could help them.

"We called earlier about Patricia," Tess told her. "I'm so sorry if we worried you, Miss Elliot. Is she in the back room?" She gestured toward the door from which the owner had emerged.

The owner glanced back at the door. "Oh, no.

I'm preparing some canvases for tonight's class, so I had to go back and finish. She was talking on the phone out here—"

"She must've gone back to the bakery, then," Tess replied. "She's not hiding anywhere in here?"

"Hiding?" the owner asked, confused. "Why would she be hiding?"

"It's a long story," Kallie said. "Is there anywhere else she could be?"

The studio was basically one giant room with a lot of long tables. They could see the whole room, and there was nowhere to hide.

The owner quickly slipped into the back and checked a restroom, and then shook her head. "She's not here. She hates to leave the bakery, so I'm sure she just went back. What's this about?"

"It might be nothing. *Hopefully* it's nothing," Kallie responded. "Let's find her first, and then we'll explain everything."

But you know it isn't, Kalliope. It's not your overactive imagination this time.

They quickly walked back to the bakery next door, which still had half a dozen customers waiting for their delectable croissants and bagel sandwiches. Kallie called out to Betsy, "Is Patricia here?"

The baker's assistant looked up from the register and smiled at them. "Oh, hi! No, she just went next door to take a phone call. I'm sure she'll be right back."

Kallie and Tess looked at each other, and Kallie suddenly felt sick to her stomach.

If she's not here, and she's not next door, then where is she?

***

"What's up, Kallie?" Cornwallis answered his phone, cutting to the chase in his usual manner.

Kallie sputtered, "We thought Patricia might be in danger, like you said. So we called her and told her to hide. And now she's gone."

"Wait, wait. Slow down," he replied. "Are you talking about the baker?"

"Yes, Patricia Evans. The baker. She's gone."

"What do you mean, she's gone?"

Kallie switched her phone to speaker so Tess could hear him, and they stepped closer to the wall. "Someone was following us. We told her to wait in the painting studio, and she said she would. But now she's gone. They haven't seen her in the studio or the bakery."

"She's a grown woman. She could've gone anywhere."

"She wouldn't leave in the middle of a shift,"

Kallie insisted. "She's a total control freak about the bakery." She glanced at the door to make sure no one heard her opinion, which sounded a little cold to her own ears. "I mean, in a good way. I guess. But she wouldn't leave in the middle of the lunch rush."

"Maybe she felt sick and went home. Heck, maybe you stressed her out and she went to get a martini." Cornwallis sighed, but continued before Kallie could interrupt. "And before you tell me that I'm ignoring the facts, I *do* realize that she might've witnessed a murder. And possibly even saw the killer. But if no one saw her being threatened, the police can't do anything right now. She's an adult."

"So what do we do?" Tess asked.

"You can ask the studio owner if she has any security cameras. Same with Patricia's staff." He thought for a moment, then added, "You could try the other shops nearby, too. How long has it been?"

Tess looked at her watch, and replied, "Fifteen minutes?"

Cornwallis groaned audibly. "I know you're worried, but people spend more than fifteen minutes in a gas station bathroom. And it's unlikely that someone grabbed her in downtown Clearwater in broad daylight. Ask about the cameras, and ask them to call you when they see her."

"We can't just leave. Not right now," Kallie complained.

"Okay, then pick a place with an eyeline on the door and have some lunch," Cornwallis sighed.

"You think we're being soft," Kallie stated plainly.

"No. I *do* think you're probably overreacting, but that's okay. It's better to overreact than underreact. But if you're just going to worry, then watch the bakery and wait until she comes back."

"Okay," they both agreed.

"And don't ask her if she was in a gas station bathroom when you see her."

Kallie hung up without replying.

***

Kallie and Tess verified with the studio owner that she didn't have any useful cameras. There was one pointing at her easel, at the opposite end of the room, but it didn't have sound.

Nothing had been disturbed in the room, so they were confident that specific camera wouldn't have caught anything. The owner, though, was kind enough to check the app on her phone, and she verified that the camera hadn't even triggered movement.

The bakery had no cameras at all.

They walked back outside and quickly spotted two cameras nearby—but they were on a lawyer's office and a bank. No way they were giving up their cameras without a formal request. Certainly not to two random women who were concerned about a baker who'd been missing for—twenty minutes, now.

"Wally's probably right, and we're going to feel silly when she comes back from the grocery store, or wherever she is." Tess pointed diagonally across the street and added, "But that place has pretty good pizza."

They crossed the street and sat outside at a by-the-slice pizza joint, ordering quickly so they could keep an eye on the bakery door.

The day was nice, if warm, and the pizza was perfect—but neither of them felt very cheerful when Patricia hadn't returned after another twenty-five minutes.

Kallie called Cornwallis again, even though she knew what he was going to say.

"I'm sorry, but there's nothing to be done about it. The police don't have the manpower to spend on someone who's been 'missing' for forty-five minutes. Especially when no one even saw her leave."

"I know," Kallie acknowledged grumpily.

"Ask them to have her call you. And then call them back tomorrow morning and check, if you don't hear back," he added. "And try not to dwell on it."

"We won't—"

"I know you, Kallie. You dwell."

Tess raised her eyebrows and nodded in sympathetic agreement.

"Go home and study. It will keep your mind off it," he added. "There's nothing you can do today."

"Fine," she acquiesced, knowing he was right. But also knowing it would bother her all night.

"Hey, one other thing. I convinced one of my contacts to check out that house," Cornwallis told them. "The one you were *trespassing* in," he added, sounding annoyed.

"Really?" Kallie asked.

Tess added, "Did he find anything?"

"It cost me extra because he swore the place was haunted," he grumbled. "But he said there was a big bag in the back yard, covered really well with some old brush."

"No way! He found the bag? Was it full of *money?!*" Tess yelped, suddenly excited again.

"I bet it was drugs," Kallie corrected her. "A bunch of heavy cocaine bricks or something, right?"

"Close," Cornwallis replied. "So close! Only it was actually antifreeze and old car batteries."

"Oh," Kallie replied, suddenly feeling miserable again.

"He said it was all toxic waste, the normal kind, that the landfill just won't take. Motor oil and weed killer. A flat tire."

Neither of them replied, and he added, "I'm sorry. Those guys probably got paid to dispose of the stuff, and then just dumped it."

"Okay, thanks, Wally," Tess replied, not sounding thankful at all.

Kallie hung up, adding, "At least it wasn't a dead body."

Chapter Ten

"Hey Tess, Cornwallis and I are going to meet down by the pier tomorrow morning before work," she called her best friend later that night. "We're going to stop by the bakery, and then he needs to talk to one of the dock workers. But he said you can't join us?"

"I'm sorry, Kal. I'm still working on this case for Winchester."

"The one in Baton Rouge?" Kallie asked, surprised. "That case is going on forever."

"You have no idea," she groaned. "And he's actually in Clarksville, Mississippi now."

"*What?!* Isn't he miserable?"

Tess laughed. "He's having the time of his life. He's trying to pretend that it's awful, but you know Winchester. If he wasn't having fun, he'd pass it off on some local paralegal and jump on the first flight home."

"Is the case really that interesting?"

"Not to me, but I'm just reviewing his broader notes. But whatever's going on behind the scenes, it must be good."

"So you're too busy to come with us tomorrow?" Kallie asked.

"Yeah, he spent two days on a fishing boat with some witness, and he couldn't upload his notes. So now I have *three* days' worth of notes to check."

"And you're swamped," Kallie sighed. "Well, one of Cornwallis's informants said he saw a dock worker arguing with Oscar sometime before he was killed," Kallie explained.

"I know, he told me. Believe me, I'd meet you if I could, but I have to pay the bills."

"I get it. And someone needs to keep an eye on your boss."

"Honestly, for Winchester to spend *two days* on a fishing boat—the guy who spends hundreds of dollars on whole-house air freshener—" Tess laughed.

"It *must* be important. Two days in a boat full of fish guts doesn't sound thrilling to me, either."

"It started out as a family law case, but I get the feeling it's going to turn into a criminal case—when he's done with it."

"I'll be sure to take lots of notes and video for you, tomorrow," Kallie added, and then reconsidered, "Maybe not video of the dock worker, unless he okays it. But whatever else we see."

"Thanks, Kal. Sorry, I have a ton of work on my plate right now."

"That's okay," Kallie replied, sincerely. "The two of us will handle it."

"Great, I'll meet you for dinner after we both get home, and we can look over it together," Tess agreed. Then she added, "And watch out for Cornwallis, will you?"

"Watch out for him? How do you mean?" Kallie asked, surprised.

"He seems like he's getting really invested in this case."

"That's his job, right?"

"Not this much. He's playing it off like he's only interested because it's our first case, but I think he might have a personal connection that he hasn't told us about."

Kallie laughed. "Well, he's not going to tell *me* about it. You're his secret-keeper, not me."

"You never know," Tess replied cryptically. "He might talk to you. I just started asking about his life — being a little nosey, you know?"

"Okay, I'll try," Kallie shrugged. "I think he'll tell me to back off, but maybe he wants to chat. We'll see."

"I have to go. Talk to you after work tomorrow. Be careful."

"Thanks, Tess. Will do."

***

Kallie could smell the fresh bread from a block away, as she and Cornwallis approached the bakery, but the delicious aroma didn't make her happy today.

She's probably right there at the register, Kalliope. You were worried for nothing, and Cornwallis was right, like always.

She wasn't sure whether to be relieved or embarrassed at that thought, but Cornwallis was reaching for the shop's door before she could give it any further consideration.

"Kallie!" a woman's voice called, and for just a second, a wave of relief rolled over her.

Thank goodness, Patricia's fine after all.

But it was Betsy, the cashier and assistant, who was yelling to her. She had both hands in the oven, removing a sheet of baked goods, and was turned around at the waist. "I wanted to call you, but I couldn't find your number."

"Hi, Betsy. What happened?"

"Well, it's what *didn't* happen. Patricia never came back."

Kallie turned and gave Cornwallis a stern look.

The breakfast rush was nearly finished, so Betsy had time to talk with them at the counter. "We were all surprised that she never came back yesterday. I mean, that was weird because she never misses a shift. But we're always telling her that she can take time off."

A young man mixing dough added, "We can keep the place running without her. The customers love her, but she needs to make time for herself."

"So at first, we thought, maybe she actually took the afternoon off," Betsy considered. "She went to take a phone call, so we thought maybe it was an emergency or something."

"We were surprised that she didn't tell us, but emergencies are like that sometimes—" the young man interjected.

Betsy looked like she felt guilty. "We were actually a little happy for her. In the past week, she's looked exhausted."

The young man turned off the industrial mixer and joined them at the counter. "But then she didn't come in this morning."

"And we're closing until lunch in. . ." Betsy looked at the wall clock, "Oh, in ten minutes. And she's still not here."

Kallie stepped behind Cornwallis and physically pushed him toward the counter. "This is our boss. Cornwallis, help them."

To his credit, Cornwallis stepped right up and explained the situation. "The police don't have the manpower to escalate a missing adult case like this, when there's no sign of foul play or injury. Not when it hasn't even been twenty-four hours. But you should call them and report it, so they're aware. Is there anywhere else she could be?"

"She has a son, but he doesn't live here. He lives with his dad in North Carolina," Betsy replied. "I haven't called him yet. But she wouldn't miss work." She shook her head and added, "I know everyone always says that when someone's missing, but it's true. She almost never even takes a sick day, and she *always* tells us."

"I believe you," Cornwallis replied. He turned around and added to Kallie, "And I believe you too."

"What else can we do?" Betsy asked.

"Call the son, talk to his dad. Verify that she isn't there." She started to interrupt, but he cut her off, "I know. But just verify."

She nodded.

"Write down all of the details you can remember. When she left, where she was going. Who she spoke to. Who *you* spoke to. Literally everything you can remember, no matter how small." He leaned forward. "You don't think you'll forget the details, but you will. So write them down, right now. As soon as we finish talking."

The young woman looked like she might start crying, but he put his hand on hers. "You can cry later," he added, gently. "Do everything you can for her right now, while you have momentum, and it's fresh in your mind. Okay?"

She nodded, silently.

"It still might be nothing. A mix-up," he added, in that peculiar accent that Kallie could never place. "We're already working on this case, so we'll just add it to—"

"What case?" Betsy asked, sounding surprised.

"I'm getting old," Kallie heard him mumble to himself with annoyance. He replied to Betsy, "We think this might be related to another case in the area. But we're not sure yet."

"Another missing woman?" she asked.

"No, it's something else."

Kallie could tell he didn't want to worry Betsy by mentioning the possible connection to the Celebration of Sandcastles murder, so she tried to change the subject back to their next steps. "The police can't get involved yet, but they have a lot more resources than we have. They'll need every detail you can give them if she doesn't come back by tomorrow."

"Okay, we'll write down our notes, and I'll call the afternoon shift from yesterday and ask them what they remember. I'm the only one who was on both shifts." Her face fell. "Except Patricia, I mean."

"Call us if you remember anything else." Cornwallis handed her a business card, and Kallie quickly wrote her cell number on the back.

When they stepped back outside, Kallie pointed across the street and asked, "Those are the only two cameras we saw. Should we give them a heads-up about

Patricia? So they can make sure to save the video?"

He looked at one and frowned, then looked at the other and shook his head, annoyed. "A bank and a lawyer's office. It couldn't be a bar and a pizza place, right?" He sighed in obvious dismay. "They won't help us."

Kallie looked at him with curiosity.

"Not without a warrant. But they won't lose their video footage in the next thirty-six hours either," he added. "Don't worry. They'll have professional video monitoring with off-site storage. Not a thumb drive in the closet. So the police will be able to get it."

"Okay. Should we go talk to the dock worker, then? It looks like we're out of options here."

Tess was right. Cornwallis does look stressed out. Is it just because of Prudence?

He said he barely knew her.

"Sure," Cornwallis agreed. "Let's go see this guy and find out how he knew Oscar."

"Hey! Hey, wait a minute!" a woman's voice called from behind them.

Kallie spun around to see the owner of the painting studio, Alicia Elliot, walking quickly toward them.

"I found this phone in my studio this morning." She held up a cell phone in a flowery plastic case. "I thought someone left it after last night's class, but now

I think it might belong to Patricia."

Cornwallis patted his pockets quickly, obviously not finding what he wanted, and replied, "I don't have any gloves. Could you put it in a plastic bag?"

"Oh! Oh, of course!" she replied, quickly running back inside her studio. She returned a minute later with a personalized paper shopping bag. Her face was crestfallen. "This is all I had, without paint on it. I'm so sorry, I wasn't thinking about fingerprints."

"Don't worry, we can eliminate your prints," he replied, reassuring her gently. "Thank you so much for this. Could you show us where you found it?"

She took them back inside and pointed toward the back of the counter. "I didn't notice it because it was on the lower shelf. It seemed like a place one of the visitor's kids might've left it, so I expected to get a call from a frantic mom." Her eyes teared up, apparently thinking of Patricia and the danger she might be facing, and she added, "But then I saw you outside. . ."

"You did exactly the right thing, Miss Elliot. Is the phone locked?" he asked.

"I didn't check," she whispered.

Cornwallis pulled a pen from his pocket and carefully poked the side button, lighting up the screen without touching it. "Good, it's not locked with a passcode."

Kallie leaned over and looked at the screen, which showed the bakery's logo, reimagined as a colorful neon sign. "And you were right, it definitely looks like it belongs to Patricia."

"She's really in trouble, isn't she?" the studio owner groaned. "*Why* didn't I make her come into the back office?"

"It's not your fault, Miss Elliot, so don't blame yourself," Cornwallis insisted. "If she hasn't returned by tomorrow morning, we'll turn this over to the police forensics office. It may help them find her."

She walked back into her studio, still looking heartbroken. Kallie and Cornwallis watched her go, and then continued back toward the car.

"I noticed there were a few missed calls on Patricia's phone," Kallie added, hopefully.

"Very good!" Cornwallis replied. "They were from the 512 area code, but I don't know off-hand where that is."

Of course, he noticed the exact area code in one second. I wonder if I'll ever be that good?

Kallie took out her phone and quickly looked up the area code, noticing that the battery was almost dead. "Austin, Texas."

"I don't want to touch the phone again, to get the exact number. Especially since it could just be a telemarketer," Cornwallis replied. "But I'll ask my contact at the police department to keep us updated."

Kallie nodded and put her own phone away.

5% battery power left – and I just charged it this morning. I really need to replace this old phone. Maybe Cornwallis has a charger in his car.

Cornwallis looked at his watch. "Let me lock this evidence in my trunk, and then we can head out to meet my contact in Owhiro. We'll only be a few minutes late."

"Where did he ask to meet you?" Kallie asked, once they'd locked up the phone, and quickly made the short drive.

"He said he wanted to meet at a diner. I guess he's meeting us on his lunch break."

"Sounds good to me," she replied. "I'm hungry, and I'm always up for a diner."

She saw Cornwallis roll his eyes, but he changed the subject, instead of commenting on her appetite. "By the way, I found a problem with Prudence's alibi."

"What? You're kidding?" Kallie replied. "Is she a *suspect*?"

"No, I'm not kidding. And I'm not calling her a suspect, yet." He pointed and said, "This is the diner, on the left. Remind me later, and I'll show you my notes on Pru."

A few moments later, they stopped in front of a small, nondescript restaurant. It had dingy windows and a tattered cardboard sign with OPEN written in black Sharpie marker.

The best kind of diner, Kallie thought to herself,

as her stomach growled. *I'll bet they have fried catfish.*

Cornwallis glanced around as the door jingled softly, then made his way, casually but directly, to a table in the rear corner of the restaurant.

"Mr. Diaz," he addressed the man at the table, quietly. "This is my colleague, Kalliope Brooks."

Colleague, Kallie noted, trying not to look surprised.

"Cornwallis," Diaz replied. "I wasn't sure if you'd come. So you believed me?"

"You haven't given me any reason *not* to believe you," Cornwallis replied.

"Have a seat," Diaz continued, pushing out a chair for Kallie and waving for the waitress.

Kallie glanced briefly at the Daily Specials chalkboard and was thrilled but not surprised to indeed find fried catfish. She placed her order, with sides of potato salad and fried cabbage, while Cornwallis looked studiously at the full menu. The place was pretty busy, so the waitress said she'd give him a minute.

"So you say you saw Oscar Lawson shortly before he was killed?" Cornwallis asked, without looking up from the menu.

Wow, short and to the point, Kallie noticed, taking mental notes of Cornwallis's technique. *Don't let the guy get comfortable.*

"Saw him when I was gettin' off work. He was

fightin' with some guy." Diaz was watching Cornwallis closely, but Kallie couldn't quite read his expression. It looked something like pleading, but she couldn't imagine why.

"Did you know Lawson? Why did you remember seeing him?" Cornwallis asked. "Something interesting about the fight?" He waved down the waitress again and ordered a grilled cheese sandwich and fries.

"I didn't know him. I'm just good with faces."

"So you didn't recognize him at the time, you just remembered when you saw him on the news, then?"

Wait, did he just look left? Or is he looking for the waitress?

Diaz reached for his glass of water and nodded. "That's right."

The waitress returned with their lunches and set down a dish of fresh tartar sauce next to Kallie's plate. The catfish was fresh out of the fryer, and so hot it was still steaming. Kallie tried not to drool while she kept one eye on Diaz, trying to read his body language.

"Can you describe the other guy?" Cornwallis asked, forking a French fry.

"He was tall and skinny. Light brown hair. Had a tattoo on his arm, below the elbow."

That doesn't sound like any of our suspects. What are we missing?

Cornwallis nodded appreciatively. "Your burger's getting cold."

Diaz broke eye contact and picked up his cheeseburger, taking a bite. He chewed briefly. "I've never seen the other guy before, either."

He definitely looked left that time. What's going on here?

Relax, Kalliope. Cornwallis and Tess both said that's not always reliable. It's probably a coincidence.

Then what's he looking at?

Kallie struggled not to look in the direction his eyes kept darting.

Does he know someone over there? An accomplice?

You're imagining things, Kalliope. Pay attention to Cornwallis—he's the expert.

Cornwallis changed the subject, and they continued eating their lunch. They discussed hockey and the upcoming hurricane season, and then Cornwallis picked up the check.

As they walked back toward their parking spot, Kallie watched the sky darken and heavy clouds begin to form. Finally, she felt brave enough to ask, "Okay, what in the heck was all that about?"

Cornwallis smiled and asked, "You're the new investigator. What do you think?"

Kallie blushed, but gathered all of the facts she

could remember. "I thought he was lying. But why would he lie about seeing a fight? It doesn't make any sense – we're not offering a reward for information or anything."

Cornwallis nodded, but didn't respond to her thoughts. "What else?"

"He was looking at you in a weird way."

Her mentor frowned. "How do you mean? What weird way?"

"He looked disappointed when you didn't look at him. When you were looking at the menu," she added. "And then when he was telling the story—the lie, I guess—he looked like he expected you to say something. Or do something. . ."

They were almost back to the pier, and Cornwallis stopped on the sidewalk and looked at her. "That's very good, Kallie. I think I might know why he—"

Before he could finish his sentence, though, the sky opened up and torrents of pouring rain came down on them.

Kallie laughed out loud in surprise, and they both looked around for shelter. The closest cover was the pier itself, so they ran frantically under the nearest section, which supported the shops and restaurants. Everyone else had run for cover, and they were alone, so Kallie started to ask about Diaz again, but the pouring rain was too loud.

But like most Florida storms, it passed as quickly as it came. Soon they were huddled under the pier for no reason, and they made their way back toward the resuming daylight.

"What were you saying about Diaz?" she asked.

As Cornwallis started to answer, though, Kallie saw a rapid movement out of the corner of her eye. She spun around to get a better look and dodged away from someone running past them, toward the steps that led from the sand up to the side of the pier.

"What was that about?" Kallie asked, annoyed. "That guy barely missed us."

When she looked over at Cornwallis, she was concerned at what she saw. He was standing silently, clutching his thigh. His face was pale.

"Are you okay?" Her eyes followed his downward gaze, and she saw blood seeping between his fingers, where they were grasping his pant leg. She gasped in shock and worry. "Cornwallis, your *leg*!"

"I think that guy stabbed me," he replied, sounding confused.

Kallie looked around wildly, but the attacker was gone.

Cornwallis seemed to be recovering from his initial distress, and he winced in pain and stumbled. "Can you take me to a—"

They both jumped in surprise as they heard a

loud, frantic yell from above them. The same dark figure came barreling back down the stairs and ran across the beach toward the nearby row of businesses on Main Street, but Kallie cringed away from him instinctively.

But the yelling above them started again. A man was screaming bloody murder up on the pier. Kallie looked at Cornwallis with wide eyes, unsure of what to do.

"I'm fine, go see what happened up there," he ordered her. He was slumped against one of the pier pylons. "I can't make it up the steps."

She shook her head and moved toward him.

"I'll be fine, Kallie. If he stabbed someone else—"

Kallie couldn't breathe, couldn't talk, but she forced herself toward the stairs. She looked in the direction where the fleeing man had run.

"He's gone, Kallie. Go see if that guy needs help."

Go, Kalliope! Cornwallis is right – this guy needs help, and this is your life now. Get a move on.

Kallie stumbled up the stairs and was met by a shocking sight. A middle-aged man was lying in the puddled rain, clutching his arm. He hadn't been as lucky as Cornwallis, however. He'd been stabbed multiple times, and the assailant had obviously hit an artery. His left arm was bleeding badly and his dark

238

eyes were already unfocused, drifting closed, as he gazed in her direction.

Kallie quickly pulled out her phone to call 911, but now the battery was completely dead.

NO!!

Kallie groaned out loud, tears filling her eyes, and looked around frantically for help.

I need a tourniquet or something. Think, Kalliope!

She checked her pockets but found nothing.

Crap, I don't even have shoelaces—what a day to wear sandals!

The pier looked abandoned thanks to the sudden downpour, so she spun around again, hoping to see someone, anyone. Even the snack shack was shuttered to keep out the rain. There were normally half a dozen artists selling their wares out here, but the cold, rainy weather had chased everyone away.

Thunder crashed in the distance, startling Kallie into action. *Do something! Find help!*

She knelt on the soaking wet boards and checked the injured man, but he had lost consciousness. She quickly felt his pockets but found nothing she could use to stop the bleeding. Awkwardly putting her hands over the wound, she applied pressure and silently pleaded for someone to appear.

Finally, she spotted a figure in the distance, all

the way at the end of the pier. The bait shop was already closed for the day, but someone had been sheltering under their awning.

"Hey!" She yelled, voice cracking, "Hey, I need help!" She didn't want to take pressure off the wound, so she hoped the person would hear her. "*Help Me!*"

Nothing.

She pulled off the guy's beanie and tried to press it against the wound enough to hold the bleeding for a minute. Basically useless, but she couldn't sit here alone and do nothing. Couldn't just watch him bleed.

With one last glance, she took off her sandals and started running, barefoot, yelling all the way.

"Hey, I need help! Hey, I—"

She grabbed the person's arm as she reached the end of the pier, stumbling a little. "I need your help, there's a guy—"

The person turned around slowly, and Kallie saw that it was an old woman. She was leaning toward the edge of the pier with a pair of giant, old-fashioned binoculars in her hands. Beside her, a small portable oxygen machine burbled quietly.

Great. I guess she's not going to be running back to the victim with me.

"Oh, hello, my dear," the old woman spoke sweetly to Kallie. "I didn't hear you coming. I was just watching the pelicans. Aren't they lovely?"

Kallie panted, terrified and out of breath. "Yes, ma'am. I need your help. There's a man bleeding down here. Can you help me?"

"What was that, dear? Bleeding?"

"Yes, ma'am. Do you have a phone? Could you call 911?" Kallie pleaded, panic growing quickly.

"Oh, of course. Let me just see. . . My phone's in one of my pockets. . . "

Kallie groaned as the old woman fumbled slowly, methodically, around the pockets of her long skirt and oversized jacket for her phone.

We're in a rush, here, lady. Please?

"How about a belt?" Kallie begged. "Do you have a belt, ma'am? I need to make a tourniquet."

"Oh, yes," she replied with a patient smile. "I was a nurse in the war, dear. I know all about tourniquets—"

She kept fumbling slowly for her phone, and Kallie looked back at the injured man, fearing the worst.

"Here's my phone. You'd better make the call. My hands shake a bit."

She handed the phone over and then reached into another pocket as Kallie started to dial 911.

"Yes, it's an emergency," Kallie replied to the dispatch agent. "I need an ambulance at the Owhiro pier, right away. There's a man bleeding and—"

She glanced up at the old woman, and to her

amazement, the woman was pulling a long strip of rubber tubing out of her pocket. "It's a spare air hose for my oxygen machine, dear. My daughter insists that I carry a spare." Kallie gaped for a moment, and the woman added apologetically, "I'm afraid I'm not wearing a belt. This skirt doesn't even have belt loops—"

Kallie could've cried with relief. She hugged the old woman, thanking her profusely, and then sprinted back to the man, with the tube and the phone.

"Yes, I'm still here," she panted. "Yes, I need *two* ambulances. There are two men injured, stabbed. One guy's bleeding really badly."

The injured man remained unconscious when she got back to his side, but she could still feel a pulse. She quickly applied the tourniquet to stop the bleeding and sat down on the soaking wet boards, exhausted. The Owhiro police station was nearby, and she could hear sirens a minute later.

"Not today, creep," she whispered, looking around for whoever did this. "You're not getting this one too."

The police arrived quickly and took control of the scene, and she looked over the railing to make sure the paramedics were tending to Cornwallis too. She stayed with the other victim—whoever he was—holding his hand, relieved to see his greying eyebrows furrow and his dark eyes open briefly – pained, but alive – after he was given an injection. He looked at her but didn't speak, and then he was lifted onto a gurney and they took him away.

Suddenly at loose ends, Kallie put her sandals back on and walked back out to the old woman, who had returned to watching her pelicans. She used her bloodied, wet shirt to clean the borrowed phone as well as she possibly could. It seemed to only make it worse.

"Thank you, ma'am, I brought back your phone," she called gently to the woman as she approached, to avoid startling her.

"Hello dear. Oh, is that *my* phone?"

"Yes, thank you. It was very helpful."

"I'm so glad, dear." She took the phone back and slipped it into one of her many pockets.

She didn't ask about the victim, or about her oxygen tube. Kallie wasn't sure if the elderly woman even remembered their earlier conversation, but she certainly didn't want to leave her alone, especially without her spare tube. She might need it one day.

"Do you live near here, ma'am? Can I give you a ride home?"

"My daughter comes to get me on her way home from work." She squinted at a large, tarnished men's watch, flopping loosely on her small wrist. "She should be here any minute now, actually."

"I'll just wait with you until she gets here, if that's okay?"

"Of course, dear. Have you seen the pelicans?"

Chapter Eleven

"What did Morrison say about the guy on the pier?" Tess asked, as they walked out of a sandwich shop the next day. Tess was being extra sweet, after the previous day's events, and had even splurged on milkshakes for both of them. "Did he have any identification?"

"Morrison said the security guard at the pier recognized him and knew his name," Kallie answered. "He's in the hospital, and the doctor said he should be okay. Eventually."

"That's all on you, girl." Tess nudged her arm, encouragingly. "You saved his life."

Kallie didn't answer, but looked down at her shoes again.

Barely. And only after I totally panicked.

"Hey, you okay?" Tess asked quietly.

"Oh, sure. Yeah, it was just scary," Kallie answered. "Marcy makes us do that first aid training at work, but I never expected to use it."

"Well, that guy's lucky you were there, whoever

he is. Otherwise, Morrison's investigation would be very different today."

Kallie blushed. "You should've seen him. He couldn't decide whether to be freaked out or proud of me."

"I'm sure he's *super* proud of you," Tess insisted. "Although he'll probably *also* assign a patrol officer to follow you around for the next six weeks."

"I wouldn't be surprised. It might be six *months*."

Morrison had actually heard the news about the attack on the pier, and her own involvement, from one of his colleagues – since her phone's battery was dead. By the time he was able to reach her, he was incredibly worried and frustrated, but he was very proud of her.

You should be proud of yourself too, Kalliope.

Yeah, right. She scoffed to herself. *I'm surprised I didn't make it worse.*

"Did he say if the two cases are related?" Tess asked.

"They can't tell yet. "

"I'm sure they're related. I mean, two homeless guys attacked on the beach in little Owhiro, less than two weeks apart?"

"Morrison said it's not that uncommon, actually," Kallie answered, frowning.

Tess looked upset by that, too, but didn't reply.

"Hey lady, you got a match?" a voice called from a nearby doorway.

Kallie whirled around, already annoyed, and suddenly enraged at this intrusion. She gave the man a scathing look. "A match?! Why would I have a *match*? Are you kidding me?"

The man flinched backward, and Tess grabbed her arm. "She's had a bad day," she told the man quietly, pulling Kallie away. "And we don't smoke."

The man didn't answer, but disappeared back into the shadows of the local bar.

"Who even asks something like that? A *match*?!" Kallie snapped.

Tess just quietly held her arm, and they kept walking. If she was startled by Kallie's outburst, she didn't show it.

"I haven't even *seen* a pack of matches in twenty years," Kallie grumbled, seething. "I mean, at least ask if I have a *lighter*. At least people still own lighters."

They crossed the street and turned up the block.

"I don't even have matches for my *fireplace*, for Pete's sake." She kicked a rock out of her way as she walked quickly up the sidewalk.

"It's not your fault, you know," Tess whispered.

"Why would it be *my fault* that I don't have any matches?" Kallie growled.

"It's not your fault that Cornwallis got hurt,

Kallie."

Kallie took a deep breath, but didn't answer. She wiped at one eye with her sleeve, but didn't look at Tess.

"This is his job, and he's gotten hurt before," her best friend added quietly. "It's not your fault."

Kallie's head hung a little lower, and she couldn't find the words to speak. Tess was trying to make eye contact, but she couldn't bear to look.

"Kallie?"

"He wouldn't have been there if it weren't for me, Tess," she replied, evenly, trying not to cry.

"Kal, he would've been there *alone* if it weren't for you. He wouldn't have had you there to help him."

"I distracted him. He wouldn't have made the mistake of turning his back on the guy if I hadn't been there."

"You don't know that," Tess answered, simply.

"Yes, I do. He told us to always pay attention and be aware of our surroundings. I shouldn't have been asking questions. I should've seen the guy."

"Kallie—"

"What kind of partner am I, if I let him down?"

"We're *not* his partners, Kal." She stopped suddenly, pulling Kallie to face her. "We're *students*."

"What difference does that—"

"Because he knows we're beginners, and he

248

chose us anyway. It was *his* decision to teach us," Tess insisted, without raising her voice. "Because he *trusts* us."

"Well, the joke's on him, then, isn't it?" Kallie growled bitterly, pulling away and continuing down the sidewalk toward the car. "He trusted me, and I almost got him killed."

"Will you please stop saying that?" Tess groaned. "He's not dying."

They got into Tess's car, and Tess looked to see if traffic was coming.

"I think I need to quit, Tess. I can't put you and Cornwallis in danger with my—"

Kallie grabbed the door handle frantically, as Tess suddenly spun the wheel and pulled a chaotic U-turn out of the parking spot. A car honked dramatically as she whipped across the road into the opposite direction.

"What are you *doing*, Tess?" Kallie yelped. "Home's the other way."

"I can't listen to you anymore. We're going to the hospital."

"What?!"

"You're going to see Cornwallis right now. And you're *not* quitting."

"*What?!*" Kallie cried out. "I can't go see him! Tess, he doesn't want to see me. And I can't face him."

"He *does* want to see you, and I'm not letting you wallow in this."

Owhiro's small hospital was only a block off of Main Street, and she pulled into the parking lot before Kallie could even formulate another argument against it.

He must be so ashamed of me. Some investigator I am, getting my boss stabbed in broad daylight.

She was sitting silently in the passenger seat, looking at her hands, folded in her lap, when Tess rapped hard on the window.

"Get out!" Tess yelled, muffled through the glass.

"Tess, I can't—"

"*Now!* Let's go."

Kallie opened the door sheepishly and stepped out of the car.

Her best friend relented a bit, now that she was standing, putting her hand on Kallie's back and guiding her toward the old-fashioned brick hospital. They took the slow elevator up to the third floor and walked down the clean but plain hallway. Tess nudged her toward one of the doors on the left.

Kallie took a deep breath, traumatized and scared of what she might find. Afraid of what he might say. How he'd look at her.

Cornwallis was leaned back in the hospital bed with his leg bandaged and elevated. He looked exhausted and pale, but two pretty young nurses were standing beside the bed, clearly joking with him. The blonde seemed to be openly flirting.

"Kallie!" he called out, when he saw her in the doorway. "Kallie, get over here."

He didn't sound mad. He actually sounded. . . *relieved?*

"Hi, Cornwallis," she replied, standing still by the door. "I'm so sorry."

"No, no, no," he insisted. He shook his head and then grimaced. "Ugh, my head," he grumbled. He kept his eyes closed for a few minutes, but just as Kallie was ready to run away, he continued, "Kallie, Tess told me you're feeling guilty."

Tess grabbed her by the wrist and pulled her closer to the hospital bed.

One of the pretty nurses handed him a tiny paper cup containing a few pills, which had been sitting on his dining table, and he swallowed them. Finally, he added, "Girl, you did great."

"What?" she whispered, stunned. "But you—"

"I couldn't *believe* it when you ran up those stairs," he chuckled, eyes gleaming. "I know grown men who wouldn't have been brave enough to go up there."

"I had to, though. That guy was screaming."

"Kallie, you didn't *have to*. You just *did*." He smiled awkwardly and added, "I'm so proud of you."

Kallie could feel her face getting hot as she blushed, and the room grew blurry as her eyes teared up.

"But you got *stabbed*, Cornwallis," she whimpered.

"Eh, it's fine," he replied, waving his hand cavalierly.

Kallie and Tess both looked at his heavily bandaged leg, and Tess raised one extremely critical eyebrow.

"I'll be back to normal in a few days. Heck, I've been stabbed before."

"*What?!*" Kallie asked.

"So is that part of the job description that we *missed*, somehow?" Tess added, sarcastically.

"Okay, okay," he amended. "Maybe I've never been stabbed *on the job* before. But I grew up in a tough neighborhood."

Kallie wondered again at his peculiar accent, and thought for a second that he might finally explain where he grew up.

"But that's a tale for another day," he deflected, as if reading her mind. "These lovely Nightingales were just bringing me a painkiller, so I won't be much for conversation. But I'm glad I got to talk to you."

"Me too," she added quietly.

Tess and Kallie left the room so Cornwallis could get some rest, but one of the nurses followed them into the hall.

"Miss Brooks," she called, as they neared the elevator.

Kallie turned, surprised that anyone would know her name, and the nurse caught up with them. "I know Mr. Green would like to see you, before you go. If you have a minute to spare?"

"Mr. Green?" Kallie asked, feeling confused.

"He just woke up about an hour ago, and he immediately asked about you."

"I think you must have me mixed up with someone else," Kallie explained. "I don't know a Mr. Green—"

The nurse smiled gently and waved for Kallie to follow her. Kallie looked at Tess, who shrugged, and they both followed the nurse to a different patient room.

Kallie looked cautiously into the room as the nurse opened the door—not wanting to intrude on someone who was sure to be a total stranger—and was surprised to see a familiar face.

"It's you," he croaked, softly.

Kallie ran across the room and grabbed his hand. "You're awake! How are you?"

Last time I saw you, you were trying really hard to bleed to death.

I've never been so happy to see a stranger before.

"I've been better," he rasped. "But I'd be a lot worse if it weren't for you. You saved my life."

Kallie blushed and hastily wiped the tears from her eyes. "I just held your hand, sir. The paramedics did all the work."

The nurse cleared her throat, and when Kallie glanced back at her, she shook her head subtly.

"I think we both know that isn't true, Miss—"

"Kallie," she answered, smiling. "Kallie Brooks. Nice to officially meet you, Mr.—?"

"Green. Endicott Green. And I'm so glad you were at the right place at the right time, Miss Brooks."

What?!

"Wait, you're *Endicott*?" Tess gasped.

"It can't be—" Kallie replied, equally baffled.

"It's not really a common name," Tess agreed.

"No, it's not. This *must* be him."

"Did I miss something?" Endicott interjected, bemused.

Kallie shook her head and then explained, "A friend of ours mentioned someone named Endicott. Someone she knew."

"I've never met anyone else with my name, but it's sure possible," he agreed. "Who's your friend?"

"We only know her as Mrs. Jackson," Tess replied. "She's really more of a friend-of-a-friend."

The nurse looked at her watch and warned them, "Mr. Green needs to take his medication and rest, ladies."

"Clementine. Cornwallis told me her first name is Clementine," Tess responded.

"Oh, sure," Endicott replied with a smile. He started to sit up and then winced in pain. "I know Clementine Jackson. Or *knew* her, some years back. She's a good woman. Heart of an angel."

"She'll be so glad to know you're okay," Kallie told him. "She was worried about you."

He looked at the nurse and whispered, "Connie, I'm not feeling very—"

"Okay, that's time, ladies. Mr. Green lost a lot of blood, and he needs to rest."

"Of course. We're sorry," Tess apologized quickly.

"Feel better soon. We'll talk to you later." Kallie added, "You're family now."

The nurse, Connie, ushered them out of the room, and another nurse pushed a cart past them.

"Thank you so much for bringing me to see Mr. Green. I was so worried," Kallie told her.

Connie smiled gently and replied, "The first words out of his mouth when he woke up, were 'where's that redhead that saved me?' Reginald had already told us all about what happened at the pier, so I knew it must be you."

Why does it always sound so weird when people call him Reginald? He does have a life outside of this job, you know.

"You know Cornwallis?" Kallie asked.

"I can't discuss his medical history, but let's just say we've seen him before," she replied with a laugh. She pressed the elevator call button for them and added, "And you really did save Mr. Green's life, Miss Brooks. Without question."

Tess stepped sideways and bumped her shoulder into Kallie's arm. "Told you."

As the elevator doors closed on them, she waved goodbye, and the tears rolled down her face in earnest.

***

"So what do we do now?" Tess asked when they got back into her car in the hospital parking lot.

Kallie had settled back down, wiping her tears and processing the overwhelming relief. She picked up a warm bottle of water, drank most of it, and considered the question. "We have to keep investigating," she replied. "I don't want to fall behind now that Cornwallis is out of the game."

"Agreed. Did you guys find out anything else when you were at the bakery? Or from that dock worker?"

"Nothing at the bakery," Kallie answered with a frown. "Patricia's staff is worried, and they say she wouldn't have missed work without telling them. But Cornwallis said the police are unlikely to get involved in her disappearance yet."

Tess grumbled in acknowledgement.

"The dock worker's story was. . . weird." Kallie thought about the interaction and shook her head. "Or maybe *he's* just weird. I was trying to use the stuff we learned in our textbooks, and he was giving me really strange body language."

"How do you mean?" Tess asked, looking at Kallie.

"I thought he was lying, and he kept looking around strangely." After all that had happened since then, she couldn't pinpoint exactly what had made Diaz seem so strange. She thought it was more intuition than any one thing. "He was acting shady, but it wasn't just that. He was looking at Cornwallis in the weirdest way."

Tess smiled crookedly. "What kind of weird way?"

Kallie frowned, recalling his behavior. "I know it sounds crazy, but all this police psychology stuff is hard." She tried to picture Diaz's face, and then added, thoughtfully, "He was talking about seeing Oscar Lawson at the dock, like an ordinary eyewitness report. Nothing serious. But his face—"

Tess nodded, waiting for Kallie to process her thought.

"He looked like a dog begging for food, but afraid of getting kicked instead," Kallie whispered, awkwardly.

Tess's eyes widened. "Whoa. While he was talking to Wally?"

Kallie blushed. "I know, I said it'd sound crazy." She added, flippantly, "Maybe his face is just. . . *like that*. I don't know."

"Kal, if that's what you saw, then I'm sure you're right," Tess replied, all trace of humor gone from her face. "But why would he look like that?"

"Cornwallis started to tell me something about him, but then it started raining. And then—" She trailed off.

"Yeah, and then the rest of it. I know." She touched Kallie's hand.

"Oh, there was one other thing. I forgot until just now," Kallie added. "Right before we got to the diner, Cornwallis said he found out something about Prudence."

"Oscar's daughter? What about her?"

"He said there was something wrong with her alibi," Kallie replied. "We were right by the door, so he told me to remind him later, and he'd show me the file."

"Alibi? Does he think she's involved in the murder?" Tess asked, looking concerned.

"He didn't say," Kallie replied, shaking her head. "But I doubt it. If he thought she was guilty, I think he would've told me more, instead of putting it off."

"Or he's just being protective of her. He seems like he wants to keep her sheltered from all of this, doesn't he?"

"Well, it's his friend's kid. Even though she's a grown woman, I don't think it's weird that he wants to protect her." Kallie shrugged.

"Okay, well, we can't ask Wally about the dock worker until he's off the painkillers, so I think Prudence should be our next research project."

"Sounds good to me. He said he had notes, so let's go to his office and see what he's got."

Tess started the car. "And now we have a plan."

She had just pulled out of the hospital parking lot, headed for Tampa, when Kallie's phone rang.

"Hey Brooks, are you feeling any better?" Morrison's voice sounded like an angel, and she slumped back in the car seat peacefully.

When he'd called the previous night, she hadn't been ready to talk about Cornwallis, and he honored her wishes. But she was glad he was checking with her again.

"Much better," she replied. "Tess forced me to go to the hospital and see Cornwallis. He's not mad at me, after all."

"Mad at you?" Morrison asked. "Why would he be mad at you?"

"He got *stabbed*, Morrison," Kallie replied, as if it was the dumbest question on earth.

"That's not *your* fault. And you saved the other victim's life."

"That's what we keep telling her," Tess yelled from the driver's seat. "Have you found the attacker?"

Kallie put the phone on speaker so Tess wouldn't have to yell.

"Not yet, but it was incredibly brazen, attacking two people in public, in the middle of the day. He's sure to be caught soon."

"It's related to the Sandcastle killing, right?" Kallie asked.

"I don't have much information on this case, actually," Morrison replied.

"We *finally* have a case in your jurisdiction, and you don't know about it?" Tess teased.

"Even though I don't know Cornwallis personally, his connection to you is too close. I don't want to damage the county's case."

"Well, that's boring," Tess grumbled.

"We understand, though," Kallie added quickly. "You'll let us know when they catch him, though, right?"

"Of course, you'll be the first to know. After Benny, I mean," he joked.

"Well, obviously," Kallie replied, smiling.

Kallie hung up, and they pulled into the office parking lot ten minutes later, making good time on the bridge into Tampa.

Tess unlocked the office door, and they immediately sat down and started examining the files on Cornwallis's desk. Tess took the file on Diaz, since she didn't get to meet him, which left Kallie with Prudence's file. They read in silence for twenty minutes, pausing to discuss some details from each file briefly, and then Kallie stopped to order food.

"Yeah, these files are really *thorough*," Tess agreed with a groan. "And I'm starving. You want pizza?"

"No, I'm afraid we'll get grease on his notes. How about lasagna?"

"Sounds good. And caffeine, please."

Kallie placed the delivery order and then sat down to continue reading. "I can't believe how much detail is in these files."

"Yeah, like I said, I think he has a personal connection with this case. I just don't know what it is yet."

"You don't think it's just because it's our first case?" Kallie asked.

"Hmm, I guess he could just be covering his butt, in case we mess up," Tess considered. "But I'm pretty sure it's more than that."

"Because he knew Oscar, maybe?"

"I know he protects his contacts, and thinks of them as close friends. . ."

"Yeah, even Badger," Kallie added.

"So that might be why. Although he hadn't spoken to Oscar in years."

"Maybe he feels bad about that too."

They went back to reading until the food was delivered, and Kallie ran downstairs to meet the driver. Tess was closing the folder on Diaz, when she returned, and had started reviewing her notes.

"So Wally knew Diaz before," Tess explained, after she moved the papers to the top of the filing cabinet and opened her lasagna container.

"Really? He didn't tell me that. . ."

"I don't think he worked with him as a contact. It sounds like Diaz was a pretty bad dude at one point. Really violent." Tess flipped through her own notes. "Wally rejected him as a contact once, a couple of years ago."

"Oh, maybe that's why Diaz was acting so

weird."

"Wally doesn't really talk about his personal thoughts in the file—"

"Not surprisingly," Kallie interjected.

"—but it sounds like Diaz claimed he wanted to go clean, and Wally didn't believe him. Like he caught him doing something dirty."

"But this time, he didn't have a choice about talking to him, since he saw Oscar," Kallie concluded. "He's a *witness* this time, not an informant."

"But if he still wants Wally to hire him—"

"Ugh. Then he might just be *lying* to get in his good graces."

"Exactly what I was thinking. Does Diaz want to be an informant to become a 'good guy,' or is he just in it for the money? Or is he still a criminal, and just trying to lead Cornwallis down the wrong path?" Tess sighed. "Why is this always so complicated?"

"He did keep looking to his left when we were at lunch," Kallie suggested. "The book says that means he's lying."

"Cornwallis told us that doesn't always work."

"My intuition said Diaz was lying, too." Kallie tapped her pen against the heavily-inked notepad, thinking. "But I don't know whether to trust it anymore."

"Wally says he trusts his intuition completely."

"Yeah, but I'm not him," Kallie sighed.

"Don't worry, Kal. We don't have to solve this alone. We'll just ask him what he thinks about Diaz, and we'll take everything in the file with a big grain of salt for now." Tess took a sip from her Diet Coke, watching Kallie. "Now tell me what you found in Prudence's file."

"Okay," Kallie agreed. "But it's not good."

"Why am I not surprised?" Tess asked, shaking her head.

"Her alibi is falling apart, and it doesn't sound like Cornwallis was very surprised either."

"Was she involved with her dad's murder?" Tess whispered, sounding horrified.

"I can't tell yet, but I hope not. Maybe she had some other reason to lie about where she was that night."

Tess rolled her eyes. "That never works."

"Yeah, I don't know why people even try," Kallie agreed. "She told the police—and Cornwallis—that she was doing housekeeping work at a hotel in Palm Harbor. Said it was her first night there, and she caught a ride with a friend."

"That sounds feasible," Tess replied.

"The friend backed her up, too. But the hotel says it didn't happen."

"Wow, so she got the friend to lie for her?" Tess asked, surprised. "Lying to the cops can get you in big

264

trouble."

"I don't think they've determined if the friend was lying or not – at least at the time of Cornwallis's notes. Pru might've gotten a ride, but gone somewhere else." Kallie looked over her handwritten notes again. "Or, the hotel could be wrong, I guess. Although they have to do a lot of paperwork for taxes, so that's probably the least likely case."

"Depends on the hotel," Tess replied with a smirk.

"I don't think it's *that* kind of hotel. Cornwallis said they had a *concierge desk*."

"Hmm, and a legit hotel probably wouldn't be paying her under the table, either. Did Wally go there himself?" Tess asked, and then rolled her eyes and answered herself. "Of course he did. That was a silly question."

"He said the concierge got the manager, and they showed him the employee schedule for the night of the murder. She wasn't there."

"Did he ask Prudence about it?"

"If so, it's not in the file," Kallie replied with a frown.

"Well, that got us a whole lot of nothing," Tess concluded with a sigh, picking up her lasagna again. "We don't have any more leads than when we got here."

"There is one other thing," Kallie said. "It might

be nothing, but there's a copy of Prudence's phone records in here."

"Did she call the killer?" Tess asked, with a smirk.

"If you tell me the killer's phone number, I'll check," Kallie quipped back. "But she *did* call her dad."

"It just keeps getting harder and harder to trust that woman," Tess groaned.

"I don't think we're going to find out much more about Diaz until we talk to Cornwallis again," Kallie noted. "But we can start looking into Prudence. We could even go talk to her."

"Do you think she'll talk to us?" Tess asked.

"Sure. We're on her side, right?"

"True. And I'm *sure* Cornwallis didn't confront her," Tess replied, sounding confident.

"Yeah, you're right. He's got a soft spot for her, so he wouldn't confront her unless he had evidence that she did something wrong."

Kallie made sure her hands were clean from the lasagna and walked over to the files. She opened the top cover and quickly wrote down a phone number in her notepad. "I want to talk to Cornwallis first, but then let's call her. Not to ask about the alibi – I don't want to alarm her – but we can ask for more information about her dad's friends."

"Okay, but let's get out of here. I don't like this

office when Wally's not here."

"Yeah, same," Kallie agreed. "I think we've got everything we need right now, anyway."

***

"Hey, you got your old cane back!" Kallie exclaimed when they walked back into the hospital room the next day.

Cornwallis's dragon cane leaned against the wall next to the bed, looking as elegant as when they'd first seen it, earlier that year.

Cornwallis looked at the cane and smiled. "I love that thing. My landlady picked it up for me and brought it over. They're letting me go home today."

"Oh, great," Tess replied, then appraised him briefly. "Are you sure you're ready?"

"Sure I'm sure. They checked me out, no harm done." He smirked and asked, "Want to see my stitches?"

"No!" Tess yelped, making him laugh.

"While I'm waiting for my discharge paperwork, tell me what you found yesterday."

"We went to your office and looked at the files for Prudence and Diaz, but now we have more questions than when we started," Kallie explained.

"Yeah, Diaz is a weird case." Cornwallis tapped his ring on the metal bedframe. "I'd love to hire him, but I just get a bad feeling about him."

Me too. Something isn't right with that guy.

"I checked on him before we met at the diner, to see if he was still involved in criminal activities, but I couldn't find anything at all."

"Does that mean he's gone clean?" Kallie asked.

"No, I mean, I couldn't find *anything. At all.* No job, no home, no relatives. No vehicle. Not even a driver's license."

"That's weird," Tess replied, confused.

"Yeah, I thought so too," Cornwallis replied. "It's like someone scrubbed his whole identity. Which wouldn't be that weird, if he were in witness protection or something."

"But if he were in witness protection, he wouldn't have met us at the diner," Kallie reflected.

Cornwallis nodded and pointed a finger at Kallie. "Exactly."

"So maybe he's working for some local criminal organization. A gang or something?"

"I haven't found anything yet, but I want you two to stay away from him for now. It's probably a coincidence. He's not smart enough to be a major player in any criminal activities, but even the bit players can be dangerous."

Kallie sighed. "Okay, we'll stay back for now. But we're running out of—"

"If neither of you is going to address the elephant in the room, then I'll do it," Tess interrupted with an irritated sigh. "Prudence is lying to us."

Cornwallis looked surprised.

"It's her *father*, though," Kallie replied, sympathetically. "It has to be some kind of mix-up. She wouldn't kill someone in her family."

"You'd kill Jack," Tess replied.

Kallie laughed. "Tess, *you'd* kill Jack, too."

"I've considered it, actually," Tess admitted with a smile.

Neither of them would really kill Kallie's horrible, entitled, drug-addled brother, of course – but she'd certainly considered it a few times, herself.

But now I know how hard it would be, to get away with it.

"Out of curiosity, what do you think Prudence is lying about?" Cornwallis asked, bringing them back to the subject.

"Nothing she says checks out," Tess snapped. "The timing, the people, her alibi."

Wow, Tess sounds angry. I'm actually pretty accustomed to people lying to our faces, by now.

"All of it falls to pieces as soon as we start checking it out," Tess concluded.

"And you don't think she's confused? Or just mistaken?" he asked. "After all, they were barely in touch for a few years."

"Are you defending her?" Tess asked, sounding confused and slightly hurt.

"I'm not doing anything of the sort," Cornwallis replied, carefully. "This is *your* case, Tess. Tell me your reasoning. What makes you think she's an unreliable source?"

Tess slumped back in one of the guest chairs, frowning.

After a minute or so, Kallie took the lead instead. "Okay, well, she implied that her dad's roommates had gotten him back into drugs again, or drinking—which we determined was untrue." She looked at Tess, but her best friend didn't look up at her, so she continued, "That *might've* just been a mistake, or she might've been trying to mislead us. Or confuse the motive."

"And she said she was at a job in Palm Harbor, which also wasn't true," Tess finally interjected. "Again, she could've just misremembered."

"But that's her alibi, and it's also full of holes," Kallie added. "She said they hadn't spoken in over a year, but your subpoena from the phone company shows a call from her—or from her *phone*, anyway—to her dad's number.

"Lasting over ten minutes," Tess added. "So it

270

wasn't a wrong number."

"Unless she's just *really* friendly with strangers," Kallie added with a smirk.

"Each one might be a simple mistake," Tess concluded, "but when you add them all together–"

"You get a pretty unreliable contact," Cornwallis completed her sentence. "Very good."

"You *knew*?" Tess snapped.

"I've known Oscar for years, but I don't know Prudence at all. She was just a kid back then," Cornwallis reminded them. "I'll admit that I was protecting her – probably to an unrealistic degree. And I'm still willing to give her the benefit of the doubt. But I don't *trust* anyone."

Wow. That sounded ominous.

"I didn't *know* she was lying—and I *still* don't. But if you two think so, then we need to analyze it and find out for sure."

Kallie heard Tess exhale, and realized that she'd been holding her breath as well.

Hoping he wouldn't call us crazy? Delusional?

"I'll reach out to some police friends and some of my other contacts when I get back to the office, and see if they have any recent information about her." He looked at Kallie, "Sorry, Morrison probably doesn't know her, so—"

"No, he's a detective, not a beat cop," Kallie

agreed. "So it'd be a total coincidence if he'd ever spoken to her."

Cornwallis tapped his ring against the bedframe again, and his face darkened. "And if I find out Prudence is involved in the murder, and she took advantage of my *kindly nature—*"

Kallie smiled at that. *A kindly porcupine,* she thought to herself, *but he really did go out of his way to help her.*

If Prudence was lying, Heaven help her.

Chapter Twelve

Cornwallis was never one to waste time, and he was back on the case before they'd even reached home. Both of their phones dinged simultaneously, and Kallie leaned forward in the passenger seat to remove hers from her pocket.

"Ugh," Tess snarled in annoyance, as the message popped up in her hands-free holder. "I can't believe she has an alibi too."

"What?" Kallie asked. "Who?" She checked her phone and saw a brief text from Cornwallis.

Cornwallis

Cousin's roommates all have alibis. Sorry.

"Aw, man," Kallie complained. "Peaches is clear? And the other couple too?"

"We didn't really think it was anyone in the apartment, though, right?" Tess asked.

"Prudence was sure it wasn't the cousin, but she didn't trust the roommates," Kallie recalled. "They weren't our first choice, but it wouldn't have surprised me either."

Since Tess was driving, Kallie called Cornwallis for the details.

"It took the police some time to reach the landlord," he explained. "His apartment is right under theirs, on the first floor. He said he heard them arguing and walking around up there all night."

"He was totally sure?" Kallie asked.

"I didn't talk to him, but the police wouldn't have said they were cleared unless the landlord was sure," Cornwallis replied. "Apparently, Peaches has a *particularly* annoying voice."

Tess, who was listening, pulled into the drive-through of a Mexican restaurant and added, solemnly, "That's probably why Oscar went out in the middle of the night. To get away from their arguing."

"Probably," Kallie replied with a sigh. "That's an awful thought."

Cornwallis apologized and said he had to go, so Kallie hung up.

She looked at her notebook and added, "We had them both marked as unlikely, though."

"I know," Tess sighed. "Who else do we have on our list of real possibilities? Anybody besides Teflon Donovan?"

They placed their drive-through order, and then Kallie replied, "I only have Donovan left on my solid suspects list – and we're not getting *anywhere* with that guy. But maybe we can get some more information from Endicott, once he's feeling better."

"Yeah, I hope he's better soon. Poor guy. I know we're pinning our hopes for Oscar's murderer on him, but he's the most likely to have some information."

"Since he saw Oscar right before he died, maybe he'll have some *suggestions*, at least."

"That makes me feel a little better about Peaches being off the hook. But, proving someone's innocent is just as important as proving they're guilty, I guess."

"Way less satisfying, though," Kallie replied with a sardonic laugh.

"No kidding."

They picked up their order at the window, and Tess pulled into a parking spot to check her case notes.

"Did Cornwallis ever hear back from Prudence about whether her dad had any known enemies?" Kallie asked, inspecting the food. "It wasn't in the file."

"I don't think so—"

As if on cue, their phones both dinged again.

Cornwallis
Pru's gone.

"You've got to be kidding!" Tess exclaimed.

"Another person involved in this case disappeared?" Kallie asked, equally alarmed.

Cornwallis

Landlady says she left town in a hurry. Maybe to her grandparents' house.

"I swear, he's trying to give us a collective heart attack."

"Wait, I have something on that." Kallie flipped to a page near the back of her notebook. "When we were at the office with her file, I wrote, 'Family in the suburbs of Grand Rapids.'"

"That must be them," Tess agreed. "But did she leave town because she has a guilty conscience—?"

"Or because someone's after her, too?" Kallie leaned over to look at Tess's notes. "I'm worried about her."

"Yeah, me too. Even with the alibi thing," Tess agreed. Kallie could tell she was trying to be pragmatic, but her furrowed brow showed her concern. "But she seems like a no-nonsense girl, with a good head on her shoulders."

Kallie texted back to Cornwallis, and they drove home to Kallie's house. There they spread out studiously, with the food and their case notes.

"We could call Prudence's grandparents," Kallie suggested.

"That's a great idea," Tess breathed with relief, plopping down on the couch. "I'd feel so much better if we were sure she's okay."

"'Suburbs of Grand Rapids' doesn't narrow it down much, but at least it's not Detroit," Kallie replied, trying to sound optimistic. She opened her laptop and started looking absently at maps of Michigan.

"Oh, sorry," Tess shook her head and grabbed Kallie's laptop. "I'm so distracted by all of these alibis. It'll be faster if I search for them."

"No kidding," Kallie replied with a laugh. "I mean, I was willing to *try*, but you're the one with the nerd skills."

"Remember to have that engraved on my tombstone," Tess replied with a sarcastic laugh. "Tess Russo. The one with the nerd skills."

"Her last name's Lawson too," Kallie added. "That's what it said in Wally's file, but I don't know if she was ever married."

"I wonder if they're her dad's parents?" Tess considered. "Well, there's a fifty-fifty chance. I'll start there, since we don't know her mom's maiden name..." She typed and scrolled on the laptop for ten minutes, her face growing more serious as time passed.

"No luck?" Kallie eventually asked.

"A little. It's easier to find a victim's family if there's an obituary," Tess complained. "You'd be amazed at how much personal information is included in obits. Names, ages, marriages, kids."

"Yikes," Kallie whispered.

"Yikes for them, but good for me," Tess answered, sounding a little jaded.

"But he was basically homeless, right?"

"Yeah, sometimes there are obituaries for the unhoused, especially former military. But Wally said Oscar didn't have any close family except his daughter." After a moment, she added, grimly, "You can't have an obituary without someone to write it."

"Maybe we can write one for him," Kallie mumbled.

Tess looked up and smiled gently. "Maybe. Let's see what I can find."

Kallie walked to the kitchen and poured them each a Diet Coke, then joined Tess back on the couch.

"I found a few people with his last name in the Grand Rapids area. None of them are named Oscar, but that doesn't necessarily mean anything." Tess showed Kallie the list. "I've read that homeless men are rarely the oldest child in their family."

"Oh, because the oldest son usually gets the father's name," Kallie nodded in understanding. "That makes sense. So his parents could be *any* of these listings."

"Or *none* of them," Tess answered with a shrug. She looked at the clock. "It's just barely five o'clock in Michigan. We can try calling them in half an hour or so; maybe we'll catch them before dinner."

"And say what?" Kallie asked, with a crooked smile.

"We'll just say we're from Tampa, and we wanted to see if they know Prudence."

"Do you think they'll tell us?"

Tess laughed. "They probably won't even answer the phone. And if they do, they might tell us to get lost. But it's worth a try."

"Just to make sure she's okay?"

"Why not?"

"Okay, let's try it." Kallie scanned the list again. "There aren't too many. And if we find her, maybe she'll be so *thrilled* to hear from us, that she'll tell us something we can use."

"I doubt it," Tess grumbled. "But we can hope for the best. 'Cause we are *seriously* short on clues, here."

Kallie put a bag of popcorn in the microwave, and then they split the list of 'Lawson' phone numbers in Grand Rapids, and started making calls.

***

"So I have good news and bad news," Cornwallis told them when they arrived at his office later that evening.

"Ugh, bad news first," Tess replied glumly.

"Donovan has an airtight alibi."

Kallie groaned. "An alibi for four a.m.?"

"Yep. He was at a hotel in Washington, DC, and didn't come back until the following afternoon."

"Couldn't he—?" Tess began.

"And the hotel has video of him entering the elevator after midnight," Cornwallis interrupted her.

"Dang it," Kallie mumbled. "I was *sure* he was involved. "He's so shady, and that hotel is just a cesspool of crime."

"And he's a jerk," Tess added grumpily.

"Well, the police are looking into him more closely, so hopefully he'll get picked up for the drugs and prostitution charges," Cornwallis answered her. "I don't know who he's been bribing to stay out of trouble, but he's under a microscope now."

Kallie crossed her arms and pouted. "Him and his stupid pear tree—"

"I still have some good news," Cornwallis reminded them. "Do you want to hear it?"

"Are you going to tell us you were just kidding about Donovan's alibi?" Tess asked, sarcastically.

"No," Cornwallis replied.

"*Fine*, go ahead," Kallie replied, slumping lower in her chair.

"Donovan might have an alibi, but his receptionist doesn't."

"What?" Kallie asked, suddenly interested again.

"She said she was in DC with him, but the police checked the flight manifest, and she wasn't on the plane. And she wasn't at the hotel either."

"He probably just made her fly coach on a cheaper airline," Tess replied, still not convinced.

"And stay at some fleabag motel," Kallie added.

"Like a cut-rate version of the McCormick," Tess agreed. "With fancy hookers and the swankiest meth in town. While he stayed in some thousand-dollar-a-night suite."

"Nope, the police checked," Cornwallis replied softly. "She bought groceries in downtown Tampa that evening."

Tess finally looked up. "She was here in town? And she lied?"

"She can't be the murderer, though," Kallie scoffed. "I mean, what possible motive could she have?"

"We already talked about Donovan manipulating her. What if he forced her to kill Oscar?" Tess suggested.

Kallie considered that, then shook her head. "That seems like a stretch. Unless he was blackmailing her for something."

Cornwallis was showing just the hint of a smile, listening to them, and Tess squinted at him.

"You think she's involved, don't you?"

"I think you should check her out," he replied, simply. "What do you know about her?"

"Not much," Tess replied, honestly. "I don't even know her name, do you?" she asked Kallie.

"Nope."

Cornwallis wrote on a notepad and tore the sheet off, sliding it across the desk.

Kallie picked it up and read, aloud, "Katerina Melnyk."

"It's a pretty common name, believe it or not," Cornwallis said. "But not so common in Florida. See what you can find."

"When we were at Donovan's office, we heard her talking about making a reservation at Rooftopz for someone," Kallie commented, considering the connection.

"Fancy. And you think it's involved with the murder?" Cornwallis asked.

"We aren't sure," Tess added. "At the time, it just seemed noteworthy, because we thought Donovan was up to his eyeballs in this. . ."

"But that reservation could be for anyone," Cornwallis finished her thought.

"Yeah, and that place is *expensive*," Kallie

added.

"But they *have* to be involved somehow," Tess insisted. "Whether it's Donovan or the receptionist. What if we just go check the place out?"

"It's a restaurant, though. We can't just stand around staring at people, like weirdos. They'll kick us out."

"See if you can find any other connections, and maybe we can get you a reservation," Cornwallis replied. "A concerned citizen donated some money to help find the killer."

"What?" Kallie replied, surprised. "Somebody gave you money to find Oscar's killer? Who would care about some homeless panhandler?"

"Besides us, obviously," Tess added quickly.

"The wealthy benefactor asked to remain anonymous."

"And that doesn't seem a little sinister to you?" Tess replied, raising one perfect eyebrow.

Cornwallis chuckled and shook his head. "I'll explain it later. But if you can find a better connection between Oscar and either Donovan and Melnyk or the crimes going on at that hotel, we might have the funds to get you into Rooftopz."

Kallie and Tess looked at each other and shrugged. "If there's a connection, we'll dig it up."

***

Kallie and Tess were studying the next morning, when Kallie's phone rang. She glanced at the number, reaching to turn off the ringer so she could concentrate, but then yelped, "Oh my gosh, it's Prudence!"

"You're kidding," Tess replied, in obvious disbelief.

Kallie held up her phone, showing the caller ID with the Michigan number – she'd saved it in her contacts as "Pru's Grandma" – and quickly answered the call.

"Hi, Prudence?"

"Hello, Miss Brooks," Pru replied, sounding stiff and awkward. "My granny told me to call you back. But I don't have any information."

"We just wanted to make sure you were okay, Pru. Did someone threaten you?"

"No," the young woman sighed. "I just needed to get out of there."

"Okay, I understand," Kallie replied, unsure of what else she could say. She didn't dare put the phone on speaker, though she wanted Tess to hear the call. Her best friend leaned closer.

Should I ask her about the alibi? About why she lied?

No way, Kalliope. She's not going to tell you, and you'll just make her hang up.

284

"Cornwallis is worried about you—"

"I know. That's the only reason I called you back," she mumbled. "I owe him that much for helping me. . ."

"He's still trying to find your father's killer. We all are," Kallie explained. "Is there anything—"

"I don't know anything!" she snapped, voice suddenly cracking. "I barely knew him, anymore! I don't know if he had any enemies. I didn't even know his *friends*!"

Kallie stayed silent for a moment, considering her options. Knowing she probably only had one chance left.

"I know this is hard. Did you ever see him with anyone who seemed out of place?" she asked, calmly. Trying to stay serene, in the hope that Prudence would do the same. "Anyone who wasn't from his group of friends, or didn't belong?"

"No, Miss Brooks," Prudence replied. But she was calmer now. "I really can't think of anyone who—"

Kallie waited, holding her breath.

"Actually. . ."

Yes. Please, Prudence. . .

"There was one guy. I didn't see him, but my dad mentioned him on the phone."

That phone call that she didn't mention, the one Cornwallis found on the subpoena records.

"He said he was going to meet a guy at a yoga class in Ozona," Prudence continued. "I didn't give it much thought at the time, because a lot of those yoga types are all *peace and love*. I thought maybe it was some kind of outreach. . ."

"But?" Kallie asked, patiently.

"But if it was an outreach program, then his cousin would've been going too. And he didn't know about it." She paused, and Kallie could tell she regretted speaking.

"Thank you so much," Kallie replied. "We'll see what we can find. And thank you so much for talking to us. We'll let Cornwallis know you're okay. And don't hesitate to call if we—"

But Prudence had already hung up.

"She said there was a guy at a yoga class," Kallie told Tess, with an odd expression, after she put down her phone. "Someone Oscar was going to meet."

"A *yoga* class?"

"That's what she said. What kind of murderer takes yoga classes?" Kallie wondered aloud.

"The kind who's searching for enlightenment, I guess?"

"Yeah, I'm not sure even a yogi can fix that kind of karmic debt." She thought for a minute then added, "Good on him for trying, though, I guess."

"So we're staking out a yoga class now? How

would we even find out which one?"

"She said it was in Ozona," Kallie answered with a smile.

"Well, that narrows it down," Tess responded. "Ozona makes Owhiro look like a bustling metropolis, and most of the residents are over 60."

"Should we pull in Isabel?" Kallie suggested.

Tess laughed. "She'd love that! She and Carlos are always so interested in our stories!"

Imagining Izzy teaching a grueling yoga class, while suspiciously watching a killer, waiting to make her move, Kallie chuckled.

"But Carlos would literally kill us," Tess concluded.

"That's true. And he's a big guy, and smart," Kallie added. "The cops would never find our bodies."

"Then I guess we're on our own," Tess sighed. "You've taken yoga classes before, right?"

"I took one of Izzy's hot yoga classes a few years ago, and. . . Well, I *survived*."

"Great, then we should be fine." Tess typed quickly on her phone. "I found the place, Ozona Flow. It's the only yoga studio in town. I'm signing us up for a class on Sunday morning at nine a.m."

"We can't, they're expecting us to volunteer on Sunday," Kallie replied. "Madeline's out visiting her parents, so they'll be shorthanded."

Tess nodded. "The only other opening is tomorrow morning at eight, though."

"That's okay, I guess. You promise I won't die?"

"From the class or the murderer?"

"*Either*, Tess."

"It's a Saturday morning, in a public place, so we're probably safe from the killer. And I'll try to protect you from the deadly yoga," she smirked. "Do you want to wear my smartwatch? It monitors your heartbeat and stuff."

"Yes," Kallie replied, without a second thought. "Does it let out a loud, screeching alarm if my heart explodes?"

"It's yoga, not high-intensity interval training, Kal. You'll be fine."

"I know, I know," Kallie groaned. "But can we please schedule a massage tomorrow night, too? I'll need it."

Chapter Thirteen

Tess drove to the yoga studio in Ozona the following morning, explaining that she'd have to hurry back to the office after the class, even though it was the weekend. "I told Winchester I'd be a little late, but he's working on Central time, anyway."

"That's fine, I probably won't survive until the end, anyway," Kallie quipped.

As they pulled into the parking lot, Tess seemed to be reconsidering. "We might be totally off-track here, Kal. Could the guy who killed Oscar really be taking yoga classes? It seems—"

"Or is he stalking the instructor as his next victim?" Kallie suggested, gravely.

"Okay, good point." Tess opened the car door. "I guess we're going to find out. The class was non-refundable since I booked it at the last minute."

"Wild horses couldn't tear me away," Kallie groaned, sarcastically, making Tess laugh.

"Here, take my smartwatch. And seriously, don't overdo it. This is an intermediate class, but it isn't boot camp. The instructor will understand if you're not ready for some of her positions."

"Okay," Kallie mumbled.

"Besides, if we have to chase this guy, you'll need your strength."

"That's a great point," Kallie replied, feeling a little less intimidated. "And what if we have to fight him? I won't be able to fight if my legs are like spaghetti."

"We're not going to fight him, Kal. We're professionals now, we don't do crazy stuff anymore." She got out of the car and closed the door.

"Tell that to the murderer," Kallie mumbled as she stood up, straightening her yoga pants, which were tighter than she'd like.

Nobody's looking at your butt, Kalliope. This isn't third grade.

She leaned back into the car and grabbed Tess's cardigan, tying it around her waist.

Tess signed them in to the class as Kallie looked around. It wasn't as nice as Isabel's studio, but there was more room. She could hear the traffic noise from the road outside, and an airplane flying overhead, probably landing at the regional St. Pete airport.

Wow, Isabel must have a lot of soundproofing at her place. I never hear any outside noise there, and Owhiro is much closer to the airport.

The studio quietly filled up as Kallie and Tess

looked around. There were a few photos on the walls, and a framed magazine article about the studio. Tess pointed at one of the photos. "This must be the instructor. She's very fit."

Kallie tied the cardigan tighter around her waist, awkwardly, and looked around at the group of students who had gathered in the small, peaceful space. There were no men, so far.

"Where is he?" she whispered. "Do you think he left because of us?"

"Maybe he's changing. . ." Tess suggested, hesitantly.

A car honked noisily outside, and then another car honked back. They could hear two men yelling at each other in the parking lot.

"This place is pretty popular," Tess remarked, glancing out the window. "I'm surprised it's not more... tranquil."

"I was thinking the same thing when we came in. It's a nice space, but it could use some soundproofing."

The other students moved into the main room and began unrolling their yoga mats and doing some preliminary stretches, so Kallie and Tess followed them. Kallie looked at the smartwatch and saw that the class was starting in just a few minutes. She unrolled her dusty old yoga mat near the wall, adding, "We'd better sit down."

Untying the cardigan hesitantly, she looked around for a place to drop it, and heard Tess whisper, "What the—?"

Turning at the sound, she was surprised to see a familiar form emerge from the rear of the studio. He looked every bit the serene instructor, barefoot and dressed in ankle-length linen pants and a short sarong. Only his scruffy beard and tattoos belied their earlier encounter.

Including the ace of diamonds tattoo on his neck, of course.

"*Namaste*, class."

"You've got to be kidding me," Kallie groaned in annoyance, as the rest of the class replied, "*Namaste*, Danny."

Kallie barely even noticed the rest of the class, although she was sure she'd be sore later. She pouted, disappointed, as they gathered their belongings to leave, and tried to ignore all of the girls flirting with her former suspect.

Jerk.

"Another washout," Kallie complained to Cornwallis, as Tess drove her home from the class.

Cornwallis grumbled in response.

I'm not sure whether I should feel guilty of suspecting that guy, or just feel stupid.

No one seems even a little surprised – except

me.

"I think I have some news that will cheer you up, Kallie," he said, suddenly alert.

"I doubt it," she replied, but she tilted her head in curiosity.

"I just got a text. Your mysterious benefactor is interested in Katerina Melnyk," Cornwallis announced. "Interested enough to send you to Rooftopz."

"No way!" Kallie exclaimed.

"Yes, way," he responded.

"That's so much better than a dumb yoga class—"

"Hey!" Tess objected from the driver's seat.

"There are rules, though," Cornwallis interjected. "No drinking on the job. And try to keep it under a hundred bucks, if you can."

"Rooftopz is pretty expensive, Wally," Tess called out.

"I *know*. I checked the menu online," Cornwallis agreed. "But a tip from an old pro – you're likely to get *more* funding if you're thrifty on the first job."

"When are we going?" Kallie asked, excitedly.

"Tonight," Cornwallis replied, laughing as Kallie gasped in shock. "Katerina Melnyk booked the suite for tonight, so you'll have to be there to see who shows up."

"We'll make it work, Boss!" Kallie chirped,

happily – memories of her earlier disappointment already forgotten.

***

"What are you getting to drink?" Kallie whispered to Tess, staring at the drinks menu at the prestigious Rooftopz outdoor dining area.

Tess was peacefully staring over downtown Tampa below, sparkling in the darkness. "We can't drink. Do they have a non-alcoholic menu in there?"

"I'm sure they do," Kallie nodded. "We even have a non-alcoholic menu at the Gecko. It's super trendy to *not* drink, right now." She flipped to the next page. "Most of our non-alcoholic cocktails are more expensive than the real thing."

"Well, at the Gecko, at least you can get a plain old lemonade instead," Tess replied. "I don't think this place has two-dollar lemonade."

"They might have twenty-dollar lemonade," Kallie replied. "Look at these prices."

"Not our problem tonight. Cornwallis's mysterious benefactor is footing the bill."

"I'm going to try this 'Pompei Pommie' – pomegranate juice with lime and soda water, and it comes with a sparkler burning in the glass."

Tess laughed. "Of course you want the drink that

arrives on *fire*."

"Naturally," Kallie grinned.

"It's probably not very subtle, though."

"Oh," Kallie answered, with a sigh and a small pout. "I guess we *are* supposed to be undercover, aren't we?"

"Yeah," Tess agreed, obviously feeling bad for her best friend. A moment later, she added, "You know what? Go ahead and order it."

"Really?"

"If this guy thinks he's being followed, no way he's going to guess it's by the two noisiest girls in the room."

"The perfect camouflage," Kallie added with a laugh. "What are you getting?"

Tess took the menu and quickly pointed at the top of the page. "Mocha Anthill. No question."

"It's not on fire," Kallie complained.

"No, but it says it's thirty-two ounces," Tess explained. "That means it'll be in a glass the size of my head. And covered in whipped cream and chocolate-covered coffee beans."

"Go big or go home," Kallie replied with appreciation.

"Exactly. This restaurant doesn't seem like the kind of place that would have crazy drinks, especially with this billion-dollar view of the city. But I guess that's their clientele. The young-and-spoiled super-rich."

"Like our suspect, presumably. Can you tell which one he is?" Kallie asked, trying to keep her eyes on the view and not look around.

The high-priced suite was in the rear corner of the dining area. Kallie had to admit, it was stylish – open to the air but enclosed with decorative wrought iron bars. Live tropical vines with yellow flowers wrapped the room in secrecy, so they could hear people partying inside, but couldn't see anything.

"Yep, I saw him come in while you were reading the menu. He's over by the suite, with some other troublemaker-types."

"Paying extra money for the seats without a view," Kallie laughed.

"Enjoying the view wouldn't be *cool*, you know."

Their handsome young waiter arrived and took their drink orders, then left them to review the menu. They perused the appetizer options, chattering happily about celebrities and gossip, and being intentionally loud. Meanwhile, Tess secretly watched the guy in the dark corner.

"Let's get the grouper ceviche," Kallie suggested.

"Yum, and I want to try the puff pastry Cuban bites."

"Do you think we could get entrees to go?"

"I think that would be pushing our luck with

whoever's paying," Tess answered, shaking her head. "But if we send an itemized bill with just non-alcoholic drinks and appetizers, maybe he'll hire us again!"

"What a *bargain* we are, with our fifty-dollar booze-free drinks," Kallie deadpanned.

"Oh, he's getting up," Tess whispered, suddenly. "I'm going to follow him–"

She grabbed her purse and started to stand up, but the waiter came around the corner with Kallie's blazing drink at that very moment. Tess stopped, halfway out of her seat, for a moment, and then sat back down, trapped.

The waiter was laughing awkwardly, and drawing the eye of everyone nearby, as the tall drink— topped by two blazing, live sparklers—lit up their whole side of the outdoor bar. Kallie saw half a dozen people grab their menus to find out what she'd ordered. When he finally set the drink on the table, Kallie's eyes were so dazzled by the blinding light, she could barely see.

Remembering Tess's earlier idea about their *modus operandi*, she laughed loudly and bounced up and down in her seat. For the *pièce de résistance*, she jumped up to hug the startled waiter, gushing, "Thank you so much! It's my birthday!"

Did you seriously just hug that poor guy, Kalliope? Totally overdoing it.

But this bar was too small to hide two amateur private investigators, and Tess was right, if their suspect knew he was being watched, he'd never guess that the noisy, seemingly-drunk girls were the ones on his tail.

The waiter glanced behind himself, and another waiter followed, carrying an enormous fishbowl of a glass, filled with some kind of brown, slushy mocha drink, and overflowing with chocolate sauce and whipped cream.

Well, in for a penny, in for a pound, Kallie thought to herself, as Tess cheered loudly too. "Happy Birthday, Bestie!" A few people looked at them strangely, but smiled indulgently, as Kallie decided they might need to tone it down before someone complained.

We've made our impact, anyway. Two non-threatening girls. Definitely not two stalkers funded by a suspicious, unknown financier with deep pockets.

When the sparklers burned down, the waiter removed them from the drink, dousing them safely in a tall glass of water. They thanked him again and ordered their appetizers, then went back to slyly watching the dark corner, where their quarry hadn't yet returned.

I hope he didn't leave.

Nah, he just got here. Relax, Kalliope.

"Wow, this is really good," Tess whispered, after finally taking a sip of her drink through its comically long straw.

"Twenty-six dollars good?"

"Hmm," she took another sip, considering the question. "Maybe. Definitely *someone else's* twenty-six dollars good."

"Is he back yet?" Kallie whispered.

"Here he comes, now. I can't believe he missed that whole show," Tess grumbled.

"His friends will probably tell him all about it," Kallie reassured her, blushing.

"And how incredibly dorky we are."

"Exactly. Should we start singing, to get his attention?" Kallie asked with a laugh.

"Mmm, I think that couple will have us arrested if we make any more noise." She nodded toward a very attractive couple, who looked increasingly annoyed at the whole situation. Apparently, this place wasn't what *they'd* expected either.

I doubt they've ever been to a restaurant with sparklers on the menu before.

"We've got to bring back some kind of report," Kallie advised, taking another sip from her drink. She could tell Tess was trying not to stare.

"I know, but I don't recognize that guy," Tess replied. "I was hoping it would be someone famous – or *infamous*, at least. But I've never seen him before."

"And you've been studying the crime blogs for years. He doesn't look familiar at all?" Kallie was dying to turn around and take a look herself.

"Ugh, he just went back into the suite."

"Well, what does he look like? Any distinguishing features or tattoos?"

"He's too far away," Tess sighed. "I don't see any tattoos or anything."

"I'll go to the restroom, then," Kallie suggested. "Maybe I can get a good look at him, if he happens to come back out—"

"Oh my gosh!" Tess suddenly screeched in a high-pitched voice, shocking Kallie into silence. "I've just got to get a picture of you in that gorgeous dress, Bestie!"

Kallie shook off her surprise, wishing again that she could turn around – just for a second.

Tess whipped out her phone, and Kallie leaned forward toward her, making kissy-lips across the table – playing along even though she had no idea what Tess had planned. She stood up and twirled as Tess took a few more pictures, and then she squealed, "Ooh, get one of me by these *flowers*!"

Tess took more pictures, as she posed by the flowering vines surrounding the suite.

Thank goodness I let Tess convince me to wear a dress tonight!

"You look amazing!' Tess cooed, "And those flowers look so great with your dress!"

They sat back down, as their appetizers arrived,

and Kallie whispered, "I hope you got a picture of him?"

Glancing at her phone, Tess whispered back, "I got about ten, but a few of them look really good. Great idea about the flowers, Kal."

"Then our mission here is complete," Kallie mumbled, digging into her dish of ceviche happily.

***

"What do you *mean*, you don't recognize him?" Kallie whined on the phone.

"What am I, the perp dictionary?" Cornwallis replied with a chuckle. "I'll send these over to TPD. Good job, by the way. They're great pictures, even if the face doesn't ring a bell."

"Thanks, Boss," Tess answered, cheerfully.

Kallie stared at the photos of the man she hadn't been able to see the night before. He wasn't what she expected. With spiky reddish-blonde hair and trendy wire-rimmed glasses, he wasn't the sinister kingpin-type she thought they'd be chasing. Even his jeans were boring.

"I'll show them to Morrison too, and see if he knows the guy," Kallie added. "I'm meeting him for breakfast in a few minutes."

"Good idea. If that guy's involved in the murder, maybe he has a record in Pinellas."

Kallie pulled into the parking lot of their usual outdoor café and saw Morrison sitting at her favorite table. They'd been meeting for breakfast ever since they'd met – long before she realized that her detective friend was interested in being more than friends.

He must've sensed her looking at him, because he turned and smiled at her.

Kallie's stomach did a somersault at the sight of his handsome grin, and she blushed at being caught staring.

Why are you embarrassed, Kalliope? Pretty sure he knows you like him, now, silly.

"How's the sleuthing, my beautiful investigator?" he greeted her, as she slipped into her usual seat.

"Insane, as always," she answered with a laugh, as Justine brought her coffee and a glass of orange juice, unbidden. She'd be back for Kallie's breakfast order, which wasn't as predictable. "And I'm not an investigator yet."

"You're not *licensed* yet, but I see a lot of investigating going on," Morrison insisted.

"Speaking of that," she replied, "Do you recognize this guy?" She handed over her phone and then scanned the menu quickly, deciding what she wanted to eat.

"Is this from *Rooftopz*?" he asked, looking at the photos.

"Yeah, how could you tell?" Kallie asked, surprised.

"I was up there for a theft case, a few weeks ago," he replied. "How did you get into that place?"

"We have a rich benefactor," she answered, mysteriously. Justine came back, and Kallie ordered the chocolate chip pancakes.

"Nice," Morrison replied, with a smile. "I don't recognize this guy, but Rooftopz isn't known for its criminal enterprise. They're pretty respectable, actually."

"Oh, really?" Kallie asked, with a disappointed frown.

"They were really accommodating in the theft case."

"Oh. . ."

"No, that's a good thing," he quickly reassured her. "If this guy's bad news, they'll probably work with us to clear their reputation."

"Us?" Kallie asked, smiling hopefully.

Morrison chuckled and rolled his eyes. "Okay, I stuck my own foot into that one. I'll meet you there before their dinner hours, and we can see what the manager has to say."

"Thanks, Morrison," she replied, happily.

***

The evening manager of Rooftopz greeted Morrison warmly, when they met later, but Kallie already had a sense that it wouldn't go as easily as the detective thought.

"And you don't know his name? What else did he tell you?" Morrison asked.

"He asked me to leave," the manager replied. "But he's not the first guy to ask for privacy. That's why we *have* a VIP suite."

We have a VIP lounge at the Gecko too. Nobody's ever asked me to leave before, but I wouldn't think twice if they asked for privacy.

I mean, isn't that why they pay for a private room?

"That suite costs five grand for the evening, on weekends," he continued. "If they ask for privacy, they get it. We bring food and drinks, and get out of the way."

Whoa, five grand? I need to talk to Marcy. I think ours is like a hundred bucks.

Morrison nodded, continuing to take notes. "Are they regulars?"

"I've seen them here before, but I wouldn't call them regulars. Maybe once a month?"

Five grand once a month?

"And that guy in particular—the gentleman in the photos— has he ever given you any trouble?"

The manager rolled his eyes. "*None* of them give

us any trouble, Detective. We run a clean restaurant here. Even with those rental prices, we wouldn't tolerate troublemakers running off our dinner patrons."

"Not even for five grand?" Morrison asked.

"Have you looked at our menu prices, Detective?" the manager sighed, sounding a little condescending to Kallie's ear.

"Actually, no," Morrison replied. But he didn't ask for a menu.

"We have families who've known the owner since he opened his first restaurant in the 1980s. Kids that've grown up eating his scallopini saltimbocca since they were toddlers. No business gathering is worth losing those people. They're family."

"Wait, business gathering?" Kallie interjected, confused.

Morrison looked at her in surprise.

"I thought it was a party. Friends hanging out, doing shots. A party," she explained, quickly. Feeling a little foolish. "Are you saying they're a *business* group?"

The manager shook his head. "I don't see why that would matter—"

"No, she's right," Morrison interrupted him. "What business are they in? This is a pretty expensive locale for an after-work happy hour. As you pointed out."

"I really couldn't say," the manager fumbled.

"They booked the space under a corporate account, but I don't–"

"Fine, I'll just get a subpoena," Morrison replied with a long-suffering sigh.

"Get a—"

"That won't hurt your business, will it?" Kallie asked, sarcastically.

"No, it'll be fine," Morrison answered her. "I'm sure their clientele will love eating in a place where the police are questioning everyone."

"Their kids will actually love it, probably," Kallie agreed. "Children love first responders."

"And they'll tell their friends at school," Morrison replied, but he was looking at the manager, not Kallie.

"Daddy, can we go back to Rooftopz for dinner?" Kallie imagined aloud, in a sing-song childlike voice. "Jimmy told me they saw lots of *police* there last night."

The manager blanched at the thought.

"Jimmy said his daddy talked to the officer for a really long time," Kallie continued. She was pretty sure she heard Morrison choke back a laugh.

"*Fine*," the manager sighed, taking a phone out of his pocket. "Let me call the owner and see what he wants to do."

The manager walked away, talking quietly but seriously into his phone, and Morrison poked Kallie in the arm, chuckling. "Daddy, don't *you* want to talk to the police too?" he added, in a cracking, childlike imitation.

A few diners looked at them questioningly, many of whom had probably never heard a police detective laugh before.

"Sorry folks," the manager groaned as he returned to the table. "I talked to the owner, and he said you can get your subpoena."

"*Seriously*?" Kallie asked quietly.

"He's not selling out his patrons," he added. "But I'd appreciate it if you could keep a low–"

"Thanks, chum. I'll make sure to have a few uniformed officers here every night, until this is resolved," Morrison promised soberly.

"Hope you don't live on tips, sweetie," Kallie added, sarcastically. "And you might want to give your servers the rest of the month off."

***

"So we're stuck there until the police get the subpoena – if they can even find a judge to grant one," Kallie explained to Tess when they met at her house. "What's our next move?"

"Let me check my notes," Tess replied.

"I still have a bad feeling about that yoga guy,

but Cornwallis said the police cleared him."

"Yeah, that guy's definitely a paradox," Tess agreed. "He's a real *suspect*, since Prudence pointed him out to us. But—"

"You don't think it was him, do you?" Kallie asked.

"He's a *legit* yoga instructor, Kal. There's no way he could've taught that class without serious training." Tess touched her leg gingerly. "My hamstrings are still a little sore."

"But the way he was running, when we saw him in Clearwater—"

"Maybe he was just *running,* though. I mean, did you see his body? He must exercise a *lot*. The other guy was probably his running partner, and they were just getting in some exercise."

"I guess so, but—"

Tess pulled out her phone and tapped for a moment. "His studio has 4.8 stars online."

"Do you think Isabel knows him?" Kallie asked, curiously.

"Ask her," Tess suggested. "You know she'll give you an honest answer."

Kallie quickly sent a text to Izzy, and then looked over at Tess's phone.

"He has great reviews," Tess continued, scanning the page. "His name's Danny Lloyd. Hundreds of students and even some other instructors say he's amazing.

"Most of them say he's hot," Kallie mumbled, looking over her shoulder at the screen.

"He is pretty hot," Tess agreed with a laugh. "A few of the most recent reviews complain that the outside noise has gotten worse. You mentioned that, too."

"Yeah, we could hear every car that drove by, and the airport traffic was rattling the windows. That was weird for a yoga studio, where it's usually peaceful."

"That was really annoying," Tess agreed. "But they love the instructor."

Kallie's phone dinged, and she read Izzy's reply, frowning. "Isabel says he's really good, too. Especially at *Ashtanga*, whatever that is."

"Oh, good. Do you feel better now?" Tess asked, looking closely at Kallie's face.

Kallie considered for a moment and shook her head. "Couldn't we just *check* on him?"

"You really think he's involved? When even *Izzy* says he's okay?" Tess asked, sounding surprised.

Kallie leaned back in her chair and sighed. "I guess not. You're probably right—"

"Hey, no," Tess interrupted her. "No way. If you have any doubts, then let's go check him out."

"Are you sure?"

"That's what we do," Tess answered, poking her in the arm. "And Wally said we should never ignore our intuition. We're investigators now, right? So let's investigate!"

"Thanks, Tess."

"But *how*?" her best friend considered.

Kallie looked back at her phone. "Izzy said he has gatherings at his house on Sunday nights. It's supposed to be for meditation, but she said all of his students go and flirt with him."

"Hmm, I wonder if we could—"

"The *trashy* students, Izzy said," Kallie interjected, sneering a little.

"We can go *undercover* as trashy students," Tess replied with a sinister grin. "We have a few hours. I can do your makeup and force you into a slinky dress."

"Oh, hooray," Kallie responded grimly.

"You're the one who wanted to investigate him," Tess answered coolly.

"Okay, fine. Do your worst."

"Nothing of mine will fit you. Let's go borrow a dress from Izzy, and she can tutor us on what to ask him, too," Tess replied with a sneaky grin.

"Isabel's dresses will be too short for me, Tess."

"That's *exactly* my plan," Tess replied, raising one perfect, devious eyebrow.

"Hey, is that–?"

Tess was cautiously looking into a dark closet that smelled strongly of pachouli, but called back, "Hmm?"

Kallie was wearing a skirt that was at least three inches too short, and so much mascara she could barely see. But it didn't matter, because no one had even acknowledged them at the party. The women were all busy flirting with the yoga guy—Danny—and he was completely engrossed with a stunning blonde who was talking about her favorite *pranayama*.

Kallie moved a few books aside and smiled. "Wow, I haven't seen one of these since Janet Monroe's birthday in sixth grade."

"That can't be good. She was a wild child," Tess laughed. "What did you find?"

"It's an old Ouija board." Kallie moved another book and frowned. "Where's the pointer thing?"

Tess grabbed her hand. "It's called a planchette, and we are *not* going to find out."

"It's just a game, Tess," Kallie sighed.

"I don't care if it's a game, or a toy, or a portal to the seventh level of winter in Alaska. We're on a case, so don't touch it."

"Because it's *spoooooky*?" Kallie teased.

"Because this entry to his house is *technically* implied consent, since the party was open to his students, and we paid for the class. But we don't need to risk a trespassing charge," Tess replied, seriously. "Also, it's a little creepy. We have enough problems without inviting a ghost to make it more complicated."

"Maybe the ghost knows something about the murder, Tess," Kallie answered with a smile. "Did you think of *that*?"

"Your Honor, the prosecution would like to call Casper the Ghost to the stand, as an eyewitness," Tess deadpanned.

Kallie shrugged. "I mean, it's Pinellas County. I'm sure the judge has heard weirder things."

Tess laughed. "Probably, but not from us. We have a reputation to protect."

"Fine, no Ouija board. But I still want to look around more, since we went to the trouble of *technical* lawful entry."

"It's a lot harder doing this the legal way, isn't it?" Tess quipped. "Come look at this closet."

"Did you find something?"

"We know Oscar was from Michigan, right?"

"Yeah," Kallie answered with a nod. "At least his family lives there."

Tess took a pen from her pocket and pushed a coat hanger aside in the closet. When it was out of the way, Kallie could see a sweatshirt that said TEMPLE across the front.

"Temple University is in Pennsylvania, isn't it?" Kallie asked. "That's where Elizabeth Kwan went to school."

Tess nodded. Kwan, their favorite reporter on the local news channel, occasionally remarked on her college days when she was in the studio. "So it doesn't sound like they're from the same hometown."

"That doesn't mean anything. They could've known each other from here."

"True. But they have *nothing* in common," Tess considered. "Danny and Oscar were at least twenty years apart in age. They don't hang out in the same circles or have the same interests—"

"Yeah," Kallie grumbled.

"I'm not shooting down your idea," Tess quickly added. "I'm just thinking out loud. How could they have known each other?"

Kallie didn't answer, but started checking out the bookshelf again.

Tess took out her phone and snapped a few photos of the sweatshirt, then continued delicately searching the closet. Kallie moved on to the bathroom, but she could hear the coat hangers clink as Tess pushed them apart with her pen.

Kallie caught her reflection in the bathroom

mirror and barely recognized herself, laughing awkwardly. Her long auburn hair was glamorously curled, teased, and hairsprayed to twice its normal volume, and her olive-green eyes were weirdly dazzling behind black mascara-clumped lashes. To her alarm, though, she found that her skirt was even shorter than it felt, and she tried to yank it down, grumbling in annoyance.

She finally looked away from the mirror, feeling amused at their undercover roles rather than embarrassed. A nearby mark on the floor caught her eye, and she bent down to check it out, immediately forgetting about her odd appearance.

"Hey Tess, could you come look at this?"

A moment later, Tess leaned into the bathroom. "Find something?"

"Do you think this is blood?" She pointed at a spot on the bathroom floor.

Tess squatted down and peered at the spot. "It's shaped like the blood droplets in our textbook," she replied. She gestured with her hand and added, "Moving that way. But in his own bathroom, it could be anything."

Kallie nodded in agreement, trying not to feel discouraged.

"Take some pictures of it with your phone." Tess walked to the bathtub, then knelt down again, squinting at the drain. "That looks like blood too."

"I wish we had one of those crime scene lights."

"I think you can buy them online. We definitely need to get one," Tess agreed.

"It might just be rust." Kallie wished she could poke it with Tess's pen, to see if it flaked like rust.

"Sure, and even if it's blood, it could just be a shaving injury or something," Tess agreed. "Especially in the bathtub."

Kallie nodded and took more pictures.

"Want to ask the Ouija board if it's blood?" Kallie asked with a smirk.

"The police are a little more reliable than a Ouija board."

"But not usually faster," Kallie added.

"Definitely not faster. But way less creepy."

"Oh, sorry!" a woman's high-pitched voice interrupted them from the doorway, startling them both. "I didn't realize the bathroom was *ocupado*."

"Oh, we're done," Kallie quickly replied. "My friend wasn't feeling well, but she's better now."

Tess, who was still hunched over the bathtub, played along. She stood up slowly, pretending to be recovering. "I was feeling a little sick, but I'm fine now. We'll get out of your way."

The intruder seemed a little tipsy, and Kallie didn't think she appeared suspicious. "Sorry, it's all yours."

"Tell Danny I'll be back out in a second, okay?" she called out as they were leaving.

"Sure, we'll let him know," Tess replied, sweetly.

Instead, though, they skipped the party completely and made their way back to the car.

That was too close for comfort. What if it'd been Danny who caught us, instead of that girl? We need to be more careful.

Tess started the car and asked, "Do you want to stop for takeout?"

"Sure, let's get tacos. I haven't eaten since this morning."

"Me neither, and I'm sure that guy didn't have anything good."

"Right?" Tess agreed, making a disgusted face. "What's the point of doing all that exercise if you're just going to eat healthy?"

***

"Do we have to tell Cornwallis about that?" Kallie asked, when they met at her house the next morning.

"You don't want to tell him?" Tess asked. "I thought we did pretty well, all things considered."

"Except for the part where I sent us on a wild

goose chase. . ."

Tess shrugged, sympathetically. "Well, we're not billing our hours, so I guess we don't—"

Kallie's phone rang, and she picked it up to see who was calling. "How does he do that?" she asked. "He always calls right when we're talking about him."

Tess shook her head. "I'm used to it, by now."

"Hi Cornwallis," Kallie greeted him. "What's up?"

"I've got a request for you," he began, without introduction. "Remember how Badger told me he saw Oscar at the flea market?"

"Of course," Tess responded with a laugh. "Badger has the luck of the devil, I swear."

Ugh, don't say that. He's so creepy.

"I went down there to ask around, and I found someone who saw him."

"That's amazing!" Kallie replied. "And they remembered him after all this time?"

"She said she recognized him when she saw the news stories about the murder," he explained. "And even better than that, she was taking pictures of the items in her kiosk, for her Instagram account, and she happened to catch a photo of him."

"Shut up!" Tess gasped. "That's got to be an almost impossible coincidence!"

"Not as impossible as you'd think, Cornwallis

groaned. "She took almost a thousand pictures that day. Every item, every angle. Probably every person who even glanced at them. And she made me stand there while she looked through every single photo."

Kallie muted the phone and laughed quietly.

"It's worse than those people who take fifty pictures of their food," he added. "She said 'Oh he looks familiar,' but I didn't realize she was going to spend half an hour looking for him."

"But she *found* the picture?" Tess asked, shepherding him gently back to the subject.

"Yes, it's definitely Oscar. He's in the background, and he's in a crowd, but I'm pretty sure he's with the two guys next to him. It looks like they're talking."

"Send it over," Tess responded.

"I want to warn you, it's not very good," he added. "It's grainy from being blown up."

"I'll clean it up and see if I can dig up anything on the guys around him. Maybe I can find something with a reverse image search." She didn't sound hopeful, but Kallie knew Tess had nerdy superpowers.

A few moments later, her phone buzzed, and Tess told him, "Okay, I've got the picture you sent."

"Great. Call me back if you find anything."

"Okay, I'll—"

Kallie looked up after an unexpected silence and

heard Cornwallis ask, "Tess? You still there?"

Tess was staring at her phone, eyes wide. She turned to Kallie and pointed at the screen.

Kallie jumped off the couch, startled by Tess's apparent shock, and ran to her side. Taking her best friend's hand, she turned the phone toward herself so she could see the screen. A moment later, she pulled it closer for a better look, and scowled.

"Tess?" Cornwallis asked again.

"We don't need to do any research," Tess mumbled.

"What? I know it's grainy and blurry, but can't you do *something* with it?"

Finally, Kallie spoke up. "We don't need to research the guys in the picture with Oscar Lawson, Cornwallis. That's my brother."

Chapter Fourteen

"Is that Jack's dealer in the photo, Kallie?" Tess asked after they'd hung up. "Does this mean Oscar really was back on drugs? Is that why he was murdered?"

Kallie shook her head and squinted more closely at the picture. "No, that's not Jason. I don't know who this other guy is, but it's not his dealer. At least not the one I've met."

"Are we going to ask Jack about it?"

"That's exactly what I'm going to do," Kallie replied, picking up her keys as her anger at Jack slowly increased. "And if he lies to me, I really will kill him."

"I'll come with you," Tess replied, standing up.

Kallie shook her head. "No, I want to take the first crack at him alone. He'll be too embarrassed to answer if you're there. I'll talk to you when I get back."

Five minutes later, Kallie was gripping the steering wheel tightly, as she drove across Owhiro to Jack's house. When she'd taken over the mortgage of her parents' house after their divorce, her mother had bought a new house for Jack – her golden child.

It wasn't as nice, and he didn't maintain it well, but why would he? He hadn't worked for it.

Parking in the street, she approached the front door, planning to knock, and then changed her mind. She walked in boldly, slamming the door behind her, startling Jack on the couch.

"Kallie! What are you doing here?"

She marched right up to him, holding her phone out. "What's this, Jack?" She shoved Cornwallis's picture in his face. "Do you know who these people are?"

Pushing her phone back, so he could see the picture, he shook his head. He grabbed the phone and looked closer. "Not that it's any of your business, but I don't even know their names. I only met this guy twice," he said, pointing at Oscar Lawson.

"And the other guy, Jack? Who's he?"

"Some friend of Jason's. I told you, I don't know his name."

"Did he kill Oscar?" she snapped. "Is he the one who did it?"

"What? Who's *Oscar*?" Jack asked, leaning back and looking at her like she was crazy. "What are you *talking* about?"

Slow down, Kalliope. You know Jack won't admit to anything willingly. You need to convince him that it's in his best interest to tell you everything.

"This guy's *dead*, Jack," she informed him. "Which you'd know if you'd spend more time in the real world, and less with your junkie friends."

"I don't know anything about that," Jack replied, suddenly cool as ice. "Like I said, I don't even know their names, but they knew each other. And none of *my* friends were involved in any *murder*."

Kallie took a deep breath, knowing she needed to hear this, but simultaneously wanting to strangle her stupid brother.

"Don't lie to me, Jack. I can always tell when you're lying."

"I'm not—"

"This isn't like when you'd steal the change out of Mom's purse, Jack. This is a real crime." She pointed at the photo irritably. "This picture proves you were with them right before he was murdered. So if *this guy's* the killer, then the cops can arrest *you* for aiding and abetting." She leaned toward him and snarled, "And I know you don't like *jail*."

Jack looked seriously alarmed for just a second, and then seemed to brush it off. He took one deep breath and calmly replied, "I'm tired of this conversa—"

"Mom said she's not bailing you out of jail anymore, Jack," Kallie stated bluntly.

"Pfft," he waved his hand contemptuously. "She does whatever I ask, Kal. You're just jealous."

"Not *anymore*, Jack. She told me that your last arrest cost her ten thousand dollars, because you left town."

"She has plenty of money."

"She couldn't go on her vacation to Mykonos with her new boyfriend, Jack."

"So?"

"You think you're her favorite, but Mom's *real* favorite is Mom." Kallie tsk'ed at him, mockingly. "You start interfering with her hunt for husband number. . . What is this, six?"

"I think so," he muttered.

"Interfere with her hunt, and she'll let you rot in jail. If you make her pick between you and her trip to Ibiza this summer, you're going to lose, *mon frère*."

"You're nuts, Kal."

But he didn't sound so sure anymore.

"Okay, but make sure you get arrested in Tampa. You've got too many enemies in the Pinellas County jail." She gave him a stern look. "And you *really* don't want to get arrested in Polk County."

"That's for sure," he whispered nervously, running a hand through his hair. "Their sheriff's hardcore."

"Look, I've done all I can do to protect you, which is more than you deserve. Either you tell me what you know about this other guy in the picture, or I'll tell the cops you're an accomplice. I'm not letting anyone else die because of you."

"Forget it," he answered, faking his bravado. "You can't prove anything."

Kallie glared at him, hating everything about him—even more than normal.

Jack stood up abruptly and walked toward the door, waving back at her sarcastically. "Bye, sis. Good luck chasing after ghosts." He opened the door theatrically, waiting for her to leave.

But his hand was shaking on the doorknob, and she knew she had him on the ropes. There was just one more tiny step to get him talking.

Kallie sighed.

Crap, now I have to call Mom.

***

Steeling her nerves, Kallie took a few deep breaths and then picked up the phone and dialed. Two rings and a click.

"Kalliope Lynn, dear. This is a surprise."

No hello. No good morning. What is wrong with this woman?

Stay strong, Kalliope. Jack knows something, and you're the only one who can get it out of him.

"You know, your brother calls me every Sunday afternoon, and sometimes on Wednesdays, too," her mother oozed. "You should try to be more like him."

Kallie closed her eyes and leaned her head back, silently.

A manipulative, useless drug addict with narcissistic pathologies. Let me get right on that, Mom.

Do it for Oscar Lawson, Kalliope.

Or do it to make your mother squirm. That works too.

"Hi, Mom," she chirped, knowing she hated to be called Mom.

"Don't call me M—"

Kallie cheerfully chattered over her insistence, "I just wanted to let you know that Jack's about to be arrested again. I'm not sure if they'll even give him bail, since he disappeared last time, but I thought you should know. Since you're the only person who can afford to spring him."

"What was that, Kalliope Lynn?" Her mother was obviously multitasking, probably plastering on a face full of makeup for her latest boyfriend.

"I said, you're going to need to bail Jack out of jail again," she repeated, louder. "Probably tomorrow."

That's a slight exaggeration, but I need to get her onboard fast.

"Oh, no, dear. He promised me he wouldn't be caught with those drugs again." She sighed condescendingly, as if Kallie were foolish to even think it. "You must be mistaken."

"It's not the drugs this time, Mother." She forced herself to be polite, so she didn't antagonize her —much as she wanted to. She needed to make sure she was heard. "He's going to be arrested as a conspirator in a murder case, this time."

"Murder?" her mother snorted. "That's very unlikely, Kalliope Lynn."

"I just wanted to let you know, because I remembered you were planning that trip to Ibiza with Enrique—"

"Felipe, dear," her mother interjected.

"Sure, Felipe," Kallie rolled her eyes. *Who can keep track?* "I didn't want you to have to cancel your vacation again."

"Oh, my *vacation*?" Her mother repeated, sounding less sure. "Well, I really don't think—"

There we go. Got her.

Kallie took a tip from Morrison and stayed silent, letting her mother's mind stew.

"Well, I'm not cancelling my trip again this year," she snapped, suddenly. "If Jack thinks he can just—" She paused, and Kallie could sense her growing disappointment and anger.

Kallie smirked, satisfied and feeling just a smidge of spite.

"Thank you for calling, dear. I need to go now. I need to talk to Jack—"

"Okay, Mom. Talk to you later."

This time, she didn't even snap about being called Mom. Kallie could practically see the gears turning in her plan.

By this time tomorrow, he'll be begging to tell us all the details about Jason's mysterious friend.

***

"Hey Tess," Kallie greeted her friend on the phone next, after she hung up with her mother.

"Hi Kallie," Tess replied. "I was just about to call you. How'd it go with Jack?"

"Almost exactly like you'd expect. He denied everything—"

"No surprise."

"—And then I called my mother, and she's denying it all too," Kallie continued.

"Not much of a shock there, either," Tess replied. "We need some *real proof* that Jack knew Oscar Lawson. I wish Mrs. Jackson could tell us more about who she saw that day."

"I was wondering the same thing," Kallie agreed. "But I don't think she saw them up close. What if we could ask an even better witness, though?"

"Who, Endicott?" Tess anticipated her idea. "I'd love to ask him, but isn't he still in the hospital?"

"Yeah, but Cornwallis said he's doing a lot better. They gave him a blood transfusion and a lot of fluids," Kallie reassured her. "I want to ask Morrison to talk to my mom – but not until we're *sure* Jack's involved."

"Well, Endicott's the only one who might be able to identify him. . ."

"I thought he'd be in the hospital for a long time, but Cornwallis said it's probably only for a few more days. So he should be a lot stronger today."

"Do you think they'd let us see him?" Tess asked, doubtfully.

"It's worth a try. We don't have to stay long."

"And ask him what, though?" Tess wondered aloud. "We're not police sketch artists, and 'a tall blonde guy' isn't exactly a dead giveaway in Florida."

"I thought I'd bring some photos and ask Endicott if he recognizes anyone," Kallie suggested, awkwardly. "Is that a dumb idea?"

Tess considered that, and then laughed. "It's actually a great idea. Like a police lineup, but with pictures, in a hospital room. And it'll be fast, so we won't bother the nurses."

"What time are visiting hours?

Tess checked her phone and replied, "One to three, and then five to eight."

"Okay, let's try to go early. I'll get the pictures ready, and print them out on my dad's old printer."

"Sounds good," Tess agreed. "I'll pick you up a little before one."

Kallie hung up and immediately mumbled to herself, "Now where am I going to get a picture of *Jack*?"

Pulling out her last high school yearbook, she flipped to his page to see if that would work – and laughed so loud that Sherman came to check on her.

"I'm sorry, sweetie," she apologized. "He just looks so young and innocent."

Sherman grumbled and walked away, heading for the garage door – probably to politely ask Benny for a snack.

"That's a great idea, Sherm. Maybe dad has a newer picture."

Her father was in his workroom in the garage, and looked up from his jigsaw when she opened the door. "My two favorite people!" he exclaimed. "You're a better person than most people I know, Sherman, so I won't count your feet."

"Sorry to bother you, Dad," Kallie began. "You

don't happen to have a picture of Jack, do you?"

"*Jack?*" he asked, surprised. "I don't think I have a picture from the last ten years or so. Why?"

"Maybe nothing. I'll tell you later."

"Your mother's ex is on social media," he replied. "Enrique, I mean. Not the other one."

Kallie laughed. "I can't believe you remember his name, Dad."

"Why wouldn't I? He's a nice guy, Enrique. Makes a mean Margarita." He considered for a moment. "Not the best taste in women, but I can't exactly blame him for that."

"I'll check his account. Maybe he has a picture of Jack."

"I wouldn't be surprised. He likes Jack."

Kallie shook her head, walking back into the kitchen. "You never cease to amaze me, Dad."

It took less than a minute to find Enrique on social media, and as Benny had predicted, there were several photos of Jack. In one, they were smiling, arms around each other like true family.

Huh. Who knew?

Too bad they didn't stay married longer. Jack could obviously use every positive male role model he can get.

Kallie took a screenshot of Jack, and then another of a stranger about the same age. She collected

330

three other photos from different accounts, until she had a small collection of men about the same age.

Perfect for an identification quiz. Now hopefully Endicott will recognize him.

She returned to the kitchen, where Benny was sneaking a piece of cheese to Sherman. "I'm going to pretend I didn't see that," she sighed. "Can I use your printer?"

"Sure, kiddo. I just replaced the ink last week," he replied casually, putting the cheese back into the refrigerator – to Sherman's dismay.

"Don't worry, sweetie. I'm sure he'll find you some bacon as soon as I leave," she promised, scratching Sherman's mismatched black and white ears.

Kallie finished printing the five photos just as Tess arrived to pick her up, and they looked them over in the car.

"These are good," Tess said with approval. "The men aren't too similar, and not too different, either."

"I'm not sure whether to hope he identifies Jack or not," Kallie replied with a frown. "Although, the nurses have to let us in the room, first. I guess I should focus on one step at a time."

"I'm sure they'll let *you* in," Tess answered, folding the printouts and sticking them carefully in her purse. "You did save his life."

"Yeah, I guess. . ." Kallie mumbled.

Why does that embarrass you, Kalliope? Even the nurse said he's alive because of you.

Only because of dumb luck.

Tess was watching her, and looked like she wanted to add something, but – to Kallie's relief – she kept quiet and made the short drive to the hospital.

"Hi, we're here to see Mr. Green, on the third floor," Tess addressed the nurse at the front desk.

"Of course, please just sign in," she replied. "Are you family, or—"

"Oh, you came back!" a voice called from behind the nurse. Kallie looked up from the visitor's log and saw one of Cornwallis's Nightingales waving at her.

"Hi Connie!" Tess greeted her cheerfully.

"Endicott will be so happy to see you. He hasn't had many visitors." She glanced at the log to make sure they'd signed in, and then grabbed two visitor's badges and walked them to the elevator.

"How's he doing?" Kallie asked, fiddling with the badge.

The nurse beamed at her, and clipped the badge onto her collar. "Much better—"

Please don't say 'thanks to you...'

As if reading her mind, Connie continued, "His stitches are healing nicely, and his vitals are much, much better."

The slow elevator stopped at the third floor, and the nurse walked them down the hall. "He should be able to leave soon, in fact."

"Already?" Tess asked.

Kallie and Tess glanced at each other, and Kallie thought she was thinking the same thing – *Does he have anywhere to go?*

"Miss Brooks," Endicott Green exclaimed as they walked through the door. "What a nice surprise."

"We wanted to check on you. Connie says you're doing much better."

The bandages on his left arm were so clean and white against his dark skin, so pristine that she could *almost* forget how many stab wounds were healing under there. How the severed artery had been—

Stop it, Kalliope!

"Connie says I can probably leave tomorrow, and Clementine found me a nice place to stay!"

Oh, thank goodness!

"That's wonderful," Tess cried. "We were worried, but she's obviously a real angel – just like you and Cornwallis told us."

"Did she come to visit you?" Kallie asked.

"She sure did," he answered with a smile. "She brought flowers, too."

Kallie noticed a bouquet of colorful flowers on a nearby table, and also a small suitcase.

"She brought some new clothes, too. And she's arranged for a home care nurse and everything," Connie explained, gesturing toward the suitcase. "And I understand the building has security. . ."

She didn't need to finish that thought – Kallie and Tess both nodded gratefully.

"Would it be okay if we show you some photographs, Mr. Green?" Kallie asked.

"Please call me Endicott," he requested. "But I didn't see the man who attacked me. I saw his clothes, he was wearing a dark hoodie – but I didn't get a look at his face at all."

"Oh, this is someone else," Kallie explained. "The police will handle catching your attacker. And I know they *will* catch him, Endicott," she reassured him.

"What are the pictures for, then?" he asked.

"I just want to see if you recognize anyone."

She glanced at Connie, who replied, "As long as it's just a few. And as long as it doesn't cause any stress."

Tess took the printed photos out of her purse and handed them to Kallie, who carefully flattened them out. She passed them to Endicott without another word.

"I'll be happy to look at them, if you think it'll help." He took the pictures and looked through them slowly, pausing for a good look at each one. His grey eyebrows furrowed twice, but he continued silently.

When he'd finished, he held up one photo. "I've met this young man."

Kallie was dismayed but not surprised. It was the photo of Jack.

"You met him?" Tess asked.

"I was in Owhiro a few weeks ago – maybe a month ago, now – and ran into an old friend. I stopped to say hello to him, and this young man was with him," he pointed at the photo. "Another fellow about the same age, too."

"Oscar Lawson," Kallie replied quietly.

Endicott looked surprised. "Yes, Oscar."

"You're sure this was the man who was with him?" Tess asked.

"Oh, sure. Oscar and I chatted for about ten minutes, so I got a good look at him." Endicott glanced at the photo again, and nodded. "Seemed nice enough. Polite, didn't rush us."

Kallie sighed and closed her eyes.

"Young men these days aren't always very polite, especially to their elders," he mused. "I don't recognize the others." He reached out to hand the photos back.

After considering for a moment, Kallie took out her phone and pulled up the other photo, from the flea market. "I know this photo's really blurry, but is this the other guy who was there?"

Endicott squinted at the other photo for a minute, but shook his head. "I can't tell – it's too blurry. I don't think so."

"Oscar didn't tell you why he was with those men, did he?" Tess asked.

"No, and I didn't ask. Are they in trouble?"

"I hope not," Kallie mumbled. "We're not sure yet. But thank you so much for checking."

Endicott chuckled. "Well, that's the least I can do. Thank you again, for everything."

Kallie blushed, but Tess chimed in, "It's her pleasure. Believe me." She grabbed Kallie by both shoulders and added, "And she's so glad you're okay."

Connie and Endicott both smiled at her antics, but Kallie replied, quietly, "That's true. What she said."

"And now I have to chase you away, ladies." Connie opened the door just as another nurse was coming around the corner with the medication cart.

They said their goodbyes, a bit tearfully, and then made their way back down to Tess's car.

"Well, that's that," Kallie groaned. "No more wondering if Jack met Oscar at the pier in Owhiro. And that means it wasn't a coincidence that they were standing together outside the flea market."

"Jack's in this up to his eyeballs, Kal," Tess replied, pragmatically.

"And that means I need to drag Morrison into

this mess."

Tess laughed. "Well, he was going to have to meet them *eventually*. . ."

***

"I told you about my brother, right?" Kallie asked Morrison, a short time later.

"Only briefly," Morrison answered. "I got the idea that he's not your favorite subject."

"He's a narcissistic, juvenile twerp with addiction issues," Kallie rounded it up succinctly.

"He sounds lovely. Did he come back into your life or something?"

She sent him the photo in a text message. "I think he accidentally got tangled up in the case we're investigating for Cornwallis."

"*Accidentally*, huh? I don't mean to sound rude, but why do you care?" Morrison asked. "It doesn't sound like you like him very much."

"I don't. But if it's related to this case, he might be mixed up in the murder itself."

"You think he has information on the case?"

"I'd love to give Cornwallis the chance to find out. I don't think Jack will tell me the details, but if we can get Cornwallis and his lawyer involved – convince him that he's protected – he might talk."

"And you want me to help?"

"Not with the case. Just with my mom," Kallie clarified quickly. "I'm pretty sure Jack didn't see the murder, but he could tell us about that other guy in the picture."

"Why, Kallie! Are you asking me to meet your mother?" he teased. "This is so *romantic!*"

Kallie laughed out loud. "Morrison, if we could live the rest of our lives *without* you ever meeting her, it would be a dream fulfilled. But believe me when I say, she's going to *love* you."

"I have to interview someone in Palm Harbor later. I'll pick you up on the way back," he replied. "I can't wait to meet her."

"Oh, believe me, you can," she replied, sighing. "I apologize in advance. And thanks, Morrison."

***

"Oh, Detective! I didn't know you were a friend of Kalliope's!"

Morrison looked at Kallie, who gave what she hoped was an imperceptible shake of the head.

No way. She doesn't need to know.

Do not engage!

He read her like a book, turning to Kallie's mother and replying, "We spoke after another murder, here in town. It was a few years ago. But she was very helpful to the department, Mrs. Waters."

Kallie felt her whole body relax a little as she exhaled.

She tries to micromanage my whole life—when she can be bothered to show up at all. The last thing I need her doing is micromanaging a relationship with the first great guy I've ever dated.

"Oh, please call me Cassie, Detective. And I'm sure Kalliope didn't do anything the department couldn't have done without her," her mother replied, with a dismissive flip of her hand in Kallie's direction.

Morrison blinked in surprise, and frowned just slightly – but didn't argue.

"I'm sorry to bother you during dinner, Cassie, but I wanted to ask you both about Kallie's brother."

"Oh, you didn't interrupt," Kallie's mother explained. "Kalliope's cooking doesn't—"

"Jack Brooks has been on our radar for a while, ma'am," Morrison interjected, clearly annoyed at Kallie's mother as she began to insult her cooking. "His rap sheet in Pinellas and Hillsborough counties is a mile long, mostly for drugs and associated offenses." Kallie's mother went pale, and she opened her mouth to argue as Kallie smirked silently.

I guess he really was listening all those times I

complained about Jack. And my mother's tendency to make him the golden child.

"It seems unusual that he would escalate so quickly to this felony," he spoke over her objection. "But if his known associates were involved, we could be looking at aiding and abetting manslaughter, at best." He looked at her mother seriously, and finished, "And murder one, at worst."

"Murder one?" her mother whispered. She reached blindly behind her for the chair and collapsed awkwardly into it.

I warned you about Jack messing up your vacation, Mom, and you wouldn't listen. This could cost you a lot more than a missed trip to Ibiza.

Kallie thought her mother would start crying, but her schmooze instinct kicked in first. "Detective," she cooed. "I'm sure we can work this out. My son is a good boy."

Kallie raised an eyebrow.

"It's possible, Mrs. Waters. Why don't you fill me in on your side of the story?"

"Jack went to all of the best schools, Detective. He had the best teachers money could buy, got good grades–"

Kallie struggled to keep silent. *What a boldfaced lie!*

"But he's been busted with drugs multiple times,

and he socializes with a bad crowd," Morrison replied gently. "And now it looks like he was involved somehow with the Celebration of Sandcastles murder."

Kallie's mother shook her head in denial, adding obstinately, "That's simply not possible."

"We'd love to prove that, Mrs. Waters. Maybe you can help us," Morrison appealed to her. "Can you give us any background on his circle of friends, if they're involved in any crime?"

"Oh, I don't know anything about that!" she replied, sounding appalled.

Kallie rolled her eyes. *Jack and I barely speak, and even I know his drug dealer's name. She probably has his number on speed dial.*

"Mom, he can't help us if you don't tell him the truth!" she finally blurted out.

"Don't call me M—"

She at least had the self-awareness to leave the demand unfinished this time.

"Detective," she cooed again, returning to her schmooziness. "My dear Jack might've had some substance issues when he was younger, but I'm quite sure his current friends are all above reproach. He said they talk about sports and get together to play cards once a week. Nothing dangerous."

Kallie sighed and shook her head, giving up.

"I'd be happy to give you their names and

numbers, if you'd like to contact them."

Kallie looked up, startled. *Is she really willing to risk what they might say about her golden boy? Could she really be that naive?*

I mean, I warned Jack that she might give him up, but I was bluffing!

"That would be very helpful, Mrs. Waters."

Kallie's mother took out her phone and opened the contact list, pointing out the names and numbers of Jack's friends. Morrison wrote them down and thanked her again.

"I'll check their backgrounds and see if anything pops. Thank you for your help, Mrs. Waters."

"You don't really think he's a murderer, do you, Detective?" Kallie thought her mother sounded genuinely worried, for the first time.

Could she really be afraid for Jack?

"I'd be so embarrassed if my only son turned out to be a killer," she whined. "I think they might even kick me out of the country club."

Okay, that's more like it.

Morrison looked back at Kallie for a moment, and she quirked up one corner of her mouth in a tiny smile.

I told you.

"I'm sure there are country clubs that don't check criminal backgrounds, Mrs. Waters," Morrison replied, straight-faced. He closed his notebook and thanked her once again.

"If that's all, I'll walk you to your car, Detective," Kallie suggested.

"Thank you, Miss Brooks."

They stepped out onto the front steps and Morrison whispered, "Wow, you weren't kidding."

Kallie laughed, embarrassed, and walked him down the stairs to his unmarked car. "I always thought Jack was the most important thing in the world to her. It's refreshing to see that she really only cares about herself, after all.

"Well, you turned out okay, Brooks."

"Thanks."

"And I can't wait to talk to your dad tonight," Morrison added with a laugh, as he opened the passenger door for her. "I have *so many* questions for him."

***

Kallie updated Tess on all of the details about Jack, as she'd promised. They sat down to study their textbook again, but Kallie noticed that Tess was staring at her phone.

"What's up, Tess?"

"What? Oh, I'm just. . . I swear I recognize this guy."

"What guy?" Kallie crouched behind her and looked at the picture on her phone. "Oh, the guy with Oscar and Jack?"

"Yeah," Tess mumbled, squinting at the photo. "I blew up Wally's picture and used the computer to clean it up a little. I thought we might get a better look at him, and now. . ."

"I've never seen him before, Tess. You think you know him?"

"I don't *know* him. . . I just think I've seen him before. I recognize those eyes." Tess slumped in her chair. "It's been driving me crazy since this morning."

"I'm sorry, I can't help. He doesn't look familiar to me, but I'm sure you'll figure it out. Probably when you least expect it."

"I guess," Tess mumbled, setting the phone down on the table with a thump. "Are you okay with this stuff about Jack?"

"Eh," Kallie waved her hand scornfully. "Jack and my mom are on their own. You should've heard Morrison rant about them on the way home. And I'm sure he's getting the whole gruesome story from my dad right now."

"They are a pair," Tess laughed.

"Oh, and Morrison told me he's setting up some

uniformed officers at Rooftopz, trying to get the owner to break, and give the police more information. So hopefully we'll be able to—"

"That's it!" Tess yelped suddenly, grabbing her phone.

Kallie jumped at the shout. "What's it? What's *what*?"

"That's where I've seen this guy. The guy with Oscar and your brother." She pointed at her phone. "He was at Rooftopz!"

"Oh, I never even saw the guy that night. Are you sure?"

"Yeah, because I actually thought, 'he's kinda cute,' and then he looked toward us and I saw those eyes." She shook her head and gave a little shiver. "So creepy."

Kallie took the phone and looked closer at the picture. "Yikes, he does have creepy eyes. He looks like he's about to rip someone's heart out and eat it."

"Right?" Tess agreed. "He doesn't even look mad. He just looks. . ."

"Scary," Kallie agreed. "Can I see the pictures you took at Rooftopz?"

Tess scrolled to the photos that she'd taken, and frowned. "You can't really tell it's him here. I think he dyed his hair or something."

Comparing the two photos, Kallie agreed. "They

definitely don't look alike. But I can see what you mean about his eyes."

She thought for a moment and then sighed. "Well, if you're right, then we finally have a verified link between Donovan, Jack, and Oscar. Even if we don't know exactly what it is. . ."

"I'm sorry, Kal. I know you didn't want Jack to be involved in this, even though he's a jerk."

"Yeah. But his dirty little fingerprints are all over it." She shook her head. "I'm disappointed but not surprised."

"Me neither."

"Well, let's go talk to him," Kallie stated, looking exhausted. "I never thought I'd intentionally go to Jack's house, much less go there twice. But I guess it's time we get the whole story. Before he gets himself killed."

***

Kallie didn't hesitate before walking right into Jack's house this time. But someone else was on the couch – a skinny young woman with dishwater blonde hair, who looked hungover.

"Who are you?" Kallie asked, not really interested. "Where's Jack?"

"Sorry to burst your bubble, Miss Nosey Nellie,"

the blonde sneered, "But Jack's not here."

Miss Nosey Nellie?

"Besides, he's *my man* now. You can just take yourselves outta here."

"Look, *Sally*," Tess began, rolling her eyes, "We're not here to steal your man." Her eyes said *'Trust Me!'* Kallie noticed, trying not to smirk. "We just need to ask him a few questions."

"I told you, he's not here."

"His car's outside. Are you trying to tell me he *walked* somewhere?" Kallie asked, voice dripping with sarcasm.

"Uh. . ."

Right, Jack's never walked anywhere since he was old enough for a Learner's Permit. He'd need to have four flat tires – and probably a gas tank on fire – before he'd walk anywhere.

And our girl Sally knows it too.

"Fine. He's here," she finally conceded. "But he's sleepin' and you're not wakin' him up."

Kallie shoved past the blonde without a further word and stomped back to the rear of the house. "Cassidy Jack Brooks, you get your butt out here, right now!" she yelled, and then banged on the door loudly.

She heard Tess and the blonde both mumble, "Cassidy?"

"If you don't open this door, I'm coming in!"

The door opened quickly, and Jack stumbled out, disheveled and unshaven, in boxers and a faded old Nickelback T-shirt. "Okay, Mom, I heard you," he mumbled, rubbing his eyes. "What is it?"

Ugh, do I really sound that much like Mom? Eww.

"Kallie," he finally clarified, sounding annoyed. "What are *you* doing here? I thought you were Mom."

Wait, is he allowed to call her Mom?

Not to her face, surely.

"You need to check your phone, Jack." She pushed him back into his bedroom to talk, but then recoiled at the stench of feet and stale beer. Gagging a little, she grabbed him by the T-shirt and pulled him back into the hallway. After she'd caught her breath, she admonished him, "We've all been trying to reach you."

"About what? I don't want to hear your lectures."

"The cops think you killed someone, Jack. Mom gave you up, and they're ready to arrest you."

Still exaggerating a little, but he doesn't need to know that. . .

"Pffft," he waved his hand dismissively. "I didn't kill anybody."

"Maybe not, but your buddy Jason is going to let you take the rap for it."

"Jason?" He scoffed again. "No way, Jason's a

good guy. He's my friend."

"He's your *drug dealer*, Jack." Kallie sneered at him. "You don't have to pay your real friends to hang out with you."

"Whatever, Kallie." He walked back into his bedroom and tried to slam the door, but Kallie blocked it with her foot.

"Jack, you need to go to the police and talk to them. Your buddies have a much worse rap sheet than you realize. They're starting to leave a body count, all around the state." Kallie looked at her estranged brother sincerely. "Seriously, tell the cops what you know, before *you* end up in jail, instead."

Jack scoffed. "They can't put me in jail for something I didn't—"

"Yes, they *can*, Jack. They might not be able to put you in prison, but they can hold you in the county jail if they have probable cause."

"No way, I heard—"

"Jack, I was *there*, remember?" she yelled in frustration.

Like he was even paying attention when I was in jail. I obviously don't have enough money to hold his interest.

"Oh, right," he replied, frowning at the vague memory. "I guess I forgot. . ."

"And while you're in jail, your dealer friend and

his cronies will assume you're spilling your guts to the police about them."

"What? I wouldn't do that, Kallie. I'm a totally loyal—"

"And does skeevy Jason know that?" she interrupted him, growing more annoyed by the moment.

"Of course he does."

"And what about his boss? He's getting those drugs from someone, and I'll bet it's not a super nice guy who wants to be your new best friend."

"He works for some Cuban guy," Jack replied with a dismissive wave of his hand. "I've never even seen him before. Jason says he's pretty nice, though."

"He's not going to be nice when he hears you're in jail, ratting him out to the cops," Kallie warned. "He's got a lot more to lose than Jason does."

"I'm not scared of that guy. Anyway, Jason will explain it all to him."

"Are you sure about that, Jack?"

"Well, no." Jack laughed awkwardly. "I guess not. But I could just text him, and let him know—"

"You can't text from jail, Jack," Kallie groaned.

"Then you could text him for me, and let him know I wouldn't—"

"Are you *kidding* me?" she yelled, more infuriated than she intended. "After the way you've treated me? I'm not calling off your stupid, druggie fr—"

"But we're family, Kal. We're a team!"

Kallie stared at him like a stranger, appalled that he would suddenly claim kinship now. She shook her head, finished. "Whatever, Jack. I give up. Talk to the police and tell them what you know. Maybe it isn't even Jason. You could help find a killer."

Jack didn't answer, so she turned and walked away. Tess put an arm around her waist and opened the front door to leave.

"There's no 'I' in Team, Kal," he called after her.

"I think there's a reward, Jack," she yelled back, without turning.

She heard him ask, "How much reward?" as the door slammed shut behind her.

Chapter Fifteen

"So you're pretty sure Jason's going to be at this party?" Tess asked as they stepped out of the elevator, adjusting her blouse.

"My mom told Morrison that Jack plays cards with his friends every week, and she had this address in her phone," Kallie answered. "Jack doesn't care about impressing anyone but Jason, so he should be here."

Tess took a deep breath and blew it out slowly. "Okay, here goes nothing. How do I look?"

"Gorgeous, as always," Kallie answered with a smile. "He's going to lose his mind when he sees you."

Tess sneered. "Gross, don't you dare leave me alone with him."

"Girl, I would rather stab myself with a fork than leave you alone with that jerk," Kallie replied. "Are you planning to turn on the Russo million-watt charm?"

"I'll try," she sighed. "Why can't I ever flirt with a nice, cute guy, Kal? Maybe with a dimple and good hair?"

"I'll order one up for you, I promise."

Kallie opened the apartment door, and they walked into a cloud of cigarette smoke. A group of men sat around a table, playing cards. None of them looked away from the game, but all of their girlfriends glared at Kallie and Tess.

"Cheerful place," Kallie muttered under her breath.

The players' girlfriends were all holding bottles of beer, so Kallie and Tess walked into the kitchen to find drinks. There was nothing but beer in the refrigerator, so they each took one.

"What do we do now?" Tess asked, quietly.

"I didn't see Jason at the table. I wonder if he's even here." Kallie took out her phone and pressed a few buttons, then set it on the counter.

As she turned back to Tess, a voice behind her oozed, "My boys told me there was some new blood in the game, but I didn't know it was you, Tess."

Kallie spun around toward the voice, gritting her teeth.

How is he so effortlessly annoying?

Be nice, Kalliope.

"Tess, you remember Jack's friend, Jason?" she introduced them, trying to sound charming.

Tess had been adjusting her blouse again, apparently exasperated with it, but her face suddenly brightened up in a cheerful smile. "Hi, Jason!"

As Kallie had predicted, their seedy quarry was immediately fixated on Tess. Jack had mentioned to Kallie in the past that Jason liked Tess, and he wasn't bothering to hide it now.

"Come to play poker? I can teach you."

Tess played along, answering sweetly, "That'd be great, Jason. I've always wanted to learn."

Honestly, he obviously doesn't know anything about Tess if he thinks that's her normal personality. Or voice. Or if he thinks he can beat her at poker.

"We don't usually get girls in the game, because they aren't good enough to keep up with us," he added. "But you're special, Tess."

"Thanks, Jason," Tess cooed. "I think you're pretty special too."

Kallie was trying to maintain the friendly act, but she was getting more irritated with him by the minute.

"You'd better be careful, Jason. She might take all of your money," she grumbled.

Jason seemed to notice Kallie for the first time. "I'm gonna go out on a limb here, and guess you don't know who you're talkin' to," he replied, cockily.

Kallie rolled her eyes. "You're the guy that pretended to be my brother's friend, and got him hooked on drugs."

Careful, Kalliope. Honesty probably isn't your

friend right this minute.

Jason laughed obnoxiously. "I don't sell drugs to my *friends.*"

"I tried to tell him that, but he insists that you two are the best of buddies."

He walked to the refrigerator and took out a beer, giving Kallie a chance to quickly peek at her phone, on the counter. The screen had greyed out, but she could see the numbers flicker.

Still recording. I just hope it can hear us over the noise from the poker table.

"Jack's okay, I guess. He does what I ask him." Jason waved his hand disdainfully. "But he's not my friend." Closing the refrigerator door, he added, "I'd like *her* to be my friend, though."

Kallie looked over at Tess, who was smiling agreeably at the sleazeball.

"I could be a great friend, and get you anything you need, Tess." He gave her a corny wink, obviously convinced that she was enraptured with him.

Jason asked Jack about Tess before, but he obviously didn't remember the 'NO!'

Or he's stupid enough to think he has a chance with her. Either way, good for us.

"But you've gotten into a lot more than just selling, haven't you, Jason?" Tess asked, flirtatiously. "I hear you're an important guy now."

"You bet I'm important," he answered, grinning at Tess like a hyena surveilling a tasty meal.

Important but not very bright, Kallie thought to herself. *If you think a gem like Tess would fall for a lowlife criminal like you. . .*

"See, Kal? I think it's pretty brilliant the way he worked his way up from a salesman to the top ranks," Tess purred to Kallie. "Pretty *fast*, too."

The young thug smiled haughtily and glanced at Kallie. "That's right, I'm brilliant. See, Tess is hotter than you, *and* smarter."

I can't argue with that. But she's a lot smarter than you, too, loser.

And this bonehead can't be smart enough to get away with murder, either, Kallie suddenly realized. *No way he's in the upper echelon.*

"When are you taking over the top spot, Jason?" Tess asked, leaning forward, exposing a little more cleavage than Kallie would've liked. "You're way better than that *Cuban* guy."

"Marco?" Jason replied with a sneer. "I'll be taking over his job, any day now. His boss likes me better anyway. Says I'm more reliable."

Reliable? Easier to manipulate, maybe.

And now we know Jack's Cuban guy is named Marco. Good job, Tess.

But who's Marco's boss?

She heard Morrison's voice in her mind, whispering, *Be careful, Brooks.*

"Yeah, I heard Marco's on the way out," Tess replied scornfully. "My friend said he made the big boss mad. Made some bad sale or something."

"A bad sale?" Jason asked, confused. "Marco's too big to make sales—"

Oops.

"I wasn't really paying attention," Tess laughed, playing off the mistake smoothly. "My friend just talks and talks and talks – he's so boring. And he's not *cute* like you," she added with a tiny lift of her eyebrow.

"You should hear everything Marco's boss says about me," Jason bragged. "He said I'm the best guy on his payroll."

I can't believe he bought that—hook, line, and sinker.

Tess is amazing with people, but I almost never get to see this devious side of her.

She can't ask for the boss's name, though. Not if she's pretending she already heard gossip about him.

"Isn't Marco's boss from Cuba, too, though?" Tess asked. "Those guys usually stick together. You know, after all they went through on the island."

"Nah, he's not Cuban," Jason answered, obviously feeling smart for knowing this detail. "Marco calls him *Búho* because he has a big owl tattooed on his arm, but I don't think he even speaks Spanish. He sounds like he's from Alabama or something."

Great, an owl tattoo. That narrows it down to about a million people in the world.

Although hopefully only a handful in the central Florida crime scene.

"If he's not Cuban, that's lucky for you, baby," she cooed. "That means—"

A door slammed in the next room, and one of the group's bodyguards suddenly appeared in the kitchen, whispering to Jason. He nodded and set down his beer. "I need to go talk to someone, ladies. I'll be right back." He leered at Tess, scanning her figure slimily, and Kallie saw her smile back enticingly.

Ick.

The moment Jason and the bodyguard left the room, Kallie snatched her phone off the counter and checked the screen. Rewinding the recording by a few seconds, she verified that the sound was working.

With a deep breath and a quick nod, they made their way, swiftly but gracefully, back to the elevators.

***

"We have some evidence to show you, but after all that talk about Cubans, we're both hungry," Kallie told Cornwallis, with a laugh, when they were in the car.

"We're in Tampa, near your office. Want to meet us for dinner?"

Cornwallis agreed, and after Tess had a chance to change into jeans, he met them at the restaurant just a few minutes after they were seated.

"Oh, hey." Cornwallis turned back and reached into his jacket pocket as he sat down at the table. "I forgot, I brought you something."

"What, for me?" Tess asked, surprised. She raised an eyebrow and asked, jokingly, "Is it a restraining order?"

Cornwallis smiled wickedly for a second, but then he replied, "No, not this time." He reached out one hand, holding a small cardboard box.

"Too big to be an engagement ring," Kallie whispered jokingly, earning an embarrassed laugh from her best friend.

Cornwallis apparently overheard her, because he blushed awkwardly and mumbled something that sounded like ". . .not someone like me."

Kallie noticed that some of the other diners also overheard her, because suddenly chairs at other tables started squeaking as they turned to see if there was a marriage proposal underway.

"She was just kidding," Cornwallis told them, quickly, but a few kept watching.

Tess took the box and frowned a little. "It's not

my birthday or anything. What's it for?"

"Just open it," he waved impatiently.

Tess carefully opened the two-piece cardboard box, pulling the lid off gently. It seemed old to Kallie, and a little tattered. "Oh, it's. . . a coin?" She held up a metal disc, gingerly. "Is it a necklace?" she asked.

The nosy diners at the other tables let out a collective groan, and Kallie heard one woman say, "Some gift, that thing's downright ugly. No wonder she's not interested in him."

"You said your parents' house in Atlanta was robbed, and your father lost his war medal," Cornwallis explained, leaning forward in his seat.

Tess shook her head, confused. "Yeah, my mom said—"

"The other piece is in there," Cornwallis gestured at the box.

"I don't understand, what's—?" Tess looked closer at the box and Kallie saw her lift up a faded piece of old fabric. "Wait, is this *his medal*?!"

"That's the bronze star that he was awarded," Cornwallis replied simply, blushing.

"Wally, that's so sweet of you!" Tess gushed, genuinely. Kallie could see that there were tears in her eyes. "Did you petition the military to issue a replacement?"

"No. No, that's actually *his* medal. His name is

on the paper folded up at the bottom of the box."

Tess gasped softly, and quickly pulled out the cotton batting and unfolded the yellowed old paper, with slightly shaking hands, Kallie noticed.

"How—? Wally, how did you *do* this?"

"One of my contacts found it in a pawn shop in Boca Raton."

"Thank you so much! My mom's going to freak out when I tell her." Tess flipped the medal over a few times, engrossed in it, and read the paper again. Finally she added, "She'll probably send you a cake, by the way."

"Sounds good," he replied with a laugh. "I work for cake."

"Oh my gosh," she yelped. "Let me pay you back for this! What was I *thinking*?"

"Keep your money," he replied, waving her away. "It's disgraceful how little they charged him for it. I don't even want to tell you."

Tess's eyes teared up even more, and she smiled crookedly at him. "Thank you."

Their waitress arrived and took their order, and Cornwallis took the opportunity to deftly change the subject. "Tell me about your interview. Did you talk to Jason Fisher?"

"Tess worked her feminine wiles on him, and he folded like a pretzel," Kallie updated him, proudly.

"Good job," he replied with a nod. "Any scheme that works is a good scheme. What did he tell you?"

Tess thought for a moment and then counted out their findings on her fingers. "Jason admitted that he was selling drugs, but he's moved up in the ranks lately. His boss, the Cuban guy, is named Marco. And he said Marco's boss has an owl tattoo on his arm, but that's pretty much all we know about him."

"An *owl*?" Cornwallis repeated, sounding surprised. "Was he from Dallas?"

Tess looked dejected, and replied, "We didn't even get his *name*, much less his hometown. Jason said he has a southern accent, though. So I guess he *could* be from Dallas." She perked up suddenly, and added, "But, guess what? Kallie managed to record the whole thing!"

Kallie expected Cornwallis to be excited, but he was frowning at the table, deep in thought.

"It's not a perfect recording, but you can hear him over the background noise," she explained, even though he obviously wasn't listening. She looked at Tess, who also seemed confused.

"What's wrong, Wally?" Tess asked.

"What? Oh, no. No, you both did great." Cornwallis still looked distracted and serious. "I think I know who they are, that's all. I need to talk to your boyfriend, Kallie."

"Morrison?" Kallie asked. "Is it one of his cases?"

"Yes, ma'am. And I think he's going to be pretty impressed with what you two found."

***

"Hello?" Kallie answered her phone the next morning, as she was trying to squeeze in some studying before work.

"Kalliope Lynn! You have to do something! Jack's been arrested, and they won't let me post bail this time!"

Whoa, that escalated fast!

I told you he was going to be arrested, Mom," Kallie sighed. "I tried to warn you."

Her mother didn't even fight about being called Mom, which meant she was really concerned.

"Didn't you try *talking* to him, Kalliope?" her mother snapped accusingly.

"Of course I did! I even went to his house," Kallie retorted, gripping the phone tightly in her fist. "You know he doesn't listen to me."

"Well, do something!" she yelled.

"What do you think *I'm* going to do?" Kallie countered. "Setting bond is the judge's decision."

"Go down to the jail and get that Detective friend of yours to release him."

"What?!" Her mother had always been a nightmare, but she'd never tried anything this weaselly before. "How *dare* you even ask for something like that!?"

"He's your broth—"

"Jack is a criminal, Mother. It's time you accepted that. I'm not going to ask a detective to interfere when Jack committed an actual crime!"

"Jack's not a bad—"

But Kallie wasn't having it. "I thought *you* might try to get him straightened out, if you thought your precious *vacation* would be ruined," she shouted angrily, "but I see you don't even care that much. You just want to schmooze your way out of it, like you always do. Well, it's not going to work this time."

Her mother started to respond, sounding flustered and insulted, but Kallie quietly hung up before she could start arguing.

Honestly, I thought she'd get him to talk to the police. At least to save her vacation.

What was I thinking?

Kallie huffed. *Well, at least now I know she treats Jack as badly as she treats me, occasionally. She didn't even try!*

Kallie stood up and stretched, and then reached for her textbook again, hoping the complicated lessons would scrub that conversation out of her mind.

She sat back down and opened the book, calling Sherman up to sit with her, but she was left frowning at the book instead.

Am I seriously feeling sorry for Jack right now? The world's second-most annoying, self-absorbed jerk?

Sherman must've noticed her tension, because he looked up at her face with concern.

"Don't worry, Sherm. I'm not going to do anything stupid. Or expensive. Jack can sit in jail overnight. It might teach him a lesson."

Sherman tilted his head curiously.

"Fine. I'll call Morrison," she told him. "But not to get Jack out of jail. Just to let him know what's going on." She leaned over and picked up her phone from the side table beside the couch.

Why am I explaining this to Sherman?

Because it's going to be easier than explaining it to Morrison, she answered herself.

The detective picked up his phone on the second ring. "When you call my desk phone, it's never good news," he answered, without a greeting, but Kallie could hear the smile in his voice.

"It's *occasionally* good news," she countered, defensively. "But yeah, not this time."

"What's wrong?"

"Owhiro PD arrested Jack a few hours ago."

Morrison paused for a moment, then answered quietly, "I can't interfere with local police business, Kallie."

"Oh, no!" she gasped. "No, I would never ask you to do that!"

He was still silent, so she added, jokingly, "Maybe for Tess, but never for Jack."

Morrison finally laughed. "Well, if Tess ever got arrested, I'd know it's because she was protecting *you*, so—"

"I just want to know the details. Can you find out if he was just arrested for buying drugs, or if it's related to the murder?"

"That'll be public record after he's arraigned," he replied. "It should be up on the website by morning."

"Uh, could you find out before morning?" she asked, awkwardly.

Morrison sat quietly for a minute, but Kallie was just glad he hadn't hung up. "I can call a friend on the Narcotics desk at the station and see what I can find out. He'll only be able to tell me if it's drug-related or not. Nothing else."

"That's enough!" Kallie exclaimed. "Thank you so much. I owe you!"

"You can pay me back by staying out of trouble, for once."

Kallie laughed. "Do you think that's likely to

happen?"

Morrison sighed, "No, but a guy can dream. Seriously, if your brother's gotten himself mixed up in a murder, he might be safer in jail. But the bad guys might come looking for *you* instead."

"Well, they'll probably do that even if I stay out of it. At least this way I'll be informed. And I can let Cornwallis know, too."

"Okay, give me half an hour to finish up what I'm doing, and I'll reach out to my friend. I'll call you back."

Kallie knew she wouldn't be able to study, so she started getting ready for work – even though it was early. She took a shower and washed her hair, including a deep conditioner to kill time. After drying her hair and moisturizing her skin, she finally pulled out mascara, just to keep herself busy.

When the phone finally rang, she snatched it off the bathroom counter like a striking viper.

"Hello?"

Why are you so worried, Kalliope? It's only Jack.

"Hey Brooks. There's a lot going on. . ." Morrison began.

"Good or bad?" she asked, unsure if she wanted to know.

"Uh, mostly bad." He quickly reworded, "A little

of both. It might help your case, actually."

"Really?"

"I called my friend in Narcotics, and he said Jack wasn't arrested for drugs," Morrison began.

"That's bad," Kallie concluded.

"Theoretically, that could mean anything. With his record, he could've been picked up for jaywalking."

"But—?"

"But I also got a call from Investigator Cornwallis. He said you mentioned another guy, related to Jack's dealer?"

"It's kind of a long story," Kallie explained. "Jack didn't mention him. We talked to his dealer last night, and *he* mentioned the boss – some guy with an owl tattoo. And another guy named Marco."

Morrison sighed, but didn't respond.

"Cornwallis said you might know who they were—?" she suggested, hesitantly.

"I'm familiar with them," he replied, and Kallie could tell he was choosing his words carefully. "After I talked to Cornwallis, I took another look at that photo you sent. The one of Jack and Oscar Lawson—"

"And—?" Kallie's heart was racing now.

"I wouldn't have recognized him, but I think the other guy in that photo is Marco."

Kallie groaned. "Jack was hanging out with

some drug lord's right-hand man *and* the murder victim? What was he *thinking?!*"

"I need to get forensics to verify that it's him. The photo's so grainy, and his hair is the wrong color, so I can't be sure. And I've never seen him dress that. . . suburban."

Hang on, Kalliope. Tess said that guy was—

"Wait! Morrison, Tess said that's the guy from Rooftopz. The guy in the suite!"

"What, now?" he asked, confused.

"I never saw his face, but Tess thinks that's the same guy we were watching at the restaurant," Kallie explained. "She said his eyes freaked her out."

"If that's Marco Acosta in the picture with Oscar Lawson, just before Oscar ended up dead. . ."

"That's bad," Kallie repeated, quietly.

Morrison paused and she heard him take a deep breath. "I can't say anything else right now, Brooks. This is getting close to classified information on other cases."

"Okay," Kallie replied. "What should I—?"

"Don't do anything yet." His voice was strained, "Let me follow up here, and I'll let you know. . . Well, I'll tell you what I can."

"Okay," Kallie repeated, her mind racing. "I have to go to work."

"Great, that'll keep you out of trouble for a few

hours," Morrison quipped, but his voice cracked a little. He still sounded worried, and Kallie was pretty sure he was trying to keep her calm. "I'll talk to you later."

***

"I know this is going to be a hard pill to swallow, Mrs. Waters," Morrison said, sitting across from Kallie's mother that evening, "But we need to consider that Jack might really be involved in this murder."

"What?!" Kallie's mother gasped. "You said you were just checking out his friends!"

"That was before we found evidence that he's connected to both the murder victim and the other suspects behind the crime. Jack has texts on his phone from the primary suspect, and a second attempted murder victim picked his photo out of a lineup."

"That doesn't mean–"

"It's too much evidence for us to ignore him, even if each piece is mostly circumstantial."

"Look," Cassie replied, suddenly dropping her sweet and innocent act, "Jack's a drug addict. That's the only reason he's friends with Jason. He's not some kind of *accomplice*–"

"You told us that was in his *past*, Mrs. Waters," Morrison replied, starting to lose his patience. "Why would Jason Fisher have texted him *last week*?"

"Jack never stopped using drugs, but it's only prescription medications. You don't kill someone for prescription drugs, Detective," she insisted, pleading with Morrison. Kallie could tell that her mother was trying to sound logical and cool, but her nerves were fraying rapidly.

You didn't like having an addict in the family, so you ignored it.

Now maybe you have a killer, instead.

And you have to consider that your own brother might've committed the murder you're investigating, Kalliope.

"I don't have a subpoena, so you don't have to talk to me, Mrs. Waters," Morrison explained. "But I wanted to give you the opportunity to tell the police anything that might help Jack. If he's not involved with the murder, he doesn't need to go down with Jason and his colleagues."

Kallie looked at her mother, wishing she could force her to talk. Wishing she'd be sensible, for once.

We don't really think Jack's a killer, do we, Mother?

Her mother turned away, putting on a show of dismissiveness, but her eyes were red with worry.

Fine, I guess we're going to find out the hard way.

Kallie and Morrison left the house silently, and

neither looked back at Cassie. Kallie's head was spinning.

Once they were safely in the car and pulling out of the driveway, Kallie asked, "You don't really think it was Jack, do you?"

"I doubt he's the killer," Morrison replied, "Although I haven't ruled it out." He looked over at her with a compassionate expression and added, "But Kallie, I *do* think he's involved somehow."

"With murder?"

"You told me that he considered Jason a friend. People do stupid things for their friends—especially their manipulative, sociopathic friends."

"I'd do anything for Tess," she whispered.

"Tess wouldn't ask you to kill anyone, Brooks," he stated, sternly. "And you're not a drug addict."

"Is Jack's situation really that bad? I thought it was just, you know, Adderall. 'Kiddie speed.' Like my mother said."

"Maybe it was, once, but not anymore. I've seen his arrest record."

"His arrest rec—"

"I know it seemed like a family joke, but he was in a lot more trouble than I think you realized. And a lot more debt."

"Oh."

"Yeah. And he might not seem like the kind of

guy who would bend over backward for a friend—"

"Try 'not at all,'" she mumbled.

"But being in debt to a drug dealer—"

"Could get him into a lot of trouble," she finished his thought out loud.

Morrison nodded.

"I wish I could say 'I'm sure he knows better.'"

"He probably *does* know better," Morrison acknowledged. "His *father's* a very sensible guy."

"Oh, no," Kallie groaned. "Poor Dad."

"I'll talk to him, but I doubt your father will be surprised."

"So it's just Mom and me who have our heads in the sand, huh?" she chuckled, self-consciously.

"Not you, Brooks. You're surprised by the magnitude, but you knew he was in trouble. Your mom, though? Definitely neck deep in the sand."

"Does my dad need any kind of protection, Morrison? Do you think those guys will come after him?"

"I'm not worried about Benny. He and Jack aren't close. And frankly, it sounds like Jack's always done exactly what they want. They don't have any reason for retribution, at this point." Morrison continued, "I'll ask him if he wants a guard, though."

"Oh, good."

"Now, *you*, on the other hand—"

"What? *Me?*"

"You're investigating them, and you're not exactly subtle—"

"Why does everyone keep saying that?" Kallie sniffed, sulking. "I'm *totally* subtle."

Morrison smirked, but dropped the subject. "And, presuming they've noticed you, Jack has probably already told them that you're his sister."

"Oh, great," Kallie frowned. "Yeah, he probably thinks he can get the creepy boss guy to marry me, and then he'll get free drugs on the Brother-In-Law Plan."

Morrison chuckled.

"I wish I was kidding," Kallie snarled.

"I know you're not going to like this," Morrison said, "But I need you and Tess to back off on Jason Fisher."

"*What?* No." Kallie glared at him in shock. "No way."

"Listen, Brooks," Morrison explained gently, "I can't tell you very much. But we're following Jason for his involvement in a big drug-running case out of Honduras—"

"What, now? *Honduras?*" Kallie shook her head, confused and annoyed. "He might be working for some scary guys, but that little poser isn't important enough to move drugs from out of the country—"

"No, but he personally took delivery at the dock." Morrison's face was sympathetic but serious. "That makes this an international case. And—"

"Okay, okay," Kallie allowed herself a moment to pout. "You need us to back off. I get it."

"I'll tell Cornwallis myself," he added apologetically. "I'm sorry, Brooks. I know this is an important case for you."

"I think we almost had him, Morrison," she sighed.

"And I'll make sure the sheriff knows how much work you put into this. And how much you *found*," he reassured her. "I promise. And the feds, too, if this helps them catch the leader."

That's a big if, she thought to herself. *Especially if it means letting Oscar's killer get away.*

"But like I said, I don't think Jack or Jason is the actual Celebration of Sandcastles killer. So as long as you stay away from Jason Fisher, you can still keep investigating."

Kallie couldn't blame him, but she still didn't feel like talking for the rest of the drive home.

Chapter Sixteen

Neither of them were the type to hold a grudge though, and soon Kallie was discussing their romantic plans with Tess again.

Tess wanted to replace the shoes that had been ruined in the first freak rainstorm, and they were grabbing lunch in the food court at the mall.

"Morrison and I are going for a hot air balloon ride next weekend. Do you want to come?"

"After as long as it took to make you two chickens into a couple?" Tess scoffed. "No way! Go do your couple stuff."

"I don't want to be one of those girls who ditches my bestie just because I found a man," Kallie added, seriously.

"Well, I didn't tell you to move to Ecuador and become a shepherdess," Tess laughed. "Go do your couple stuff and then come back here and eat ice cream with me, and tell me all the details!"

"That's a plan," Kallie answered with a smile. "Let's make a dinner reservation for that evening."

"That might not work. You never know how long you're going to be gone, with a hot air balloon."

"That's what Morrison said too. Why not?"

"There isn't really any way to steer them. You just go wherever the wind takes you. They have a truck that follows you—chases you, actually—they call it a 'chase vehicle,'" she added with a laugh. "When you land, they load the basket into the truck and you drive home."

"Have you done it?"

"Wally did it with his ex-wife, during their honeymoon. We were just talking about it last week."

"Wait, *what*? He told you about his *honeymoon?!*"

"He said it went just about as well as the whole marriage did. They ended up getting caught in a freak storm, and they were blown almost down to Port Charlotte before they could land safely." Tess smirked and added, "She was in a silk dress and heels, and they got ruined by the rain. And then they *both* had to help the pilot bundle up the balloon in the mud, and get it into the truck. He said she yelled at him the whole drive back."

Kallie sat staring at Tess, baffled.

Tess laughed quietly to herself. "And the hot air balloon was *her* idea. . ." Suddenly her eyes widened and she looked horrified. "Oh, but your trip won't be like *that*!" she backpedaled. "It'll be beautiful, and *so romantic!*"

"Morrison sounded like it was going to be a nightmare too," Kallie replied, reconsidering. "Maybe I should cancel—"

"No! I didn't mean to scare you. Just, um, don't wear a fancy dress and heels."

Kallie looked down at her jeans and ratty Converse low-top sneakers. "Not much risk of that."

"See, then you'll be fine." Tess quickly grabbed her food order and tried to change the subject.

"I'm going to check their reviews online, again," Kallie mumbled, picking up her phone.

"So what do we do next? Since we've been ordered to drop our primary suspects?" Tess asked morosely, as she sat down at the wobbly plastic table with her tray of tacos.

"I think we're at the point where we need to ask Cornwallis."

Tess frowned and shook her head.

"I mean, we're *students*, Tess. We're supposed to ask for help when we need it."

"So, what, we call him down here to the mall food court?" her friend asked, sarcastically.

Kallie snorted. "He's not *Winchester*, Tess. I'm sure Cornwallis has been to his fair share of food courts."

"I'm not ready to give up yet. I don't want to

378

disappoint him."

"He's not going to be disappointed by questions. He *likes* teaching us. But if you want to keep trying, I'm fine with that," Kallie agreed. "So you tell me. What's our next step?"

Tess picked up a taco and unwrapped it, but then held it at eye level, thinking. "We could go back to the pier, but the police have already collected all of the evidence."

Kallie nodded, taking the lid off her lo mein noodles.

"Who were we investigating before we found out about Jack?" Tess pondered aloud. "Maybe we could try to track down the guy on Mr. Hayashi's video again?"

"I don't think we have the resources for that. We'd be looking for a needle in a haystack." She picked up a broccoli floret with her chopsticks. "Especially after all this time."

"The police are looking into Patricia's disappearance now, and they have way better research amenities than we do. Donovan has an alibi for the murder, and there's no way he'll let us within a hundred yards of his receptionist. Who else is there? Are we forgetting anything?" Tess asked.

"Maybe we should stick with our strengths," Kallie suggested. "Cornwallis has his operatives, and we can't compete with that. . . Not that we're *competing*," she corrected herself quickly.

"No," Tess agreed, blushing. "No, we're not competing."

"Even if it feels like it, occasionally," Kallie added. "But your strength is online research, and nerdy stuff like that," Kallie continued.

Tess squinted at Kallie, the hint of an evil eye brewing.

"Cornwallis can't compete with your technical skills, and he knows it," Kallie concluded, pragmatically.

"Okay, I'm going to take that as a compliment for the moment," Tess mumbled. "What do you have in mind? It's not like I can hack into the county surveillance system."

Kallie grinned, imagining the possibilities.

"I mean, if I had enough time, maybe I could *finesse* my way in. Social engineering, not hacking." Tess considered the idea for a minute. "But I'd *really* hate prison, Kal."

"Me too. So let's think of something legal." Kallie continued, grumpily, "I can't believe we're starting over! We almost *had* Jason and his seedy bosses."

"Yeah, but we can't '*interfere,*'" Tess replied, sounding as frustrated as Kallie felt.

"Actually, now that I'm thinking about it. . ." Kallie reconsidered. "Morrison only told us to back off of Jason."

"Are you thinking—?"

"Jason's off limits, and Donovan and his receptionist are bulletproof. But that still leaves—"

"You want to investigate *Búho*?" Tess asked, looking alarmed. "Kallie, I don't know. That guy's a—"

Kallie shook her head. "I'm sure he's involved, but we don't even know his name, or how to find him. I was actually thinking of Marco Acosta." She paused uneasily, waiting to see what Tess would say.

She's going to call you crazy, Kalliope. Because you are.

"That's not completely crazy, actually," Tess replied, thoughtfully. She stared at her tacos and tapped one fingernail on her tray. "We know his name, now. And we know what he looks like – even though he apparently changes his appearance a lot – because we just saw him three days ago."

"And we know he's in that organization, because Melnyk made his reservation at Rooftopz, and we saw him with Jack. He's the linchpin holding this whole thing together."

"But what's his motive for killing Oscar?" Tess sighed. "We've got nothing until we know that."

"We'll have to figure that out ourselves. But I think he should be on the list."

"Agreed," Tess replied. "What else do we have?

Have the ballistics results come back on the bullet? If it's an unusual caliber or something, maybe we could call local gun shops?"

"That would take forever, and it was probably sold out of someone's trunk, anyway."

"Well, let's think about it. Your noodles are getting cold." Tess finally took a bite of her taco.

"We can check with Cornwallis about the ballistics and the medical examiner's report, without losing points," Kallie suggested, picking up a twist of lo mein with her chopsticks.

Tess nodded. "And ask him if the police have gotten anywhere with the local security cameras."

"That doesn't count as asking for *help*," Kallie concluded.

"Right," Tess agreed. "Not at all."

"We're just following up on the forensic results."

"Good, and I want to start looking up Acosta, as soon as we get home," Tess added, squeezing a packet of hot sauce into her second taco.

Kallie smiled, dunking an egg roll into a tiny cup of duck sauce. "I knew you would."

***

They hadn't thought of any more leads by the

time they got home, so Tess was reading from her textbook again, while Kallie reviewed her photos from the pier.

"What happened with this e-scooter?" she asked, holding up a photo on her phone. "Did Cornwallis find out anything about it?"

"Oh, I forgot about that," Tess replied. "He said he went back the next morning and it was gone. He didn't know if the rental place found it, or if it washed out into the Gulf."

Kallie looked closer at the ruined equipment. "It was covered in barnacles, so it had probably been out there since before the murder, anyway." She swiped to the next photo. "I hope the rental company found it, and it's not out there with the dolphins and manatees."

"Are you reviewing all of your photos from the case?" Tess asked. "That's a good idea."

"I'm hoping it will give us an idea of what to investigate next."

After half an hour, though, Kallie sighed and threw her phone on the couch in frustration. "Can I see your pictures?"

"From the pier?" Tess asked. "Sure." She took her phone out of her purse and handed it over to her best friend.

"My phone is so old, the pictures are terrible," Kallie added with an annoyed pout. "I would've sworn I got some good shots, but they look awful."

"Maybe they'll be better when you download them to your laptop," Tess suggested. "But you can look at mine in the meantime."

Kallie opened the photo app on Tess's phone and scrolled back to the pictures from the night on the pier. She flipped through them slowly, looking for scenes from the waterfront. "Here! This is what I was looking for." She quickly flopped down next to Tess on the couch and showed her the picture.

"The dolphin statue from the restaurant?" Tess asked, leaning over to see the photo.

"What? Oh, no," Kallie quickly took the camera back and zoomed in on the lower right corner. "I was pretty sure I saw something in the water when we first got there. Remember, I kept looking after Cornwallis pointed out the wheels?"

"Yeah, I noticed you were still looking for something." Tess squinted at the photo again. "So what was it?"

"There wasn't anything in the water. I think it was a reflection."

Tess frowned and took the camera back, zooming out on the picture and back in again, squinting. "I don't see it."

Kallie sighed, "I can barely see it in your picture. I took mine from a slightly different angle." She picked up her phone from where she'd thrown it, in her frustration, and opened the photo app again. "It's so *grainy* when I blow it up," she groaned.

Tess grabbed the phone and grimaced. "We've *got* to get you a new phone."

"They're so expensive," Kallie whined.

"Well, I mean, this one is from about 1986," Tess teased. "We could get you a 1998 model for about five dollars, and it would be an improvement."

Kallie laughed, despite her annoyance. "Did cell phones even exist in 1998?"

"I doubt it," Tess replied, smile fading from her face. "I actually do see a reflection in this picture, but I can't tell what it is." Tess tilted her head, looking at Kallie's phone, and then zoomed in and sighed in frustration. "I'm just going to email it to myself, okay?"

"Sure," Kallie replied, with a consenting wave. "I don't think you'll be able to see anything. Instead of just grainy, it'll be grainy and bigger."

"We'll see," her best friend smiled. "I have a pretty good imagination."

Kallie heard her phone make a whooshing sound as Tess emailed a few of the photos from the old phone to her laptop – where she could view it with her high-quality graphics software.

Tess flipped through Kallie's photos from the night at the pier, again, admiring them. Even though they weren't the best resolution, she commented on the angles and perspectives. "You're a really good photographer. Like Renee McGuire said, you should practice."

"So I can take pictures of cheating spouses?" Kallie sighed.

"Gosh, I hope not," Tess replied, looking appalled. "We're not going to be *that* kind of investigators. It'll be good for crime scenes and stuff. If we're going to do this, we need to get serious about our technique."

"Look at us, getting all professional. You're absolutely right."

"We really need street cred," Tess laughed. "In the mean ol' dirty city of Owhiro."

"Watch me do a brooding stare," Kallie added. "Like on the forensics shows." She squinted and frowned, staring thoughtfully across the kitchen at the freezer door.

"Oh, that's very good. Very Humphrey Bogart."

Tess's phone dinged, and then Kallie's phone buzzed an instant later. They both jumped guiltily.

"That's gotta be Cornwallis."

"Why do I suddenly feel bad about joking while we're supposed to be working?" Tess asked.

"Like he was watching us?" Kallie cringed.

"Like Mrs. Miller in seventh grade?"

"Well, it's not like he's *paying* us," Kallie sighed. "We're allowed to have lives." She picked up her phone to see the message.

Cornwallis

Ladies, on your way to the office tomorrow, could you please pick up pizza from that place in Palm Harbor? I'll pay you back.

He never complains about you having fun, Kalliope. That guilt is all you.

"You know, Wally never tells us to be serious, unless we're in a situation where there's some danger," Tess said, shaking her head. "I don't know why I feel like we got busted for whispering in class."

"I was just thinking the same thing," Kallie replied. "He's really so nice."

"And he's trying to keep us from getting ourselves killed. Which is also kind of a decent personality trait." Tess added, "I like a guy who wants me to keep breathing."

"I mean, we've only almost gotten ourselves killed about five times in the past year. He might be overreacting a little," Kallie replied with a sardonic laugh.

"Good luck telling him that. I think he's attached to us now."

"Like stray cats."

"Exactly," Tess nodded. "And now he feels obligated to teach us how to avoid provoking murderers."

Kallie realized they'd gotten off-track. "What were we talking about?"

"Hmm? Oh, right!" Tess responded. "I was looking at your photos from the pier. Let me go check that reflection you mentioned."

While Tess went back to her laptop, Kallie wrote herself a note to pick up two pizzas from the place in Palm Harbor. It wasn't on their direct route to Tampa, but she didn't mind a little side journey for their mentor.

"Hey, come here and look at this, Kal." Tess had her graphics software open, and she waved Kallie over. "I can actually see the reflection here. I think there was someone hiding *under* the pier!"

Chapter Seventeen

"We definitely need to get you a better phone," Cornwallis replied with a whistle.

"That's what I said!" Tess added with a laugh.

He looked at Kallie with admiration and took off his glasses. "I can't believe you got this shot, Kallie. Even with your junky old phone," he joked.

"Hey," Kallie scowled. "It's not *junky*."

"Obviously not," Cornwallis replied, sincerely, looking back at the sharpened photo. "The resolution is still grainy, but the reflection is crystal clear."

Kallie and Tess both waited, anticipating his response.

"You've got a great eye, kid." He finally looked up. "You could do great work."

"So *you* see the same thing *we* see?" Tess asked quietly.

"Yeah," he sighed. "There's definitely someone down there. I don't know how you saw his *reflection* in the darkness when I didn't even see *him*. And I was standing about ten feet away from him. With a flashlight." He chuckled.

Kallie frowned. "No, I just thought you were—"

"Don't you start making excuses for me, Kallie," he reproved her, gently.

She snapped her mouth shut, embarrassed.

"We all have different skills, and my pride is that I knew you girls had something special," he continued. "We'd make a great team—if I wasn't ready to retire."

Cornwallis had originally agreed to mentor them specifically because he was ready to retire, but neither of them liked to hear it. Kallie crossed her arms awkwardly and turned her eyes away.

He looked at Kallie and Tess, and obviously saw them both frowning. "No pouting, you two. We're not done yet. This is an excellent start, but what else have you found?"

"I interviewed the last two store owners from the shops on the pier," Tess blurted out, to Kallie's relief.

Did we accomplish anything else? Think, Kalliope.

"Any luck?"

"No," Tess answered, sounding a little guilty again. "None of them have security cameras. They take everything expensive home with them, since the pier is so wide open at night. And I asked the dollmakers if they saw anything, but they leave at seven o'clock."

Cornwallis nodded, and then looked at Kallie.

"I talked to Morrison about the cameras near the bakery, but they haven't had any luck yet either."

"Sorry," Tess mumbled.

Cornwallis rolled his eyes, and Kallie thought he was going to reprimand them for not finding enough clues. For letting a killer stay on the streets for two more days, when he should be locked up.

For disappointing him.

Instead, he took a chewed-up ballpoint pen from a coffee cup on his desk and scrawled something in his notepad. Kallie couldn't read it until he picked it up and showed them:

THIS JOB SUCKS.

Kallie saw Tess frown in confusion and suspected her own face looked the same.

"This job is *hard*, ladies. Most days you won't learn a single thing."

Kallie slumped back in her chair.

"Witnesses see nothing. Cameras fail. Promising leads fall apart."

They both watched him silently.

"You can't blame yourself. Just work harder tomorrow." He shrugged. "Now get out of here. Leave a man alone with his cold pizza."

They nodded and stood up to leave.

"Actually, wait a second," he called, stopping them. Cornwallis took his car keys out of the top desk drawer, and fumbled for a small key on the ring. Spinning his chair around, he used it to unlock the bottom drawer of his filing cabinet.

"Take this with you." He held out a black bag to Kallie.

Kallie frowned and took the small purse-sized bag, which was surprisingly heavy. Sitting back down, she put the bag on her lap and unzipped it. "A camera?"

"I can't afford to get you a new *phone*," Cornwallis replied, jokingly. "So this will have to do for now."

"Cornwallis, this is a *good* camera. I can't take this."

"It's not new, but it's in good condition. And you have a great eye." He waved her away again, "Now scram."

"Are you sure?" Kallie asked, awkwardly.

"Take it. I'll expense it or something."

She looked at Tess, who was nodding encouragingly.

Kallie smiled crookedly, and stood up to leave, clutching the black bag to her chest. Tess opened the door, and they trudged wearily to the top of the stairs.

"Wait, one *more* thing," he called again, stopping them in their tracks. "I got a tip from a friend at the station. Some uniformed officers went around with a photo of Patricia and asked people if they'd seen her."

"Just now? After all this time?" Kallie asked, distressed.

"But someone recognized her!" Cornwallis declared.

"You're kidding," Tess responded, looking suspicious at the news.

"No, it was a regular from the bakery," he explained. "He said he saw her on the beach with a man."

"And he remembered that?" Kallie replied skeptically. "I see the cashier at the Thai restaurant all the time, but I wouldn't remember if I saw her on the beach."

"The witness said she was stumbling, and he thought she was drunk. The guy was holding her up and helping her walk, but he said he had a weird feeling about it." Cornwallis paused and added, "I mean, she's not a twenty-year-old kid on spring break."

Kallie grumpily conceded, "Yeah, okay. I'd remember if I saw the Thai restaurant cashier stumbling around and being held up by a strange man. So now what do we do?"

"You said she wears a lot of jewelry, right? Get out there with a metal detector and see if she dropped anything."

"After all this time?" Tess repeated.

"Their tracks will be gone, but if she dropped anything, let's hope it got buried in the sand and it's still there."

"Okay, it's worth a try," Kallie agreed. "I think my dad has a metal detector in the garage. I'll see if it still works."

"Good, let me know what happens," Cornwallis replied, going back to his pizza.

"And finish chapter eight," he called after them, as they reached the stairs again. "Pop quiz on Monday. You've been warned!"

***

Kallie arrived at the pier bright and early the next morning, with a bottle of ice water, her new camera, the borrowed metal detector, and a vague understanding of how to use it. It had been windy earlier, but the weather had settled down nicely.

She turned on the metal detector hesitantly, and a few lights started blinking.

It works! This is already going better than I expected!

She stood up and waved it around hopefully, but it didn't make any sound. A green light flashed occasionally, but she couldn't tell if it was working or not.

Well, what do you expect, dummy? There's no metal!

Kallie took her car keys out of her pocket and carefully dropped them on the sand. Then she picked up the big, clumsy metal detector again and waved it over them. Once. . . Twice. . .

"Beep!" went the awkward machine.

Yes! Success!

Bending down, she picked up her keys and dusted them off before putting them back in her pocket.

Lucky for me, it's early, and no one can see me out here looking foolish.

"Hi, neighbor!" a cheerful voice called from behind her. "First day searching for gold?"

Dang it.

Kallie spun around and saw a short, middle-aged man in a loud Hawaiian shirt approaching her. He was also carrying a metal detector, but his looked much fancier—with more dials and blinking lights.

"Hi," she called back, trying not to look embarrassed. "First time. What gave it away?"

"It's easier if you hold it this way," he replied, and Kallie was pleased to see that he demonstrated with his own detector, instead of getting handsy behind her—like her previous golf instructor.

Changing her grip, she found that it was indeed

more balanced and easier to hold.

"Thanks! Um. . ."

"Marvin," he replied.

"I'm Kallie. Have you ever found anything good down here?"

"I come here almost every morning. I've never found buried pirate treasure, but I've found lots of coins. And I found a lost wedding ring once," he added enthusiastically. "The owner lost it while she was on vacation from Minnesota, and she gave me a hundred-dollar reward."

"That's wonderful," Kallie replied.

"A bunch of us come out here all the time, but never any pretty girls like you."

"Oh, I'm, uh. . ." Kallie stammered at the uncomfortable statement, but he quickly changed the subject, yet again.

"Mine's a ZapFinder 3000. What's yours?"

"I'm not sure." She held up the contraption and read the tattered old label. "Oh, it's a ZapFinder One, actually. It must be an old version of yours. I borrowed it from my dad."

He began showing her around the area near the pier, guiding her to the places where he'd found items in the past. Unfortunately, his flirting was becoming more obvious. And annoying.

"I don't see a wedding ring on *you*. . ."

"A friend of mine might have lost something out here, actually," she quickly interjected. "And I just wanted to see if I could find it for her." She wasn't sure exactly why she was telling a tiny lie, but she just didn't quite trust him.

As they approached the Celebration of Sandcastles festival site, she saw a familiar Bentley SUV parked right in the front row, with a goofy spoiler and an unmistakable sticker on the back window.

That's the same tacky car we saw right next to Patricia's van after the murder, Kallie recalled, cringing at the gaudy decorations.

"Wait, is that car from Texas?" she wondered aloud.

Didn't Cornwallis say Marco's boss, the guy he calls Búho, is from Dallas? I'm sure he did!

When we find out his real name, I'll bet we find out he drives a Bentley. And now he's back at the scene of the crime!

Everything points back to them!

"How do you know it's from Texas?" Marvin asked, jarring Kallie from her thoughts. "It has Florida license plates."

"It's that flag sticker on the back, see?" Kallie pointed at the rear window of the car. "That's the Texas flag, with the big white star on the left side. Because it's the Lone Star state."

"Oh, I see it. You're so smart, Kallie."

Kallie rolled her eyes at the awkward compliment, in spite of his help. It was so weird, with him following her around like a puppy.

Is this how Tess feels all the time? It's so irritating.

"I see more than *one* star out here," he cooed, staring up at her.

Kallie gritted her teeth and tried to ignore him.

Don't be rude, Kalliope. You need his help.

Ugh, why did I ever want Tess to teach me how to flirt? This is so much worse.

"You're more beautiful than all of the heavenly—"

"Hey, Marvin? Let's go look over there, on the other side of the pier, okay?" She quickly moved away from him, calling, "If we split up, we'll be finished sooner."

"If you say so, Kallie," he stared after her—she could almost feel his annoying eyeballs locked on her back.

A sudden chill ran up her spine, and she grimaced.

Was that a 'danger' chill or a 'shut the heck up and stop staring at me' chill?

I've never needed to know the difference before.

398

Could this guy be more dangerous than he seems?

She glanced back toward the festival zone, and saw Marvin staring at the ground, waving his metal detector over the sand strategically.

Nah. He's harmless.

After ten more minutes of searching by herself, though, she knew she needed his help. "Are you sure this is the most popular area?" she called out.

He quickly stumbled back to her side, exclaiming, "Oh, yes. I'm always near this section of the beach, because I love to come here in the fall and watch the pelicans dive in the water. I could watch them all day, swooping in to splash around and look for fish."

"Okay, thanks, that's—"

"Swooop! Splash!" he added, cheerfully. "Swooooop!"

"Okay, I'm just going to—"

"SPLASH!"

I am so apologizing to Tess in the morning for envying her beauty. I might even bring her a key lime pie.

"Swoop—" he mumbled, walking back toward the festival grounds.

I had no idea this was her life. And she doesn't even flirt with them.

And am I the only person in the county that isn't

out here watching the pelicans? Maybe I'll ask Morrison about that.

The blinking lights on her metal detector started to fade, and she smacked it gently on the palm of her hand. That worked for a while, but in a few minutes, they started to fade again.

Great, now I have no choice but to talk to him.

See, this is why you should carry a purse, Kalliope. You could carry spare batteries in there and avoid awkward conversations.

"My scanner's out of batteries, Marvin. I should probably head back to the car."

"Okay, Kallie," he replied with a nod, but he was staring at something on the ground. "Could you come see this?"

Kallie sighed and walked back across the sand toward her new helper.

If he's trying to lure me in for a kiss, I'm going to—

"Oh my gosh, Marvin. I think that's her bracelet!" she yelped in surprise, interrupting her own negative thoughts.

"Do you think so?" he asked, bending toward the sparkling metal, partially buried in the sand.

"Don't touch it! It must've been uncovered by the windstorm this morning." She knelt down for a closer look and saw a broad strip of silver and a bit of blue peeking out of the sand. That made her feel even more certain.

I don't recognize it, but it certainly looks like her style. She loves turquoise.

She took some photos with her new, official camera, carefully keeping Marvin in her line of sight while she bent down for a better look.

Seriously, Kalliope? Do you think he's going to smash you over the head with that giant metal detector? He's harmless.

What if he's just pretending to be a nice guy with a crush on me? What if he's really a criminal, working with Marco and Búho?

What if he IS Búho?

Okay, now you're being paranoid, Kalliope.

She finished taking her photos and stood back up, brushing the sand off her knees, and took out her phone. "I just need to make a quick call, Marvin. We're going to let the cops handle this one."

"Okay, Kallie," he replied, happily.

But as she turned away to dial Morrison's number, she saw a quick movement out of her peripheral vision. Turning to look, she felt a sudden jolt to the back of her head. Knees buckling, she stumbled sideways, but turned just enough to see a figure grab the bracelet from the sand.

Are you kidding me? It was Marvin all along?

She swore at her own stupidity, as dizzy spots filled her vision and she struggled to stay conscious.

Not so paranoid now, am I?

But no, there was Marvin, shouting at the top of his lungs and chasing after the shadowy figure.

"You come back here with that! That's not yours!" he shouted, running as fast as his slippery loafers would carry him, sliding across the sand until her attacker had disappeared beyond the pier.

A minute or two later, he had trudged his way back to her side. "I'm sorry, Kallie. I tried to catch him," he mumbled, sounding like he might cry.

"I know you did, Marvin. You did great," she replied, sincerely.

He might be weird, but I have closer friends who wouldn't chase down a dangerous attacker for me.

"I'm calling the police, Kallie. You stay there and rest until they get here." He dialed his phone and then added, "You might have a concussion. Just rest and wait for the police."

***

Morrison was running down the hallway so fast that he passed her, backtracked, and slid into the hospital ward sideways. His eyes were wild. "What happened to you? Kallie, your *head*!"

Kallie held the ice pack in place, hoping to keep the goose egg on her noggin from getting any bigger. "It's nothing, Morrison. I just got hit on the head. They said I don't even have a concussion, but it hurts a lot." Her eyes teared up, in pain and embarrassment.

I was so stupidly worried about Marvin conking me on the head, I wasn't paying attention to my surroundings. I can't believe I let that guy sneak up on me.

I knew better!

And worst of all, he stole Patricia's missing bracelet.

"We found evidence that Patricia was there, Morrison," she explained, as he knelt down in front of her and took her hand. "At least I think it was hers. There was a bracelet in the sand, near the pier. It was probably covered by the sand right away, but then uncovered in the wind storm this morning, so—"

She realized she was babbling and closed her mouth.

"That's great, Kallie," he mumbled, leaning against her knees, obviously more concerned about her injury than the bracelet.

"But the guy stole it. The guy who hit me—he grabbed it and ran away," she whined, feeling another wave of embarrassment and self-pity.

He touched her chin and looked at her eyes closely. He seemed very serious, and she thought he might be angry.

"I didn't mean to lose it, he just—" she stammered, wishing he'd smile and forgive her. "I'm sorry—"

"*What?!* Brooks, there's nothing to be sorry about." His gaze softened. "I think they're right about you not having a concussion. I might not be a doctor, but I see a *lot* of head trauma, and your lovely eyes look okay to me."

She smiled crookedly and stared back at him adoringly for a moment, and then realized they were being watched by about twenty doctors, nurses, and other patients. She blushed shyly.

"Oh, wait. I took pictures!" She yelped, pulling out her new camera and handing it over.

Morrison looked at the photos and nodded. "I'll send these over to our forensics team later and see what they think. But they can wait." He sat down on the bed next to her and hugged her, and she gently placed her head on his shoulder, wincing at the contact, trying not to cry.

***

"I think we need to talk to that guy again. The

404

cashier guy," Kallie said, pouring a measuring cup of baking powder into the mixing bowl, the next morning.

"I think they were wrong about the concussion," Tess replied, leaning across the counter. Picking up a sheet of notebook paper and reading the handwritten notes, she shook her head. "That was supposed to be a *tablespoon* of baking powder."

Kallie took the paper from Tess, then looked down at the measuring cup in her hand. "I hate baking. If I wanted to be a chemist, I would've gone to MIT," she grumbled. Dumping the whole bowl into the trash, she pulled the flour canister back out of the pantry and started again. "At least I didn't mix in the chocolate before you noticed."

"At least I *noticed*," Tess replied with a laugh. "Those would've been some nasty muffins."

"I should open a bakery and call it 'Nasty Muffins.'"

"Are you okay, Kal? You seem really distracted." Tess's face was serious. "Look at me. Is it your head?"

"I'm just worried about the case," Kallie replied. "It feels like every lead is slipping through our fingers."

"Well, worry about it later. You're about to dump a quarter cup of salt in the bowl."

"What?" She looked down at her hands and laughed at herself. "Quarter teaspoon, quarter cup. What's the difference?"

"Edibility," Tess answered with a grin.

"Maybe you'd better finish these."

"I think that's a good idea." Tess stood up and chased Kallie out of the kitchen, then pulled a funnel out of a drawer and poured the extra salt back into the box. "What were you saying about the cashier guy?"

"He was one of the last people to see Patricia Evans, right?"

"The flower shop manager who moonlights at the bakery, you mean?" Tess asked. "I think the police already talked to him."

"They talked to him about Oscar. Not about Patricia."

"Are you sure?" Tess replied.

"No, but they questioned him *before* she disappeared. They probably don't even know he was working at the bakery."

"Okay, let's try to find him. He'll probably be at the flower shop."

"I know the police are looking into her disappearance, but since the bakery is in Clearwater, I doubt they're focused on her in relation to Oscar's murder," Kallie reasoned.

"It's worth checking," Tess agreed, stirring the muffin batter.

Kallie set the digital kitchen timer for the muffins and added, "And if the flower shop guy didn't

406

kill Patricia and dump her in a shallow grave–"

"Nice."

"—then maybe he saw something. He seems like the kind of guy who knows how to watch a room."

***

"There he is," Kallie whispered, trying not to stare across the trendy flower shop, when they arrived later.

The cashier-slash-manager-slash-bakery guy was sitting at the register, chatting with a woman holding a pot of red gerbera daisies.

"Well, that was easy. Let's go talk to him," Tess replied.

"You think he'll talk to us?" Kallie asked.

"We're not monsters. Besides, we're not even cops, so he has no reason to avoid us. Let's just ask about Patricia, and see what happens."

Kallie picked up a small pot of violets as a decoy, and they got in line behind the daisy lady.

"Just be sure you don't overwater it, this time," he was saying. "It'll probably be safer to plant it in your yard."

"But, Lionel, the last ones—"

"You brought me the last one, and it was

definitely overwatered," he interjected. "If you leave it in the pot, don't water it more than once a week."

"But—"

"Promise me, Edith. *Promise* me you won't water it more than once a week."

"But, I just—"

"Give it a try. If it dies, you can bring it back. But only water it every Sunday. That's all."

The woman finally agreed to the new watering schedule, and she carried off her new plant in a cardboard carrier. She looked worried.

"Sorry about that, ladies. Serial over-waterer. Can I help you with that violet?" he asked. "Another one that's easy to overwater, I'm warning you."

"Actually, we wanted to talk to you about Patricia Evans."

"Oh, she's wonderful with plants," he answered, smiling broadly. "A real green thumb, that one."

"When was the last time you saw her?" Kallie asked.

"I filled in for one of her employees at the bakery," he replied. He thought for a moment, frowning. "Oh, but that was two weeks ago. But, we just had our seasonal sale, too. I remember she picked up a native milkweed plant for her butterflies."

"And when was that?" Tess asked.

"It was. . . I'm not sure. Let me check with one

of my girls." He waved down a young brunette and asked, "How long ago was our spring sale, Julia?"

"It was three weeks ago, Lionel," she replied quickly.

"That long?" he asked, surprised. "I guess I'm better at remembering watering days than actual days. Could you see when Patricia was last here?"

"Sure. We have a frequent buyer program, and she's a gold member," the brunette explained to Kallie and Tess. "Let me check." She headed for the guest services counter and they saw her searching on the computer.

"Did you check at the bakery?" he asked.

"Yes, and they haven't seen her," Kallie replied, hesitantly.

"Haven't seen her?" he repeated. "Is she missing?"

Can he really be unaware that Patricia's missing? I haven't seen it reported on the news, but they definitely know each other.

Or is he bluffing? Pretending ignorance?

"They haven't seen her for over a week," Kallie clarified, watching his facial expression.

He frowned again, looking concerned. "Several of us watch out for each other's shops. If she went on vacation, she definitely would've told me. And her employees would know, obviously."

Julia waved for them to join her at the computer, so they walked across the store, bemused.

How could he work so nearby, and be friendly with Patricia, and not have heard the news?

Maybe he just avoids gossip?

But if he's only pretending to be unaware that she's missing, why could that be?

"Lionel won't tell you. . ." Julia whispered, when they met her at the computer. "He's a very private man, and he'd be embarrassed if he knew I was talking to you."

"What is it?" Tess asked, confused.

"Betsy told me about you, and how you're trying to help. So I thought you should know. He and Patricia dated. They were off-and-on for years, before Patricia got married. He's a bit older than her, but he called her 'the one that got away.' And he never married." She blushed and added, "Since she got divorced, I think they both—"

"Thought it was their second chance," Tess murmured.

"Oh, that's so sad," Kallie sighed.

"We've been trying to keep her disappearance from him, and it hasn't been on the news yet," she looked heartbroken. "If you can find her. . ."

"We'll do our best, Julia," Tess reassured her. "And the police are looking too."

"And we won't tell him about this conversation," Kallie promised.

The young woman thanked them and walked back over to Lionel, and Kallie and Tess watched her go.

"That's so sad," Kallie repeated, forlornly. "After all that time, they almost got back together."

"You know what's *really* sad?" Tess asked. "We need to consider that he might be faking it. That they may have had a lovers' quarrel that ended badly."

Kallie's shoulders slumped as they left the store. "And that makes him our next potential suspect. Sometimes I hate this job."

"I'll look up his background when we get home," Tess sighed.

Chapter Eighteen

Tess called Kallie that evening, and she sounded like she was almost in tears. "I'm so sorry, Kallie," she sighed. "I have to fly to *New Orleans* tomorrow."

"What?" Kallie asked, confused. "New Orleans?"

"Winchester is still on that case in Louisiana, and it's getting pretty serious. He needs me to come down there."

"Don't be sorry, Tess," Kallie reassured her. "Cornwallis and I will stay on the case, and keep checking up on the remaining suspects."

"Send me anything else you find, okay?" she suggested. "I'll keep researching in the evenings while I'm at the hotel."

"What's he getting into down there, anyway? Didn't you say it started out as a domestic dispute or something?"

"Yes, but it's *evolving*," Tess responded, mimicking Winchester's southern drawl. "He's going out to some small town, and for some reason, he thinks I'll be able to help him."

"In the bayou?" Kallie asked, incredulously.

"Apparently," Tess scoffed. "Can you imagine me in hip-waders?"

"Being chased by an alligator? Absolutely," Kallie replied with a laugh. "Don't worry about it. I'll keep checking into things here, while you're gone, and update you in the evenings. You'll be staying in a decent hotel with internet access, right?

"Oh, trust me. Winchester's pretty big on hotels—" Tess reassured her.

"Yeah, I can't imagine him sleeping out with the water moccasins."

"He'll probably drive us back to New Orleans every night, if it comes to that."

"Or Baton Rouge, or something," Kallie agreed. "There are other big cities in Louisiana. You'll both be okay."

"I'll be bringing my laptop for work. So just email me anything you find."

"How long will you be gone?"

"I'm not sure. I mean, he's been down there working on this case for over a month, already. I don't even know why he wants me to join him."

"Okay, so hopefully not for too long. Have you told Cornwallis?"

"Not yet," Tess sighed. "I hope he won't be upset. He really wanted us to focus on this case for our training, but I have to pay the bills."

"I'm sure he'll understand – he's working on another case now, too. I guess he has to pay his own bills while we do this one *pro bono*." Kallie shrugged and added, "Besides, working with a lawyer is a whole 'nother good skill set, for our eventual profession."

"I'm basically just a glorified secretary," Tess replied, self-consciously. "Although—"

"That's not true. Winchester obviously doesn't want you down there to take dictation. He can do that over the phone."

"And he *has* been, for a month," Tess agreed with a groan.

"I hope it's something exciting," Kallie grinned.

"Me too. Although maybe not *too* exciting." Tess paused and then added, "Who am I kidding? Winchester is a semi-retired Southern lawyer with a Mercedes SUV and high blood pressure. There's not going to be any excitement."

"Yeah, he probably just wants you to witness a signature or something," Kallie sighed.

"Yeah," Tess pouted.

"Well, I'll keep poking the bears up here while you're gone, and maybe something will turn up."

"Okay, but tell Cornwallis before you do anything. And be sure to stay out of trouble," Tess added.

"Me?" Kallie replied, sounding aghast. "I'm never in trouble!"

"Mmm-hmm. Can you drive me to the airport tomorrow morning, Miss Poirot?"

"*Mais oui*, my dear. Email me your itinerary."

***

"Look out, here comes trouble!" Isabel called as Kallie walked into Studio Alvarez the next morning. She'd dropped Tess off at the airport, but the house felt too quiet, and her dad was spending the day with Anna.

"Aunt Kallie!" Lily shouted from the couch, where she was sitting with her mom. "Did you bring—?"

Kallie stepped aside theatrically, and Lily shrieked, "Sherman!"

Her adopted dog dashed through the doorway and bolted for the little girl, wagging his tail like a lunatic. Lily hugged him, and he licked her face and nuzzled her ears.

"And just like that, I'm invisible," she joked to Isabel.

"To both of them," Izzy laughed. She patted the couch seat and called, "Come on up, Sherman."

The fluffy black-and-white dog jumped up onto the couch and carefully squeezed in between them, snuggling up to Lily. Once they had both settled back down, Kallie sat down and kissed Lily on the forehead, ruffling her curly dark hair.

"How's my favorite girl?"

"Daddy's making a sea turtle, Aunt Kallie," she pronounced seriously.

Carlos was at the easel, as always. Kallie sometimes wondered if he ever did anything else anymore, outside of work. But she knew Lily was learning to swim, so he was definitely helping with that too.

He looked away from the enormous drawing and waved a charcoal-stained hand at Kallie. It was still funny to see the huge, muscular former-bouncer poised at an easel, creating a beautiful work of art.

Although he definitely wasn't spending as much time at the gym anymore, either. He didn't need to, now that he was in management, but she knew he was splitting that time between his family and his art, which both made him happier than Kallie had ever seen him.

The giant charcoal and chalk drawing was actually a small cluster of sea turtles—baby ones. Kallie and Carlos had once seen a nest of them hatching behind The Lazy Gecko, and watched the tiny creatures romp adorably across the beach and into the surf. She suspected he was drawing them from memory.

"Remember when we saw the baby turtles that night?" she asked.

"I was always so mad at Marcy for putting out

416

those ugly amber lights during hatching season," Carlos answered with a smile and a shake of his head. "It made it so hard to watch the customers outdoors and make sure everyone was safe. It felt like she was sabotaging our job."

"Until we finally saw a nest!"

"I'll never forget it," he replied, adding some dark stripes to the turtles' shells and a bright sparkle to their unusual, charming eyes.

The sea turtles didn't usually lay eggs near the bar, because they liked a quiet spot with no impediments on the sand. Hardly an apt description of the popular beachfront nightspot. But one had managed to find a quiet location for her eggs, and the local conservationists luckily noticed the nest and carefully marked it. Once it was roped off with posts and bright plastic tape, Marcy and her bouncers guarded it ferociously, warning patrons to stay away.

Marcy had cried happy tears when the tiny turtles finally hatched, and Kallie had been sniffling right there with her. Watching under the ugly amber lights, she had seen Carlos and her friend Mike standing just as awestruck as she felt.

"Is this a commissioned piece, or is it for a gallery?" Kallie asked.

"It's for a local artist's collection at the Ringling Museum in Sarasota, actually," Izzy replied, proudly.

Carlos didn't reply, but Kallie could see he was

blushing.

"Carlos, that's amazing," she gushed. "I mean, it's totally *understandable,* because your drawings are spectacular. But it's still awesome!"

"People come from all over the world to visit that museum," Isabel agreed. "I was telling him to get ready for commissions from Paris and Milan."

"That's silly, Izzy," Carlos mumbled quietly.

"It's not silly at all, really," Kallie responded. "Your work will be hanging with some of the greatest European masters—the Ringling Museum is world-famous."

"Don't make me nervous, Kal," Carlos chuckled awkwardly.

Lily, who had never known her dad as anything but an artist, was bored with the whole ordeal. "Can Sherman stay for lunch, Aunt Kallie?"

Not wanting to intrude, she started to say no, but Isabel interrupted, "Of course he can. And your Aunt Kallie is going to stay too."

"Thanks, we'd love to," Kallie replied, "If it's not too much trouble."

"Not at all. Carlos's mom finally gave me her ropa vieja recipe, so I have a batch cooking right now."

"Nice!" Kallie responded happily. "And yum!"

"All I had to do was give her a grandchild, apparently," Izzy laughed. "It was worth the forced bedrest and labor, though. Wait 'til you taste it!"

"I'm sold. Can I help with anything?"

"You can tell us all about your latest case, of course," Carlos answered. "Izzy's trying to be polite and not ask, but we're both dying to hear all about it."

"Don't we need to make sure–?" She was going to ask about Lily's young ears, but the toddler was already half asleep, cuddled up with Sherman.

Kallie stared at the adorable scene for a minute, then replied, "I wish I had more to tell you. Our main suspect is pretty elusive, and we don't know much about him. But we got a pretty good photo of him at—"

"Oh, wait until Carlos's mom gets here!" Isabel interjected. "Or she'll make you start over from the beginning."

Carlos washed his hands and then picked up Lily and carried her across the garden and into the house. They sat back down in the kitchen, preparing for lunch.

"Hey, what happened with that yoga instructor?" Isabel asked. "The guy with the studio in Ozona?"

"We never got anywhere with that guy. He had a really popular class, and Tess said the yoga was really good. I guess he was legit."

And I was ready to throw him to the wolves, I was so sure he was shady.

419

I guess my intuition doesn't work quite as well as Cornwallis's does.

"I've only been there once, but one of my instructors raves about his classes," Isabel replied. "And she said he's really hot—"

"Izzy, I'm right here," Carlos replied with a laugh.

Isabel swatted him on the arm. "I was thinking we should set him up with Tess, if he's single."

"With Tess?" Kallie asked, crinkling up her nose. "I don't think he's her type."

Or do you just feel guilty for suspecting him, Kalliope?

"She likes yoga, and he owns his own business," Isabel rationalized, while taking silverware out of the kitchen drawer. "Besides, she needs a boyfriend."

Kallie shrugged. "I'll ask her when she gets back from Louisiana."

I'm obviously not the best person to be assigning romantic partners, since I was completely oblivious about my own boyfriend. So maybe Isabel's right.

"Anyway, I'm glad that guy's in the clear," Izzy replied with a laugh, opening their new rice cooker. "I don't need some murderer ruining the local yoga cred. That could've really damaged my business."

"I'm sorry I worried you. He really seemed like

a good suspect."

"Oh, I wasn't worried, Kallie," Isabel insisted. "I knew he was one of the good guys. He went to Temple, the same school my sister attended, after all."

"Sure, we saw his sweatshirt from Temple University, in the closet," Kallie acknowledged, remembering their search.

"Not Temple *University*," Isabel shook her head, fluffing the rice with her fork. "Temple College. It's about an hour north of Austin."

Wait, what?

Did she just say Austin? Why does that ring a bell—?

"This rice came out perfectly, Izzy," Carlos mentioned. "I mean, it was always great, but it's different somehow."

"I know, it's the brand your mom recommended. I like it a lot better."

Kallie stared at her plate, vaguely listening to Izzy and Carlos, but her mind was in another world.

It can't be. The crime boss, the guy they call Búho – he's behind the murder. And Marco Acosta. Right?

But Patricia's phone. . .

Slowly, the pieces fell into place. One by one.

"Oh my gosh. Izzy, I know who committed the murder."

"*What?* What did I say? Rice?" She looked at Carlos, who shrugged.

"I have to go," Kallie called from the doorway, already on her way out.

Carlos looked surprised, but he laughed and replied, "Go solve that case! We'll keep Sherman."

Sherman lifted his head from where he was cuddled with Lily and sleepily wagged his tail.

"I'll call you later!"

Chapter Nineteen

Kallie texted Cornwallis from the car, and then she called Morrison. "Can you meet me in fifteen minutes? I know who killed Oscar." She took a deep breath and explained everything, right down to the ropa vieja.

She thought he'd argue, but he apparently heard something urgent in her voice. "I'm just over in Clearwater, Brooks – I'll be right there. Don't do anything until I get there."

Kallie pulled into the strip mall parking lot and looked around warily, but there were only two other cars nearby. She sat impatiently, tapping her feet anxiously and biting her nails until Morrison arrived, with another officer. She'd met Officer Ramos before, and waved nervously to her.

Morrison walked to Kallie's beat-up but beloved old car and leaned on the door, starting to ask for an explanation, but she gestured to wait. Kallie quickly called Tess, and put her on speaker.

"Hey, Kal," Tess's voice called out, sounding a little tinny on the speakerphone. "Wally told me you figured out the killer. Who is it—?"

"Let's not get ahead of ourselves, ladies. We're just going to ask some questions," Morrison interjected. "We're not accusing anyone of murder."

"Can you please just go in there and check?" Kallie pointed at the strip mall behind them. "I'm really sure, Morrison."

"Officer Ramos and I will go check," he reassured her. "Stay out here, in the car. Seriously."

"Do you think I'm right?" she asked, hopefully.

"Just stay here, please," he sighed, without answering her.

Kallie agreed, but as Officer Ramos got out of the car and the two of them crossed the parking lot, she craned around to watch through the back window.

The phone crackled, and Tess's voice broke up. "—losing the signal, out here. —call you back." And the line went dead.

Feeling suddenly alone, Kallie whimpered softly to herself.

Across the parking lot, she saw Morrison open the door, and she could immediately tell that something was wrong. Even from that distance, she could see that the yoga studio was abandoned. All of the colorful decorations and bamboo trim were gone. They both drew their service weapons cautiously, and Morrison glanced back, presumably to make sure she was still safely in the car.

Kallie's stomach lurched.

Please be careful, Morrison. Please.

Even with the windows rolled up, Kallie could hear a loud crash inside the studio, and Officer Ramos took off in a flash. Morrison was right behind her, and they both disappeared into the building.

Kallie whined aloud, heart jumping into her throat. But there was only silence. She wanted to get out of the car and see what was happening, but couldn't risk distracting him.

Another minute passed, and another. Still only silence.

What are they doing? The place isn't that big. What's taking so long?!

A single loud bang jarred her to the core, and she knew in her heart it was a gunshot. She wrapped her arms around the headrest tighter, terrified. Her teeth were clenched so hard that her jaw ached.

Suddenly, a man darted out from the side of the building and looked around frantically. Without thinking, she honked the horn of her car loudly to let Morrison know the man was outside.

What if Morrison can't chase him, Kalliope? What if he got shot?

But her plan backfired. The man saw Kallie, and his face immediately contorted in wrath. He ran for her

425

car, so fast she was stunned into stillness for a moment. She finally jammed the lock down on the old car with her elbow, just as he grabbed the handle and tried to wrench it open. Now that he was only inches from her face, she could see the same familiar playing card tattoo on his neck.

I knew it was you! Aargh, why did it take me so long to figure it out?

Danny Lloyd began smashing his elbow against the driver's side glass, eyes wild, determined to get through to her. Kallie didn't know if he was intent on punishing her for bringing the police, or just trying to steal her car and escape – she was frozen in terror. The old glass wobbled and started to crack near the top edge, as Kallie frantically looked around for some kind of defensive weapon. She grabbed her trusty umbrella, but knew she'd need something stronger.

She lurched backward and climbed awkwardly over the armrest, falling clumsily into the back seat. Her instinct told her to get out of the car and run, but she was terrified, knowing he'd attack her. She pressed her body against the rear door, as far from him as possible. Her only hope was to jump out as soon as the old car's driver's side window gave out and shattered— which seemed imminent.

He's probably exhausted from being chased and from beating on the window. Maybe I can outrun him back to the yoga studio.

Maybe he wants the car more than he wants to kill me for exposing him.

Wishful thinking, Kalliope. He knows you're the one who figured it out.

He bent down and stared at her, seething with rage, as he smashed the window again.

How could everyone think he's so hot?! He's a psychopath!

One more elbow to the old glass, and the window buckled. She grabbed the rear passenger door handle and hoped the old hinges wouldn't stick, for a change. The madman shouted with fury, and smashed the window one last time. Finally, it shattered into a million tiny squares of safety glass, raining over the seats and onto Kallie. She held her breath and yanked the rear door handle.

And it stuck.

No! No, no, no! Open!

He seemed to calm down instantly, leering at her over the seat – knowing she was trapped. Helpless. His sudden, eerie composure was almost as terrifying as his previous fury. Reaching through the broken glass – bleeding from a hundred tiny cuts on his arm – he serenely unlocked the car door, opening it casually and getting into the driver's seat.

Kallie backed up as far as she could, holding the umbrella up as an ineffective shield. She was trapped with the madman inside her tiny car, with nowhere to go. He smiled nastily and growled, "I knew you saw us. Near the bakery. In the car. At the pier. You couldn't just *mind your own business.*"

That was him? Every single time?!

How long has this paranoid freak been following us?!

"That stupid old man ruined *everything*," he muttered. Then he took a deep, cleansing breath and seemed calm again. He turned in the seat and reached back for her, and Kallie gasped and closed her eyes. She backed against the door, handle digging painfully into her spine, sobbing, and screamed as loud as she could.

Danny Lloyd's teeth rattled audibly as the taser hit him in the side of the neck and pumped fifty thousand volts into his skin. He froze and shuddered in place before collapsing, slumping over the seat. A moment later, Morrison was tearing the rear door open and dragging her out of the car. He picked her up and carried her away, with one hand covering her hair, brushing the glass off of her. Kallie glanced back, gasping, sobbing, and saw Officer Ramos with her taser, guarding the incapacitated yoga instructor.

"I stayed in the car this time, Morrison," she told him, with a choked laugh, through her hysterical tears.

"I know you did, Brooks. I know." He held her protectively, watching Officer Ramos.

"Did he shoot you?" she whispered.

"Nobody got shot." He set her down in his car's

passenger seat and brushed more glass off her face gently. He looked relieved, but so very concerned. And something else. "You were right, Brooks," he told her, with a lopsided smile.

"I'm *always* right, Morrison," she sniffled.

"Rarely," he replied with a chuckle. "But you're right when it counts."

Kallie heard the police radio buzz to life, and then a call, "This is Olivia Ramos, Dispatch. We need two ambulances at the Ozona Flow yoga studio." She gave them the address.

"Two? I'm not hurt, Morrison," she argued. "It's just a little glass. I don't need an ambulance."

"I'm going to have them look you over, just to make sure. But the other one isn't for you."

"You said nobody got shot, Morrison," she whined quietly.

"Hold on, and I'll show you." He left her sitting in his unmarked car and walked back into the yoga studio. He was gone for several minutes, and she could barely resist following him. The ambulances arrived quickly, and Ramos pointed one of the paramedic teams inside.

Somehow fighting the urge to join them, she kept waiting, heart in her throat.

What's taking them so long? What if Danny's friends are in there, waiting to attack them? Why don't they hurry—?

Finally, the paramedics came back outside, pushing a gurney. There was someone on it, unmoving, bloody.

No! Morrison!

This time, she couldn't stay still. She darted from the car and ran to the stretcher, afraid of what she'd see.

What in the—?

"*Patricia?!*" she gasped.

The bloody and bruised bakery owner opened one blackened eye and looked up at Kallie from the stretcher. She smiled just a little in recognition, and then disappeared as the paramedics hurried her into the ambulance.

Morrison smiled at her from the doorway and nodded. "Good job, Brooks."

***

The next morning, Kallie took a deep breath and explained everything she knew, while her friends listened silently. Morrison had stayed with her all night, with Tess playing a supporting role on the phone, as she alternated between hysterical sobbing and increasing pride in her work. By morning, she mostly felt relieved.

They had all gathered at their breakfast café,

and Justine was just as interested as the others.

"We had a few suspects in the beginning," Kallie explained. "But once we found out my brother knew Oscar, and we saw that photo of him with Marco Acosta, I was pretty sure he was involved in the murder somehow. I mean, I tried to deny it at first. But Jason always bothered me, and then we just kept finding *so many* facts that tied them to the case."

"You weren't still following Jason, were you?" Morrison asked.

"No, as soon as you told us to back off, we did," Kallie assured him. "It's a federal drug case, and we wouldn't want to mess that up. But every clue *still* seemed to point back to them."

Morrison hadn't been able to tell Kallie much about Marco's boss, except that his real name was Flynn Ingram. His criminal background was classified, but Cornwallis used that limited information to verify that – as Kallie suspected – the dreadfully tricked-out Bentley SUV belonged to him.

"We saw Marco's boss drive past Patricia's bakery van on Main Street, on that video, right after the murder," Tess agreed from the speakerphone. "That big Bentley SUV with the tacky purple neon lights around the license plate is totally unmistakable."

"And even though no one could tell us anything else about him, I saw the same car parked at the beach, right next to the festival site in the daylight, and it had a Texas flag sticker on the back window." Kallie mumbled, "Honestly, that guy is so cheesy."

"Just proves that money can't buy taste," Tess agreed from the phone.

"Ladies, the case, please?" Cornwallis interrupted them.

"Patricia had that call from Texas on her phone, too. It came in right before she was abducted," Kallie continued. "And then Cornwallis told us Marco's boss was from Texas. I swear, *everything* pointed to Acosta and the guy he calls *Búho*."

"And he almost certainly saw Patricia talking to the police, when he passed her that night," Tess added. "So he had every reason to make her disappear."

"It all seemed so *obvious*," Kallie sighed.

"Then how did you figure out it was Danny Lloyd?" Isabel asked.

"You told me, Izzy," Kallie replied, wryly.

Isabel smiled and blushed a little, confused, and Carlos winked at her. "We were talking about rice," she replied, looking bemused.

"We saw that college sweatshirt in his closet," Kallie continued, "and we thought that meant he was from Pennsylvania. . ."

"No, but it was from Temple *College*, where my sister went to school," Isabel corrected her. "Oh. In Texas."

"I suspected Danny Lloyd from the start," Kallie replied, trying not to grit her teeth in annoyance. "Prudence mentioned him because he just seemed wrong, somehow – and I felt the same way. And then he was acting so crazy and hostile, the first time we saw him in Clearwater."

And you should've trusted your instincts, Kalliope.

"And I thought, 'What if *he's* the one who called Patricia from the Texas phone number?' And then I thought about the guy in Mr. Hayashi's video, on the beach, running away from the crime scene in the dark. *He* saw Patricia too. He ran right past her side mirror, while she was talking to the police."

"Was that *him*?" Carlos asked.

"He's the right height and build, on the video," Kallie replied. "And Patricia said the guy she saw was tall and lean—"

"Nobody else we interviewed was built like that," Tess agreed from the phone. "Jack's tall, but he's not athletic. And Jason is shorter than Kallie."

"Marco Acosta is about five foot eight," Cornwallis confirmed.

"The crime scene team found a pistol in Danny Lloyd's belongings," Morrison added. "The sheriff is holding a press conference at noon. No word yet if it's the weapon that killed Oscar Lawson, but forensics is checking the ballistics for a match."

"If he'd just played it off, though," Kallie mused, "If he'd invited Morrison and Officer Ramos into the studio and offered them tea and a complimentary lesson—?"

"We didn't have any proof," Morrison agreed. "He probably would've gotten away with it."

Kallie stirred her coffee, considering that idea.

"I can't tell you much right now," Morrison added, "but it looks like Danny Lloyd may be connected to a murder in Texas from three years ago. A kidnapped woman who'd been kept in a secluded cabin, about an hour east of El Paso."

Kallie thought about that for a moment, and then slammed her hand on the table in frustration, making them all jump. "*That's* why the yoga studio was so noisy!"

Carlos and Isabel were both staring at her in alarm, but Morrison nodded for her to go on.

"The students only started complaining about the airplane and traffic noise *recently*," she explained. "Meaning it was a normal, quiet yoga studio at one time. But then he pulled off the soundproofing and used it all in one room."

Isabel recoiled in horror. "He was creating some kind of *prison* in the yoga studio?"

Kallie saw Morrison nod almost imperceptibly, and guessed her idea must match up with the case in Texas.

"He didn't dare go out and buy a bunch of soundproofing, in case the police were watching him. He had to use what he had on hand." Kallie scowled angrily. "He was planning another kidnapping."

"Was *that* the motive for Oscar's murder, then?" Tess asked from the phone.

"Wrong place, wrong time – like we originally thought?" Kallie suggested. "He said Oscar ruined everything. So maybe Oscar saw Danny Lloyd trying to grab his next victim, that night at the festival grounds. And he tried to help her?"

"And Lloyd killed him for it," Cornwallis asserted.

"And then Patricia saw him running away from the murder scene – even though she didn't know what she'd seen. So he kidnapped *her*, instead," Tess concluded.

"Which means Patricia must've been in the studio when we took our class," Kallie added, sounding appalled. "How many students walked right past her in that hidden chamber?"

"We'll have to hope he confesses," Cornwallis added, frowning. "Presuming that was the murder weapon in his belongings."

"This is all speculation, but it's not unreasonable," Morrison interjected. "A decent lawyer will try to get him a plea deal. Maybe then we'll find out for sure."

***

Morrison showed up at Kallie's house at quarter to twelve with three pints of ice cream, taking his place as Kallie's temporary press conference cohort. He handed pints to Kallie and Benny, as they sat on the couch and called Tess.

"I still don't understand what Oscar was doing with *Jack*," Kallie wondered aloud, as she pried the lid off her mint chocolate chip ice cream. "It doesn't make any sense."

Morrison shook his head. "The medical examiner said Oscar's toxicology results came back clean. Not even alcohol. So whatever they were doing, it wasn't drugs."

"But he knew Jason and Marco?" Kallie asked.

"Maybe he knew Marco from the old days," Benny suggested. "Before he was clean."

"Dealers will sometimes pay vulnerable people to work as a lookout. Maybe they tried to hire him for the Honduras transaction," Morrison suggested. "But since he was clean, they wouldn't have any leverage to force him."

"So he didn't do it?" Tess asked from the phone, hopefully.

"No, we've already identified their lookout for that deal. It wasn't Oscar."

Benny made a pot of coffee as they waited for Tampa News Twelve to cut to the sheriff, and chatted with Morrison about fishing, football, and Kallie.

"I'm exhausted, Tess," Kallie told her best friend on the phone, as Sherman hopped onto the couch next to her. "I might ask Marcy if I can take tomorrow off."

Tess scoffed, "You need a vacation, Kallie! Why don't you come to New Orleans for a few days? I'm sure Winchester will get you a room in this hotel!"

Kallie daydreamed about New Orleans food and music for a moment and smiled. "Let me think about it. I'll ask Marcy if it's okay."

"We both have suites!" Tess added. "And there's gumbo!"

The television cut to the press conference, and Sheriff Hall was already speaking. "—arrested a suspect in the Celebration of Sandcastles murder last night in the tiny community of Ozona, near Palm Harbor. Our St Pete forensics team has just confirmed that ballistics from a weapon found in his possession are a match to the round that killed Oscar Lawson on the night of—"

"What did he say?!" Tess asked from the phone. "I can't hear! Did he say it was a match?"

"Yes, it's a match, Tess," Benny called out to her. "You got him!"

"We got him, Kallie!" Tess yelled. "Our very first official case, and we got the killer!"

The news station had switched back to the anchor desk, and Kallie heard just a snippet from another story.

"—other news, local billionaire and hotelier Barton Donovan has been arrested this morning on charges of drug smuggling and human trafficking. Donovan's legal representation released a statement saying—"

Kallie smiled and turned off the TV. It could wait.

Detective Morrison was smiling at her like he'd won the lottery, they'd solved their first official murder, and she had ice cream and coffee.

Kallie Brooks wasn't sure if life could get much better.

Thank you so much for purchasing and reading *Margarita Malevolence*. I'm extremely grateful and hope you enjoyed it. Your feedback and support are always appreciated, and they allow me to continue Kallie's journey.

Please consider leaving a review online at your favorite bookseller or on Goodreads.

* * * * *

<u>Also by Tanya Westlake</u>:

Bloody Mary, Bloody Murder

Piña Colada Calamity

Mai Tai Malice